The Occupation of Eliza Goode
Shelley Fraser Mickle

© Copyright 2013 by Shelley Fraser Mickle

ISBN 978-1-938467-69-1

Published by

an imprint of Morgan James Publishing

5 Penn Plaza, 23rd floor
c/o Morgan James Publishing
New York, NY 10001
212-574-7939
www.koehlerbooks.com

Publisher
John Köehler

Executive Editor
Joe Coccaro

Front cover photo by Ernest Bellocq.

In an effort to support local communities, raise awareness and funds, Morgan James Publishing donates a percentage of all book sales for the life of each book to Habitat for Humanity Peninsula and Greater Williamsburg.

Get involved today, visit www.MorganJamesBuilds.com

Also by Shelley Fraser Mickle

Barbaro: America's Horse
The Assigned Visit
The Turning Hour
The Polio Hole:
The Story of the Illness That Changed America
The Queen of October
Replacing Dad
The Kids are Gone; The Dog is Depressed
& Mom's on the Loose
Jason and Elihu—A Fisherman's Story

For my book club,

The Page Turners,

which gives me unconditional friendship and,

with other book clubs,

keeps the love of reading alive.

The Occupation of Eliza Goode

A Civil War Novel

Shelley Fraser Mickle

NEW YORK
VIRGINIA

PART I
DISCOVERING ELIZA

Chapter 1

She was one month from seventeen. It must have been about two o'clock, March 9, 1861, on South Basin Street in New Orleans, when she was called into the room where her mother and Preston Cummings sat. There, she was told of the promise—for a price, that is—made when she was four, to be his upon her seventeenth birthday. So it was that Eliza walked into the game room of the parlor house where every night Madam Francine allowed men to wait, where they played cards until they were invited upstairs by one of the "boarders," whom Madam Francine affectionately called her "veshyas" and where, if the men did not have one girl in mind, she would choose one for them, bringing first one to the table, then another, as though merely saying hello.

"Yes, here, Eliza. Come here." Her mother's voice rises, no doubt, bursting with what she thought was her spectacular advance planning. "I have a surprise."

Wearing a lavender day dress with white piping at the collar, its hem sweeping across the thick mauve rug, Eliza stops where they sit: her mother and Preston Cummings together on a small settee. The windows, heavily draped in purple velvet, let in only a slit of light, so the chandelier's prisms of glass scatter rays of shell-pink across the ceiling, like butterflies in flight. And the ceiling, Eliza notes, is already strangely leaking a smoky *naranja rojizo* of emotion that she cannot yet read.

Tall vases of jasmine lace the air with a honey sweetness, which is the calling card of the purple arts, eventually giving rise to a legend that nineteenth century New Orleans prostitutes often wore snips of jasmine as perfume, prompting an opening of, "Want a little jas'?" And since all brothels employed piano players to play what, jocularly, they called "ass music," the idioms were bound to slide and merge to take shape on the tongue as *jazz.*

"Yes, here, Eliza." Her mother reaches for her hand as Preston Cummings leans over a hat of beaver felt in his lap and takes her other hand, cupping it in his own wide palm. He is now forty-eight. There seems never to have been a time when Eliza did not know him. But today his face wears an odd, disturbing expression, nothing like she is used to seeing when he's taken her for rides in his carriage, taken her to the park, and bought her sweets on Esplanade Avenue, year after year.

Today his eyes burn with strange emotion; but then, over the last five days he has often been highly emotional, ever since Lincoln was inaugurated—though most often the emotion has been rage.

He wears an expensive suit of black broadcloth with cuffless trousers over his boots. A satin waistcoat sets off the stiff white of his shirt, and as he pulls her closer, rubbing his thumb across her hand, Eliza catches the scent of sweet cherry smoking tobacco—his favorite, the one he always uses in his pipe

"Eliza, my dear. Come closer. Yes, right here." His voice too is different—thick and liquid. But, as usual, there is his swarthy handsomeness: hair and mustache whiskey-black, sharp ancestral French features, long nose, high cheekbones, eyes glittery dark. His right ear folds over at the rim, a defect since birth; and his manicured fingers wrap around a walking stick where, in the handle, is hidden his Arkansas toothpick, the renowned dagger of the time. "Yes, sweet Eliza, your mother and I have a surprise."

Oh, how thin her mother looks in an afternoon gown of *violeta rojizo* highlighting her hair. As she squeezes Eliza's hand, Eliza notes that her mother's hand feels fish-skin damp and her voice changes to the tone of speaking to a very small child: "Remember, how I always told you of a life where you would never want for a thing? How you would be the center of a great man's life? That you would one day have a wonderful new future? Well, this is your future—Mr. Preston, as you have known him, is now Mr. Preston Cummings, to be someone else quite different again. You see, darling, I promised years ago that on your seventeenth birthday you would be his. To be his only. And with such patience all these years, he has waited! What a prize he has won! What do you think of our surprise?"

Dear One,

What a stupid dummy-girl! Why had I not even guessed this? How had I misread all the signs? Was it only a child's wish to have a father, to be out in the world closed to me? O! I was such a stupid puppet! Why not wail and cry and kick on the floor, screaming no, no, no; I would not have it? Ah! But you see, in that moment I understood what I always knew but now grasped in a way I could not ever have been told. I was a whore's child. This was our world—my mother's and mine. This was my intended occupation. Who was I to flail against it? It had fed us. To be one man's only was a prize—to be a courtesan! O! Poor stupid mother! This was what she chose as best for me.

Quietly, I turned and went out of the room, my feet and hands marble. My very breath narrowed to a wheeze. My world had stopped, and I slid off. Until I could find another to climb onto, I would keep my life in its ice bucket.

That night, I grew two hearts. There was the one, open as ever to whoever walked by. The other, darkly labeled, No Entry. This was where I carved out a sacred spot—where no one had a right to look into. I myself guarded it furiously. My holy of holies. At least this part of me could never be sold.

Chapter 2

There were more than three hundred letters. This was not the first I read, but the first to allow me to touch Eliza's innermost life, and they came to me by way of my Cousin Hadley, who believed—rather desperately and mysteriously—that they could save her.

"Susan!" Hadley first called from a downtown Boston convention center where she was attending a national conference for anesthesiologists. "Did you know we had a prostitute in the family?" Hadley's laughter was explosive.

I had not heard from Hadley in eleven years, except for an occasional Christmas card. We lived so far apart, and her medical practice seemed all-consuming. But then, her Mississippi accent, and her smoky, sexy voice that was always disarming—especially in light of her professional accomplishments—gave her away. "Well, did you, cuz? Did you? An honest to God Civil War prostitute related to us?"

"Hadley, is this really you?"

"Yes, it's your twit of a cousin who sent Mamaw Masters to the whiskey bottle at least twice a day. So, now tell me, Susan, did you know about our relative Eliza? Did you ever think we'd be kin to ...?"

"Well, no." I chuckled now too. "Hadley, I'm so glad to hear from you!"

"Yeah, well, I lost touch. Had to retrench for a while—like a decade." Another loud laugh, followed by a hacking cough, and, "A divorce will do that to you."

"Yeah, I know."

"So anyway, can you come over here to Copley Square, the Marriott, and meet me for supper? This blasted conference on pain management is pure agony. Besides, I have something to show you. Something that's going to really get you worked up, Susan. Can you come? Please, please, please?"

"Of course."

In my family, Hadley is what we affectionately call a nervous talker. Even when she was nine, and I was a college junior, when we shared two weeks of a summer vacation at Mamaw Masters's Mississippi lake house, Hadley had poured forth a babble so endless, our grandmother disciplined her—whenever it was needed—by ten minutes of a scarf tied over her mouth, into a forced silence. And in comic rebuttal, Hadley kept talking in a made-up sign language, punctuating with her eyes. Of course even then, Hadley's ease with language—she would eventually speak three—was a sign of her knife-sharp intelligence. I don't think there was anything written down in any book anywhere that Hadley could not master, once she aimed her mind at it.

I had last seen her at a family reunion in Mississippi in 1993, when she had been thirty-seven years old, just getting settled in a medical practice, newly married and with her only child, Jack, who was, at the time, three years old. And I too had married, this time to my old and original love, Caleb Montiel, who came to me with a house full of children and a sweet, passionate love that was beyond any hope I had imagined. Now at Caleb's and my ripe age of fifty-nine, just at the peak of what I liked to call our *full maturity,* we had taken on a new freedom beyond raising children, to be at the heights of our careers, yet newly worried. In the third summer after the terrorist attack on the World Trade Center, when our country was in the midst of a war, Caleb and I were feeling eerily as if we were on the edge of being back in the America of our youth, the '60s, when divisions between people were as palpable as knee bones. It was almost impossible to pay attention to going on with an ordinary life. Nothing felt ordinary anymore. The future, if not exactly on hold, felt at best left to vague and struggling imaginations.

But why was Hadley calling now—and me in particular—and with such news?

"You see, Susan, I want to show you how I found out about her, our relative, the soiled dove. Did you know that's what women were called back then—soiled doves—I mean, women in the 1800s who sold their bodies to make ends meet?" Another belly whoop, and with it, I realized her laugh was so cultivated with a forced joy that I could not help but wonder what it was hiding. I assumed too the cough that followed was the remnant of a cold or an allergy. Boston's August humidity can be hard on those with allergies.

"Get this, Susan: Our dear departed relative was a public woman who impersonated an officer's wife and was burned alive as a spy." Then Hadley harnessed her news to a lower level. "You see, I've been cleaning out our grandmother's cousin's house in Bells, Tennessee, helping to move her into a nursing home. Bells is only about a hundred miles from Clarksville. As you probably know, it was occupied by the Union Army for the whole of the Civil War, and that's where our dear departed relative was burned as a spy. And in our cousin's attic, I found the most amazing cartons of old things. So, okay, you'll meet me here, I mean here at the hotel near the convention center? And be prepared to stay late. You're not going to believe what I have to show you."

In my study in the big house on Irving Street in Cambridge, where I moved after marrying Caleb, I watched my computer screen dim to sleep mode. I now had an inkling of why Hadley had searched me out. After years of being a rather successful writer, I found that people were always bringing me one story or another that they had either lived or found, wanting me to set down what had spoken to them in some personal way but which they themselves felt inadequate to capture in words. These stories always held more than the promise of a fictional entertainment. They were wishes, sometimes desperate, and almost always subconscious, to express something about themselves they were driven to know.

And, as you might imagine, quite often the stories were god-awful. Wronged husbands, bitter ex-wives, mistreated employees or wrongly accused bosses; almost always what they brought me were stories about revenge or about making something right. But Hadley was family. And I owed her more than a professional ear. "Sure, Hadley. I'd love to see what you've found. What time?"

"Seven? The Harbor Grill?"

"I'll be there."

****

Downstairs, I heard the bell on the back door and knew that Caleb had come home for lunch. He was writing a book in his office at the Harvard chemistry department, where he had taken a position after being a senior research scientist at the Sloan Kettering Cancer Center in New York. He frequently walked home in the middle of the day as a welcomed bit of exercise, and to also, I knew, check up on me. Not that I needed checking up on. But age was spewing glue into my joints, so that carrying groceries up the porch stairs or baskets of laundry up from the basement could take many minutes and effort. Caleb's desire to protect me and my desire to protect him from whatever— overwork, bad reading light, a leaking faucet, worrisome news from one of the kids, anything at all that Time or Happenstance threw up as an irritation, if not an outright danger—had become the daily conversation of our love. It was hard now to tell what brought us together so frequently—a desire to spend time side by side or a defiance of the Time that would eventually part us. Under our outward, and orderly, serenity, there was no serenity at all.

I came down the stairs into the kitchen. "I had the funniest call today."

"Hmm?" He was taking plates from the cabinet.

"My Cousin Hadley called and told me we had a prostitute in the family. I don't mean now. Like in the 1860s or so. Soiled doves, they were called, apparently."

He looked at me—one eyebrow up, one down—and put a can of tuna in the electric opener. "I always suspected that."

"I take that as a compliment."

"And I meant it as one."

"I haven't spent any time with Hadley in over ten years, not since we went to that family reunion on Sardis Lake. Do you remember?"

"Yes. Quite a looker, as I recall."

"Oh, yes. Hadley has it all. Always did. The smartest woman in our family—at least as far as getting degrees is concerned. And she married a great guy, I thought. I really liked Rick—an orthopedic surgeon, wasn't he?"

"I think so."

"Anyway, Hadley's here at a medical conference. But she sounded a bit strange, I have to say."

"Strange how?"

"Overwrought. Certainly worked-up. And I'm meeting her tonight to find out about what."

"Fine. I have a journal club meeting. So I'll get supper there."

I looked across the table where now we were sitting, chewing the last bits of our sandwiches. Caleb's light hair was gray now, almost throughout, and his eyes, blue, snuggled under creases, studied me in a soft, tender way.

"What?" I asked.

"Hurry back."

****

That evening, driving across the Charles River on the Massachusetts Avenue Bridge and patiently winding my way toward the parking garage at the hotel, I rolled over in my mind what I might say to Hadley when she asked me what I suspected she would ask me. So, pulling into the parking garage, I was practicing, "Gee, Hadley, this is interesting but ... tied up with something else right now ... I'll file it and ..."

I popped the trunk for a bomb search, then took the parking ticket from the attendant and walked inside. The Harbor Grill opened off the lobby where people were walking through or sitting in groups, visiting in the plush furniture among lush plants—obviously lots of conventiongoers, anesthesiologists like Hadley. I lingered at the door of the restaurant and looked over the tables to see if I spotted her. She might look very different after eleven years. Or maybe I had arrived before her.

Someone touched my shoulder from behind. "Cuz." I turned to the sound of Hadley's explosive laugh. "Fooled you, didn't I?"

"Well, yes."

Hadley, thin to the bone, her hair tinted blond and cut in the latest, shortest style—back brushed in swats and air blown into different directions, so it stuck out like petals on a daisy—was also wearing blue-framed glasses with square lenses. Beneath them, I saw something of the same eyes I'd so admired when she was a ten-year-old: impish and eager. But now, over forty, those eyes had swapped eager for anxious.

"I was sitting at a table by the window. You looked my way, and then—"

"I'm sorry. I just didn't—"

"It's okay. I knew you probably wouldn't recognize me." She laughed, rubbing me on the shoulder in an affectionate way. Looking into her face, I saw there the same even, lovely features. Counting up, I realized she was in her late forties. And while I usually think women find their most complete bloom in their thirties, I also had come to know that aging had changed in our culture. A woman on the cusp of fifty is often now only, finally, at the height of her physical power. I studied the changes in Hadley's features that had been merely chiseled by age: the short nose, the flawless skin, her expressive mouth—oh, that mouth that even when she was a child, and even in its constant manufacture of words, was mesmerizing. Hadley's eyes and mouth worked in concert, reeling you toward her, connecting you to her, loving you in their unwavering acceptance and curiosity. Some people are said to speak with their eyes, but it was Hadley's mouth that was the natural flirt. She simply loved people, always had, the absolute complete human species, one at a time and even in great numbers, much like fish drawn to spawning grounds. Now, rubbing my arm affectionately, she cooed, "Let's go in. I've ordered us a drink. I knew you wouldn't spot me."

With a barking cough that she covered with her hand, she folded her other arm across mine, holding me by my wrist. "Damn summer cold; nothing's worse." She flipped her white shawl tighter across her neck as we walked back into the restaurant to a table by the window. "You look just the same, Susan. Years only make you better. You always were so naturally pretty."

"You fudge, but thanks."

"And, as you can see, I've gotten into flaunting the latest styles. I think at this conference I blew the mind of every one of my colleagues when I gave my paper on Epidural Morphine for Control of Postoperative Pain in this outfit." She brushed her hand across herself and laughed in a burst again. "Whatever new style comes out, I get, even if it doesn't suit me. I'm into trying anything and everything. It's quite fun at least."

"I love it." I sat down, gesturing to her whole outfit: the tight black pants, the white sweater and shawl, the silver jewelry, the black patent heels, and then I added, "Especially those blue, square glasses. As our youngest child, my namesake, says, *you rock*."

Hadley laughed. "How old is little Susan now?"

"Twenty-three."

"Lord, time is a bitch. Doesn't hold back, does it?"

"And what about your Jack?"

She unfolded her napkin and put it to her mouth to cough again, then in a few seconds, told me, "My little Jack is fourteen, just on the diving board of manhood. He has no use for me. Mothers are a nuisance to boys becoming men."

"Just remember," I said, "they come back. When he's nineteen, it will all be sweet again."

"Really?"

After a few more exchanges about my family, Caleb and the five children we raised, some adopted by Caleb and his first wife, none of our own, Hadley looked around the restaurant, distracted.

Suddenly, she stood up. She waved her hand toward the waiter at the next table. "Where are our drinks? I ordered them twenty minutes ago. And what about menus—why don't we have any menus?" She wasn't saying any of this in an irritated way, but in a comical way, as though the world had stopped and she needed to restart it.

The waiter nodded, waved his hand and trotted off to get

our drink order. Abruptly, Hadley sat down and picked up her purse. "Now in here, I have a sample of what I want to show you." Her purse was big enough to hide a ham. Reaching inside, she rooted around and brought up a plastic bag with a folded piece of paper inside it. "This is just a sample. A copy I carry with me as sort of a talisman, a reminder, you know, of someone who lived a very difficult and amazing life. But after dinner, I'm going to take you up to my room where the real stuff is. I found a whole briefcase of these. Three hundred and seven in all. And this one is the appetizer. Look."

She spread the slick Xerox paper out on the table between us, moving the candle, flattening the paper on the white tablecloth as if about to curate an event like a docent leading me through an exhibit.

"Now, Susan, you're not going to believe this. Not at first. It will take you a minute to figure it out. But you're quick, so I'm not going to time you. But now, listen." And she began to explain in a low, cough-riddled voice: "This is dated the 16th of April 1861, New Orleans, when she was only seventeen. And here, this is what I know you'll want to see too. This is truly amazing. Look." She pulled a cardboard envelope from her purse and reached inside to take out a photograph, one of those black-and-white portraits we associate with the nineteenth century. She passed it across the table to me.

I held the photograph, my fingers carefully on the borders. Its size, about three-by-five, was awash with a dark background, which threw the image of the young woman in the center into a vivid clarity. The irony of what I had thought earlier about Hadley's age now hit me fully, for in the nineteenth century, seventeen was an age of full womanhood, in terms of trials and responsibilities. And what struck me as odd about the photograph was not only that the young woman in the image was standing at a balcony with her hands resting on it, her left wrist bent slightly in a graceful gesture, but her expression was not dour or stiff or posed, as was usual at that time. The young woman was stunning. She was leaning a little forward, slightly smiling, her skin china-white, her face heart-shaped, with her head tilted in a thoughtful pose, her eyes looking directly at the camera or at the man's eye behind it. She wore a dress that looked very much like a dressing gown, a robe in an Asian style. The fabric appeared embossed in a swirling pattern and crossed over itself with an open V below her neck. It was sashed at the waist. The woman's dark hair was pulled upward and back in a swooping style, no doubt pinned somehow. And her face, one side in a grayish shadow, was so perfectly proportioned, she looked cherubic and playful, yet her face seemed shockingly so much like Hadley's, even in Hadley's twenty-first century sleekness, that I looked up and back, comparing the photograph with Hadley's face, as she looked back intently at me, smiling in amusement at my realization.

I blurted, "Hadley, this looks so much like you, it's unnerving."

"Isn't it, though? Except for this. Look at this." She put a finger on the photograph near the shadow of the young woman's cheek beside her left ear. "Isn't this a mole? Looks to me like she had a beauty mark here, maybe drawn on or real. There's no way to know. She never mentions it in any of these." She patted the Xerox letter. "And obviously she's wearing some kind of very chalk-like makeup to set it off. Her skin is as pale as an eggshell." She held up the letter again.

"And that was written by her?" I asked.

"Yes. Eliza Goode. They're all signed Eliza Goode, or at least after she took on the name of Eliza Goode. She started out as Eliza Hamilton. Was born and raised in the most upper-level house of prostitution in New Orleans at the time and promised as a courtesan to a prominent banker. Surely she anticipated a future such as that, but then, well, you'll see ..."

For a moment Hadley looked at me, smiling, teasing me with silence. "And there are three hundred and seven letters?"

"Mmhmm. Most of them upstairs in the briefcase that I brought with me."

"Hadley, these could be worth a great deal of money, if indeed they reveal a personal story of that time and if she mentions any prominent historical figures. Does she?"

Hadley's cough grabbed her. She stopped a moment, tending to it by hacking into her napkin and saying between coughs, "Like, oh yeah, they do. U.S. Grant is in here. And Stonewall Jackson and Sherman. Even Lincoln. And central to her whole story is a minor character, the officer I mentioned; actually he started out as a cavalry officer, Bennett McFerrin. Good Scottish name, don't you think? He never did anything to mark his place in history. But you won't believe how he and Eliza came together. These letters cover the first two years of the Civil War, beginning in New Orleans, ending in Clarksville, with, you know, after she was … like, well, how I told you."

"Burned alive?"

Hadley put her napkin down, composed now again. "Yeah. But let's not dwell on that. It's too sad. This is what is going to get you. Read this." But then, "No, wait, I want to read it to you. You need to get the full effect."

She pulled the letter from me—carefully though, I must add. Hadley was handling the paper and photograph as if touching one of her infant patients whom she was about to usher into a dreamlike anesthetized sleep.

"Dear One." She looked up to read my eyes and reaction. I nodded, encouraging her to go on, not knowing at the time what response she was anticipating from me. She read in a low voice, almost a whisper.

"Though we may never know one another in this world, here, these words will link us, and I know that one day you will come and find them, and in them, me."

Glancing up to see how the words were reflected in my face, enthralled as you might imagine, Hadley then smiled and looked down to continue.

"Outside, as I write this, the sound of celebration pouring into the streets reaches into these windows like the highly tuned excited yelps of an animal about to hunt. The War of Rebellion has begun. And I fear for what it will mean, yet plan now, this day, this night, to ride it to freedom."

"Wait," I said, unable to restrain my curiosity. "You think this was written in a house of prostitution or bordello, something like that, in New Orleans, when she was seventeen?"

"Right-on, cuz. As I said, upper-level kind of bordello, cream of the crop. She was born into it. Her mother, Agnes Hamilton, followed some handsome seagoing bloke to America who promptly dumped her, pregnant with child. Typical story, really, but at least Agnes was not one of the prostitutes France put on a boat and shipped over here. But now listen." And Hadley turned to the letter again, glancing at me, enjoying my captivation.

"Only last holiday, shortly after Christmas, there was an upcountry gentleman here who stopped by the Louisiana Military Academy on his way down (he keeps a monthly appointment with Lotty) where his manservant was told by another a most disturbing story. Apparently on Christmas Eve the superintendent of the Academy, a Mr. Tecumseh Sherman, was in his office burning niter paper for his asthma, attended to by his vigilant servant, and this gentleman Sherman was carrying on something fierce about what he had just learned from a newspaper handed him, that South Carolina had seceded. He was railing in a most distressed way about the stupidity of us Southerners, doing so twice as boldly because he had come to be so fond of living here, knowing Louisiana as he does now and loving it. And saying we are bound to fail, that the seceded states have nothing with which to win a war. He called us mad—committing a crime against Civilization. And then of course, as we now know, after South Carolina, Mississippi, then Florida quickly followed. And in January, we Louisianans pitched our hat into the ring of the Southern Nation. I hear now that this Mr. Tecumseh Sherman moved to St. Louis and is running a streetcar company. I must say, his words passed on as they were on the bitter lips of Lotty's regular do not bode well for us in my eyes, yet ring in singular whispered opposition to the shouts of celebration and expectation of those who dance in the street below this window at the official notice that we are now at war.

"Apparently a fort, fired on, has marked the beginning, though President Lincoln, I hear, was confused as to which fort it should be. Learned this last night from Rose, who from one of her regulars (a boot maker who keeps a seasonal appointment), just returned from Washington where he was, three weeks ago, ushered in one day to measure the President's feet and overheard the President himself speaking with his cabinet member, a Mr. Seward, I think, and also his young secretary, Mr. John Hay (who is apparently quite handsome and in possession of a healthy masculine tickle, since often he frequents Mrs. Wolf's where Lotty's cousin is one of the most

*frequently asked for). Lincoln apparently did not intend to force
an issue to war but believed a heated skirmish would unite the
North, uttering something to the effect that the seceded states
will come to their senses and soon request to be readmitted.
This boot maker, proud that he was not suspected to be a spy...
but then, he is the least likely thing you would think of as a
spy—a spider of a man who brings Rose lavender soap every
time he keeps his appointment, as if bearing jewels from Egypt.
If anything, I suspect Lotty's cousin of being the one to make
things up—certainly she's loose with what she knows.*

*"Seward supposedly proclaimed to Lincoln that the war
would last no more than ninety days. Just think—three months,
no more. Apparently the President was considering forcing the
issue with one of the three Florida forts, but clearly we know
now he chose this one in South Carolina instead, resupplying
it to make clear it was to remain a viable Union fort. But now
the fiery shouts here outside make me doubt any seceded state
will bow to come back in. Yet, if the war might be, indeed, no
more than three months, I must ride it quickly. I am a bird
teetering on the edge of a leaf, afraid the air will not hold me.
Dare I trust it?"*

Hadley looked up, coughing again, wiped her face with a
tissue and then:

*"Companies are drilling not less than a mile from here. I can
hear shouts of soldiers and the firing of practice rounds. Ned
Tatum is joining up, he says. And I do not doubt it. And good
riddance. As close as a brother as I will ever have, since he and
I have shared childhood in this house for all of my seventeen
years, he is due a setting free, which maybe the army will afford
him. Never have I known such a tormented soul, nor one I wish
more to relieve the suffering of. He torments me, crushing me
between affection and disgust as he does. And with the recent
death of his mother, there is nothing here now keeping him.
Charlotte too says she will go, packing and planning to follow
the army marching from here when it forms. Fanny from Mary
Wittle's house down the street too. And after last Tuesday, I
know that my freedom, like Ned's, is either in an unknown
destination where one day I will, quite by surprise no doubt,
find myself, or it exists only in death.*

"I have told no one my thoughts to date. But tonight I will confide in Delia. I will need her help. Being a leased slave, she knows how to keep a secret better than anyone I have ever known. And so, with my love to you—you, my Dear One to come, who I imagine will one day in a distant future find and know me here as only I can make my life known,
Eliza Hamilton."

Hadley put the letter down, reading my face, which must have been a bit creased in wonder. "Amazing that she was only seventeen when she wrote that," I said.

"A week over seventeen, to be exact."

"And so educated. How, I wonder?"

Hadley smiled. "You'll see."

"And it must have been right after Sumter. Had to be."

"It seems."

"And you found these letters in our relative's house in Bells? They were just up in the attic, with no explanation?"

She nodded. "Apparently she's Mamaw Masters's distant cousin. And the dear woman has no idea about the letters—well, her mind is gone. She couldn't answer any of my questions."

"So now, read that first sentence again." As I was trying to piece the facts together, Hadley seemed to be playing with me in an uncharacteristic quietness. I felt as if we were in the middle of a childhood game, once again, and she was urging me on to unravel a mystery: warmer, you're getting warmer, or no, colder, colder.

Looking down at the ending of the letter, Hadley read slowly, *"Though we shall never know of one another in this world, here—"*

"Do you think," I interrupted in my excitement, "she wrote these letters to no one in particular but to some imagined future?"

Hadley smiled. "When you see what I have upstairs, you will know this for sure. She didn't know it was I who would finally read them; and I'm too much of a scientist to believe in something so mystical as that these were intended for me personally. Yet there is part of me that believes exactly that. And now it is my luck or misfortune to have found them. It's me she imagined."

The waiter came with our dinners. We stared at each other in silence, not wanting to say a word in the presence of anyone. I was curious as to why Hadley called finding the letters "luck or misfortune." But frankly, my mind was trying to fold itself around the stunning material in the letter. Hadley was way ahead of me. And she was also digging into her spaghetti carbonara at twice the speed.

Groping at the facts, I summed up what I thought we knew: "So Eliza was planning to run away? Was going to leave that house in New Orleans?"

"Yes, along with Ned Tatum, another child of another public woman who lived there with nineteen other women and Zapa, a homosexual man who helped keep the place up and served meals. The parlor houses apparently operated something like a family within them, and then in the following letters you will see how Delia, the slave who came to work there, played a vital role. You see, often widows would rent out slaves they owned to help with expenses, trying to hold on to their property—and property Delia certainly was. Owned by some woman in Natchez, I believe. Rented for ..."

Hadley then rooted in her purse and pulled out a package of Kleenex. She was sweating profusely across her forehead and neck. "Fifty dollars a month." Her cheeks shined with perspiration. "With ten kicked back to the widow toward purchasing her freedom. Wonder how that bill of sale would have read: *You are now the sole owner of the body and soul you were born with*?" She laughed, dabbed at her face, and then abruptly stood up, her dinner half-eaten. "Let's have dessert upstairs."

I stood to follow her.

"Put this on my room charge," she said to our waiter, then wiped her neck with her shawl and flipped it across her chest. "Come on. You're not going to believe what I have upstairs."

Chapter 3

I stepped aside for the crowd emptying from one of the elevators, and our Aunt Ellen stepped out, accompanied by her husband, Arthur. "Aunt Ellen?" I was sure that it *was* Aunt Ellen, though I had not seen her in several years. But I was well aware that the strangest coincidences can occur, such as the time I saw my college roommate in the House of the Vestal Virgins in Rome, which, meeting there by chance gave us a hearty laugh. So seeing Aunt Ellen there was quite possible, in my mind. And as I was about to call out to her again, Hadley barked, "No," grabbed me by the sleeve, and said, "That's not Aunt Ellen, just someone who looks like her. What would Aunt Ellen be doing in Boston?"

Taken aback, I didn't argue. Besides, Hadley was pulling me into the elevator and busily pushing the buttons, acting as the elevator operator for everyone else who got in—shutting the door, "which floor, and for you, which floor, right away, yes, good," laughing, punching all the buttons.

But of course, even though it was possible that Aunt Ellen was at one of the other meetings at the hotel or even had come to Boston with Arthur for a Red Sox game, there was also the chance that I had confused her with a stranger.

I had the distinct feeling Hadley wanted to avoid our relative at all costs, which made me wonder what Hadley was hiding.

The elevator door opened on the eleventh floor. In her room, Hadley threw off her shawl and kicked off her shoes. She bounced on the bed. "You want to order dessert or see the rest of the letters now?"

"The rest now. I'm intrigued."

"Told you. I knew you'd get caught up in this."

She walked to the closet. She took from it a black briefcase, thick and heavy like the kind used in movies loaded with spy gadgets. I almost laughed as she put it on the bed, but she beat me to it, popping open the locks, chuckling. "This is the briefcase I found in our cousin's attic. It must date from the forties. I bet her husband sold Fuller Brushes." She stood quietly, looking down, then at me.

The papers in the briefcase were covered in a tea-colored gauzy material. "When I found them," Hadley said, lifting the fabric, "they were in two parts, each sewn into this linen. Someone had opened them—I assume our relative who is now in a nursing home. Her mind is gone too much to answer my questions about them. All she says is 'passed down, passed down' and shakes her head yes, yes, smiling at the attention my question gives her. But you can see in her eyes that the light left there is not connected to any real knowledge about these. What she knew about how they got in her attic she's forgotten, and now she has no hope of remembering. But, and here's the thing, she had a partial family history drawn out, stored in her attic. And there was Eliza Hamilton Goode listed on a branch with her great-great-grandmother's sister, Tilly. But the branch trailed off into unknown territory with a question mark. Anyway, it blows my mind to think that Eliza's fingers sewed these papers into this linen. I guess it was the way she planned for the letters to be preserved."

"You know, Hadley," I pointed out again, "these could be worth a great deal of money."

I was thinking that perhaps Hadley was hiding some financial trouble, like an overextension of her practice, a bad investment, or some other kind of unfortunate slip-up that good people can make and that the letters could afford her to dissolve.

She looked up, startled. "Oh, I would never think of selling them. They've come to be to me ..." She opened the linen and pulled out the first few sheets of paper. "These have become so personal to me. It would be like selling part of myself now. I couldn't ever part with them."

She tenderly handed me the letter on top of the others. I took it over to the chair and sat. Hadley lay on the bed, propped on one elbow. It was the quietest and most peaceful I had seen her that day. She watched me read. On the dried yellowed paper, the handwriting, though beautiful and executed with great care, was still a bit difficult to read. I would stumble silently over a word and have to go back and fit it into the sentence so the thought was then complete.

17 of April, 1861, New Orleans, South Basin Street

Dear One,

I can sit still no longer than a fly in the streets of this city. My whole body is afire with the excitement of what I am planning. We, Delia and I, sit on our secret as if it were diamonds sewn into my hems. And of course there is the arduous silly decision to make about what exactly I should do with all my hoops and hems! I must have more elaborate plumage than anyone of any age in this house. For it has been my good fortune or curse to have been given a dress by almost every courtly rich gentleman to have come through this house, every year as I have grown, which of course has kept the mantua-makers happy on Rue de Ursaline, and has made me what Mama dreams, seeing me in the finest. It is no longer a simple matter, though, for Delia thinks I must not follow one of the companies forming near here, for they will be taking the train from New Orleans to some other city and there joining an army under the command of some general. And the devil himself, Mr. Preston Cummings, when, no doubt he discovers my absence, will guess the railway and be waiting at the first stop to board to hunt me out to drag me back like some trophy to be served up at his whim, a side dish. Dear One, I cannot begin on him, just yet, but only here in beginning say—beware of anyone who wants to tell you over and over, "Tes jolis yeux bleus, bleus comme les cieux, tes jolis yeux bleus on ravi mon âme, etc." Rubbish! So Delia says I dare not leave my grand wardrobe behind. According to her, my looks are my ticket. And I guess Delia knows more than anyone that skin and the fabric swaddling it are indeed the tickets to freedom, if not survival. And so, Delia is planning my escape by talking with her husband, Quashi, at the Royale Stables. I am to head off to find a cavalry or some other group, mustering in near here in Mississippi. Mr. Preston would never think of seeing you on a horse, Delia says. Make it an old one, I say, short and calm. No cheval fringant or I shall break my neck. We make fun, but underneath we are as scared as a sword swallower with a stubby neck. It is only a day's ride, she says. But she doesn't have to travel it and arrive alive! She trembles for me, and I for myself. Delia says lean on the angels. I say yes, Ciel m'en préserve! Two days more and I am gone.

You, Dear One, you are in my dreams too,

Eliza Hamilton.

I looked up at Hadley. "She was fluent in French?"

"Oh, I don't think completely. But a good many phrases, that's clear."

I looked down. "My own college version is not good, but I'm guessing she has said something here like, 'Your pretty blue eyes, blue as the skies, your pretty blue eyes have delighted his soul.' And she ends with something like, 'Heaven protect me.' Is this right? You're the one, Hadley, who has a talent for languages."

She watched me with eyes glossy from what seemed a fever. "Yes. You're perfectly right."

"So how was she educated? How did she know all this?"

"The next letters will tell you. But think about it, growing up in one of the finest brothels in New Orleans in the middle 1800s, don't you suspect that any number of wealthy men from foreign countries moved through the Port of New Orleans with a hearty testosterone tickle he was eager to scratch?"

I laughed and then, "Umm, does seem plausible."

"And more than plausible. Eliza Goode, as she became, was extraordinary to begin with. You'll see."

I stood up. "I better get back."

"Our desserts haven't come."

"I can see, though, Hadley, you aren't feeling well."

"Nothing I can't live with or die from." She laughed deeply, then lost the sound in a cough. "Besides, you're to take those." She pointed at the suitcase.

"I'd love to. Because, you know, of course, I'm bitten."

"No doubt."

"When do you want them back?"

She closed the briefcase, snapping the locks with a crisp metal sound. She picked it up by the handle and held it out to me. "Never. They're yours."

"But Hadley, they're not. I can return them after some months, after I've put together things within them; or better yet, I'll copy them. I'll return the originals. I can send them back by registered mail in a few days. Because you said how much they mean to you."

"They do. But no. They're yours now. I've gotten all I need to from them. What I need next is what you make from them."

Her eyes looked even more feverish. Her mouth wore a playful curve, taunting, flirting, making me feel like a kid she'd blindfolded and led into a room and now was about to whip off the fold to let me see where I was. I said what I thought she expected: "You intend for me to write something from these? A story, a novel, a non-fictional account that will pull them together?"

"Yes, something that will make me *feel*." She smiled oddly, her eyes glistening with fever and obvious emotion. "Make me feel what Eliza felt, Susan. Look, I'm a physician. I read fast. I'm trained to digest facts without emotion. So yes, I've read these letters. But I want you to put them all together and give me what she lived, so I can feel it."

For a second I absorbed that, stunned. *Why,* I wanted to ask, or at least to come up with some tactful way to probe her strange answer. She was now turning down the bed covers, moving about with such agitation, I knew I didn't have long to keep her attention. "Wait," I started. "You want to live Eliza's life—or rather, relive it. And through what I might write about it? I don't understand. This seems—"

"Right—crazy. Well, most likely I am. And maybe certifiable too. But now, Susan, think: Haven't you at times wanted to crawl into someone else's life to have them lead you out of a place so confusing you've lost all direction?" She then gazed at me with such intensity, I was alarmed. Suddenly, she laughed, loudly, bitterly. "Oh! Well, the look on your face tells me you don't have an ice cube's chance in hell of knowing what I'm talking about! You've lived your life with few mistakes or at least not big ones. But I haven't. And now I have a decision to make. Eliza made one too. She ran to escape her life. She lived with shame. And she apparently did something quite remarkable, considering why she died. But how, Susan? How? Did she come to terms with her past? When she died, was she at peace?"

I struggled to digest what she told me. In an ending quip, she added, "Indulge me. I know it's unreasonable to expect you, or anyone, to really understand me. But let's just say you'll be dealing with my magical thinking—like a little child's wish. If I can understand Eliza's life, I might have a chance of figuring out my own."

Her eyes widened. She smiled. "At the least, this will be fun."

I nodded.

Part of what she told me *did* resonate with what I had felt at times in my own life: a sense of isolation, of being unknown. Her longing for connection was palpable. I also sensed a torment at the center of her life, and it occurred to me that her obsession with Eliza was a way to distract herself from that. Quickly, she added, "So how long, Susan, do you think it will take before you can write this up in some way that will bring it all together?"

"About six months, maybe. Why, Hadley?"

"Six months is just about right. Try not, though, to take longer."

"Why?"

She gave me no answer. Instead she laughed, a manic, bitter-sounding laugh, and pulled a pair of pajamas out of her suitcase. They were black-and-white striped, the cartoon version of what a jailbird would wear.

"I'm sorry to end the evening so early, Susan, but I'm battling this cough. I think I should go to bed."

I studied her for a second. Her face was shiny with sweat.

"Sure, Hadley. Get some rest. It's terrific to be back in touch, and thanks for calling me. I'll take good care of these." I held up the briefcase.

On the way down in the elevator, a feeling of unease made me want to turn back. In the lobby, as security men glanced at the briefcase, I was amused, thinking they might be considering stopping me and searching it, though it was not customary to search briefcases going out of a hotel, only coming in. And with my worried look, I guess I could have fit the profile of a female middle-aged lunatic or suicide bomber. Ordinarily, I would have let myself enjoy that thought, but the suspicion that Hadley was hiding something disturbing was more insistent, so that outside the hotel door and three steps toward the parking garage, I turned back.

Quickly, I walked through the lobby to the elevators. Back up on Hadley's floor, I plunged down the hall and knocked briskly on her door.

"Who is it?" Hadley was streetwise and cautious.

"It's Susan again. I remembered something, Hadley."

The door opened.

"Hadley, are you seriously ill? Is something going on with you you're not telling me?"

"Oh sweet, smart cuz." She hugged me while whispering in my ear in a childlike, lilting voice. "I'm fine, Susan. I'm just as fine as fine can be. Now go home to your wonderful Caleb and start bringing Eliza to me."

Many times over that next year, I would ask myself how things would have been different if I had believed her.

Chapter 4

Driving home across the Charles River, turning down Irving Street, I was eagerly looking for a light on in Caleb's upstairs study. Always good at digging under the surface for cold facts, he could, surely, sort out my trigger-happy imagination and put to bed the disturbing scenario I was cooking up. While pulling into the garage and taking the briefcase out of the backseat and carrying it to the porch steps, I was putting the final touches on my explanation for Hadley's odd, manic behavior: Hadley was sick, seriously sick. How else to make sense of the feverish eyes, the sweating, the chills, the on-the-edge desperate request of me and the remark about six months as perfect to pull together Eliza Goode's letters?

Hadley was dying. *Hadley was dying?* Rehearsing the words did not yet carry feeling. But *yes,* I speculated, Hadley had been given a notice to a limit of time—a definite, serious limit of time, not the everyday far-in-the-back-of-the-mind knowledge that one day we all die but an up-close announcement, within sight and breathing. What else could explain the whole evening, the request, the manic tone? She had contacted me with this one particular thing in mind. She was expecting some kind of realization or meaning, maybe even a source of serenity through

what our family history could reveal through me. *Through me.*
I was caught up in the drama of my imagination.

Opening the back door and calling, "Caleb," I had no idea
how close I was to the truth, and yet how far I was from the
engine that drove it.

The door closed with its bell jingling and Caleb called,
"Here!"

I found him in the living room, sitting in his father's old
chair, re-slipcovered about five times now, drinking a glass of
wine, listening to a Willie Nelson CD. *You were always on my
mind,* trailed out to greet me in Willie's odd, scratchy voice.
The emotion of the song sank me. I leaned on the frame of the
doorway. What I had only been thinking now washed over me
with full meaning. Hadley and I hadn't been close, not since her
childhood, really, but still, tonight had been extraordinary. I
spread my fingers on the heavy wood moulding, pushing back
for balance as if my clothes were water-soaked. This house had
seen its share of death already, with Caleb's father. And tonight
Hadley had become more than family. Our imaginations had
coalesced, and while probably neither of us could have sensibly
explained how it felt to be united by Eliza Hamilton Goode's
long-gone life, it, *she,* Eliza, whoever she was and the intrigue of
what she had left, was indeed a force now with its own calling.
The last thing I needed to be, or could be, was a savior of some
kind. But I felt that was exactly the role Hadley was leading me
to take.

"Are you okay?" Caleb took the briefcase from my hand.

"Hadley has something really wrong with her." I sat on the
couch. "I could use your thoughts on this."

He poured me a glass of wine from the bottle on top of the
grand piano. Jeans, loafers, a starched white shirt open at the
neck with sleeves rolled and a long scratch on his right arm from
where he had been pruning a tree in the backyard—it was so
easy to love this man. His calm acceptance of whatever I brought
him that ruffled the waters—a child's fever, bad grades, a college
kid's maxed-out credit card or DUI—horrors—seemed only a
matter of course to Caleb. He would analyze the problem, assign
it an agenda, and then step back to watch it through. My fear for
him always, over all these years, was overload.

As he handed me the glass of wine, I asked, "How would you put together an obvious fever, a chest-rattling cough, a rushed meeting with a distant cousin, namely me, and then a desperate request that I write something for her?"

"Desperate?"

"Yes, I'd call it desperate. She asked me if I could finish it in six months."

"Sometimes you can work that fast." He grinned. Unable to resist teasing me, he then added seriously, "But is it something worthwhile? I mean, what she asked you to write? Tell me."

For the next few minutes, I did, giving in detail my meeting with Hadley and what I had noticed about her.

He rubbed his right eyebrow, an unconscious habit. With his other hand, he raised his wine glass and took a slow swallow, and wryly asked, "You want me to do a differential diagnosis?"

"Well, you *are* an expert on cancer. You've pretty much seen it all. And I'm assuming the worst. Very serious, at least. So I thought you might know what she's hiding."

"Why do you think there's something she's hiding?"

"Because all this is too odd to be only what it seems."

"Fever and a cough—could be any number of things: emphysema, lymphoma, a lung infection, even depression. Something as benign as acid reflux can cause a hacking cough. Also, just what she said: that she is fine, that it is only a summer cold. Why do you suspect more?"

"Why would she be looking me up after all these years and with this intense request?" I opened the briefcase.

He came over and put his hand on the letters, feeling the bulk of them.

"Remarkable," he said, "that little pieces of paper can convey the feel of a whole life."

****

It wasn't until later when I reached into my purse for my reading glasses that I found the note that Hadley had secretly placed there.

Susan, let's meet in some exotic place in three weeks and talk about Eliza's letters. I'll want to know all you've figured out by then. Here's my home phone in Laurel: 601-599-4233. And also my cell: 601-342-6659. Leave a voicemail if I don't pick up. It seems I'm in the OR half my life. Hadley.

****

That next morning, I called Hadley's room. When there was no answer, I called the desk, and the clerk told me she had just checked out. Next, I called her cell phone number, and after it rang three times, I heard, "Okay, take Storrow Drive and skip Copley, but I think you're about as dead wrong as a raccoon stealing golf balls as eggs. And I don't care if you are tough as nails, growing up in Haiti and all, at this hour, nobody expects the long way," and then, "Hello. Oh, Susan, I'm just getting in a cab on my way to the airport. And don't you think taking Storrow Drive in eight a.m. traffic is insane?" She laughed raucously. "But I can't change this cab driver's mind for love nor money. Not that I've offered him love." She laughed again, then coughed. "You see, he's lived here two months and knows it all." She coughed again. "If I miss my plane, I'll sue him. So how are you this beautiful a.m.?"

"Hadley, I'm worried about you. Have you seen about your cough? Maybe you need some antibiotics."

"Sure thing, cuz. Antibiotics. I see living with Caleb has turned you into a family practitioner. Antibiotics, though, sweet cuz, aren't my charm just now. This thing has me by the throat, as they say. But I'm ..." She laughed, and then coughed the laugh away.

"Hadley, I'm wondering if there's something you're not telling me. That there's something really—"

"Yes, there is, Susan. There really is something. And when you count the letters, you'll wonder if I'm playing a mean trick on you. But—" There was a loud blast of a horn. "You're crazy too!" Hadley was obviously yelling out the window and laughing. "If you can't drive it, park it!" Then, "Susan, I gave you only half the letters. The rest are in Mississippi. I put them in a safe at the Jackson Hancock Bank." She giggled. "Think about that— Eliza Goode in a Jackson, Mississippi, bank! You see, on my way back after finding them, I had to stop for a medical conference in

Jackson. And I was so afraid something would happen to them. I had time to make copies of only the first half, so I stashed the rest. Besides, I wanted you to get to know her before you knew too much. Ha! Does that make sense?"

"Hadley, I have this feeling you're hiding some—"

"Oops. I just spilled my coffee. *Pardon, pouvez-vous me prêter ...?* Hey, Susan, have you found my note? Yes, I want to meet in three weeks in Costa Rica. I'm going down there to work in a clinic, helping to fix cleft palates, pro bono. Some days I think about joining Doctors Without Borders. But that's out of the question now."

"Hadley—"

"We're entering the tunnel, Susan. See you in three weeks in Costa Rica. I'll send you the name of the hotel."

Either Hadley had faked a cell phone break up, or she really was going down into the tunnel.

****

That next week, I'd had time to read through only the first few letters. If I had only the first half of the three hundred that Hadley said existed, then Eliza Goode had indeed written enough to give me a very significant portion of her life. But it was Hadley herself who haunted me now.

Three times that week, I called her. But a recorded message told me the voicemail was full and could not receive anymore calls. I got the number for her office, her practice in Laurel, Mississippi; and again, each time, there was no return of my call, even after the secretary, who took my message, promised that Hadley would get back to me. Every e-mail I sent her also went unanswered. Finally, I stopped trying for a few days, not only perplexed but seeing my hunt for her take a cartoonish turn: Had Hadley managed to snuggle down on the planet, disappearing as mysteriously as Osama bin Laden, who was still a prime item in the news? Right then it occurred to me that Hadley might be doing this on purpose.

I remembered how, as a ten-year-old, she could beat me in chess, making me feel duped by a kid half my size but twice as clever. Her mind was so quick, thinking three steps ahead and delighting in leading you to a place that only she knew. I recalled too, how long ago now, during that vacation we'd spent together, she secretly had taken from my suitcase a favorite lipstick, a bookmark, my watch, a pearl barrette, something inexplicably dear that I didn't know how I had lost. And then at night there the lost item would be on my pillow, or propped up on the sink beside the faucet when I went to brush my teeth. It was enough to make you question your vision. And when you realized that it had been Hadley all the while, turning your life into a salad and watching you deal with it, you wanted to kill her, while at the same time you were ignited by the delight in how she had reunited you with a favorite thing. How alive you felt in that instant of surprise. How much you appreciated the existence of the thing itself as never before! All that was coming back to me now, but Hadley had been a child then.

Well, I could outfox her. If not smarter, I was at least more experienced. Helping Caleb raise five kids had made me a master at spotting manipulation, if not outright lies.

I called information and got the number for her family home in Oxford, Mississippi, where her father, my uncle, had been a physics professor at the university. Four years before, when he died, I remembered seeing at his funeral Hadley's two older brothers, who were blurred figures in my memory, as well as Hadley too, who had been a distant figure disappearing into her own car instead of the funeral entourage. A bit strange now when I thought of it. Why not the family's car, with them, and at the gathering later? In that rushed few days, I had not even had a chance to say more than hello to her, awkward as that is when someone is shut away in grief. I knew, though, where her parents had lived all these years, and I dialed the number, sitting in my upstairs quiet study, waiting for Hadley's mother to answer. But someone else picked up. A young girl's voice told me, "She's not here. Mrs. Masters moved last month and rented the house out to me. My little boy and I need a place. And she said if I stayed here and took care of it, she'd let me have it cheap."

"Where did she go?"

"To her sister's in Omaha. She's a widow now too. But I don't know how much longer they're going to last in that winter up there. The last time Mrs. Masters was down here, she told me she's thinking about going into a retirement home. Hope she doesn't sell this place out from under me."

"Thank you. Can I have the number, please?"

"You're not a bill collector, are you?"

"No. I'm family."

Thinking back, I realized the last time I had seen Hadley's mother, Nora, was at my mother's funeral two years before. Big family reunions were the only occasions I'd spent any time with her. "Tally's girl, looks just like a Robinson, though gets those eyes from her mother's side of the family," was how I was most often introduced. And now, remembering Hadley's mother, I brought up in my mind what was there: a fuzzy picture of her standing at a picnic table beside Sardis Lake—a short, stout woman in her late middle-age with a sweet, thin-lipped smile and short hair the color of an orange cat. Hadley had gotten her mother's elfin features and pretty skin, but it was her father who had contributed the magical combination that became Hadley's extraordinary mind. Nora Masters, I remembered, had a quick way of judging who you were and what you did. Like many throughout the Masters family, and Southerners in general, she was socially conscious above all else. How often the expression "quality people" peppered the Masters family's speech—a term, I eventually learned, that was brought from Stuart, England, during colonial times—a true Americanism that hung on in the South long after the rest of America let it go. "Bakers' bread, what the quality eat," said Huckleberry Finn. "Not lowdown cornpone."

Hadley and her mother must have fought like mad crows when Hadley was coming of age.

When Nora Masters answered the phone, I quickly identified myself. "Mrs. Masters. This is Susan Masters, Tally's daughter."

"Oh, Tally's daughter. How nice to hear from you. Are you here?"

"No, I'm in Boston."

"I remember now. I last saw you at your mother's funeral. And you—Robinson eyes?"

I laughed. "Yes, Robinson eyes."

A few more exchanges and then, "Mrs. Masters, Hadley was up here recently at a meeting, and we spent some time together.

But I haven't been able to reach her since. Even her home number doesn't pick up. I thought maybe you'd know another number where I can reach her."

"I don't know anything about Hadley." The tone of her Mississippi softness changed.

"You haven't talked with her lately?"

"Frankly, I don't give a rat's behind if I ever do. Pardon my French, but Hadley has disappointed me beyond forgiveness. I don't consider her any longer a member of this family. She has ruined my family."

Her anger stunned me. For a minute I didn't know how to go on. Then, "You aren't in touch with Hadley at all?"

"She knows better than to call me. She has to live with her own self, because no one else can stand to."

Deviously, I said more than I knew: "So you don't know anything about Hadley's serious illness?"

"If Hadley's sick, she hasn't told me."

"I guess if you're not speaking, she wouldn't, though."

"No. And I really don't care to know."

"But what if she is? What if she has something very, very serious? Do you know how to get in touch with her?"

"I don't know anymore than you do."

As a final ploy, I added, "Just in case, I'm going to give you my phone number. I think Hadley's in trouble. I'd appreciate if you let me know if you hear from her. We're doing some business together, and I need to talk with her."

"Of course she's in trouble. Hadley doesn't know anything else. And she's got you fooled too, I can see. If you don't already know, you will soon. Hadley's a master of lies. Now, if you don't mind, I have a luncheon to get to. Nice to hear from you, though. Your mother's funeral was real sweet. And I sure miss Tally. He was a wonderful brother-in-law. I wish we'd taken more time to visit."

"Are you telling me that Hadley's faking who she says she is? That she's not even—"

"No, I'm not talking about any of that. She's a doctor all right. But I can't talk about any of the rest. Hadley is dead to me now. It's the saddest thing in the world to lose a child because she hurts you so."

The conversation ended like that—so strange that the only way I could feel settled with any of it was to repeat, "But if you hear from her, you will please tell her to call me?"

She made some bland sound and hung up.

****

I went down into the kitchen at four a.m. for a glass of milk and a fine, fat Mallomars cookie. Chocolate never fails to sort out what jars my anxiety muscle to the point of throbbing. And if Hadley was disappearing from me, I simply couldn't find out why. At least not right now. Standing up to put my glass in the sink, I watched, almost hypnotically, a fat, shiny black roach brazenly walk across the counter and slide down into the sink and begin feeding at the drops of milk I had poured out. He must have slipped in, baby-sized, by grubbing down in the glue in a grocery sack. I grabbed a spatula to bong him on his fat back and wash him down into the disposal, where I'd grind him out into the city of Cambridge's pipes. Instead, I held the spatula in midair, anticipating the sound of what I would hear while squashing him and the feel of his beetle-back cracking under the pressure of my hand. At that moment, I could not bear feeling that murderous, although at any other time, on any other night in another year, taking him crudely out was what I usually would have done without a second thought.

"What's up?" Caleb's voice startled me. He stood in the kitchen doorway, his string-tied pajama bottoms hanging on his hips and his hand scratching his chest.

"I think we have a new pet."

Caleb walked to the sink.

The roach was tiptoeing into my milk glass, which I had conveniently turned on its side for him.

Caleb looked at me.

"I just couldn't kill him. I think I'm losing it," I admitted.

He put a Mallomars in his mouth, and while chewing asked, "He looks like a Rufus to me. Should we call him Rufus?"

My answer of laughter is the only explanation I can give for how we lived that whole next year with the scratching presence of Rufus scurrying around our house at night. Totally without logic, completely out of tune with how we would have handled him at any other time, I can only say that our need to do something opposite to the roaring violence that was running rampant in our world was what drove our acceptance of Rufus into our home. And since we also knew that living with him would seem revolting to anyone else, we kept him our secret. We didn't introduce him or speak of him to any dinner guests.

The next morning early, a FedEx truck drove up to the house and the driver got out and walked up onto the porch to deliver to me a plane ticket to Costa Rica, along with a handwritten note.

See you in three weeks. The Crowne Plaza Hotel. And don't forget Eliza. Bring her to me.

Hadley

Chapter 5

Aweek later, I sat in my upstairs study reading Eliza Hamilton's letters. Those that I had, I planned to read through in a few days. I was looking for a single longing in Eliza's life—what I call the emotional engine behind every story, if not behind every life, carving the total down into a single driving hunger that I could feel. So who she was and what she did would come out of that. *That* was my thinking. But my goal was shot to hell the minute I read through the first five letters. Layered with rich fact and thought, and carried on her looping, elaborate handwriting, reading them took the whole afternoon. I found myself leaning back, barely able to mentally digest all that she had written in only a few letters. Going through all one hundred fifty could take weeks. One in particular struck me with a nagging curiosity.

Dear One,

Now that we have found each other, even many years apart, and are about to begin this long journey of my escape together (me again, you for the first time), I must stop and tell you what is apparently most unusual about me. When exactly I discovered this rare trait, I cannot say—maybe about four—for certainly I remember that night when rushing into my mother's room, driven by a nightmare of hideous monsters, I saw an amarillo aura across the ceiling, the tint of goldenrod and fresh butter, and could instantly read the mood as joyous, rojizo heated by a secret physical pleasure that intuitively I knew was similar to touching my own skin's secret places. Mr. Preston Cummings was there with my mother, both sitting up in bed as I burst in, chased by the bad dream. And the nightmare's violeta azulado followed me to be quickly swallowed by the amarillo hue on the ceiling. Both my mother and Mr. Preston leaned over me—cooing sweet reassurances, hugging me and wiping my tears. This most strange ability that I had been bequeathed, I soon learned to keep hidden. For occasionally blurting out something like, "Why! It's verde amarillo in here!" I so discomforted those in the room, I was suspected of being a witch or a voodoo spirit slipped in from the Islands. For a while I was even feared! Maybe all children name by color what they feel. But I never outgrew the painted emotions I could read, and also found that my other seemingly otherworldly trait was the one I could let out to entertain. "Here, listen to this," Hattie Louise in her better days often said, standing me in front of a gentleman from Buenos Aires or Vienna or Rome, even once Cairo, and as soon as he spoke, I imitated his language and spoke back. Simply, languages seem to me songs, the melodies of which I can instantly sing. Some nights in the main parlor I entertained for an hour, speaking the languages of various visitors from France, Germany, once a rather old gentleman from Portugal. Blessing or curse, I can read what either warns me or becomes a torment. Only when I sleep is this power quiet. And lucky for me, my dreams—during, at least, my childhood— were either unremembered or washed of all color.

What these gifts led me to know, intuitively too, as though some great being spoke to me from far away, not in language but in feeling, was that in my second decade I would undergo some momentous transformation. Now, Dear One, think me possessed or of sick mind or only a girl-woman of silly notions. At times to be envied. At times to be pitied. For never did I ask for the power that keeps me so fiercely awake to this world.

I read this short letter over at least five times. How strange that she slipped in that phrase, *me again, you for the first time.* Clearly she had written this letter at a different time from the others, and much later. After all, the letter was undated and had no address. Was this a mistake or a manipulation?

The concrete act of what I was doing suddenly struck me with quirky resentment. Damn Hadley! She had spun me into a web with both her and this Eliza Hamilton, whoever she may have been—battening down my life with a huge stack of hand-written letters from a dead woman, imploring me to bring her back, through words, to life. And while, ha! I had written fat books before under the pressure of a deadline in the midst of household confusion, this time my promise to Hadley gave a whole new meaning to the word *deadline.* I was put out with myself for letting her manipulate me like this: planning a rendezvous thousands of miles away when I was expected to have something on paper to bring back Eliza's life. What did Hadley think—that I could throw this together like doing a load of laundry?! There is always a moment in creating a human being on paper in which I am frozen in awe of the power of the imagination, not only to create a world but to conceive itself. More than a little magic was required. And also that holy moment in which you wait to see if your creation will breathe. I wanted to throttle Hadley around her thin silk-scarf-decorated neck. I shut the briefcase and looked down through the window at the front yard grass.

Some nights now, Caleb and I could hear a roar from Fenway Park where the Red Sox were playing in their best season in decades, apparently even headed for the World Series. Every day too, the airways were splattered with mudslinging and the pitched intensity of a presidential campaign. Only weeks before, a few miles away, the Democratic National Convention had introduced as its keynote speaker a young man of mixed race, of a Kansas mother and an African father, who, in an impassioned speech, certainly looked presidential, at least on television. And how ironic *that* felt as I began the early steps in researching Eliza's life when the unspoken fear of miscegenation drove so many unrelentingly to war. Amused with that thought, I let out one quick guffaw, wondering if perhaps all along the nation had been hatching its own idea of who it was to become. Certainly every day, Eliza's world looped up into mine, as too, every week, we could see on PBS photographs of those killed in war—in Iraq, this time—that is, if we dared to look. Nearly a thousand by that summer; more than three thousand wounded. And so many of the wounded were amputees; in fact, nearly all. I could not help but be struck by that: how *this* war, like the Civil War, was being paid for dearly in missing arms, hands, legs. After all, wasn't that partly our fascination with the Civil War: the horror of it? How supposedly well-balanced men could line up across a field to march forward to butcher each other and be admired for it? Aside from the Civil War's being the defining test of our democracy and the necessity to remove the stain of slavery, wasn't it really Lee, Grant, Lincoln, gallantry, carnage, Southern arrogance, the determination of the Union, the heroism of Chamberlain's Maine company at Gettysburg—weren't these what transfixed us: the sheer insanity of all existing together, the befuddling scope?

Two nights before leaving, 1861

Dear One,

I have so much to tell, so much to set down for fear no one will ever know what it was like and why—to be promised, given, owned. Yes, let it all be known that I had my reasons—I was not bad or cruel or cunning as Hattie Louise, who is dying— drying up like an old pea in a burned pot—says I am. She lies in her swathed bed as if already in a funeral robe, calling me here, calling me there—do this, bring that—and at each fetch rebukes me for not appreciating what my mother has done for me. And all the while, sitting on her French sheets with her dog Caesar beside her as though he too has bought her favors. The old hag's skeletal face haunts me, and she's not even dead yet. She's been in this house since a young woman, and Madam Francine takes care of her now because she says Hattie in her heyday was desired by more rich men in the city than a free fifth of aged whiskey. In short, my Dear One, I was "allowed" to be born here, in this house—a rarity Miss Hattie reminds me of since I could have just as easily been ripped out of my mother's womb by Dr. Gilmore (who is so obliging, still)—as so often so many here are—(the house sings with the voices of the unborn). Supposedly I am privileged to be in one of the finest—and it is true—a parlor house of great renown, and to have been promised to Mr. Preston Cummings, one of the richest bankers in New Orleans, to be his courtesan upon my seventeenth birthday. Ascending to the level of a courtesan is admired here. My mother has done a great deed for me. But Mr. Cummings smells bad—like overly sweet cigar smoke and onions. His face is marked with the pits of smallpox—only some, but still, it is a face I loathe to look upon, though there once was a time when ...

I looked up from the letters. Several of them stopped in mid-sentence as if she had come to a place where the pain was so sharp, she had to clench her teeth. Her girlish voice vacillated between seeming mature beyond her age and being just what I had once been—seventeen: a woman, and yet not quite knowing what a woman knows.

As I searched in my imagination for who she was then—not yet Eliza Goode but instead Eliza Hamilton, barely seventeen—blending what I knew from the letters to what I was also reading from history, I felt that I could see her, there on the wall of my study, not yet moving but waiting. Since I am wary of anything that smacks of the fantastic—even consider myself immune to what science might prove to be merely a wish—my desire to recreate Eliza must have opened a particularly intense tunnel in my imagination. And I stepped through, as it seemed she did now too from the wall into my study, so that quickly, I began to see her running, barefoot, through fog, a black floral dress billowing at her ankles. She is more beautiful than even her photograph promised. Behind her, chasing, carrying his shoes, so as to steal out through the backstairs and onto the brick street, is Ned Tatum, the tormented young man who has grown up with her in that parlor house, the most renowned upper-level house of prostitution in all of New Orleans at that time. And, "You hope ...," "Shhhhh," "No ...," "Then don't get near." "Oh, but I will." Their panted exchanges hiss. Running behind her toward the St. Louis Cathedral in the four o'clock dawn, Ned is in black pants, a white shirt, flopping dark hair, his long nose tubelike and crooked at the bridge, his face pitted by the smallpox that nearly killed him when he was five. His lips curve in a feminine fullness; his ears twist oddly, like knots on trees, lying close at the lobes and then, comically, straight out. In the last month he has begun wearing rings—one on his right thumb and little finger, three on his left hand. A confused sexuality wars secretly inside him, muddied even more by how he feels about *her*. While they were children, he would chase her up and down the backstairs, into the kitchen by the stable and out into the courtyard, stopping to dunk her in the watering trough, after which, she would dunk him, while their bell-like laughter bounced on the courtyard walls. In the evenings they put on magic shows in the main room for the "visitors"—simple, sweet shows that could have been a mockery of their childhood's innocence in being so unlike the lewd, suggestive sketches that Madam Francine directed using the boarders as actors. All during their growing up, Eliza and Ned were surrounded by the erotic air, perfumed every late day with the smell of sex itself as it literally began to feed them, as it had since their births.

Probably Ned loves her more frantically because his desire is safe. They both are certain that she will never return it, and therefore, he will never feel the pressure to be the man he is not. Yet resentment of her, fueled by his self-loathing, could grow into a smoldering hatred to tip over into murderous desire.

It was the night before when he had told her, gleefully, the news he had overheard while running an errand downtown. Knocking on the door of her small bedroom on the third floor next to Hattie Louise's, he had called, "Eliza?" then rushed in to find her writing letters, reclining on her bed with the pink crocheted coverlet under the mosquito net that most of New Orleans used.

"Thought you'd want to know, your fine banker—"

"Mr. Preston Cummings?"

"Yes … has entered the code duello."

Her breath caught. Ned nodded, smiling viciously. "Suppose he'll be killed—you'll be stuck here forever! Old Hattie Louise, that's who you'll be." He sneered. His eyebrows tightened.

Eliza smiled, thinking: *He does not know my recent vicious thought. Why! Only just now I'd been thinking the perfect solution to the Mr. Cummings problem is to have him dead.* "How?" She sat forward, hiding her letters under her day dress. "How has this come about?"

Ned moved closer, gloating with information. He was quick to tell what he'd overheard. And quick to spill out how it all met the intricate ritual of the code duello, which was as complicated as it was insane. A visiting gentleman from Savannah, a banker himself who had arrived in town only a few days before, had climbed the steps to the door of Preston Cummings's bank while Preston himself ushered the visitor in. Suddenly, the Savannah banker looked up and simply stated aloud what might have been only a passing thought: "Why! In Savannah we have liveries with trim work like this."

Whether the Savannah banker meant his comment to be an outright insult was beside the point. Preston Cummings took it as one and flicked his glove at the man, so that an hour later their seconds were meeting to busily work out the details. By noon the next day, one or both of the gentlemen would supposedly be lying stiff in a grave.

Eliza got up, her stomach churning with nervousness. She took a deep breath and held it. She pushed aside the cloth bag she had been packing. Ned did not realize what the bag meant. He was consumed with his own announcement that he was joining one of the companies leaving by train in a day. Dare she hope that Mr. Preston Cummings would indeed die in a duel—of all things!—and on the eve of the war she was planning to ride to escape him? Entering a duel at the outbreak of war made him seem twice as impetuous. "So it is for sure? You know?"

"Yes. And if he is killed, you'll never leave here. Whore. Slut. A Hattie Louise. Hattie Louise. You'll be an old Hattie Louise, forever here, here ..." Twirling his fingers in the mosquito net, Ned shuffled in his thin black slippers. And the cheap glass in his rings flashed red, pink and a garish blue.

What hurt her more than Ned's words were his wormlike complexion and comically protruding ears. His taunt, after all, was mostly air, like their childish quarrels. *Poor Ned.* All her life he had squeezed her between feeling sympathy for him and disgust. They each wore lives that their mothers chose as the only way they knew to provide for them. But loved, yes. At least, Eliza had been loved. In fact, loved to the point of feeling smothered. But poor Ned, his mother, swarthy, pressed to be acceptable white, double-dipped into the cosmetics of the time: zinc oxide for face powder, lead and antimony sulfide as eye shadow, mercuric sulfide as lip reddener, belladonna for sparkling eyes, dilating her pupils to look dizzy with desire. And from these finding herself suffering from lead poisoning, facing a slow death. She was also anemic, depressed, and no doubt had a touch of creeping syphilis. She overdosed herself with a bottle of laudanum. Dead three months. Eliza and Ned were locked in a kinship, blistering tight, complicated and sad in what she called *rojo violeta*.

He was as much of a brother as she could ever have. And yet only last week, suddenly, he had thrown his desire on her in a kiss, wet and slobbering, up and down her neck, her face. *Mine, mine, Eliza, be mine,* pawing with a desire so flagrant, it could be nothing but hollow. Pushing him away, she had stepped back, sickened, then saw his hurt in her doing so, blistering the walls in *lobo gris*. And quickly she said over and over, *O, Neddy, sorry, sorry, I'm so sorry.* Which he saw as only pity, a pity that inflamed his wound.

So there in her room when he told her about Mr. Cummings, she pushed, "What else, Ned? Tell me all you know."

And so she learned how the code duello had, by prescription, been meticulously followed, all the while Ned savoring his knowledge. If Mr. Cummings had flicked his glove in anger it would not have been accepted. Oh no, to do so would not have met the requirements, for anything less than cool, gentlemanly behavior would have required that the Savannah banker be horsewhipped instead of fought. So Preston Cummings had slapped his glove at the Savannah banker's cheek as if he'd been popping a fly. Furthermore, if the banker had been of lower social rank—well, he would not have qualified for a duel in the first place.

Immediately, the Savannah banker had sent his attorney as his second to meet with Preston Cummings's second, an officer from Cummings's bank. Meanwhile, the duelists themselves had attended a bankers' meeting and luncheon, acting as though nothing out of the ordinary had happened at all. Nonchalance was part of the intricate game.

The Savannah banker had napped at his hotel while Preston Cummings kept an appointment to be fitted for a new waistcoat. So it was there at the tailor's, while Ned Tatum was on an errand, that he had overheard Preston Cummings commenting that the next day's weather forecast promised a good day for dueling.

With an average of ten duels fought each day in the city—most often at a location named the Oaks—Ned could have taken Preston Cummings's remark as merely morbidly amusing. But it was the look in Mr. Cummings's eye that said otherwise. It held choked rage. That both gentlemen should be Southerners on the cusp of a war made no more dint in their idiocy than their belief that they would each grow even richer from the war. That is, one of them, since dying in a duel, would make keeping appointments at the bank difficult.

By the time Ned was nearly finished telling all this to Eliza, he was afire with the rumored specifics: Cummings's second had won the coin toss. He chose the weapons. The Savannah banker's second had been allowed to choose the venue: pistols at dawn at ten paces in St. Anthony's Garden behind the St. Louis Cathedral.

"Just like a Savannah boob—choosing a church rather than dueling at the Oaks. Bet he's figuring the Almighty's on his side." Ned's eyes expanded in excitement.

"For God's sake!" Eliza ran out of her room. As she passed Hattie Louise's door, she was stopped by a cry. "My pot, Eliza! Empty my pot." Eliza, ducking in, grabbed the putrid chamber pot at the side of Hattie Louise's bed, where Hattie Louise was propped up on pillows with her Pekingese, Caesar, beside her.

"There. Take it there. Clean me here." All the while, Eliza did so with loathing. Hattie Louise took the moment as another opportunity to deepen the taunts she relished even more now that her rants were the only power she could feel against *that,* the gentleman named *death* waiting on the doorsill. "An ungrateful child, spurning what your mother worked her heart out to arrange. You are a selfish, evil girl, Eliza. Promised to Mr. Preston Cummings, one of the city's finest, since you were four. And him paying one thousand dollars for the privilege of it! What kind of honoring of your mother is that? Hmm? Hmm? You ungrateful child! Your mean nature will sour your life, Eliza. I've watched it grow since you were born. It will be a canker you cannot cut out. It will kill you! Kill you!" she cackled.

Finished, Eliza turned to run out, but on the bureau by the door was the lunch Zapa had left that Hattie Louise was too sick to eat. Quickly, Eliza tore a corner from the meat and put it into poor Caesar's mouth, who waited so patiently with his mistress for the death he could not know of. Then Eliza was out, down the hall, with again Ned trailing her, down the backstairs and out into the courtyard, past the oval-stone watering trough to the kitchen where Delia was bending over the stove, shoving in a pan of cornbread. Ned caught up, hissing behind her, "I hear the Savannah banker is a crack shot. Count to three and ... bye-bye, sweet life, Eliza, you'll never—"

"Shush, Ned."

"Watch yourself," Delia said, pushing Eliza back so as not to be burned at the stove. Delia, wiry, arms with sinewy muscles like bailing wire, eyes like spots of clover in a dark field, always kept drooped lids to hide her crafty intelligence. Her features were wide but doll-like. Born into slavery on a plantation near Natchez, Mississippi, she had never been anywhere else until her master died, and his widow, like many, wanted to move to the city for a more active social life. So the widow sold off the land and most slaves, then leased out Delia and her husband, Quashi—Delia at Madam Francine's parlor house as a cook and Quashi at the livery, as a farrier and skilled tack craftsman. Each were worth, on paper, one thousand and twelve hundred, respectively, so "hiring out their time" was keeping the widow from having to feed and clothe them, plus dropping a sweet monthly fee of fifty dollars for each into her pocketbook, ten of which she credited to Delia and Quashi to buy their own selves from her.

And true to the culture of slavery, Delia had acquired—and by now perfected—the trait of obsequiousness, flattering any white person she might be in the presence of, while practicing a learned reluctance to tell any of them the truth. At thirty-five, she had given birth to seven children, three dead, the rest sold, and she told no one, since as a young woman at the plantation where she worked in the fields, a visiting guest once asked why her children were so dirty, and when she answered the truth— that she was too tired from being in the fields all day to often bathe them at sundown—she was flogged for "complaining." Eliza is the age of what Delia's first child would now be. And over the last three years, Eliza had spent so many hours in the kitchen—for the parlor house, shut away from society, breeds, by necessity, a soul-aching loneliness—that Delia has forgiven Eliza for the feared white pigment of her skin. Besides, Eliza is unlike anyone Delia has ever known. Eliza, Eliza Goode-to-be. To Delia, a mysterious magic wormed itself into the girl-child, and Delia has often witnessed it at work: Eliza copying languages as if knitting them off her tongue from the threads spun from the mouths of visiting men. The way Eliza can "read" a room, discerning moods as the tints of colors thrown from skin like sweat or smells. If Delia didn't know better, she would think the child had been touched by the island spirits, in which many in the city believe. But no, Eliza is Eliza. She possesses her own brand of magic.

And then as Eliza stood before Delia on the afternoon when they both learned of the duel, Delia misread Eliza's excitement, thinking Eliza was about to give away her plan to follow the hordes of men rushing to answer Jefferson Davis's call for an army, until Eliza whispered in Delia's ear, "Preston Cummings is about to fight a duel."

"What?"

"Ned says so. He overheard."

Ned bowed and repeated proudly the details. Then he picked up a square of cornbread and walked out.

Delia turned to Eliza, hissing a whisper: "What does it matter if he is dead or not. You are leaving from here. Quashi has picked a horse for you. No matter how this war ends, either way, *I* will be free. But you—"

"Delia, I'm afraid."

"Good! It'll keep you alive. Now here, cut this foolishness. Pray the gentleman from Savannah shoots Mr. Cummings's head off."

"I've already been wishing it, Delia."

****

That night, the news of the duel passed between the rooms as if an eel had slipped up out of the great river to curl in each ear. And, as usual, Eliza's mother, with her chestnut hair framing her chinalike forehead—and smelling of the fresh springs of jasmine pinned over her left breast where the waxy green leaves fluttered on her skin as she breathed—insisted that Eliza sit at a dining table with her and Mr. Preston Cummings. His burning eyes held the only giveaway that he had another man's death on his mind. But then, Eliza had seen a similar lust in his eyes before.

And on that night, the eve she was praying to be his last, at one a.m. he opened her door, parted the mosquito netting, lifted up the pink crocheted coverlet and her nightgown, so that she found her mind on the ceiling, crawling there, as he on her, wondering: *Was this lust for me there, even as I was five and six, the whole of my growing up? How had I missed it? Why had it not assumed at least a color in my thoughts? But already, from that day in March, five days after Mr. Lincoln's inauguration when I had been told of the promise, he had not waited. No.*

Right away, one month from her seventeenth birthday, on the back stairway, he had forced her hands on the stairsteps, and taken her from the back, lifting her skirt as if tearing open an envelope, and there opening her mind to where she could feel what Hattie Louise accused her of—a rising, cunning meanness, which now tastes like silver, *a putrid vinegar bronceado* that keeps coming up over and over in her throat. Before then, she regarded him as a father. And now he is a father-beast who splits her heart's memories like firewood on a stump.

So on the morning of the duel, he might just—might just, and ... so, if dead, couldn't he then solve all my problems, if not cure my heart?

****

Ned Tatum reaches the iron railing of the fence around the back of the St. Louis Cathedral just after she does. The sun is barely up. A scattering of people are already there. Eliza's fingers wrap around the cold iron of the fence. The air seems to taste like metal, as if she has licked the fence railings. Her throat tightens. The air has a blood-orange tint, *naranja rojizo*. Her heart pounds so hard, she can see it lifting the cloth of her bodice. The carriages draw up. They park by the side of the cream stucco building. The cathedral's spires are pink fingertips in the early sky, praying. As a young child, she had once stolen inside, alone, wondering about the idea of God—looking for Him, this one whom so many seemed to either fear or look to for gifts. The walls of *azul cielo* were splattered with the color of hope. But after no sightings and no answers, she walked out the side door where now the swish of skirts and pant hems swipe the fence as the onlookers turn to watch the doors of the duelists' carriages open. The horses snort; their harnesses creak. So everyone knows now: There has been no last-minute change. The code duello would allow an apology to be offered on the way there, when a simple response could be sent, a mere "Oui." But the fact of the carriages appearing report that the prescribed time has elapsed. Now no apology *can* be accepted.

Preston Cummings steps down from his carriage and enters the church. Eliza cannot see him now. She leans her head upon her upper arm. She can still smell him on her. She imagines the sound of his fine black boots on the church's floor. There will be the wax smell of the candles as he moves through. And then out into the garden behind it, where he reappears now, and she can study his black suit and gray pants, so elegant, really. And a top hat, of all things. He is finely dressed for this event of killing. The strange fire that she felt in him the night before is there still, but now seems frozen in a single intent. And she marvels that this lust for killing is so close to the other physical lust. He is smiling. And then suddenly he stops and lights a cigar.

The Savannah visitor follows, walking around to the other side of the walkway while Preston Cummings takes a few puffs of his cigar, then puts it on the corner of a stone column as though he will be back for it momentarily. The gentlemen's seconds stand with velvet-lined boxes holding the pistols. As the duelists take them, the seconds together pace off ten steps to mark the duelists' stations, then move to the safe margins near the fence.

Eliza hides behind a burly man, peeking around his back to

see. Preston's face is so familiar to her, she can't really *see* him. There has never been a time when she has not known him. He held her as a young child. He bought her elaborate dresses and tiny little shoes that imitated grown women's things. He taught her French, playing with her, hiding all across the back parlor under velvet curtains, under tables, in the closet, laughing. And then on her eighth birthday he gave her a tiny sterling silver vase to hold, a tussy mussy, with a pink rose inside. She then was just like any grown lady in New Orleans, holding the beautiful silver as they rode in his carriage behind his high-stepping black horses, the purpose of her prized gift to cover the smell of the street manure. The horses' harnesses creaked, his hand rubbed her knee, and she giggled, bouncing with the springy ride, in and out, through the streets. For years, his love—or what she thought was his love—inched around her, raining over her, playing parts in her made-up stories, her games. Her mother had never mentioned *the promise* to be kept on her seventeenth birthday. And even then, he did not wait, not even the three weeks to make his promise complete.

Father-love twisted is rotted meat, force fed. Her stomach flips. She cannot bear to think of all this now. No. *Hope only. Hope only.* She might be set free.

Now against the cathedral fence she leans down and peeks under the burly man's arm. Ned Tatum breathes behind her. She could identify his breathing anywhere with his twisted nose making the air go in and out like a butter churn.

Preston Cummings takes his pistol, facing the Savannah banker as they walk to the stations that the seconds have paced off. His skin is sun-drenched, toasted like caramel, his hair under the top hat shining blue-black. The sun rises and throws a lemon ray across the back garden. The Savannah banker seems unhinged now as he steps toward his firing station and nearly trips.

Preston's boots sound out on the walkway. His second calls out, "Are you ready?" Preston and the Savannah banker answer in unison, "Present." Eliza mouths her wish and even prays, for she might as well not take any chances that there is no such thing as this man named God, who can supposedly make anything happen. *Sweet God, go ahead and kill him. Please make him dead. Make him dead for me. If you do this, I will believe in you. For I doubt anyone else can perform that deed. I sense the Savannah banker is going to need your help.*

She catches her breath, feeling that with these wishes she is becoming what Hattie Louise says she already is. Well, so be it. She forms the words in a silent whisper over and over: *Die! Die! I hope you die!*

Preston Cummings raises his pistol, waiting, as any gentleman should, for his opponent's pistol to be in firing position, and his eyes slide beyond his target. There he sees her. *He sees.* His face registers his stunned reaction as he catches the words on her lips. He ducks his head as though trying to read again what he cannot believe, indeed cannot believe that she is even there.

Ned Tatum chokes on his own spit and begins hiccupping.

"Fire," one of the seconds calls.

The shots ring out. The Savannah banker's bullet grazes Preston's arm as he turns away from watching Eliza. Preston's bullet catches the side of the Savannah banker's neck and severs the poor man's carotid artery. As if a tight bag has been slit, blood spurts in a pulse-driven rhythm.

Saved by leaning to read Eliza's evil prayer, Preston Cummings turns to look where she had been standing. But she is gone, running, her own life now in a vise-grip of panic.

Chapter 6

How convenient it would have been if Preston Cummings had been shot in a more important body part and pronounced dead on the spot, unable to pursue Eliza or remember what he had read on her lips. Instead, his second rushed to him with a bandage for the slight arm wound, while the poor Savannah banker was lifted onto a stretcher and hauled off to the funeral parlor. Immediately, the clean-up crew went to work on the pools of blood seeping into the cathedral walkway. By then, Eliza was long gone, running to her room to grab her carpetbag to meet Quashi, to get the horse and go. Where, she was not sure. But no other option was open now. She could not even wait another day as she had planned.

Hurry, quick, aidez-moi! What might he do? Kill me? Want to, certainly. But no, no, no, he had said over and over, many times, he loved me. Love? Bah! It had all been fake, make-believe, actor's paint. All had changed so completely, so terribly! Behind me I heard Ned, his funny breathing, his feet like a rushing duck thrashing on the brick street. And in an upstairs window of the cathedral I caught a glimpse of a priest watching me—no comfort, I assure you.

She had seen before that look in Preston's eye when he read

her lips. She knows what it can lead to. She had once watched him at a gaming table reach across and take hold of a man's hair—incensed by the way the man threw down his card on the table—and dragged the poor man to the back hall where he beat him senseless with his cane. He was just about to plunge the jewel-handled Arkansas toothpick, hidden in the cane's handle, into the card player's throat, already splitting a thin, pink bleeding line, when Madam Francine rushed to put her hands around him, patting his face, cooing in French. She succeeded in giving him a drink of a calming herb in her silver tumbler, which she said had once served medicine to the King of France. With other "customers" she would have simply called the bouncer, Sabine, and bodily ushered the drunkard out. But not Mr. Preston Cummings. Oh, no, not him—not who had been coming to her "boarding house" for sixteen years, dropping enough fifty dollar bills to support all twenty "boarders" for more than an entire year. Also, most recently, on the eve of Lincoln's inauguration—in fact, only weeks before—when on March 4, Eliza had watched Preston Cummings pick up the New Orleans paper, coldly staring at the article, and rail that "Lincoln, that frontier baboon, the most dangerous man ever set loose in office—what a pity that no one has had the good sense to rid us of him in a duel before he could get a foot in the White House."

True, Preston Cummings's objection to Lincoln was born of a complex, long-running grievance. Often in loud complaint, he railed against the Federal government for placing high tariffs on European goods and allowing Northern businesses to raise the cost of theirs to match, giving rise to the belief that Northern wallets grew fat at the South's expense. And even though most of those tariffs were repealed before Lincoln's election, to banker Preston Cummings and thousands of others, the offense cut to the bone, fueling the conviction that the North was dead set on destroying the Southern way of life. "A dictator. That's what we've got now. You wait and see. Baboon Lincoln will show who he really is. Dictator! Someone ought to shoot him now and save us the trouble later. We are but sweet people wanting only to protect what we love."

No, it was not at all uncommon that Preston Cummings would mix brutality with tenderness, not when the Southern code of honor valued men's bravery above good sense. It was distinguishing brutality from bravery that was the sticky point. He had already killed five men in duels before the morning he added the Savannah banker as the sixth. So Eliza knows only too well what his temper can lead to.

Now as she runs through the back courtyard, Ned is again behind her in leapfrog strides, bringing him up close, trying to unhinge her.

"So, you were lucky this time. Maybe you won't be a Hattie Louise, at least for ten years."

"Oh, stop it, Ned. Stop!"

"So, what will you do? Move to the apartment he has picked out for you? Think that he will marry you? Yes, marry you, Eliza! Be accepted into the city's social life? Ha! *I don't think so, Eliza. I don't think so, Eliza.*" This last he singsongs, and his voice is comically tuneless.

She trips Ned at the watering trough and pushes him in.

"Delia!" She whisper-yells: "Send word to Quashi, now. Now!"

Delia comes to the kitchen door, reading all the code words of what Eliza is saying. She looks up. Ned is climbing out of the trough, shaking himself like a dog, pretending to not care. Eliza runs into the kitchen, where she can whisper closely to Delia: "He wasn't killed. And, oh heavens, Delia, he caught me wishing he was!"

"Gracious, child!"

Above them in the courtyard, Madam Francine pushes open her French doors onto the cool morning, and then opens the black iron bars to step out onto the balcony, calling, "Delia, are you there?" She holds her dog, Lu Lu, letting the poodle sniff the air. "See, my pretty, what a lovely morning. Delia. Oh, Del-ya!"

Delia comes out of the separate kitchen house and looks up.

"Poached today. And ham. Oh, and a little hollandaise." Madam Francine's dressing gown is purple satin. Always she wears purple as a symbol, and a reminder, that she is a master of the purple arts. Today her gown has a winged collar, stretching upward to hide her aging neck, and just below her waist are two specially designed pockets covered with Swedish cotton lace— one to fit her dog, the other, her pearl-handled pistol.

"Yes, ma'am," Delia calls. "I certainly shall. And quick as can be. What a pretty gown, Miss Francine." Then to Eliza: "Hurry. Get your bag and run to the back of the Gallatin Street tannery. Wait there. I'll get word to Quashi."

Madam Francine puts Lu Lu in the specially made pocket and closes her window, pulling the heavy velvet curtain. Eliza tiptoe-runs up the back steps.

Ned is now at the kitchen door. "For me too, Delia. Poached and ham. I'll be back in dry clothes." Then he taunts, "Where you going so fast, Eliza, Eliza, promised to the man who didn't die-za, die-za."

Delia turns back to the kitchen. Her helper, Zapa, is putting new firewood under the cooking pots. Today he borrowed one of the boarder's rouge and rubbed it on his lips. Ned eyes Zapa with self-loathing disgust, hating what he knows he himself is but cannot admit, and belittling the one who wears his inner and outer self with such ease. "You better wear gloves, Zapa; you'll hurt your pretty hands. They don't take men in the regiment with such hands," Ned jeers.

"Who says I want to be part of any regiment? I have no intention of going to this stupid war. It will last only a few months anyway."

"I've joined."

"You?" Zapa laughs.

"I have."

"They must already be desperate."

The rage in Ned's eyes is akin to that of a cornered animal. "When they requisition my rifle, I might come back and kill you."

"Go ahead, my sweet pea."

Ned turns and heads up the backstairs. A hush cloaks the house. No one will wake or move until nearly noon. From upstairs, Eliza hears Ned's footfalls on the backstairs. They match the rata-tat-tat rhythm of the military drums in the distance.

Dear One,

The way I had to leave, abandoning so many pretty things—French muslin, taffetas, silks. O, I did not intend that! I grabbed only one bag. Here I was flying off with three dresses, four underskirts, one hoop, three chemises, as many pairs of stockings, two underbodies, my makeup box, a hair piece and this writing material and my hopes, ignited by fear! Until that moment at the cathedral, he had not even guessed how much I loathed the thought of what he and my mother had concocted for me—playing with my life as if I were a chip on a game board. Courtesan or not, the arrangement came to me—to me! So suddenly and unexpectedly. What I believed was fatherly adoration had now become soot. The disease of having been betrayed I had caught, and it was curdling my stomach as if I were being reamed from the inside out. As for my mother, why! I think I have been trying to forgive her since the very moment of my birth. Simply, she knows no better. And now, I could not feel who I was! As if I had been living underneath the lid of a music box, my life suddenly closed and was being reopened onto a cruel, foreign place. Separation à l'agréable was not even a possibility. O! I can't explain the depth of my confusion! And now, the war. A way, so suddenly open! He was never one to be denied or even contradicted, so the rage I unlocked in him would never let him let go of me now.

I grabbed my one bag, and hurried, imagining how it would be when they realized what I had done. No one in the house awakes before noon. By lunch the chatter, as usual, would start. No doubt it would focus on me and Mr. Cummings, and, perhaps the fact that, on this day, my seat at table would be empty, (for there is always a heavy lunch of the best meats and milk and vegetable accompaniments; Madam Francine spares nothing in providing the nourishment needed for the long nights.) and then, the mystery that no one can find me.

Every day at noon when the house wakes up, it is like a beehive. Women, women talking all the time, all the time, this and that! Playfully teasing, becoming crude even as the day wears toward evening as a way to prime the mind for what will be a night's work. I laugh now remembering: Pillow fights, contests of wind-breaking, naked dances in which the most giggled flesh wins. Yet every day, like clockwork, at four p.m., the house suddenly grows quiet. Zapa sets piles of clean sheets in each of the twenty rooms. He places fresh flowers by each bed. And always the flowers are mixed with jasmine, lovely fragrant jasmine. Indeed, the women wear jasmine pinned to their frocks, often if not always. The flower itself has become a badge of who we are. And then Zapa fills the basins with water and drops of purple permanganate of potash with which to privately cleanse the men's organs de plaiser. (Madam Francine is always so careful about disease.) Then Zapa will set the dining tables and chill the wines. Everyone will be so elegantly dressed, taking their places in the large parlor rooms with their flashing chandeliers: Ramey the Butler ready to open the door, Cal at the piano, tinkling a gay tune into a rollicking beat, accompanying the fine food, the elegant dishes, the clink of champagne, the playing of cards by those who wait. And then, by the time the evening ritual is well underway, it will be known: I am gone. I will have escaped my life!

But, passing Hattie Louise's room, holding my breath against its sour smell, I heard Caesar whining, mistaking the sound of my footsteps for the sign of breakfast. I did not stop. I rushed down the backstairs, carrying my running bag, knowing Delia would be keeping Ned out of sight in the kitchen with a plate of food, and my mother would still be asleep, as the others. Then I heard, "Pretty Eliza!" Madam Francine's voice stopped me. I was just outside the courtyard door, the two carriage horses looking out their stable doors, neighing for oats as though dueting with Madam Francine calling through the bars of her window, bars that supposedly protect us all: "Eliza, up so early? Here, come here. Come have breakfast with me. Don't tell me you have been worried about Mr. Preston Cummings! Why, I told him last night if he lost his sharp aim this morning, I'd never speak to him again! And I have just now received word he has survived! Ah, but sweet Eliza, don't you know he's not likely to die from anyone else's shot? Only mine!" Her laughter, like the sound of a boiling pot, is usually contagious.

But today I was terrified into silence. She suspected I was fleeing. Yet if anyone would have been for me, it would be she, who is a mother to us all. It was the money that would be the stickler—ah! How indeed would they hash that out? Would she have to return it? Apparently Mr. Preston Cummings paid very *dearly to wait for me!*

Well, for what he thought he bought he can wait for all eternity now. Or until the gates of Hell swing open for the both of us.

"Oh, but I am in a hurry, Madam Francine," she calls. "I am on the way to the apothecary for Hattie Louise. She's in need of more calomel and laudanum. And I promised I'd search out jimsonweed to make her a soothing tea."

Clearly, Madam Francine has sensed that Eliza is in the midst of fleeing, but Eliza is not yet sure what she will do about it. As they each keep up a charade, Madam Francine sweetly replies, "I know, dear. But you can at least have a glass of juice before you go. The apothecary is not even open yet. Delia! Move along."

Eliza exchanges a look with Delia. Delia nods, picks up the breakfast tray and follows Eliza as she climbs the stairs again, quietly. Down the hall, Eliza knocks on the door to Madam Francine's room.

"Put it there, Delia." Madam Francine points to the round table in the corner, set with white linens and silver. Vases of jasmine perfume the room. Madam Francine's dressing gown swishes. Her henna-tinted hair is pulled upward in wings and secured with silver combs. She does not yet wear her daily make-up, a heavy dusting of powder, giving her aging skin even more translucence. Her features are pretty: full lips turned upward by years of greetings, as though playing hostess to nightly parties that are not just parties but a lucrative business equal to the most successful man's holdings in the city. Her face, a bit jowly, sports a sharply sloping nose, hugged by close-set eyes that, somewhat birdlike, are mesmerizing. It is there, in her eyes, with their playful faded blue, like sun-bleached violets, that she practices her power. It's said she can persuade even the most stubborn to be led. And often she is described as being as tough as a cast-iron pot and as wily as a starving squirrel. More than once it's been said that she could battle a rattlesnake and give him the first two bites.

Few know of Madam Francine's past and how it has fueled her strange ambition, of the promise she made to herself and of which, recently, she confided to Eliza, how at fifteen, defiled by a man of the church—while praying alone (God help us!) on knees, her back to him—she vowed to live on her own terms. The trauma caused her to fester, so that in time she became obsessed with fashioning a life where she could say *yes* to only those men she chose, and also to say *when*. Eventually her vow matured into a habit of mocking life, defying it to be none other than the grandest of jokes, and now at forty-nine, with her waist disappeared into plumpness—courtesy of the crèmes and sauces that are her specialties—she lifts Lu Lu scrambling from the pocket of her gown and puts the dog on the floor as it whines. Delia takes a compote of livers from the silver tray and sets it on the floor in front of Lu Lu.

Madam Francine gestures to Eliza to sit. Delia turns to leave the room, giving a knowing look to Eliza, mouthing, "Hurry."

"Come, Eliza. Sit with me."

"But Hattie Louise is in pain."

"Yes, I know, dear. But let's have a little breakfast. Mr. Cummings won't be here for a bit. He's getting stitched up at Dr. Gilmore's."

Eliza gasps. She knew he would hunt her, but now she is caught. "Will he even try to kill me?" Oh, she had not meant to blurt that! *Que le ciel m'en préserve! I have no more control over my stupid self than if I were three!*

"At least, not right off," Madam Francine wryly replies.

Eliza jerks, standing up to run, but then sees that Madam Francine is joking, laughing with her head thrown back. And Lu Lu is whining. The room blooms pink, a *clavel rosada*.

"I think he wants more from you than that, Eliza. However, if you frustrate him too much, he may indeed come to that." She chuckles.

It is clear now Madam Francine is artfully hiding the seriousness of Eliza's predicament. "So, my darling Eliza, tell me—you don't like this match your mother has made?"

"I had no say in it! None! And now the one who has been like a father to me is a beast. And worse, I learn he long ago bought me!"

"Oh! And how I wish I'd charged twice what we agreed on. You've grown so lovely, Eliza. Twice as pretty as your own mother, who is stunning indeed. Why! You're by far the most beautiful girl I've ever had here—indeed, that I may have ever seen even."

Eliza's foot taps the floor. Her fingers wad the cloth of her skirt. Lu Lu smacks and licks her lips. Eliza watches a fuchsia tint on Madam Francine's chest heat and spread. She and Eliza might jest, but underneath, both are aware of the dark threat of twisted lust and where it might lead.

Eliza glances beside the door at the magnificent étagère filled with blown-glass statuettes. Everything in the room testifies to Madam Francine's educated taste: the carpet that is burgundy velvet, the walls papered in a French lavender print. The mosquito bar on the mahogany bed is made of lace and a basket of flowers is suspended from the tester. Around the walls are costly oil paintings of nudes and of men and women in the midst of intercourse, which are painted in brilliant reds and yellow hues, all copied from *The Kama Sutra*. Throughout her house, Madam Francine has drawn themes from the Sanskrit Hindu erotic literature, even advertising herself and her boarders as artists who employ the sixty-four sexual arts described in *The Kama Sutra*. At dinner she calls her girls veshyas, which in Sanskrit may mean prostitute, but in *The Kama Sutra* is elevated to meaning "artists in Kama," a knowledge to be learned and revered. At the foot of her bed is a statue of Kama himself, a handsome youth holding a bow and arrow, ready to pierce his subjects with desire.

Madam Francine is not unique, only rare.

Driven by her own choked rage, she entered the oldest of professions by guile, then milked its complicated culture. She never had a lack of young women knocking on her door, asking to work there. With shipments of females arriving in the "new world" to grow the population, young women were forever falling on the sharp reality of fraudulent marriages, widowhood or abandonment, to then face starvation. If they had children, their prospects couldn't have been worse. Crossing the ocean, enticed by rags-to-riches stories, they found themselves working as servants or seamstresses, the only occupations available to them. And with their average wages of only two dollars a week, joining the demimonde was a beckoning side street. Arrested for prostitution, women listed their occupations as servant or seamstress. More than half were immigrants, almost all under the age of twenty-five; half had children.

So Madam Francine never had trouble recruiting beautiful girls to work in her elegant parlor house, splitting to them twenty percent of the forty dollars she charged each male for his visit, giving each girl weekly earnings of no less than thirty dollars. Her price was exorbitant, and certainly out of the ordinary since the average public woman in a common bordello earned no more than ten dollars a week. Madam Francine had the pick of whoever walked into the demimonde seeking a living. But then, Madam Francine was anything but ordinary.

Most girls held the belief that "it would be only for a little while," and, if they had to give away their children to one of the city's numerous orphanages, well, they believed that too, was "only for a little while." Soon, none were amateurs. All became thoroughly versed in what Madam Francine advertised.

Dear One,

Here! I set this down, once and for all. So you will know how it was and what my mother gave up for me, as well as what she hoped to secure for herself. For the demimonde is more varied than common myths would have you believe. Indeed, the classes of those who make their living such are of four—at the top, the parlor house, of which Madam Francine's is the most famous in New Orleans, if not the entire South. Next, the Bordello. Then the crib prostitute who is the public woman soiled beyond measure. And finally, those who walk the streets, who by then are ruined with disease or drugs or butchered by abortions. Indeed, Madam Francine is rare in that she recently learned to employ a French device, a cervical cap of beeswax, to keep her veshyas working and thereby often now avoiding abortions or the opiates commonly used to disrupt a female's cycle. It would seem that Madam Francine pays well enough for everyone working for her to escape this depressing future. But, ah ha! That is the sticky part. How many think of "future," or are even equipped to think of it? Only three here can read and write. And you have never seen such spending as they do! Why! The most exquisite and costly lingerie is simply a business necessity. And dresses. O, my! Each of us wears the most expensive, the most fashionable, every night. Going to the city shops is one of our greatest delights. Where else are we free to go? Besides, how many here have forethought or money management sense? Tomorrow is not a word in anyone's vocabulary. My own mother, pregnant with me, with no place to turn, knocked on Madam Francine's door, and so was taken in. Scottish, beautiful, poor, she quickly became one of Madam Francine's most desired veshyas. And so, there it is—our fear— our future, that is, if we ever take a moment to see it. And that, of course, is what Ned loved to taunt me with. And what my mother wants to prevent for me, as for herself, since, when Preston Cummings was promised me, I could arrange for her to live, eventually, with me. Her future was as linked to mine as if we were still connected by skin.

Thus, the scale of four was what most slid down as age robbed appeal. Many then took their own lives, as did Ned's poor mother, who out of pity for her, and for Ned, Madam Francine protected until the end. As she then protected old Hattie Louise. Otherwise, Madam Francine is as hard as any, pushing out those who fail to be asked for when she sends out her invitations—O, yes! Madam Francine discreetly sends invitations, embossed, hand-delivered by a hired courier or Zapa, and she secures new "boarders" every few years. On the street or in the houses, there is that secret spoken invitation: the simple sprig of jasmine pinned to the bodice, so as to utter in a flirtatious, discreet way, "Want some ...?" Rarely do any say no. Indeed, Madam Francine has become one of the most powerful entrepreneurs in the city. She has done so through her own intention and what she calls a desire to escape being a femme couverte, the property of a husband. Only in Mississippi can a woman own property, thanks to a law troublesomely made in 1839, which Madam Francine laughingly says still does not suit her, since she cares nothing for Mississippi men, at least not for the long haul. No. The story she tells has her coming, as a young girl, from France to the great Port of New Orleans, where she found work as a cook. O! She has the most artistic feel for creating exciting dishes from scant cupboards, *thereby saving expenditures through cleverness. And she was, as a young cook, so successful, she was never without work, and found she loved, absolutely could not be without, the feeling of her own earnings. So she took them and parlayed them into purchasing her first parlor house. Then the next one, and next, until now she is the owner of one of the finest properties in the city. Three stories and brick! She is even considered an equal to the businessmen who are in the top rungs of New Orleans society, except she has no protection from the law—ah, she laughs, she exists outside the law, and is so well protected by virtue of her associations, does not need it! Besides, her law, she says, exists under her skirts and in the pistol in her pocket! O! How easy she makes it seem—presenting to each evening visitor a bill with prices for not only the choice of his veshya but also the elegant food and wines with prices doubled. O! How she relishes her power!*

"Yes," Madam Francine says now, looking at Eliza and spreading out wrinkles on the tablecloth with her jeweled fingers. "I've always thought you wouldn't be suited for what your mother planned for you. But she was set on it. And I thought, well, maybe. You are very special, Eliza. In one way you are like me—too independent-minded to lead only one life. And particularly one that someone else chooses for you. So, I suppose you have decided to run away? Hmm?"

"A regiment is leaving tomorrow. The word has gone all up and down the street. Some of us are planning to follow it. It's said that all sorts of people are following it. The army will need cooks and blacksmiths and laundresses. And—"

"Ah, yes ... and ... so which will you be?"

"Whatever is needed."

"I have no doubt you can pull the strings to your own life. But remember, Eliza, your mother and I have only your best interest in mind. I think you may be back. Hmm? Well, if so, then, no regrets. And, either way, you mustn't hate us."

"Having a father become a beast is enough for now." Eliza imitates the mocking laugh she's heard so many times from Madam Francine.

Delia suddenly bursts in. "Mr. Preston is coming up!" she

says, leaning against the door. She slips Eliza's running bag under the table.

Madam Francine stands up. Lu Lu begins barking. Eliza notes a *smoky noir* seeping under the doorsill and then hears a knock.

"Quick, Eliza." Madam Francine pushes Eliza into her armoire. "Squat down." She lifts heavy skirts over Eliza's head. Eliza now hears Madam Francine open the door and Preston Cummings breathing loudly.

Scorched sienna of clamped rage leaks through the hinges of the armoire. Eliza looks through the keyhole. His arm is in a sling. His cheeks are heated to a color that could be mistaken for a rash. She smells the sweet cherry smoking tobacco that seems to have seeped into his very skin, an odor as ephemeral and airborne as smoke itself.

"And so Francine, where is Eliza this morning?"

"Look at you! How well you have weathered the duel, Mr. Cummings. You know I don't permit anyone here this early."

"Today is different. I need to see my darling Eliza."

"Oh well, she's run to the apothecary to get medicines for Hattie Louise! Oh, Preston, as you know, Hattie is having a most terrible time. St. Anthony's Fire, the doctor thinks it is."

"I have to see Eliza."

"Yes. Well, would you like to wait for her downstairs?"

"Perhaps I'll go meet her on her way back."

"Yes, you could. Or, think about this—she should be here in only a minute. Why not wait in the gaming room? Delia will bring you some nice hot chicory coffee. Hmm? I'll break one of my daytime rules for you, Preston. If you're quiet, you can wait downstairs."

"Perhaps so. Ten minutes of waiting won't hurt, I don't suppose."

"Of course it won't."

Eliza hears the last of Madam Francine's purred suggestions, then his footsteps going out, and Delia chattering behind him. "Cream or black? And you want a sweet biscuit with it, Mr. Cummings?"

"Quick. Hurry!" Madam Francine opens the armoire and hands Eliza her running bag. "May the world smile on you,

Eliza. Let this war bring you fortune. And until then ..." Madam Francine quickly goes to her dresser and from a box pulls out a roll of paper money and coins that she hands Eliza. She then reaches out to hold Eliza in a motherly embrace, whispering, "Quick! If he suspects, I'll deter him awhile. *Aller. Je vous souhaite bonne chance!*"

"And you'll explain to my mother?"

"Ah, is there such a thing as explaining anything to your mother? She'll make you her own story."

Downstairs, as Eliza enters the courtyard, Delia's skirts swish around the corner and she whispers, "Quashi says he will ride with you to people he knows in Mississippi." She pushes a bag of food in Eliza's hands. "He's got a pass. As soon as Mr. Cummings hears what you have really done, he'll be headed straight to the train station. The regiment is already packing supplies there."

Eliza touches Delia's face. "You have been my angel, Delia."

A scream escapes the third floor. Doors bang. Eliza hears the shocked voice of what sounds like May Ellen's, whose room is across from that of Hattie Louise. "She's dead. It has happened. She is dead!"

For a moment, Eliza turns, startled by the little dog Caesar running down the stairs, passing under Delia's skirt and scurrying into the courtyard. Eliza hurries through the gate onto the alley toward Gallatin Street. Her feet skitter on the dirt road. The city is fully awake now and noisy with the excitement of war.

Chapter 7

Eliza rounds the corner and hurries down the shell road behind the tannery. Here, there is a wide receiving area where wagons bring hides to be made into leather goods, which is why, no doubt, Quashi chose this as the place where he could easily bring a horse to her. But he is not here yet, and she steps into the shadow of a doorway to keep very still and hidden. Leaning a little, she can see down to the corner, and, as usual, the street is teeming with its everyday crowd of cake sellers, knife sharpeners and fish peddlers. Yet today the sudden fever of war crowds the street even more, and a mood of hysterical gaiety throws a glow of *azul cielo* over all, as if everyone on the street is wearing a shawl.

Always when she is here, she feels stalked or endangered. Gallatin Street, a magnet for Spanish, German, Asians and a hodgepodge of Americans, is thick with saloons, dime hotels, bagnios, offices of prizefight impresarios with underworld connections and other shady businesses. More killings happen here than anywhere in the city. But then again, a girl secretly meeting a slave to ride off with him will hardly be noticed either.

But Quashi? Where is Quashi? She has seen him only a handful of times when he has visited Delia in the kitchen. She's not even sure she could pick him out of a crowd. And what if he does not come? What if she is forced again to consider taking the train to escape? Yes, it will be crowded, and there will be that chance to hide among many. But also, at every stop from New Orleans through Mississippi to Memphis, Preston Cummings could be there, hunting for her, lying in wait.

Public horsecars rattle through the streets, adding to the usual clangs and shuffles of the city. She hears someone yell, "Pokey Southrons! Get a move on! You're gonna miss the whole Second Revolutionary War!" Hundreds are being swirled into the war's call, like a tornado blowing a path out of the city. Folly? Fantasy? Or was it blind arrogance, when that very Sunday night, after Sumter, Jeff Davis called for one hundred thousand volunteers to trump Lincoln's call for seventy-five thousand? The 1860 census had counted the North at twenty million and the South at only nine, with nearly four million of those slaves, half under the age of sixteen. A mismatch or a subconscious death wish?

But Eliza is riveted only on her escape and watches anxiously up and down the alleyway. The tannery smells of blood and drying hides. Her legs tremble. She reaches into her left glove where her skin is itching from a nervous rash and scratches her wrist, raw, then goes to the corner to look up and down for Quashi. The livery with his blacksmith shop is not far. Why is he taking so long?

Soldiers in twos and threes walk down the street wearing new, dashing blue uniforms fashioned from what they think is appropriate. Butternut gray of the Confederacy is not yet standard; besides, the war is supposed to be so short, why go to such expense now?

Eliza hurries back to her hiding place and reaches into her running bag to finger the bills, curious about what Madam Francine has given her. Turning into shadow, she squints at the coins and bills: a total of twenty. Twenty! Twenty dollars! Was this a joke? Could Madam Francine not even spare the price of one night with a veshya? Burning liquid comes up in her throat. She squeezes the bills in her palm. What if Madam Francine had done this on purpose? And if so, why? *Why?* Was Madam Francine trying to assure that she would fail and have to return?

Or, more likely, be forced to do what she had been raised to do, as if to prove that she had no right to think above those who had raised her. Or worse, to prostitute herself night by night, as if on the street, sliding down the caste system they all feared. But then, another thought, even worse than the first: What if Madam Francine's affection had been, all along, only painted artifice like Preston Cummings's? Was Madam Francine no more a substitute grandmother to her than Preston had been a father? And if that were indeed true, how could she continue to live knowing this? Even the thought squeezed her stomach to nausea. Why, why had she been so unwilling to look at what her unique sense could have revealed!

She leans on the brick of the tannery and sinks to her knees.

Quashi. O, please, Quashi, appear! Is there nothing to do but wait? Wait? How awful to put one's future again in someone who may never appear!

She can hear out on the street now a drum and horn and loud singing. The manic revelry becomes so loud that her memory trips back, taking her thoughts to the summer when she was nine and such mania was similar but terrifying. Yellow fever had gripped the city in such a daily horror that a defiant frenzy took hold while the plague, which they called Bronze John, spread with its yellowed flesh and blood oozing from lips, gums and nose, and then the final retching of the feared black vomit as organs collapsed. Daily, a wagon manned by slaves had rolled through the streets, their voices calling, "Send out your dead! The dead here! Any dead around here, today?" In one week, one thousand went to the cemetery.

Funeral pyres had burned into the night. Cadavers piled up in cemeteries and brought such a stench that people walked the streets with handkerchiefs over their faces. Men dug trenches to push the bodies in like bad fish. Nightly, at Madam Francine's, visitors drank toasts to Bronze John, and gamblers over-bet in wild abandon. Two "boarders" died. Ned fell sick. His mother refused the usual remedies of bloodletting and purges, nursing him instead with ice and cold baths and the jimsonweed tea that Eliza's mother made him. Miraculously, he recovered. Madam Francine visited the houses of her ill regulars and nursed them either back to health or to their deaths, then attended their funerals. Eliza's own mother had nursed up and down the street, carrying her wildcrafting bag, where she kept herbs and mushrooms, pulverized and dried, the ones she so fervently believed in. Her reputation for new ways of cooking and healing burgeoned as she learned even more from the city's hodgepodge of cultures: Native American, African, Caribbean, French, Creole and Cajun. She added bay leaves to her collections to ward off bugs and made tinctures of wormwood, cloves and walnut hulls to keep parasites from the intestines. Certainly her efforts edited her and Madam Francine's reputations. They might be who they were, but still they added to the legend that prostitutes could have "hearts of gold." No one knew that mosquitoes carried the virus; it was simply noted that fall came, the air chilled, Bronze John moved on.

Hoofbeats now come down the alley. She sees Quashi turn the corner on a hearty bay while leading a small gray horse whose hooves curl at the toes like elf's slippers. The mare is tacked up in a sidesaddle, which looks so old it could have dated from the Revolutionary War. But clearly Quashi has oiled it so that, at least, its leather will not snap and kill her outright in a fall.

"Miss Eliza." Quashi touches his straw hat and dismounts, nodding toward the horse on his lead. "She's the only one I could borrow. If you've got five dollars, you can have her. Man owns her knows she's worthless, but I'm not a horse thief."

"Oh, Quashi! I can't spare five dollars. How do I know what I'm facing—tomorrow, the next day?"

"Yes'm, I know. Anyway, I'm going to take you up where I know people. I'm expected there this evening. Got horses to shoe. And in the morning, they can pass you on to others farther up. Delia says you'll make your way over to the train one day, just can't catch it near here. You send word, and I'll come get the mare next week."

Eliza puts her running bag on the saddle. How strange— Preston Cummings taught her to ride, taking her to the park on ponies he rented at the livery. But she's never ridden much. Quashi gives her a leg up, and she settles her skirt around the pommel of the sidesaddle and fiddles her foot into the stirrup. "And that please, Quashi." She points to the cloth bag still on the ground. "Food Delia gave me. No doubt her famous cornbread and sugar biscuits."

Quashi smiles. "Thank the Lord and Delia too." He mounts his horse and rides onto Gallatin Street. Across his horse's rump are the leather bags with his farrier supplies. Eliza's mare follows, its stride choppy and rough. People cross in front, bumping even the mare's nose, stepping out of the way at the last minute, and if they happen to look up and see Eliza, their gaze lingers.

Crossing Gallatin, she and Quashi head toward the east side of the city. Eliza reaches up and ties her hat tightly under her chin and bends the brim to hide more of her face. That morning, when she woke in the dark to rush to the duel, she had grabbed what she had worn the night before. After all, no one in the house owns many day dresses; it's the formal wear they dote on. So she notes now how obvious she seems, wearing black floral taffeta that is certainly not a day dress, or riding habit, or even the tea dress appropriate for later in the day, but instead the elegant wear of night, swishing with the mare's movement like swamp reeds. Her hat has a black veil and a wide brim. Those on the street look twice, as though either not believing what they see or to enjoy the visual feast. *O! It was a wrong choice already. Why had I not thought this out?*

As they cross the narrow street a short distance from Madam Francine's, Eliza hears a familiar high-pitched yelping. Quashi turns, as does Eliza in her saddle. Trotting toward her, lost and panicked, is Caesar. He recognizes Eliza, and perhaps too the smell of Delia's food that Eliza carries, and he runs faster, harder, yelping louder. "Quashi. Stop!" Kicking free of the stirrup, Eliza slides from the saddle and reaches down. She grabs Caesar with one hand. "No, Quashi, don't get down. I can myself." Quickly she remounts, for the mare is, if nothing else, low to the ground. She cradles Caesar under her arm. *How could I dare leave him destitute in the gone-wild city?* "Hush," she whispers to his excited whining at feeling safe with her. She rubs her face against his silky head and already regrets rescuing him, for when he lifts his head, there looking at her is the memory of old Hattie Louise and her curse.

They travel east, and on the corner a colorful movement catches Eliza's eye. She tightens her reins for a slower look. Walking down the street with two other men is Ned. He is wearing the flashing red and yellow of a Zouave's uniform: a fez with a blue tassel, a turban, a tight-fitting red jacket and baggy pantaloons over white leggings. *How fitting*, she thinks. And then, *O, Neddy, please, please find peace*. She ducks her head even more so he will not see her.

It is a mile to the bridge. Then they are on the road into Mississippi. She plods, watching Quashi's back as he travels on his bigger horse a length ahead. Caesar has fallen asleep, limp in the crux of her arm. For the first few miles, she chatters, trying to engage Quashi in the conversation that seems always on the tip of her tongue. "Beautiful marshland. I like marshland, don't you? And what do you call those tall bushes there. Do you know, Quashi?"

"Umm," he answers to each of her questions. Or "Don't rightly know."

So she tries conversation more personal. "Delia says she and you have known each other a long while. Is that so?"

Only a grunt comes back, nothing more, so Eliza begins humming to herself, accepting the *verte hue* across Quashi's shoulders, where she reads the truth: that he long ago gave in to his tumbleweed life and cares not a whit for talking of it. His neck sways with his horse's movement. He is thin to the point of looking slightly starved and has so few teeth that his lips are a collapsed cave.

So okay, Dear One,

Imagine this—me, rocking to the motion of the mare whose perfect name I decided was Worthless. Two miles out, kicking her every other stride to keep her going, and holding Caesar snoring his elf-snore in my arm, I kept staring at Quashi, staring at his head, seemingly as withered as a dried apple under a straw hat, thinking of him and Delia and how they had children and lost them, sold away, and that they had never been really married, since being property they could never be united in a way to be free of their master's intent. And then the moment came, as I knew it was bound to: my thoughts of what I might be losing by leaving the only place I knew. The picture of my mother bloomed in my mind. I imagined her lying

languidly amid her silk sheets in her lavender gown, yawning,
stretching, coming awake. And her waking fully to the scream of
Mary Ellen's finding Hattie Louise, and Mr. Preston Cummings
being pressed into service, even with his wounded arm, to be
gentlemanly helpful: calling for the funeral carriage, helping
Madam Francine dispose of the body, maybe even going to
the funeral parlor himself to follow up on arrangements. So,
ah, he was busy. They were all distracted. For a while, I was
safe from any search. And to distract my mind from thinking
of my mother more (my mother, O! Sweet, weak, wonderful,
awful mother!), I kissed the top of stupid Caesar's head and
told Worthless I thought she had great potential if she would
only raise up her back proudly and move quickly on her elfish
toes. And then, rudely ...

It is five miles across the border into Mississippi when
Quashi points and whispers, "Patroller," signaling the man
riding toward them on a tall roan horse. Instantly, Quashi stops.
Blocking them is a heavyset white man with a clock-round face,
a member of the militia that patrols the lower part of the state
to catch fugitive slaves. With the outbreak of war, rumors have
led slave owners to believe their property might be emboldened
to flee. Written passes are always required when slaves travel,
and now Quashi holds out the pass, written by the owner of the
blacksmith shop to whom he is leased. Laws against teaching
slaves to read and write are to make sure those, such as Quashi
now, had not forged his own pass. And if his answers and pass
are unsatisfactory, the patroller is empowered to whip him on
the spot.

"This is Quashi, my aunt's man, escorting me," Eliza quickly
offers. "I am on my way for a visit up-country to my cousin.
He knows the way and ..." *O! How I chattered on. My golden*
tongue on a mission to let us quickly pass.

"Says here," he reads loudly, " 'to shoe horses at Laurel
Plantation.' "

"Oh, yes. And that too. My cousin is there." Eliza smiles her
most fetching smile and tilts her head.

And I must say I was enjoying the moment. For I could
actually behold that heavyset, stupid man change from wearing
a mean rouge glow on the top of his head to a sea-washed verte

cap, in a sort of drunken-with-love swoon. I knew I could do it. And also that he would let us pass and admire me for as long as he could see me, at least the outline of me on poor Worthless. In departing, I whispered, "Come on, Worthless, step lively! We have to hold up our fine impression." I hate to say, she didn't give a fig about her impression or mine.

By dusk Eliza and Quashi enter the dirt road beside the cotton fields a few miles from the great river and the plantation where Quashi is expected. Riding close to the river, Eliza can hear a steamboat pass—its loud music, and the same feverish revelry heard in the city. They can then hear the sloshing water of the boat's wake, and from the thick bank foliage, cooing doves and bobwhites.

They ride through pinewoods, going out of their way to miss being seen at the great house, and follow a path to where the slave cabins and outbuildings take up a clearing of five acres between cotton fields. There is a stable here, to where they head, horses already tied and waiting. Light will be enough to shoe at least three before dark.

"*Howa, yebo, yebo,*" children chatter, running to meet them, mixing African words with plantation English. Little ones, barely toddling, are chased by older ones who are their caregivers. And behind them are two women with wide skirts and colorful rags wound over their heads, with baskets balanced there filled with just-picked vegetables from the meager patches behind the cabins. Three men call to Quashi in a truncated language of their own, mixing African with English and sometimes French, offering a cacophony of greeting, "Lo Quashi. Day 'bout gone. Aye, but enough left. You no ride lickity clippity, hmm?" Deep, melodic laughter. And then, the silent moment in which they stop and look at her.

Eliza knows they will change now to what Delia calls using the "sweet mouth," flattering her, creating their own sense of safety. "What a beautiful alabaster child!" Eliza looks around until she realizes the slave woman is talking about her, and now one woman reaches up to touch her dress. Caesar barks hysterically, no more fit to protect her than a circus mouse. Eliza hands Caesar down to one of the women and dismounts. One of the men takes hold of Worthless's reins and leads the mare to the stable.

"There's two here now for you, Quashi," one says, directing them to the shed row where horses are waiting to be shod. But halfway there, he points. "Massa." Across the field is a man on a dark bay, trotting in their direction. Quashi glances at her and points. "Hurry there." To one of the women, he says, "Hide her."

Eliza runs quickly to the nearest building where the woman leads her. She steps through the door, and then, stunned at what she sees, stops. She is obviously in the infirmary. Five women lie on the floor in the labor of childbirth, covered by filthy, thin blankets and attended by one woman, apparently a midwife.

The one who has led her here throws a blanket over Eliza and motions to the floor. Eliza rolls herself in the dirty cloth, scrunching her nose at the smell, reluctant to lie on the floor as the woman suggests. Instead, she sits against the wall, folding her knees to her chest. The woman points to her hat. Oh, yes, her hat. "So pretty." The woman reaches to touch it. Eliza takes it off. The woman throws a scarf over Eliza's head and whispers sardonically, "Guess we can do nothing 'bout the color of your skin. You best get down. Put your whole self under this blanket, lest he comes in here."

"Is he likely?"

"Always he checks to see who's birthing."

Eliza scrunches farther down against the wall, ready to roll onto the floor at the sound of footsteps. Over the occasional moans of the laboring women, she can hear outside the sound of men's voices—the white voice, and then the low throaty responses of his property. And mixed with them is the murmuring of the laboring women who hold birthing beads, rolling a string of them in their hands, focusing on them as their pains rise and wane. Finally, she hears the sound of Quashi hammering horseshoes, the clink and bang of metal, the whoosh of the bellows raising the fire, the stomp and snort of horses.

She peeks from under her scarf and sees that from under a blanket over the bent knees of one of the women, the midwife pulls a screaming baby, and then the doorway opens, and in the spray of light, a scarlet *rojo ladrillo* of pride floods across the floor. The outline of a man takes shape. Eliza rolls against the wall and lies flat, pulling her blanket over her head.

"How many today?" he asks.

"Five. By day clean, five," someone answers.

"And by end of the week?"

"Three, most likely."

Eliza holds her breath, peeking through a space in the blanket where the fabric is worn thin. Often she heard Delia say *day clean* for *dawn*. She wishes away the sound of him and his shadow across the floor. But instead she hears him walk across the packed dirt and glimpses him bending down to study the laboring progress of each woman or else at the product of her birth suckling at her breast. Then there is the sudden outburst of a scream mixed with the sound of the man's riding crop hitting flesh. Eliza flinches; her body reflexively jerks. She pulls the blanket taut, so that through the fibers she can make out the form of the woman lying on the floor across the way. Earlier, Eliza had been aware that this woman had given birth, had held up a fine, big son, naked and squalling. But now the man is leaning over this woman, yelling, "What have you done?! What?!" The sound of his riding crop cracks again as it comes down on the woman's thigh. Her high-pitched weeping is like that of a wounded animal. "Get up! Get up!" Again he hits her, then grabs her by the arm and pulls her up. He pushes her with his arm like a rod against her back to the door, yammering as he goes, "Tomorrow you'll be gone, gone. Do you hear that— gone. First thing in the morning, you're going to auction in New Orleans."

He turns, looking out over the room. "And any of you who do the same, will get the same. You'll be sold, or worse." He then brings his whip down on his own boot, and the woman flinches, her weeping now a whimper.

After the door is shut, Eliza lifts the blanket from her head and looks across the room. She watches the midwife go to pick up the wrapped bundle on the dirt floor where the woman had lain, and soon she realizes that the midwife is holding the newborn, dead. Either its mother had rolled on it, smothering it, or had choked it.

A stifled weeping moves through the room. The other women roll and moan, the pain of their birth labor now twice as hard with new grief and fear laid over them.

Dear One,

*How hard it was! I was hoping that by day clean, I would
be far away from there. I was horrified. I had never even
attended a birth! It was more than I could almost endure. I
was distraught by all that was around me and that I was at
the mercy of Quashi and each one of those hiding me. At any
moment, I could be discovered. Then, of course, I'd have to lie
my way out of why I was there and what I was doing—like a
raccoon in the midst of stealing a pie. And with one good look at
me, the master of that place might guess who and what I was,
and a whole new set of complications would arise. I lay, my
nose in the fibers of that awful blanket, wishing for the earth to
swallow me. And then, finally, I lifted the blanket and stood up.*

*I, who grew up in a parlor house, had now been lying
with the natural end product of what Madam Francine sold
so easily. Pregnancy, being what everyone I had ever known
feared worse than death, had put me here, knee deep (literally)
in it! And then the sweet, flowery smell of valerian root floated
across the room. The midwife was pouring the root tea from
a heated kettle into a mug, and I certainly knew all about
that from Mama. How often I had picked the white flowers,
macerating and drying them, as mother taught me, to ease her
backache. And then I witnessed the most amazing thing! From
a woman lying in the corner, two babies were coming—twins,
and as the last slid out, I walked close, mesmerized at this
event. And I saw that over one's face was a filmlike gauze. The
midwife handed the first baby to me, and she held the second,
imploring, "Help? Here." She pulled the embryonic sac from
the child's face and put it in a kettle. And here I was thinking
how Mother would love to see this. I remembered the day
she had read, as best she could, asking me to help, an article
in the Picayune about a slave, given an award by the South
Carolina Assembly for discovering plantago as an antidote
for venomous snake bites. Botanical remedies were Mother's
obsession; she was always searching for the cures slaves often
knew of. But then, being a hypochondriac would certainly lead
her in that direction!*

When I considered all that I had just witnessed, and what

I had now to bear in memory, I realized I could have expected it on any of the grand Mississippi plantations, what with slave holders tending to renew their stock every seven years, ever since March 1807, when President Jefferson signed into law the prohibition of the importation of slaves. The only source of renewing slave labor was exactly this—breeding them, encouraging reproduction at the rate of rabbits.

When Eliza could no longer hear the planter's voice outside, she still didn't dare to show herself, as yet. Instead she held the twin that the midwife had handed her, covering him with the blanket which recently hid her. She watched the midwife boil the sac into a tea and feed it to the child, telling the slaves' belief that being born with a caul was a sign that the child would have great luck in life and, also, be protected from ever drowning. Drinking the tea was a way of making the most of that. The mother, still lying on the floor, reaches now for the twin Eliza holds. She makes a clicking sound with her tongue and looks up gratefully at Eliza.

Eliza pulls the blanket from the newborn's face, and as she hands him to his mother, the newborn roots at Eliza's arm, then seems to instinctively turn and root at his mother's breast. "Such a beautiful baby," Eliza whispers. "And now, here's the other. Both tres beautiful. Very handsome."

"*Ewe.*" The slave woman reaches under her babies and, with one finger, holds out her birthing beads. "*Sala Kahle.*" She chuckles.

"Oh no." Eliza shakes her head, smiling. They both laugh.

"So that you might have the same luck," the woman insists.

Realizing they are a gift, Eliza takes the string of shell and wooden beads and slips them over her head, then goes from one woman to the next, bringing sips of valerian tea, giving a hand to hold, whispering encouragement. *And so I saw, I had lived my life removed from the regular world. So encased in what Madam Francine had built, I was as secluded as these who had never traveled except when sold. My mind stood on the edge of a great chasm, to be filled with what I could not even imagine. I had stepped into Delia's world. And not even her telling me of it would have given me this day.*

By dark, all six newborns were swaddled, lying in their mothers' arms, who nursed them, sitting on the floor, leaning against the walls. Eliza listens to the mothers' cooing, the puppylike grunts of the newborns.

Quashi is at the door. "Miss Eliza?" He holds a lantern and Caesar.

"Quashi!"

"Come."

She picks up her bags and follows him on the dirt road that is lined with more than twenty slave cabins. There is a cook's shop with hanging cauldrons, a cooper's shop with buckets stacked about under a porch, all lit now with lanterns as the work continues. Quashi, still carrying Caesar, who chews a scrap of hoof that Quashi trimmed from one of the horses, leads Eliza into a cabin. Its floor is dirt, its door broken, unable to be closed. Hens and ducks walk in and out at their leisure, searching out roosting spots. Half-clothed children crawl after each other on the floor, chattering, rolling and wrestling in play. Then heavy silence falls as they see her. Apparently, this is home to ten slaves, two families, the adults standing by the fireplace staring at her.

"Sophie," Quashi says.

A small woman comes forward saying, "*Yebo, Quashi*," and touches Eliza's dress. "Pretty, so pretty. *Kuhle*, yes fine."

Apparently this is where Quashi stays whenever he comes for a day of horseshoeing, and now the woman takes the bags from Eliza and sets them on the dirt floor against the wall. Quashi hands Caesar to one of the children, who passes the squirming dog among the others. The children kneel on the dirt floor, barking back at Caesar in high-pitched yipping. A timber-wolf-gray, the *lobo gris* of resignation, rises like a fog to the bare wood ceiling. Eliza breathes it, the weight of it filling her chest like a cold.

The women set out bowls and pour in cooked vegetables, a stew anchored with pigs' feet, the skin still on, boiled to hairless white. Eliza reluctantly sits on the floor, next to the children, wadding her skirt about her, bemoaning the beautiful taffeta being so soiled. Caesar scrambles quickly into her lap. As Quashi eats, leaning with the other adults against the wall, he studies her, occasionally smiling as she mimics the children's speech, chattering with them as they with her: "*Kulungile*, good." They slurp the stew. "Ummm." They all lie that it is delicious. Eliza thinks of the food Delia gave her and goes to open the bag and divide portions of Delia's cornbread. Holding out their hands, "Yes, *ewe*. *Nceda*, please." The children clap. Eliza smiles, copying them. They seem to laugh at everything she does. The adults, too weary to rise from where they sit, smile languidly.

"Here." Quashi pulls a mattress to her as the others settle onto the rough cloth stuffed with moss from trees. She lies listening to the faraway sound of a train, which reminds her of why she is fleeing, thinking of him, of Mr. Preston and the beast he became, and she shivers, then watches a patch of moonlight paint itself across the floor. She shoos away the duck that walks across her feet. Caesar is cuddled in the arms of a slave child, the dog's beady eyes closed, his breathing raising and lowering the child's arm across his side.

A hole opened in me like a yawn of cold across a sore tooth. Maybe that alone can explain my sudden decision. For, before daylight when Quashi woke me from a fitful sleep and motioned to follow him, I stood in the stable beside the man who was now to take me farther up to yet another plantation to others Quashi knew. He was a short, thin man as dark as whiskey, who wore the name of Elijah, as wrinkled as a spool of baling wire, and he instantly bloomed a putrid gerbe d'or as he brushed his eyes across me. He had been given a pass to deliver three milk cows to the next plantation, and they were hitched by rope to the saddle horn on the mule he rode. I turned to Quashi, and for a full two minutes put my hands over my eyes and let loose a river, I mean a bewailing equal to a three-year-old whose doll has been broken. Silly, stupid girl! I suddenly thrust five of the precious dollars Madam Francine had given me into Quashi's hands. "Here. Here! Give this to the man who owns her. Yes, yes. She has to be mine."

Quashi handed Caesar to me and took the dollars. So that's how I rode off before the sun was even up, on Worthless, whom I now owned as the only living thing I could touch from the only place I had ever known.

Chapter 8

Two days later, Eliza found herself sitting by a spring-fed pond, looking into her bag and gasping. There, on the satin skirt of one of her favorite dresses, a plum plaid with a full skirt to fit over a hoop, is a green-brown puddle of duck shit. In the night, one of the children must have stolen over to unzip her bag and look in, and thus left it open for the duck to visit.

And the only other two dresses in my bag were so wrinkled, I pulled them out, buried my face in them and let loose again, crying myself into a wretched case of hiccups. I pulled out my hoop, which I had dismantled in sections to fit inside my bag— for I could not ride a horse wearing one—and took it down to the pond to wash off. There, my girlish weeping simply mixed with the brackish pond water. I then threw all I had washed over bushes to dry and sat down to cry more.

Now it is dusk. She has been riding alone all day. She had followed this path into woods and found the pond. And now, for two days, she has not had a bath or change of clothes. The custom for most was to bathe about once every seven days. At Madam Francine's, out of necessity, a daily bath was mandatory. And now with the soil of travel, a daily bath seems a priority. Sitting here, hiccupping, she unbuttons her dress to slip into the pond and wash. Down to her underclothes, peeling them off, hanging them on branches, she is unable to really believe she has come to this: traveling like a hunted animal. Worthless grazes nearby, the reins cleverly tied to the stirrup so the mare will think she is tethered—a trick that Quashi taught her. And Caesar is digging in the pond mud to unearth worms or any other thing his nose sets him to hunt. Eliza scratches her leg, clawing long streaks of red, then walks into the pond and sits down. No energy to swim with, no energy to get up even to walk or wash, she sits and waits for her crying to stop.

Sunk, simply sunk by the awful travel with Elijah, she presses her chest where her feelings seem tangled in a knot. The memory of the day will not let go. Through the whole of it, Elijah had not spoken to her, not any of the fifteen miles they traveled together. As the sun changed from its April mildness to practicing summer, throwing heat down as though flipping them in a skillet, Elijah took off his shirt and rode ahead on his opinionated mule, Flo. At least the mule seemed to be named Flo, since all day Elijah yelled, "Flo, no! Flo, Flo, no! Heeah, Flo!" as the mule stopped every fifteen minutes to back up into the dairy cows tethered to the saddle, making an awful traffic jam of mooing and bellowing and hee-hawing until Elijah beat all of them back into line and then forward again. Worthless, bumped and cow-kicked so often, became prancing-nervous to keep from even getting close to a cow. Wider and wider the distance grew between Eliza and Elijah, until he must have been a half-mile away. But she could not risk losing sight of him.

Where was I going? Where indeed was I going? And then I saw the lampblack, raw noir of his wanting to lose me. All the while, in murderous silence he rode with his bare back exposed, riddled with lash marks, scarred into the shape of tree branches, as though I were the one who had whipped him. I closed my eyes to spare me the sight, trusting Worthless to follow. He seemed to do whatever he could to make my trip miserable— telling me no, we could not stop when I most needed to relieve myself in some accommodating thicket when we passed one. Telling me we could not tolerate a moment to stop to rest or to drink from the canteen Quashi had given me. Not even for the horse or Caesar, if not for me. "Hayi," he would say, "No. No. Not here. Later." But anywhere else and later did not come.

That night again, Eliza slept in a crowded slave cabin where Elijaj had led her, then left her. This time a family of pigs shuffled in and out with the ducks and chickens. And again she slept near seven children who peeked at her through half-closed eyelids all night. When in the morning Elijah did not come for her or pass her on to anyone else, she rode out before sunup on her own, kicking Worthless along, who was reluctant to leave the stable. Caesar tucked his head up under her arm and slept. All her food was gone. Her skin, mosquito bitten, smelled of sweat and of the mildewed moss mattress where she had lain. Her hair was lank, tucked up and twisted under pins, hidden under her hat. For miles and miles she rode, with no destination, past fields with hands working in gangs, hoeing the newly seeded cotton.

At the head of each gang stood a driver, a slave himself, who, in keeping with all plantation culture, held a whip, a short stick with a square leather thong tied to it. He had been given instructions to inflict a dozen lashes on any refractory slave in the field, and if the punishment was deemed ineffectual, the driver was to report the unmanageable one to the overseer, the hired white administrator of the plantation, who then could flog that slave with as many lashes as he pleased, but rarely to death, since that would amount to being an unsound business practice.

Later that day, Eliza closes her eyes against the memory, splashing her face with pond water. It is cold. She did not think to bring soap. Why soap? She had never intended to be in a fix like this. She climbs the bank behind bushes, flailing her arms, kicking her legs to air-dry them, then dresses slowly, pulling on clean underclothes and a soiled dress over her damp skin, and while stuffing her hair up under her hat, Caesar begins his high-pitched, hysterical barking and runs to the path she has followed to the pond. There is the sound of horses and men's voices. She rushes to a fallen log and squats.

"Eh, here? There's a horse loose."

"Done pitched its rider, looks like."

"No, its rein's tied. And a stupid dog."

"Shut your blow hole, yippy thing. Where's your owner—bucked off in mud?"

"Dead as a hollow tree? Where, little yippy? You gonna tell us?"

"Don't look like."

"He's mine." She stands. Better to be seen than found. "Hush, Caesar." She straightens her hat. "I stopped to water my horse. I'm traveling to see my aunt."

All three stare at her. There are, as yet, no words on their lips, though their tongues are licking. Even in her disheveled shape, Eliza is a delicious vision, especially for three farm boys who've rarely seen anyone from New Orleans, much less a seventeen-year-old girl with an advanced degree in the art of enhancing beauty. They are struck dumb but not useless.

The biggest and oldest gets off his horse and walks toward her, taking off his hat. "Jesse Marks, miss. And there's Robert Drury and Lem Polk. We're on our way to join the company forming ten miles from here. You alone?"

The others dismount.

Eliza straightens her hat again and tucks her hair further under the brim. "My mare seems to have gone lame. I thought I'd rest her here awhile, and by morning she ought to be sound."

The one named Robert, muscular and strong, his hair like a fox's coat, his eyes a sweet bachelor-button blue, and with pale skin freckled and sunburned, nods at her. "No woman ought to be traveling alone out here. All sorts of people running wild with war talk. Might use it as an excuse to thieve and run amuck. We'd be honored to escort you."

"I appreciate your kind offer, Mr. Robert Drury. But I shall be fine. I don't have far to go. I thought I might spend the night here. I know it appears unseemly and much unexpected. I simply can't think of an alternative. And this pond seems safe enough. I thought I might make a bed of leaves up under those trees."

The one named Robert looks at the one named Jesse. And the one named Jesse looks at the one named Lem, who himself seems barely seventeen.

"The least we can do is stay with you and set up a watch," Robert says. She notes that his expression is intense, his face held tight in concentration as if he is about to run his head through a brick wall. This same sort of look she has caught at times on Madam Francine, giving away her secret ambition to succeed at any cost. Although with Robert Drury, Eliza senses that it is other men's admiration he is hungry for.

Jesse adds, "Mind if I take a look at your mare?"

"Please do. I'm hoping she just has a stone bruise."

Jesse Marks goes to Worthless and lifts her front foot. Eliza watches the lanky way he moves, awkward, even spiderlike, and how his tan shirt hangs on his shoulders. He seems vulnerable and sweet. The hair on his arms is blond and thin, and although he has grown a mustache, it is spare and struggling. He looks back at her. His voice is a soft tenor with not the slightest tone of arrogance. "Some point in the past, she's done foundered. I imagine she's sore-footed from travel. If you don't give her no grain, she ought to be okay. Rich hay, corn or oats'll make her more sore-footed. Just let her graze. Keeping her lean is better for her feet too."

"That's easy. I didn't bring any grain. I expected to be at my aunt's long before now."

"I suppose that means you have no food for yourself?" Robert Drury looks at her with genuine concern.

"Well, no."

"Lem, get out our food bag. We're going to serve up this little lady a fine camp supper. One she won't ever forget."

Dear One,

Imagine me sitting with my head back against my saddle, Worthless watered and bedded for the night by three farm boys who knew more about caring for a horse than I ever would. And eating roasted wild pig that they rode off and shot and then brought back to cook over a fire they made. I spied pokeweed and wild onions, with which to make a salad and sauce to baste the pig. Don't ever think I was a dim-girl-light who didn't know how to get the most out of any male, especially when the male was so thirsty for a female he practically sipped the air I breathed. They had no more idea than a tree with worm wood what I was, and what I knew. I trusted the simple verde azulado I read on their shaved faces. I doubt any one of them was much over twenty. Robert Drury was clearly suspicious of me; but that was his way with everyone, I sensed, and could also tell he was intent on succeeding in the army. He was after glory, while Jesse Marks would have married me in an afternoon and taken me home to run his house. Sweet Lem Polk was the one more than halfway in love with me after the first look—he was verily dazzled, his eyes swimming every time he looked at me. Simply, none of them had enough know-how to suspect who I might be. But the thought was surely a wish-dream in their chemistry, and I was not about to lie down and sleep beside them, certainly not since Mr. Preston Cummings, the father-devil himself, had ripped sleep open to be, forever afterward, a torture-pit of dreams.

Lem, wrought-up and nervous, began telling how his neighbor drove three boys to muster in at the same place where tomorrow they would find themselves. "Says they ask two questions. Then you sign a paper saying you're in good health and promise to defend Mississippi from the Yankee invaders for ninety days. You get a uniform, a blanket, a pair of boots, and eleven Confederate dollars a month."

"So what's the two questions?" Jesse asks, glancing at Lem. He slaps a mosquito on his arm and gives Lem a teasing look. Then he glances at Eliza to make sure she's watching.

Eliza leans on her saddle, which is propped on the ground, and she holds a pork bone for Caesar to chew.

"They ask how many teeth you got," Lem says. "And how old you are."

Jesse laughs.

"Teeth to bite the paper off a cartridge to load your gun, right?" Robert says. "So, Lem, what you going to do about not being eighteen yet? Lie?"

"Naw," Jesse teases, "he's going to be a cook for the infantry till his birthday, then shoot a Yankee, right, Lem?"

Lem twists his shoulder, offended. "I got just as much right to defend my mother and sister and Miss Eliza here against the invaders as anybody else. Maybe more, since I got this. My uncle give it to me." He turns to his saddlebag and takes out a new Colt .44 with a long metal barrel that shines in the firelight. He rolls it over in his hand. "He give it to me this morning."

Robert and Jesse examine the new firearm, clearly impressed.

"Well, I guess birthday or no birthday, you will be right smartly armed."

Lem smiles. "Besides, my uncle give me a trick."

"What? To shoot from five miles away?"

Lem takes off his boot and reaches into it and pulls out a piece of paper. The number eighteen is written on it in dark ink. "When the mustering-in officer asks me if I'm eighteen, I'll say, Yessir, I'm over it." He then stuffs the paper back in his boot, looking pleased with himself.

Robert and Jesse laugh, admiring the younger boy now. Eliza smiles too, thinking of Ned and the teasing he took from the men visitors each night. It was teasing that often tipped over into ridicule. She sits up. "Lem, did your uncle give you the new pistol after you already had one of your own?"

"Yeah, he did."

"So now you have this one and the one I see there in your belt?"

"I do."

"Have you thought about selling your old one? For a reasonable price, I mean?"

She has surprised them into silence. The fire crackles, and Caesar gnaws his bone, growling. She goes to her bag, pulls out a dollar and lays it on the ground by the fire. "Would this be about right?"

Lem looks from the money to her. It is a meager amount, an insult in fact. But Eliza's face wears innocence. "More than enough, ma'am." He takes away the dollar and hands Eliza his old pistol. "I'll swap this dollar for Confederate. Bet they'll let me when I muster in."

"And will you load it?" Eliza asks.

"I will, ma'am. And in the morning I can give you some lessons on how to shoot it."

She cuts her eye, underlining her meaning. "Oh, I have a good idea already. But a few new lessons won't hurt." She smiles a soft, sweet smile and strokes the gun.

Robert chews on a homemade toothpick, watching the exchange. "I think you've made a real good decision, Miss Eliza. No one should be out here without a firearm to defend herself. And in the morning, we'll escort you right up to the doorway to your aunt."

"That'd be nice, Robert. Thank you." Of course in the morning, she would come up with a fit story to shoo them off.

"And now, look what I got." Jesse pours dark, golden whiskey into each of their drinking cups and begins singsonging, *"Here's a little for a boy over eighteen. Three swallows for the little, pistol-toting lady. And four for the two big, bad men who are off to shoot Yankees."*

They drink, laughing. Eliza secretly pours her share on the ground. Madam Francine's veshyas never drank with men; faculties could not be compromised. She smiles as Jesse, who has a beautiful Irish tenor voice, sings one song after another, until he and Robert are droopy-eyed drunk.

Dear One,

You think I got an hour's sleep? I named that pistol Mama Mean, and with it in one arm and Caesar in my other, we curled up like wild forest vines so I could peek through my eyelashes at the three sleeping men, drunk with drink and war. Which I was more afraid of, I can't name—them or rolling over and accidentally shooting myself! But when for a few moments I dozed off, I awoke with such a panic, a putrid taste came up in my throat, and my finger was one second from firing the gun. There sat Jesse, quietly beside me, his cheery boyish face just staring, staring. "O, I'm so sorry, Miss Eliza. I didn't mean to alarm you. I had to come close for a look that can last. What I mean is, one that I can carry with me, Miss Eliza."

He slunk off. And I held my face as frozen as a mask. A month before, I would have smiled and believed him. Preston Cummings has left on me a mark so deep that now it has become my own biology. I am changed. And I fear beyond even death itself that I might never again walk with hope and light on this earth's topside. For the rest of that night, I lay watching those three near me pretend to sleep too.

Chapter 9

Over those next few days, Eliza became haunted by what she called her *mind's scraps,* memories that heckled and spurred her as she traveled—first, a short way with Robert and Jesse and Lem, while she played one of her famous games on them, chattering, "There, look, I see my Cousin Thomas, coming through those woods on his horse, Blue. Don't you see him? Oh, yes, he's playing a game with me, riding a short way, and then hiding. Thank you, Robert Drury, and Jesse Marks and Lem Polk. You have been the kindest gentlemen to escort me this far. But I won't need you now. Thank you, thank you." And off she went on her own, kicking Worthless toward the left fork of the road, Caesar under her arm; Worthless shuffled along as though miraculously recovered, while the three farm boy-warriors stared after her, their mouths slack in wonder. And yet, where the left fork went, she did not know.

Until she was out of their sight she kept pretending, pretending, waving as though someone were, indeed, far down the lane. And she kept calling out to her imaginary Cousin Thomas, while Robert and Jesse and Lem headed to the Mississippi company forming only miles away. She stops. At a store at a crossroad between cotton fields, where the road dust covers the porch like chalk, she ties Worthless to a post. She puts Caesar down to scamper toward some children running toward her, then climbs the stairs. While the children pet Worthless and Caesar, she goes inside, where the bare wood floor creaks under her footsteps. Behind the counter a thin, old man, pale and bent, leans over to look as if she were a vision stepping from a church's stained glass window. Under the study of his eyes, she buys cheese and bread and a hunk of ham whose scraps she can feed Caesar. But, "No, no we don't take none of that, not now," he says, shaking his head, as she spreads out a bill on the counter. "I want only the kind Jeff Davis puts out."

"Well, he's not got much out. Besides," she says, clicking her tongue, smiling coyly, "you mustn't be in such a rush. This will be good for a while. And ..." She places the coins in his hand, tickling his palm in a saucy move that she learned from her mother. He seems paralyzed in ecstasy as she turns to leave, opening the door, hoping she is not leaving too much of a whiff of pond musk to spoil the effect.

In the road, two barefoot children ride Worthless double, up and down, hollering and yipping with Caesar squashed between them. Older children scamper behind, brandishing sticks as whips. She drops her bag to go after them, and when she does, the biggest boy leaps in, grabs it, and heads off into the woods while the others jump off Worthless and run behind the store. The clever little devils had planned this.

"You sorry pus pocket!" she yells, running after the boy and warning, "You're not stealing what you think you're stealing. That's my snake! Ever heard of Colleen the Cobra Charmer in New Orleans? Well, that's who I am! One look in that bag and you're a dead pus pocket!"

The boy stops. He stares at her. Then, calling her bluff, he opens the top of the bag and grins a mouthful of rotten teeth. He pulls out the money on top, not bothering to reach in further. When he throws the bag down, Mama Mean goes off, shooting a hole in the bag and tearing leaves off the tree behind him. The boy takes off like a rabbit in a burning field.

Eliza chases him to the edge of a swamp, sometimes riding Worthless, sometimes leading the mare with Caesar hanging on to the saddle like a crab on a rocking boat. But the mosquitoes and swamp muck, along with her belief that what is left of her money will soon be of no value anyway, encourage her to turn west. She is now heading back toward the great river, riding Worthless, carrying Caesar, with no destination.

At nightfall she gives Worthless her head. The mare, smelling water, brings them up to a lake, scaring up a flock of wild turkeys that run, gobbling, from the brush in frightened chatter. The birds' abandoned nests are deep with pine needles, and here Eliza decides she will spend the night, even though the smell of the nearby swamp is putrid. She unsaddles Worthless and lies against the creaking leather of the saddle with Mama Mean on her stomach, an inch from her fingers. Caesar curls beside her. But consciousness will not let go. Sleep is like a skittering melody that someone far away is singing, and in the space between, faces and leftover voices swarm like winged ants, flitting from one moment past to another, through all of her life, or so it seems. So sometimes she is eight, or four, or fifteen, or six. And one mind scrap repeats like the regurgitated taste of spoiled meat, taking her back, over and over, to those early days of being eight, following Ned to school.

****

It was only four blocks away—that school—and her mother agreed that she could go. It was the school where nuns taught city children in three rooms. "Read this. What does it say here? Yes, recite the multiplication tables to ten." But never did they call on her. Ned, yes, he was sometimes included. But in keeping with their blab-school methods, the children recited aloud at the same time different memorized lessons. But no one ever stood by her desk to hear her recite what she had perfectly memorized, could even soon recite in three languages. Throughout the day, she heard, first from one nun to one child, then another, their voices singsonging in their body-concealing cloth, *"Be good, now. Be good as God wishes you to be good. Be good."*

Well, she was good, but why did no one speak to her?

Then Sister Bernadette (or was it Bernice?), who liked to kneel, looked into her eyes and called her the Mary Magdalene Child. "You must pray, every day, twice a day, to Saint Mary

Magdalene. Ask her how to give your soul back to God."

"Who is Mary Magdalene?" Childishly misunderstanding what she had been told, thinking that Sister Bernadette was asking something about the bottom of her shoe, she asked too, "And what would she want with my sole? I never gave it away in the first place."

"Don't be impertinent. You know full well that seven demons were cast out of Mary Magdalene's soul. I suspect there are at least eight in you. Maybe ten. Perhaps an exorcist would be of help to you; that is, if your mother will spend money for that. *Mais en attendant*, do these sums."

"Pray, pray, Eliza. Pray for your soul."

Soon she knew without understanding: She was foul in a way she could not name.

And then, Fanny McKnight from Mary Wittle's house was walking down the street, crossing over to be with Eliza and Ned as they came out of the school. Fanny, then, was eighteen, freckled and thin, newly arrived at Mary Wittle's bordello around the corner from Madam Francine's.

Ned skips ahead. Eliza helps carry one of Fanny's boxes of silk lingerie, bought on Rue St. Ursaline. "So, you've been to school, have you?" Fanny touches Eliza's corkscrew curls bouncing on her shoulders.

"Yes. But nobody there will speak to me."

"Ah, well, as they say, girls aren't made for education. Draws too much energy to the brain and away from the ovaries." She laughs. "If you ask me, it's a good trade. But no one's asking me. And so, sweet Eliza, don't fret about it."

"But I know my lessons as well as Ned. As well as anyone. But when I speak to the nun, she turns away."

"It's 'cause you're a whore's child."

"A what?"

"Ask your mother. She's the one to tell you that."

The next morning, running into her mother's room, she watched her beautiful mother sit up in bed, stretching, yawning, her nightgown a sheer lavender. The color rising from her mother's skin was sweet-sleeping plum, and she wailed, "My head. Oh! Eliza, what a headache I have! Be good and bring me a whiff of valerian. Mash it with the pestle, darling. That's right, put it in that net bag. Ah, if only men could do for me what the forest does!"

Then her mother pulled Eliza into the wide V of her lap where she brushed and wound Eliza's hair on her thin fingers. "My beauty. My love. You are the most wonderful thing that has ever happened to me. Now, Eliza, be good; run down to the kitchen and tell the cook I'm ready for my morning coffee. Chicory-laced, strong as a rutting ox."

And so, "What's a whore, Mom?"

"Who said?"

"Fanny McKnight. And the nuns inside their heads."

"It's only a word. There is no such thing in this room."

"But what does it mean?"

"Nothing. Absolutely nothing."

"But it must! Fanny McKnight says it's why no one at school will speak to me."

"No one at school will speak to you because they are afraid of you, afraid of your great power. One day, you will live as none can even imagine. I promise you. You will have nothing to worry about, ever, sweet Eliza. I have it all planned. Now, be good and go down by the river and hunt out some nightshade and aloe. I promised Ellen Ann I'd treat the sores on her leg."

Soon after, Eliza stopped going to the school. She stayed home and studied the lessons Ned brought back. She read on her own; she sat and talked to the visitors from foreign cities. Her mind snacked on glimpses of the outer world like nourishment for the starving.

****

Always now just before sleep, she relived in her mind *that* day, the day in the game room with Preston Cummings when her mother told of the promise. Made when? When she was four? For a thousand dollars. What a bargain!

No, she had not let that go without a response. The next morning she had sat on the bench at the foot of her mother's bed, waiting for her mother to awake. And as soon as consciousness swept over her mother's face, Eliza blurted, "No. I do not want this. I can't believe you made that ... that plan. You and Madam

Francine. How dare you!"

"What!" Quickly sitting upright, her mother swept her hair away from her eyes. "What do you mean?"

"I will not be his. I won't be anyone's that you or anyone else chooses for me. Not Madam Francine. Not anyone else in this house. This is mean."

"Don't use that voice with me, Eliza. What do you want? What do you expect? I have done my best for you, always. And now—"

"Your best is not what I choose."

"You don't have the right to choose."

"Who says?"

"Oh, heavens! Don't do this to me, Eliza. I can't breathe. My chest. Look, my heart is beating too fast. Oh, mercy! I'm sunk! Someone help me! Help me!"

Hattie Louise, not yet so ill, rushed into the room. "Gracious child, what?" Her address, "child," did not refer to Eliza. Every woman in the house was a child to Hattie Louise, and the address was her endearment.

Eliza's mother pointed to Eliza, sitting on her bed. "This. This is what is wrong. My ungrateful Eliza. She refuses the arrangement with Mr. Preston Cummings. Can you believe it, Hattie? To turn down such a future? One I have worked so hard to secure?"

Eliza walked out of the room, accompanied by much whooping and hollering that caught fire like lightning-struck brush, up and down the hall. There was the unspoken understanding that all must be kept from Mr. Preston Cummings. It was as if Eliza had broken out with a hideous boil that had to be hidden. Soon, her mother was on a valerian root high and she, Eliza, was the talk of the house.

****

Though her emotions were sealed, Eliza's mind could not erase the nightmare memory of Preston Cummings coming up the backstairs, the businesslike sound of his boots in the stairwell, his pushing her onto her hands, raping her, animal-like, as if all along he had been hiding in camouflage, wearing the costume of father, *until now, until now, until now.*

So the next morning, as soon as she could, she knocked on Amalee's door for her help. Amalee, nineteen, dark curls like cuttings from shaved wood, was the newest of Madam Francine's recruits and the closest in age to Eliza. There, in the comfort of their blooming friendship, Eliza told of Mr. Cummings and implored Amalee to give her the knowledge of the beeswax cervical cap. Hoping of all hopes that she would not from this first time become pregnant, but instinctively knowing that this first would not be the only, she took what Amalee gave her and learned to use what she prized most now. Then the wash of relief, when, weeks later, blood poured.

Dear One,

With my mind traveling over my life, despair took hold that I did not know how to part from. Indeed, there was a memory I should have recalled above all others: of my being fourteen, riding a public horsecar through the city to watch people get on, studying, memorizing how they spoke to each other, paid their fee to the conductor, greeted each other without sexual innuendo—without touching or stroking each other's hands, arms, legs, thighs. They did not part with a promise of a future secret pleasure, issued in a tone of purring. I watched them fit into the world. And soon, I could too. As if at sea, sighting a lighthouse, I saw that no one could tell that I was a whore's child unless I told it. Why! Soon, from only looking at me—anyone could think I was the daughter of a rich, renowned family. Dear One, I was a bird who could fly from branch to branch! It was only the stain inside me that could break through, to betray me. If I let it, if I let it, if I let it.

Chapter 10

Eliza wakes to the sound of Caesar's scream. She sits up to look for him in the early morning fog over the pond. Caesar's head and front paws dangle from an alligator's mouth. The reptile is halfway onto the bank where it must have lunged at Caesar as he hunted in the mud. Eliza picks up Mama Mean, the handle still warm where she has gripped it through the night, and fires. But Caesar is gone, disappeared and no longer yelping. The alligator's jaws crunch bones as it backs into the water, oblivious to the bullets Eliza fires over and over, striking only mud. And then, there, finally, one lands in the alligator's left eye. A burst of blood. The alligator flips in a death dive, half its brain spilling out into the water.

Eliza vomits. Her body is stuck in panic, and she lies down to feel the earth under her and to let dizziness pass. Then she sits up, frantic, realizing that where one alligator is, there may be more. She grabs her bag and unties Worthless and rides off, whipping the mare with the ends of her reins into a stubby gallop.

Spent, the mare stops. Eliza lifts her head. Her hat is held on only by the strings around her neck. She sees too that she has been gripping Mama Mean and riding one-handed, as though any minute she might have to kill something else. But how many bullets did she fire? How many were in the gun in the first place? She looks in the chamber. Yes, well then, let there be only one other thing she has to kill.

Her skin itches. She is so dirty, she repulses herself. But how can she get into any other pond? Not now. Not after that. But how else? How else can she get herself together? Where else can she go? Who can she become? Should she try to find the way to where Robert and Jesse and Lem would be?

No. Yes. Well, if nothing else, that Rebel company is supposedly forming only ten miles away. Ten miles somewhere. But which direction?

All morning she rides, letting Worthless choose the way. Maybe the mare will smell a farm or town where Eliza can pretend her way into a bath and even wash her clothes.

By noon, she is so hungry she stops in a field where she spies chickweed. Pulling up the whole plant, she then bites off the roots and eats the stalks. Ordinarily, if she had means, she could boil them up with onions and add a little jelly on the side. She smiles, thinking of the recipes her mother and Delia have taught her. From her mother's wildcrafting for her many medicinal needs, and from Delia's imitation of Madam Francine's talent with food, Eliza realizes she has a store of knowledge for these fields and woods.

Milkweed by the road catches her eye, but when she leads Worthless to examine the plant closer, she recognizes it as the poisonous form, so instead she pulls up handfuls of tall grass for Worthless to eat. The mare's grinding her meal with her back teeth is a comforting sound, and in the silence of their solitude, it is a loud sound. How surprising that she misses Caesar so much. His presence and trouble had been comforting, other than his piercing eyes reminding her of Hattie Louise.

She gets on Worthless and turns away from the sun, which seems as good a decision as any other. In another hour she is near what must be the Yazoo River. She has heard Madam Francine's visitors speak of the pretty river branching off from the Great Mississippi with its good fishing and clean water. Dare she? Dare she bathe and change clothes and perhaps even spend the night?

She ties her rein to a stirrup to let Worthless graze. She puts her bag behind thick brush and removes her clothes. Slipping into the water, she nervously feels the muddy bottom and thinks that where the current is strongest is certainly where no alligator would likely be. She moves farther from the bank. And yes, it is a solid bank, no swamp. But still, what could be here—snakes if not alligators? Panthers, bobcats, bears? Her mind concocts a list of horrors. And the memory of Caesar's scream will not go away.

She floats, letting water fill her ears, and looks up at clouds and wonders: *Has this been a mistake?* Why not accept the future her mother had arranged for her? What was so wrong that she could not accept the fake, concocted world in which a man she felt affection for as a father could be transferred into the one she would give physical pleasure to? She had been surrounded by that all her life. So wasn't *that* what she should have expected? Why did she expect anything? Was a whore's child entitled to want, to be anything other than a whore's child?

A bird calls on the bank; another answers. Rowing her arms, she turns toward the whistling sound and realizes that she has floated on the current a long distance. She begins treading water. She is not a good swimmer. Only from the times Mr. Cummings took her to the city's beach has she learned to travel in water. *And the memory of his teaching me, laughing, laughing. "I won't turn loose of you. Trust me. Trust me. Yes, that's right. There now. Look, you are doing it, you are swimming. I told you to trust me."*

And here she is. No one in sight. Only herself and birds and goodness knows what lurking in the river grass to kill or poison her with a single bite, like the great black moccasin, there now, curled on the bank. She feels what must be a scream caught under her tongue. But such a sound is only for blockheaded, stupid, flighty women. Besides, what good would such a sound do here? Who would hear her? Too, she does not have on a stitch of clothes. Oh, yes, she is most certainly the daughter of a whore, feeling comfortable in skin punctuated only by a little black ribbon holding up her hair. But then, she is going under. The current has caught her and is pulling her down. Could she actually be drowning? And if so, be found naked, with legs all scratched. *That* should be enough to make anyone, with any sense of vanity, fight to live, or laugh at. Yet neither appeals to her. She stops all motion to swim. And so, let it end like this.

The deeper current is swift. In the dark water, she opens her eyes and sees her hair floating across her face.

O! How so much I was missing what I had known. That was the surprise. That was my awakening. Imagining being free was not at all like being free. I was ten seconds from not being at all!

Suddenly she is in touch with a driving force, insisting that she kick and defy the water, to come back up to the surface. Her mind even makes a cruel joke: *What about those fires of Hell that the nuns at that school so eagerly talked about?* Is she headed for them? Well, at least she would arrive *there,* soaked. Not ever did she think she would miss anyone she has fled. Or this. She touches her body where it responds in pleasure, no matter who gives it.

Be good, Eliza. Bring me my slippers. Be good, Eliza. Eat your greens. Oh, how I love you, Eliza. What a good life I will make for you. Her mother's voice is sewn into every part of her mind.

Fighting the current, she finds the strength of the river is greater than hers. Could it be that now the decision to live, to save herself, is not hers to make? She kicks and pushes, thrusting her arms. Her lungs are about to burst. Then, there, the surface, there: a slice of sunlight playing on the water. She breaks through and sees Worthless, a dot on the horizon, placidly grazing.

Eliza dog-paddles to the bank. Here she can walk, out of reach of the current. She is a long way from Worthless. Walking in the shallow water on her knees, she can keep most of her nakedness covered, though there is no need to. No one is here to see.

Reaching the bank and her bag, she pulls on her least-soiled dress, a gray plaid silk. She pins up her hair and affixes her hairpiece, tying it in with a blue ribbon from her bag.

Deciding to be alive felt in need of a celebration. At least the ribbon was clean. My skin, sunburned to the shade of a ripening apple, the veil on my hat a nuisance anyway, I tied it up over my hat, curled the brim, put on my hairpiece and stuck pins through it and the hat, took a deep breath and climbed on Worthless.

****

Riding across the field and into thick woods, she finds a dirt road that is well enough traveled to keep it free of grass and weeds. Surely, this leads to somewhere.

Perhaps five miles she has traveled, until the sun is behind her, dipping toward the horizon. The shade from the trees falls on the road in long swaths, and she breathes in the smell of honeysuckle. Worthless grabs bites of grass growing on the roadside, then suddenly stops and whirls. Eliza bobbles and reaches for the mare's mane. Deer burst from the woods and run in the road, then leap into the thicket on the other side. There is a roll of distant thunder. But no, not thunder, hoof-thunder, a two-four beat with no pauses, the sound of a great number of horses coming fast. Worthless, sensing something of a herd behind her, whirls again, her head high, sniffing, excited.

Eliza pulls the mare's head with one rein, kicking, rocking in the saddle, forcing the mare over into an opening of trees. There, from under leafy cover, Eliza looks out. A tall sorrel horse trots in the center of the road toward her, its wheat-yellow mane flowing. The rider, in a dark-blue jacket, almost black, rises and falls in the saddle, posting to his horse's powerful trot. Behind him is a cacophony of clanking sabers, saddle irons and spurs. Worthless backs up, frightened. Eliza's head smashes into a branch, covering her face with leaves and nearly tearing off her hat. She grabs the saddle's pommel, attempting desperately to stay on.

As the officer trots by, his horse sidesteps, startled by Worthless, half-hidden in the trees. The rider, agile in the saddle, rebalances, tightens his reins and glances to see what has spooked his horse. His eyes and Eliza's exchange a look of surprise. He twists in his saddle to look back at her as his horse trots on. And now riding past must be nearly fifty men on horseback, riding in twos. Some are elegantly dressed in what seem to be old military uniforms, sabers gleaming. Others wear farm clothes, as if out hunting. But all their horses are groomed and fit.

Rattling now after the last are three buggies. The large spoked-wheels jump roots and spin through the rutted soil. As they pass, Eliza sees two women, elegantly dressed, one in each buggy driven by a manservant.

Coughing as the last one raises dust, Eliza kicks Worthless into a trot behind them.

And then coming toward me, riding to the back of the column, was that officer who had passed me earlier. He was galloping his horse now, its strides needing few bounds to cover the distance of the many others trotting. He circled me and slowed to be beside Worthless, who was doing the best she could to keep up and seemed to fear being too close to the last buggy's wheels. I regret to say I was a graceless rider, bouncing—well, way too much. But I was too busy holding on to worry much about my impression. "Captain Bennett McFerrin," he said, touching his hat. "Are you in need of help?"

"O, no."

I decided to put all my eggs in the basket of simplicity.

We exchanged looks. I did not have time to study much about him but gathered a single impression: deep-set eyes, blue, with a serious kindness in them. And all of him, so upright and polished: his posture, his seriousness, his baritone voice that no doubt could boom orders to hundreds ... and yet those soft, thoughtful eyes that were looking at me in thirsty curiosity.

"No?" he asked, holding his horse to match Worthless's shuffle.

"No."

"Are you traveling far?"

"No, not at all."

"Your mare looks troubled."

"Yes, she has sore feet, but together we get where we need to go."

"Are you sure you don't need help?"

"Yes, I am sure. But thank you."

"Well, then," and off he went, galloping to the front again.

Little did I know that I had latched onto a cavalry raised by Virginia Military Institute graduate Bennett McFerrin, sweeping up from lower Mississippi to add a unit which, in three months, would be called to Virginia to a place named Manassas. It did not matter, either, that I did not know that it was the wives of three of the officers who were in those buggies, accompanying their husbands. Or that in the buggy behind which I trotted as close as I could, (Worthless willing) was Mrs. McFerrin, twenty-five, beautiful, loath to ever let her young husband out of her sight. She too was counting her minutes as preciously as I had just finished counting mine.

At least here was something to follow.

Chapter 11

W hat Eliza wrote about those first few days after following the cavalry was an attempt to blunt a regretted decision. I knew her well enough now to sense the armor around her words. *"O! How I was in such need of something familiar. When suddenly I saw someone I knew, simply, I, well ..."*

In her fifth letter documenting those first days, Eliza lowered her guard to either weaken the power of the words over her or to cleanse herself with those who would become her *Dear One*. And I was beginning to see that Dear One was meant to save Eliza as much as Hadley was counting on me—through Eliza's story—to save *her*. Day by day, a grip was tightening around the three of us as the story began to tell itself with only a little help from me.

That first afternoon, Eliza trotted Worthless behind the last buggy, following the cavalry through rising dust, past camp guards and into the expansive acreage of empty cattle pastures requisitioned from a wealthy Mississippi planter. The location must have been in the county near the Yazoo River, maybe between Jackson and Vicksburg.

Worthless stops, her nose practically bumping the small

carriage that had spun to a halt. Eliza grabs the saddle, bobbing once, then sitting straight. Here, a village is virtually rising in a pasture. Tents arranged in rows sport their canvas like meatless bones. Men have converged here day after day, and come still, several hundred already.

What she could not know was that in less than a month all would travel to Corinth to blend with hundreds more forming two regiments, for Jeff Davis and his generals assumed the Federal Army would strike first at Memphis in an attempt to split the Southern nation apart at the Mississippi River. Yet at about the same time that Eliza was trotting Worthless into the camp, President Lincoln was deciding that Memphis should not be the first battleground. Pressing concerns were changing his mind.

Some in his cabinet pushed to let the South go. After all, it was a hot place, full of mosquitoes. So why not dismiss the secessionists? Let them become a nation spreading southward, annexing South America if they were so able. Meanwhile, the North would take on Canada, building an empire upward, and/or start a war with Europe to distract the citizenry and unite them against a foreign foe. Surely, the secessionists would feel differently, sobered by a world war, and come back into the Union. Yet Lincoln found another concern even more pressing: The Federal volunteer army had signed on for only ninety days, and by mid-July, his troops would be itching to return home. His army might very well drop their war tools and leave the city of Washington exposed, to be captured and occupied.

Already the Confederate general Beauregard was amassing an army of thousands just outside of Washington at a creek thirty miles from the White House. The first battle must be there, at the Manassas railhead near a creek called Bull Run. And it needed to be a defining battle, one to put an end to the war.

Eliza dismounts from Worthless, holding the mare's reins. She tucks up closely to the back of the last carriage. There is the hum of a great number of men's voices drilling in companies, arguing, singing, mixing with the sound of horses calling to each other in high-whistling whinnies. Somewhere metal is being pounded. Eliza reads a bright *violeta* of anticipation over all, and also a palette of men's emotions: some grieving at leaving home, some adventure-seeking, some doubting their courage, others ignited with anger at the Yankee invaders and almost all fearful of cowardice.

Why! It was a whole human array, a makeshift village, even a post office and infirmary. Grass worn to bare dirt, puffing dust in clouds around moving feet. Some soldiers seemed no more serious than out hunting, cooking meat on open fires, wearing clothes no different than what they might wear to hunt or plow. Their rifles, hunting rifles too, not at all what I expected suitable for war. And around me coughing, constant coughing, like punctuation in a conversation. Everyone must have been suffering from ague or throats irritated from dust. On the far side of the camp I smelled a latrine. On the other was a tent for shoeing horses and storing grain. Worthless lifted her nose, sniffing—machine oil, cooking meat, sweat. It was a nostril stew.

And then, everyone was dismounting. Eliza didn't know what to do. Who was she? Who could she be? The cavalry officers went to the buggies to escort their wives to tents. And then Captain McFerrin walked toward Eliza. Quickly she ducked behind his wife's carriage. She watched him hand the reins of his horse to the driver of the carriage—a slave, it seemed, a wiry man nearing middle age, eyes like dark grapes and a wizened face that glowed with a lively look. Then the captain's wife appeared, seeming weak, stepping from the carriage by the help of her husband's arm. She was dressed as a planter's wife—classy gray-blue dress, not too flounced but hoop-skirted and silky, her hair swooped up under a blue hat with a tied veil. She was tall and regal, beautiful to the point of everyone wanting to stare.

Again Eliza's and Captain McFerrin's eyes met—his full of a studious bewilderment at seeing her again, so that she looked away, turning quickly, leading Worthless she knew not where. More of what he looked like stayed with her, not that he was tall or outstanding in any way, other than an acceptable handsomeness, but his eyes again met hers in such an open statement of curiosity. She couldn't help but smile. She had startled him for the second time. His blue uniform, obviously one issued when he was at VMI, is buttoned to his chin. His white deerskin gloves are soiled with streaks of harness oil from his bridle reins. When he moves, his spurs and saber clank in their own little tune. There is a boyish quality to his face and in the way he moves. His mouth is mostly hidden under a wheat-colored mustache, and on one side of his chin there is a slight scar as if he were wearing the badge of a boyhood accident with nonchalance and pride. She is especially amused at seeing that the color of his hair is so similar to that of his horse and is topped by an impressive hat unconventionally decorated, not with a plume as the other cavalry officers have, but with a pheasant feather—brown and rust and white. His face is suntanned to an apple glow, as obviously unfit for the sun as her own. Yet in a moment's exchange they share the gleeful mystery: Just who exactly is she, and why is she here?

The camp is ripe with smells of recently cooked meat and smoking tobacco and horse droppings. Near the horse's picket line to which members of the cavalry are tying their horses and unsaddling them, Eliza spies a vivandière. The wagon is parked under trees. A plump woman, plainly dressed, her stomach popped out to the size of a melon, is seated casually on a stool next to her wares. The wagon's open canvas flaps display liquor and other items she is selling. Eliza walks toward her, Worthless in tow.

"Need a little something?" The vivandière touches the red cotton scarf on her head but doesn't get up from her stool. Her expression states that she clearly doubts Eliza is there for goods.

"Maybe." Eliza sweeps her hand across the rows of tents. "How does this work?"

"What?"

"Here. This place."

The woman laughs. She tightens her scarf. "I see. The officers have all claimed their wives now, and you are left, standing. Your tent's there." She points away from the main grass path to a tent with closed flaps under trees at the side of the camp. "You're in the business of keeping the men's spirits up—least that's the way the officers in charge see it." She laughs again, deeply, raucously, winking, her face twitching in amusement. Eliza reads the old woman, the way she assumes that Eliza is one of the public women who have followed the army here. Indeed, the only other women dressed nearly as elegantly as Eliza are the officers' wives. And even after days of sleeping on the ground and killing an alligator and bathing in river water, Eliza is not diminished. If anything, her body has been animated by her fight for survival. Now the officers' wives are walking with their husbands to their makeshift quarters. Captain McFerrin and his pale wife enter a tent separated from the rows that house the soldiers. Eliza turns, studying all around her. Four laundresses, dressed in plain clothes, their blouses sweated through, stir clothes in black pots on open fires, and chatter.

Suddenly, Eliza hears a familiar voice: "Eliza!" Fanny McKnight trots toward her, leaving two other women in the path. All three are more elegantly dressed than any of the officers' wives. Fanny hugs Eliza. "It is you! How did you come? When did you decide? Amalee, Ellen, it's Eliza from Madam Francine's!"

"Shhhh. No need to broadcast it, Fanny."

"Oh, but you look … what is this, leaves in your hem? Eliza Hamilton, have you been sleeping in the woods?"

Amalee is now hugging Eliza. "Are you okay?"

"I am."

Then all three dip into the puzzle: "Where'd you get the horse? Did you ride it all the way here?"

"Six days!"

"And slept where you could?"

Eliza nods.

Fanny smiles. "We rode the train."

"Yes, right along in a car, back of the boys." Ellen giggles.

Fanny, splendid in green silk, twenty-eight now, no doubt feared staying at Mary Wittle's much longer. Amalee, who so recently gave Eliza the magic of the beeswax cervical cap to arm herself against Preston Cummings, or to at least prevent him from leaving her *with child*, wears red taffeta plaid and a hoop skirt wide enough to hide a man. She grows quiet, studying Eliza, and then tells her, "*He* found out you left right after you did. I heard he hunted in every train, managing to climb aboard and inspect the cars even as they were pulling out. So anyway, that's why …" She nods at Worthless.

"Yes," Eliza whispers. "Please don't tell anyone I am here."

Ellen giggles. "No one here knows where any of us came from. Oh well, I guess I know a few of the boys, but they're not why I'm here." She whispers, "It's the officers, Liza, who have the money. And they're nice too. I think it's war that's made 'em perk up and act chivalrous. Lieutenant Mallory in charge of artillery bought me lavender water from Miss Wallace here last night."

The vivandière smiles. "Paris Water."

"I bet you're starved." Fanny takes Eliza's hand. "We've got lots to eat in our tent. But hey, what you going to do with your horse? You won't need her, staying with us. We got off the train at Vicksburg and hired a coach to follow the boys here."

Eliza strokes the mare's neck, combing her mane with her fingers. "I've grown really fond of her. Besides, I own her."

Fanny laughs. "Hey, we could buy our own buggy and your mare can pull it!"

Ellen points to the picket line. "Let's slip her in with the cavalry horses."

The four of them walk as though they are not attracting the attention of hundreds of eyes, leading Worthless to the picket line to slip her in between two cavalry horses. But before they reach there a manservant approaches, the one Eliza saw earlier driving the captain's wife's carriage. He takes the lead rope from Eliza's hand, asking, "You have grain for her?"

Eliza shakes her head no. The slave replies, "I've been told to provide for her." He pulls the saddle off and tilts it against a tree.

"She can't have corn. She's likely to founder."

McFerrin's slave nods, looking at Worthless's feet. "I see that. I got grass hay. And beet pulp."

The sun is throwing a firelike line across the horizon. Walking to the tents, Eliza turns to see McFerrin's manservant feeding the horses up and down the line, slipping feedbags over their heads, Worthless among them.

The four women now chatter inside their tent, which is set apart from all the others. Cots are arranged with an aisle between. After making a supper of ham and bread and roasted potatoes on a fire outside, they eat while sitting on the cots. Eliza notes the mirrors hanging from the center pole, the light trunks serving as tables. She listens, knowing only that she is slicing the aching solitude that she has lived with over the last few days.

How relieved—being with someone familiar, someone who knew me even if I wished not to be known. I was putting off thinking—that's what I was doing. Listening to them laughing, their chatter so like what I had always known. Fanny, regaling us with her previous night's work: "The nicest lieutenant, really, treated me like a queen. Away from home where six children and wife wait for him, he buried loneliness inside of me. Red beard—red hair all over, and liked it hard and quick. Wonder what a general will feel like?" And Amalee, so sad, really, for she had told me of the uncle who called it awakening her to her due pleasure, using her since she was three, and thereby unleashing in her a physical craving she could not ever fill. Amalee's sweetness was like water poured over my sunburned skin. And yet I could not fool myself, for I knew her friendship could never be deeper than a thimble's length; her personal cravings would not allow it. I was too exhausted anyway for anything other than to snuggle into familiarity and sleep.

✳✳✳✳

With the oncoming night, it begins: one soldier or officer after another coming to the tent, Ellen standing by the door flap, smiling, arranging the evening's work.

A sergeant sees Eliza sitting on the cot, her back turned to the door flap. "What about her?"

Fanny's voice is matter-of-fact: "Eliza, you're on."

But Eliza snaps, "No."

Ellen's voice does not reveal her feelings as yet; instead she explains about Eliza: "She's been traveling all day. I expect she's tired. Try tomorrow."

Then Ellen, before leaving, bends over Eliza and whispers. "You'll have to step-to. We can't feed you for days. Tonight, yes, but tomorrow, no."

Eliza soon is in the tent alone. Ellen has joined Amalee and Fanny—each in one officer's or soldier's tent, then another's, which Eliza knows has provided their livelihood, earned on previous nights, and, according to what they've told her, sometimes even during the day. Ellen, Amalee and Fanny slip into their "purchaser's" tent or walk arm in arm as he pridefully parades his manliness past his cohorts. Eliza sees that indeed the vivandière has been accurate: The girls are tolerated here, if not welcomed, as a means to keep up the soldiers' morale.

At first Eliza tries sleep, but when it does not come, she slips out and walks across the grass path near where Worthless is tethered.

The mare seems content, tied to the picket line with the other horses, her eyes closed, her back foot cocked at rest. And in the dark, awash with moonlight and campfires, Eliza locates the laundresses.

For a moment, she stands watching them putting their fires to bed, spreading coals under the washpots, wiping sweat from their faces, flapping their skirts to cool their legs. She walks up, close now. With a soft tone, she tries—for she's not at all sure how to do this—"How is it I could go about doing what you do?"

"Wash, you mean?!"

"Yes."

"You?"

A large one with red cheeks freckled the color of a potato skin, laughs, bending over as though the idea is killing her.

"I'm not making a joke. I want employment. I want to be a laundress."

Another, short with a plain plaid skirt caught between her thighs, replies hoarsely, "Hon, you don't just say you want to. Lorry there's married to a private. Me and Vita's hired on by the company of Mississippi Rifles. It's all prearranged. Each company hires four. That's all. And that's us. The men pay on the day they get their rations."

Red Cheeks adds, "Besides, your hands don't look like you've washed none."

Eliza repeats, "I have to be appointed? By an officer?"

One of the others chirps, "Yes, darlin'. Company commander. That's the way it's done. And we are the four. And there's no need nowhere else. You best stick with what you're dressed for." They snicker.

As Eliza walks away, she hears them mimicking her speech. And so begins the downward slide of the next three weeks, into what Eliza calls the "Hell Bench," where she waits her turn to enter what she would pay with all the money she could ever earn to forget.

Every night, men glancing into the tent ask for her; then Ellen's voice after three more days, and even Fanny's and finally Amalee's, who despite their affection for Eliza know Ellen is in the right. "Who do you think you are? The Queen of France? Who also is, you might remember, not above pleasuring the King before supper."

"Oh, yes, Eliza. We've let you sleep three nights now. You ain't sick. Your forehead's cool as a apple peel. Your body's not lost a ounce—not since *we* been feeding you."

"We was willing to give you the benefit—tramping out in the woods like you done, running from Mr. Cummings. But it's over."

"You better bet it is. We done fed you our own food, bought by the sweat of our own brows." Followed by an unavoidable giggle, "Sweat, anyway. And you are not my child, and you are not my mother. And even my own child and mother would earn their keep. Out, Eliza. I mean it now—out!"

Her bag, packed with her few things, they throw into the pathway between the tents. Their act is a commotion. Close by, camp duties stop; eyes stare. Eyes watch all four of them all the time anyway, but this is only a bit more interesting than anything else on this day. Eliza is down on the ground, picking up her things: the brush, the comb, her underskirts that Ellen has thrown out of the tent with Fanny and Amalee watching, silently.

"Ellen, please. Amalee, Fanny, I ..."

And now, I became what I was—seventeen, alone, afraid, homesick with what was worse than a longing, for I did not want what I had run from but what I could not yet imagine for myself. I had cast myself out of my own life with no other in sight. And so I begged. I begged in a way I am ashamed of and can only forgive myself for because I was so young—a dumb, silly girl, depleted. Ellen, please, please.

It took a good five minutes, for Ellen enjoyed it so. Finally, Fanny first, then Amalee—both bent down to help her repack her things. Then Ellen stepped aside so Eliza could go back into the tent. At nightfall, Ellen brought in two men. They were not there for themselves, but for a friend by the name of Major Richard Morgan.

His story was simple, though convoluted and began with the two enlisted men—farm boys from a hamlet in Louisiana— who recited Major Morgan's history to Ellen at the door, Eliza overhearing: A wife and three kids, a farm, nothing fancy but nice, and then typhoid taking his wife and kids. And the grief hits him so hard the town begins to think he will pass away too. The townspeople feed and visit and look after him until the outbreak of war, which seems to jolt him back into what he knows. For he is a veteran of the Mexican War, and war reminds him of what he can do, of what he has been groomed for; and he is quickly mustered in as a major. He has been here now in camp seven weeks and doing oh so much better, acting right normal, and it's been noticed that he's been admiring Eliza. Some time with Eliza might just be the spark to pull him all the way through. This last spoken with a smile, the innuendo followed by a new Confederate ten dollar bill decorated with the photo of Lucy Pickens, wife of the governor of South Carolina.

It wasn't all that strange, really, being escorted down the tent row path to Major Morgan's tent, remembering the fathers who brought their sons to Madam Francine's. I kept thinking with amusement that this was like that, only in reverse—the younger taking me to the older. And while part of me regarded the story of Major Morgan's pitiful plight as mere fiction for fun, the moment I walked into his tent, suspicions vanished. He was the most simple, dignified man I could have imagined. Dignified to the point of awkwardness, for there was stiffness in the way he stood. He bowed. He actually bowed as I walked toward him! A short beard, brown hair, the sides all gray, a mustache as full as manicured grass, and dark eyes as empty as the eyes of Worthless when she plods to where she does not want to go. He took my hand. "My dear." And then, "I'm so sorry." He actually said, "I'm so sorry."

I wanted to laugh, thinking that night he got more than his worth of Confederate dollars, for all he wanted was to sleep beside me, and O! How fine that was, seeing as how being a whole night away from Ellen and Fanny and Amalee was more than all right. Usually they came back to our tent cots, liquored to sickness. "Now here," he said, and placed in my hand other Confederate money for the next night and the next, until finally he could perform, and truthfully I must say, feeling his hands petting me, holding me tightly, crying, wetting my hair with sorrow and relief, I felt what I never would have expected: good. That surprised me. And yet, here it was—the fact I had awakened something in this pitiful, lost man that reconnected him to life. I could not deny that as good.

No, she could never deny *that* as anything less than of value. It was what followed that twisted the good into what she would have paid to forget. Over the days and nights, his affection awoke. She went to his tent every evening now, the money good, the money easy. She was feeding herself, pushing the thoughts of the future and present into a section of her mind she called "O well."

O well, it would not be this way forever. O well, this was only for now. There were rumors the companies would all be heading somewhere else soon. The officers were just waiting for orders. The camp had grown to nearly four hundred. With what I was doing, I had to see no one. I slept in the day, visited Worthless, sometimes rode her at the edge of the fields. There, I watched the cavalry practicing its drills: serpentines, dismounts, charges. Captain McFerrin had now joined his men with other militias, their uniforms making a hodgepodge quilt that I supposed would disappear once the Confederate Army distributed real uniforms. I saw his wife sitting in the shade of trees, watching too. Her manservant stood beside her. Usually she held a glass of lemonade. She was so ethereal in appearance, always wearing pastel shades reminiscent of summer rains. I could not help but admire her. And whenever she looked at her husband, I could actually see a flushed color of affection stitching a path between them, and also a mysterious azul gris I could not name. But she always looked away when our eyes met. I assume she had seen where I stayed. And then part of the torment of what happened is thinking of what she, as others, decided about me. For it was only at the end of those three weeks ...

Major Morgan began to know—not just to think but to know as those given to obsession know—that he loved Eliza and decided he could have no life without her. He got down on a knee, there in the tent in the quietness of one night, professing a love that could not be extinguished. "If you will only let me be your husband, Eliza, oh, Eliza, I will treasure you always. I know I am older, much older. But you will be well taken care of. You will truly now be an officer's wife. I cannot ..."

Although his earnestness was touching, all she felt was the putrid ash that Preston Cummings had set loose in her was now being loosed all the more. So she looked away, sickened with the thought of being this old man's wife, a wife to anyone, in fact. What was any of *that* about? Never knowing anything between any man and woman but a wanting of flesh, she stared back at him, baffled and empty.

Dear One,

O, how can I tell you what I did without you despising me? I stood there like a rooted weed. I did not even put my hand on his as he held it out to me. Instead, I adamantly shook my head "no" and ran. Out through the door flap of his quarters into the woods, I didn't care where I went. Only that I could not fathom how I had unleashed this obsession in him. Yes, I had seen the deep creases in his face, and the lines sorrow had written there. But I didn't know about a darkness so deep that its inverse was the panicked light from which he spoke to me. I should have seen in him what I had only a year before seen in poor Ned Tatum's mother—the leaking away of all will to live and a desperate reach for anything to tether oneself ... so I rode off on Worthless, my heart still marked "No Entry," and frightened by what I had unleashed in him. A wanting of flesh, I understood, but this other ... I stayed in the woods two days. I wildcrafted, eating whatever I found. And then dirty, so hungry it was akin to panic that must have been a rehearsal for starvation, I thought, Why not? I am as desperate as he. I will marry him and be an officer's wife, whatever that is. It will be a nice little life, no doubt, the details of which I might not know, but will feel out, day by day, inch by inch. I was even thinking of how I could now write to my mother, tell her where I was. For how much I'd been wanting to, knowing she would be sick with worry about me, the closeness between us not being easily broken, despite her selling me as she had. I daydreamed myself walking into the camp post office, mailing the letter. "I am fine, Mother. No need to worry. I am even now married to an officer." And Major Morgan could even give me the protection I would need from Preston Cummings, should he ever find me. And that's how we went back, Worthless and I—riding into camp inch by inch, a minute at a time. As I did, every eye I passed burned into me. So many eyes, so much silence. And the catcalls, the murmurs: "Evil winch." "Murderous strumpet." Then I saw a group of men digging a grave. I saw a casket outside the tent where only two days before I had been. It was Amalee who told me this: That very morning Major Richard Morgan had stood before his company in drill formation and raised his pistol to his head, placing the barrel in his mouth and fired. But not before he said my name.

Chapter 12

Apparently it took days, days of silence, for the response that Eliza could only feel was coming. She felt it first through the thunderous whispering that rose from the camp, rows at a time, and then farther out as the story of Major Morgan and the "girl," the "public woman," "the whore" who "spurned him" and then "did this to him" rolled like a sphere, until she became the evil one doing the evil thing she was clearly made for. What a scandal! And a scandal is always so easy to love. So it would not die and would not cease growing; even the word "witch" was overheard several times. As this whispered clattering spread from tent to tent, campfire to campfire, Eliza could only tremble while reading the shades of enmity on shoulders and backs turned to her when she walked by. At the doors each night that Ellen held open, no one, no one at all, called for Eliza.

Ellen and Fanny and Amalee, patient, supportive at first, dropped into silence too. They spoke through their looks and motions, outwardly saying: "Everybody'll forget. In time, they'll forget. It'll be over. And then you'll be back in business, Eliza. You'll see ..."

But they could not and would not support her for long.

And the camp's scorn did not lift.

It was perhaps on the fourth night after Major Richard Morgan murdered himself, wrapped in her name as he was falling, that the oldest of the farm boys, Jim Lukens, who bought Eliza for Major Morgan on that first night, came to the tent. Ellen was holding open the flap. It must have been about seven at dusk, banjos playing, men at cards, campfires being turned under in the early summer heat. "It's Eliza I'm come for." He put the Confederate dollars in Ellen's hand, dollars with Miss Lucy Pickens still brightly smiling on the bills.

Eliza, sitting on her cot with her back turned to the door, sees in a sideways glance that Ellen is looking into Jim Lukens's face. Savvy if not kind, Ellen is looking for a sign of his intentions. Perhaps he is crafty too and knows that lust is what Ellen is looking for, and *that* certainly is what he can reveal. For it was clear he coveted Eliza from the minute he saw her and from the time he came to walk her down the grass path to Major Morgan's tent that first night, obviously wondering, wondering what it would be like to have her himself. No doubt, her beauty and girlish energy were a light he'd have given almost anything to rub against, but he had been honorable in seeking her for the older man, the one who had nothing to live for.

But now, "Jim Lukens is out here asking for you," Ellen calls to Eliza.

"Who?"

"Man who came for you the first time, on account of Major Richard."

"I can't."

"You will."

"He'll kill me."

"I doubt it. You're still so dumb, Eliza. He was wanting you the first time he came for the old man. And now he's in the clear is all."

"How can you be so sure?"

"If I'm not, what else you got? You're dead in the water here, Eliza. Go now; the others will see and change. You'll be back in business. Hop to. Wash your face. You look pasty."

She goes out through the door flap. He looks at her. Tall, thin, his shirt unchanged from the day, sweated through, his blond hair tangled under a field hat, he doesn't smile. He doesn't speak. She reads a grayish red on his shoulders, a mix of lust and anger and what else? She's not sure. He takes her upper arm and half-leads, half-pushes her, not to the tent where he stays but to the woods beyond the picket line where the horses stomp and chew grain in their feedbags. It is where he knows their sounds will be muffled. And he says not a word, does only what must have gnawed inside him for days, releasing the ash-red feeling that has no place to go but onto her: hitting her quickly like the strike of a rattlesnake, across the face, his fist raking across her left ear, smashing her nose, then holding her down, raping her, pushing hard on the ground, so hard she cannot breathe.

Staying silent, she gasps only, through all, strangely, so strangely silent against what would seem elemental survival, never saying *stop, don't,* or weeping, but uttering only the sounds of what her body insists it release; and *this,* even muffled by the stomping of horses and their gnashing of grain, until finally, he stops, rolling back, exhausted himself, and she slips away, crawling, wiping semen on the grass, then running, her hand over her left ear to stanch the blood. The world suddenly is muffled and distant, heard as if she is under water.

He comes after her, but by now she has reached the picket line where Worthless is tethered and squats there under the mare, mixing in between the mare's legs and those of the horse next in line. She rolls into a ball, a solid lump between their hooves, thinking that if she is not trampled, she might survive. She holds her hands over her chest to stifle her heart's pounding. The horse next to Worthless snorts and stutter steps. But Worthless herself reaches down to sniff, but otherwise stands stone-still. Eliza gags and swallows down the putrid taste of fear coming up. She puts her face between her knees to concentrate on the smell of sweaty skin and skirt, holding on to them as a tether to sanity as she hears him walking nearby, knocking bushes, trampling brush in his search for her. Lord what is wrong with her ear? Her ear! Blood is trickling from it, and sounds are muted. Her fingers feel over her face and neck, coming up bloody, then find around her neck, beneath her dress, the necklace of birthing beads that she was given that day on the plantation where Quashi led her. Lord, what is wrong with her ear? Her ear! She tilts her head, trying to hear how close he is. Blood drips on her skirt. She squeezes the beads, her fingers going from one to the next. *Save me. Save me. Save me this time. This time. Please, this time.*

With a whacking sound, leaves fall aside as his arms knock them. He is very close now but perhaps will not think she would dare hide among horses, certainly not in among their legs. His footsteps are heavy, crude; he makes no attempt to be subtle. When she thinks he has given up wanting to find her, she peeks through her arms. *Yes, maybe. Where is he?* She tilts her head, concentrating hard because her eye is bloody and swelling shut. Then she sees him walking from the woods back toward the camp. A little bit longer, waiting, she then comes out. Her saddle is propped near the end of the picket line. *Good. O! Thank you. Thank you.* She bridles the mare so quickly that the bit hits Worthless's teeth, and the mare shakes her head. *Sorry, sorry. But no time now, help me here.* Then throwing the saddle on Worthless, she cinches it, then fumbles with the stirrup trying to get on. Adrenaline catapults her onto the mare's back. She turns. Riding faster than Worthless is willing to go—in a half-lope, half-trot on the sore-footed mare—Eliza heads back toward the Mississippi River with no idea of where else she can go.

Chapter 13

*D**ear One,*

All that night I rode—rode the poor mare Worthless until she could barely stumble forward. I rode into the little town of Crystal Springs and saw right off that it was a train stop on the Mississippi Central—so Mr. Preston could be there, searching for me. Touching my face, which earlier had burned like lamp oil had been poured on it and set afire, I now felt nothing. Strangely nothing. There was only the odd shape of it—the puffy swelling that told me I was likely to be unrecognizable to anyone who knew me before Mr. Jim Lukens got even for poor dead Major Richard.

I just did not know how unrecognizable until ...

She dismounts Worthless and leads the poor horse to the livery to finagle some hay for the mare. And now it is clear, so clear that her head seems to ring with the realization of it: She has lost every worldly good, except for one. And that one she is still wearing—the beeswax cervical cap gifted by Amalee. So at least she still has *that*; the use of her body can always be her treasury.

But when the owner of the livery sees her, he gasps. She

touches her face and feels a hideous shape, a deformity to her cheek that feels as if she is touching something foreign, not a cheek or face at all. And she is fully aware that her eye will not close and must look hideous, bloodied and drying out like a shriveling plant. The sight of his seeing her, and the ordeal over the long night, depletes what strength she has. She collapses in a hay pile, clenching Worthless's rein as if it is a lifeline to firm earth.

"There now. Oh, miss. How'd this happen? But no mind. You've had a bad fall, I see. Did your horse spook?"

"Yes, bad," she whispers, tilting to hear since all sounds are muffled—thankful too that his imagination prompts a lie.

"Blasted mare," she manages to say, standing up to wiggle the reins, hoping to make Worthless look a little less dead. "Not at all trustworthy."

"You come in here to the office and get some tea. Supper too if you have a mind, and I'll feed your mare."

"Thank you, but I have to confess: She didn't succeed in throwing me off. I may not look like much of a rider, but I am. Instead she bolted and ran me into a tree limb, and when she did, she spooked even more, took off running and ... I lost my bag. I haven't a penny." But she sees he has trouble understanding what she says; her words sound thick from a swollen tongue, and her lips will barely move. He gets her drift, though.

"You can send me money when you get where you're going."

"Yes, then."

That night, *he* slept in the hayloft; *she* in his bed in his office. And there she bathed in a tin basin, washing her bruised body the best she could, removing the beeswax cervical cap and tying it into her ripped underskirt. She doubly regrets now leaving Mama Mean in the tent with Amalee and Ellen. But then, if she'd taken her revolver with her when Jim Lukens came for her, she wouldn't have used it. Shoot a man who rightfully took vengeance on her for causing the death of his older friend? No, she could not have done it.

She sleeps only for those minutes when total exhaustion insists. And then in the morning, it is there in the livery owner's shaving mirror that she sees what has been done: the purplish bruises, her eye swollen open, her mouth mostly paralyzed in a grimace, her mouth drooling, and almost all sounds stolen by the damage to her ear. She has to tilt her head to catch spoken words.

Dear One,

I now looked like the witch I'd been called. I cleaned myself as much as I could and knew that I would have to somehow feed myself. I walked into the store across the street and did what I knew I would have to do—steal. I took a can of beans off a shelf and rolled it in my skirt, then pretended to hold my skirt with my hand, wrapped around the can. Of course I would have offered services to sweep or clerk—but who would accept my offer looking as I did? Besides, my mouth was still oozing blood; I needed time and attention. I was amused thinking that now I might have the perfect disguise from Preston Cummings— maybe now there would be no need to worry about the railway or his lurking. I owned perfect freedom—the repulsion of every other human to be near me! Even in that store, I felt a young man nearby, glancing and glancing away. And then, a boy of about fourteen bumped my skirt, and the stolen can fell and hit the floor.

"There! You!" The storekeeper hurried from behind the counter.

"Who? Me?" The boy was startled.

"Yes, thieving rat." The storekeeper took him by the upper arm, and as the boy squealed, the storekeeper threatened, "I'm taking you straight to your father. The sheriff too. Nabbed you in the act, I did. Don't squeal like a pig; you know you're a thief."

The boy kicks the storekeeper. Eliza freezes, watching the storekeeper glance at her. As he does, she notes his face recoiling at her hideousness. No doubt he categorizes her as riffraff of no consequence. And now he swipes the boy with a broom, forcing him toward the door. "Confess, confess. Own up, thief."

If the nuns of my childhood were right about Hell, I will certainly be sent there. For I said nothing. In my silence, I let the boy be blamed—too ashamed of who I was and what I had done to own my thievery, when suddenly the young man on the other side of the store, who'd been glancing at me, stepped up.

And lo! I saw—it was Lem, Lem Polk. He stared, then asked, "Eliza?" My name I read from his lips, but in his eyes I could see his memory of me, his desire for me, and then I found my own memories of him: the nascent Rebel burning to fight, selling me Mama Mean for a low price. I would have shut my eyes and nodded my head to his question. But my eye would not close. He had seen me steal; there was no doubt in that. Shopping on the other side of the store, he had noticed me and wondered ... had crept close, and now reached down to pick up the stolen can to say, "Actually sir, this rolled off the shelf. The boy did not steal."

The storekeeper looks from the boy to Eliza to Lem and then, "I've had this boy steal in here before. Makes perfect sense he'd do it again."

"Maybe. But I saw the can roll from the shelf myself." Lem nods.

"Maybe. I can't say you didn't." The storekeeper lets go of the boy.

Lem reaches for her elbow. "Cousin Eliza, how long have you been in town? Come, there's something I want to show you."

She takes his arm. Working the charade perfectly, Lem escorts her to the door, while the storekeeper drops his accusations. And there, outside on the boardwalk, Lem guides her to a bench as his eyes dart across her face.

"Eliza, how'd this happen?"

"An accident. I know I must look raw." She laughs at her inability to say "raw" and senses that her laugh resembles an animal sound.

"We have to get you help."

In truth, I was so glad to see him, I wanted to grab hold. Instead, Dear One, I gave him a teaspoon of truth and a barrel of concoction. I told him in my garbled speech—taking extra time for my tongue to do the work which my mouth could not— that my aunt, whom I was going to see on the day he met me, had died. That the inheritor of her plantation despised me for reasons I cared not to go into. And even abused me (letting his own imagination fill that in). Then I said I was thrown out "with nowhere to go. No money. No other family. The war displaced everyone I knew. And then yesterday, my horse threw me, running under a tree limb first." I waved my hand across my face as explanation.

"Worthless?" He cocked his head in disbelief.

My blaming everything on that poor half-dead horse was bound to raise suspicions.

"Yes, Worthless," I repeated and attempted a smile. "I am certainly that now too." When I reached up to feel my smile, I felt my hideousness. Bah! Beauty come, beauty go. At least I wouldn't have to deal with the complications of that anymore; and yet, how was I going to be without it? It had always been my mainstay.

"Don't underestimate an old mare," I added.

"Here. Let's go down here. Easy now. That's right." He took me by the arm and led me to the doctor on the next block. A serious little man, who put a poultice on my eye and a dark salve on my face and asked too many questions, all of which Lem answered for me. And then the doctor said, "What a sorry event, for I can see that at one time you were very pretty."

"Will it come back?" I put my hand near my face. "The movement, I mean. I seem paralyzed here."

"You are. Apparently a nerve has been damaged." He gave me a jar of the black salve. "Movement might come back, might not. You'll have to wait to see."

Outside on the street again, Lem turned to me. "Miss Eliza, I'm heading for Corinth. Have you heard? Governor Pettus ordered all local militias there." His face twittered with excitement. "We're to form the great Rebel Army. My company's taking the train in the morning. Would you welcome the chance to come with me?"

I was prepared to say yes with a vigor of relief. But before I could answer, he threw into the mix: "Robert Drury—remember Robert, Eliza? He has made sergeant! Good old Robert— would you believe? And he's coming into town tomorrow to hire a laundress for us—for our company. I know that would be greatly beneath you, but it would be employment and ... excitement. Soon there's to be a great battle. You could be a witness to history seeing the North whupped and no Yankee left to invade. By any long chance, would that suit you? If so, I will recommend you to Robert. I'm sure he'd quickly agree."

O, how I was due a fat slice of good luck! I hugged him, left black salve on his shirt and a look on his face that bespoke more than delight.

That night I slept at the livery again. In the morning, I led Worthless to meet Lem where we would board the New Orleans and Jackson Railroad en route to Corinth. Robert Drury was there too and made good the offer Lem mentioned. Robert looked at my face and pursed his lips to keep from reacting. Lem pointed out which car I should ride in, but first went to tie Worthless in the open car with the cavalry horses. I insisted on going there too—I'd grown so fond of the old mare, as if her welfare and mine were as tied together as sunlight and flower. And much to my surprise, as I stepped into the car with Lem to tie Worthless behind us amidst a jangling of spurs, came Captain McFerrin, leading his fine sorrel. He tethered it there beside me.

One glance, and a glance away, then his forehead furrowed with puzzlement in seeing me, then furrowed again in the pain of looking at me. Yet his eyes did not veer away. I could see in them a struggle of recognition. Then he took off his hat, with its fine pheasant feather, to nod at me, then put it back on. Since I had last seen him, he had grown a beard: wheat-brown, the color of sun on sand, and a mustache to match. His skin, finally now suntanned to caramel, set his eyes in such high contrast— blue and intense—that I looked away in embarrassment.

"You are badly hurt." His voice carried a warm concern.

I nodded.

"Have you seen a doctor?"

I nodded.

"Can I help in any way?

I nodded no.

I knew that he had heard all the rumors at the camp where Mr. Morgan died. Perhaps he had even heard of Jim Lukens running me off, if not beating me nearly half to death.

He stared at me in sympathy and concern, then nodded in understanding and stepped down, most likely to go to where his wife was traveling or to the car with other officers. He looked back at me once more. Now I was troubled far more than I expected to be. For if he, as well as Lem, recognized me in my hideousness, that meant that Mr. Devil himself, Preston Cummings, could as well.

I found the car with the other camp followers and joined them in a seat where I kept my head down. And where, so hungry for sleep, I sank into it.

The train signaled a boarding call. On the station platform, the Crystal Springs mayor wound up a speech and ended with a prayer. Men lined up to board, to shake hands with the mayor and with other bystanders, then climbed on to lean from the train windows.

Beside the tracks, women waved handkerchiefs, some crying, others letting loose a long, hardy cheer, others waving flags and hats. Sitting where she was, her head nodding on her chest, even with her loss of hearing, Eliza sensed the send-off and the train's engine peppering her sleep.

The train roared toward Corinth; and despite the warm day's sun pouring over her, she found the first real sleep she'd had in weeks.

Chapter 14

For three days, the train rolled toward Corinth, frequently stopping along the way to add more militias, and each time, the cheering bystanders gave a rousing send-off. With a population of one thousand, the city of Corinth was thought to be the perfect hub from which supplies could be sent all over the South, for it was here that the great railroads—the Memphis, the New Orleans, the Charleston, the Mobile and the Ohio—converged in what would become known as the vertebrae of the Confederacy.

The train stops. Rising from her seat, Eliza stands in line behind the other camp followers: three prostitutes in front, their perfume wafting back in a sweetness mixed with sweat. Lace and feathery trim float as they descend from the train. Ten other laundresses follow, their long skirts hoopless and plain.

Eliza walks down the train steps and finds Lem waiting for her. "I'll get your horse, Miss Eliza. Wait there." He points to a field where some of the cavalry are already leading their horses.

"Thank you." She notes how young and eager Lem's face is, notes too the flush of infatuation looping from him to her. Clearly he was having what Madam Francine called "a spasm of the heart." Even in her hideousness, he desires her, which deepens her bafflement at the nature of men. Does nothing deter them?

Standing in the field next to the station, she keeps her head down, wishing she had a scarf or her old hat to conceal her face. Ducking, as cavalry soldiers walk near her leading their horses from the train, she then lifts her head to look for Lem and instead glimpses Captain McFerrin coming toward her, leading his sorrel.

In the muffled clink of his spurs, she notes the kick-up of dust and quickly puts her hand up to avoid any closer look at her face. His horse is so tall; she steps back, thinking they will pass. But his eyes are steadily set on hers, and his expression is so sympathetic that as her eyes dart up, then away, they are drawn back by his, to hold hers in a shared gaze. He stops in front of her, his boots shined to a high gloss, his hat with its pheasant feather dusted from practice drills. "Are you feeling better?"

She tilts her head to catch his voice. "Yes." She smiles but feels how strange that her mouth will not move. "A friend took me to a doctor in Crystal Springs. He gave me a salve. It is an ugly salve, but it seems to be working." She laughs ironically and knows her words are slurred. "Thank you for asking."

"I wonder if I might ..." He pauses, then says, "My wife is not well. I am getting her settled there." He points to the Tishomingo Hotel facing the railroad grounds. "The camp medical officer will attend her as needed, and could be of service to you too, if you like." He pauses to see if she will reply, and when she doesn't, he adds: "My wife has a will much stronger than mine. I tried to keep her from coming, but she overpowered me." He smiles with lines creasing his face above his beard. "And I was wondering if you might—that is if you are available and if you feel better—be employed to help look after her?"

She reads his lips and tilts her head. Then, "Oh. I ..."

Her shame paralyzes her. Voices in her mind raise questions: If he knew of the scandal at the former camp, did he believe the rumors? Was he aware of what she did, how she "earned" her living? And then her mind answers her with: *Most likely.* Followed by, *Of course.*

Finally she says, "I don't do that sort of work. I've never done that. It would be inappropriate of me to accept."

"I see. Yes, well, then forgive me for asking."

He looks closely at her again. "Is there any way I can help you?"

"No. Thank you for your concern, though. But I am, I assure you, quite fine. And now if you'll excuse me, here comes ..." She nods toward Lem leading Worthless to her. The two men, Lem and Captain McFerrin, nod to each other.

She takes the mare's reins and begins stroking the horse's forehead.

Lem points to the Irish woman leading a mule cart with laundry pots inside. "Go to Molly Evangeline—there. She's the head laundress for our company."

Captain McFerrin touches the brim of his hat and leads his horse away.

"Molly Evangeline McCarthy'll watch out for you." Lem again takes Worthless's reins, and while guiding Eliza, explains, "She'll help you find some other clothes too."

Eliza looks across at the woman Lem refers to: short, fat, deeply freckled, hair the color of an apricot and shifting a wad of snuff under her lip. She wears a gray cotton skirt and striped apron. Her good-natured smile reminds Eliza of a painted doll at a street fair. Eliza touches her own rumpled silk dress with its stains and rips from the night that Jim Lukens raped her.

"Good luck, Eliza." Lem gives over the mare's reins, then turns to join Robert Drury, who nods at her with Jessie Marks walking beside him. Neither can help but stare in disbelief of her vanished beauty. Then all three break off to join where rations are being handed out. A long line of men is forming.

Eliza watches each receive bacon, flour, sugar, coffee, rice, beans, molasses, vinegar, soap and candles.

Suddenly she hears a voice so trumpetlike that even her damaged ear cannot block the sound.

"Eliza! Eliza Goode!" Molly Evangeline yells. "Ain't you the one Sergeant Drury hired to launder? Well, come'ere, then. Come'ere! He said you was good. I thought he meant 'good' was your surname! But then he told me your real one. Oh, I guess I forget it now."

Eliza walks forward, leading Worthless. She hesitates for a moment, and then looking at the large woman who takes a handkerchief out of her pocket and spits into it—who now was to be her instructor, if not quite a savior—she says: "No, you heard Sergeant Robert Drury very correctly the first time. I *am* Eliza Goode. I do spell it with an *e*, though. G-o-o-d-e."

"Honey," Molly Evangeline laughs, handing the mule's lead rope to Eliza, "I don't care if your last name is Shit Mary or Alice B. Loose. All I cares is if you can wash sixty pounds of stinking clothes in a pot of lye soap. Now here, take King Charles's rope and tie him with your mare there." She hands over the mule's rope and points to a tree. "King Charles ain't no good on Tuesdays and Thursdays, but he's a damn fine mule the rest of the week. When we left home I promised him a girlfriend. Looks like your mare's it."

Smiling, Eliza takes the mule's rope.

So you see, Dear One, the name I so surprisingly took was part joke on myself and part prayer. I added the "e" onto "good" for no reason except that I wanted to distinguish my new self in some way. If this was to be my new life that I was crawling into, then let me come out the other end as changed as a moth from a chrysalis.

****

That first night, Eliza helped pitch her new home—the tent that Molly Evangeline McCarthy stored in the mule cart. Helping too were the other two laundresses, Eleanor and Colleen. Eleanor, the wife of Robert Drury's drill sergeant, was a big-boned woman with rough, dry skin and a need for a jolt of rum every morning as an eye-opener. Colleen was the young bride of a lieutenant—brown-haired with protruding front teeth and small sharp features reminiscent of a beaver. Molly Evangeline was herself the wife of the company's second lieutenant. So soon, all four had a makeshift home with utensils, clothes racks, a mirror on a string. Outside they strung up clotheslines between trees and made a site for the fires to heat water for the laundry pots. Late into the night they stacked kindling.

Right away Eliza noted that in terms of physical strength, she came in a pitiful fourth behind Molly Evangeline and the others. Hoping they would not use that against her, she soon took on attending the washpot fires double time. Wherever she went, she collected kindling. At first, the laundry method was new and hard: heat the water, fill the wooden buckets, pour it in the tubs, rub the clothes on a washboard. She learned that sitting on a stool saved her back when using the washboard while scrubbing shirts and pants up and down on it in a steady rhythm.

Every day too she took on the duties of caring for King Charles and her own dear Worthless. Every night she refilled their water buckets and every morning staked the mare and mule out to graze.

"Eliza Goode, here, take this here."

"Yes, good, Eliza Goode, take this over there."

"More washin' for you, Eliza Goode."

Eliza Goode.

Her new name echoed across the camp.

Molly Evangeline, Colleen and Eleanor were kind by not asking about her wounds, even if they did occasionally pronounce "Goode" with a tinge of teasing in it. But then they each had to be good every day when men came forward with their laundry to be washed and dried and returned in due time.

Forty cents for shirts and pants, small things thrown in free. The washtubs were big enough to stir several men's clothes at once. It was the hot water that was dangerous. Soon blisters from burns spotted Eliza's arms along with insect bites.

Some of the men said each day while paying her: "I'm so sorry for you, miss."

Several overpaid, whispering, "Maybe you'll find a doctor, one who can fix ..." and not knowing how to say what they meant, ended with, " 'Cause , miss, I can see you was once mighty pretty."

Her mind, using her once girlish-chattering voice, silently retorted in anger, *You're one to talk—pretty as a hog's behind.* And, *I don't need your pity, Mr. Filthy!*

Shame could lose its sting, she found, when coated with anger. She also heard in her semi-deafness the leftover voices of her mother and Madam Francine, even the detested Preston Cummings. Their words mingled: "Beautiful, so beautiful, Eliza. Indeed, you may be the most beautiful I have ever seen."

Every day, voices awakened me to where I was—not just in Camp Clark in Corinth, Mississippi—but in my life. Only hard physical work softened the voices. Only the press of many around me kept me at the here and now. By May 27th, the day after I arrived, 1,500 men were in that camp. And more companies were arriving every hour. At night, the camp looked like 5,000 lights.

Always there was talk: some saying there would be a big battle next week. Some, that there would be no war at all. Days were shaped by the camp's rules: bugle calls at dawn for roll call, assignments to the men for guard duty, then drill—drill, drill, drill in the belief that confidence in battle would come from the touch of elbows.

No one was allowed off the grounds without permission from their company's captain. One man in the mess of eight learned to cook, and most often badly. All were sleeping on the ground with nothing but blankets. Pillows would bring good prices. Yet no one complained, for war excitement glazed over discomforts. The sound of banjos, guitars, fiddles, and men's voices broke out in song at all hours in revelry similar to a hunting camp.

And the fights! O, Dear One, the fights! With companies arriving from all over the state, men saw others they had known in the past. So friendships or vendettas were picked up and carried on. Four or five fights broke out each day. I overheard a private say, "I hated him back home, but I hear now he hates the Yankees, so I think better of him." And always whiskey flowed. For infractions due to drunkenness, the wayward one was often tied to a tree and left there until sober.

Finally tents arrived—one handed out to each eight men. Now the camp was a wall of white. Canteens were handed out too, and haversacks. As the camp swelled by the thousands, it took on a more permanent appearance with chairs and tables in front of tents. Men played cards and wrote letters home. And now on June 3rd, my own letter. I wrote it while sitting on an upturned bucket after tending the mule and mare. I sent it from the tent post to go by train to South Basin Street. "Dear Mother and Madam Francine, I am sure you wonder how and where I am, but rest assured, I am fine, though not near. I regret if I have caused you sleepless nights and warranted worry. I am riding the war far, and it is exciting! Never say I was *foolhardy or stupid. Say only that I threw my life on the back of the future, and rode it without once being thrown. Yes, I am surviving grandly. P.S. Madam Francine, I appreciate your generous monetary going-away gift. If I were near, I would repay it, for I have suddenly grown quite rich. Devotedly, Your Ungrateful Eliza."*

Amused at my lies and sarcasm, I walked back from the P.O. I was also distracted by what had happened the day before: three deaths in camp, one from being accidentally shot, one by drowning in the river nearby, the other from dysentery. There was fear that an epidemic was breaking out. And on top of that, there were rumors that spies had been caught and were soon to be hanged.

That humid June morning, Eliza awakes to the bass chatter of men's voices mixing with birdsong. Eleanor and Colleen, being slow risers, roll from side to side, stretching and complaining before they are up.

Quickly Eliza paints her face with the black salve, musing at how the medicine colors her face as if she could lay claim to an Indian ancestry. She wears the clothes bought in Corinth: a skirt of gray cotton, a white blouse that ties at the neck, a flowered apron that hides dirt. She also now has a hat to pull down over her eyes, as well as a scarf to pull up over her chin.

"Hurry and get that first load in," Molly Evangeline orders, stoking the fire under the laundry pots.

Eliza sees in a nearby field Captain McFerrin's company of cavalry performing drills: serpentines on horseback, columns of two multiplying into fours. Then one man dismounts to hold the mounts of four others in a drill for hand-to-hand combat. The horses' muscular shoulders and haunches glisten with sweat.

She finds herself searching for the bobbing hat whose crown wears a pheasant feather. Often she catches sight of him waving his arms in directions to his company, then galloping his sorrel in blazing speed to stop and spin with his sword flashing in sunlight against his horse's side.

She recalls his voice asking her to help look after his wife and wonders why *that* had so frightened her. By far it would have been better than this, stirring men's stinking clothes in a pot with water heated by coals that are never allowed to go out.

She touches her face and can feel her fingers tracing her nose, her mouth, the whole of her cheek. She goes into the tent to look into the mirror that Eleanor tied to the tent pole. When she smiles, her lips move. They move crookedly, but they move. Her eye can open and close enough now that she no longer has to sleep with a wet cloth over it. But even so, she is still hideous.

The week before when she ventured into town for supplies, a child saw her and ran. She is still a visitor from nightmares.

She glances out the tent door and sees that the fire under one of the water pots is about to go out. Eleanor and Colleen have gone into town; Molly Evangeline has gone to visit her husband. Eliza rushes from the tent to throw wood on the fire, and as she does, the hem of her dress brushes the coals. There is a puff of smoke, then the blaze of fire.

Looking down, she sees flames rising toward her waist. Wild with panic, she beats at them and jumps from the heat. At first she thinks it is her own voice screaming, but instead it is Molly Evangeline's. "God help! She's on fire. Fire!" Molly is running toward her.

Suddenly someone throws himself around her, pushing her to the ground, and she feels the wrapped tight-hold of arms, and the force of them taking off with her, rolling, over and over across the ground, throwing dirt up over her, into her face, over her skirt, over the whole of her to stifle the flames.

He must have been walking from the hotel across the street when he heard the cries—my hands above my head, my skirt ablaze and jumping as if I could leap above them. For several long minutes, Captain McFerrin and I were bound together, both of us on the ground, his legs among mine, and his arms throwing dirt to stifle the flames with one intention save any other: to keep me for whatever was going to be my new life.

When we stopped tumbling, I heard low in my ear, "Are you all right?" His mouth against my hair, my good ear, my hideous face. "Let's stand up and get a look."

My skirt was burned up nearly to my waist. My blouse was torn and changed permanently to the color of dust. But I was standing. My thighs were on parade. Yet I was all in one. I seem to have survived. I looked down at myself and then at him and then I laughed. For the first time in over a month, the sound of my laughter was the sound of my laughter. It was no longer a muffled sound from a swollen, unfeeling mouth. It was no longer, either, the laugh from a girl. It was instead the laugh of someone who knew—deeply knew—the shortness of life in all the mystérieux singularity of it. Never before had I felt my existence such as that.

He laughed with me. "Looks like we have indeed saved you."

"Saved for another day at least." I looked up at him. "And I thank you."

He bowed. "You are most welcome." He then walked back to chase down his hat.

Molly Evangeline McCarthy spread her own skirt over my thighs, then put her arm around me and guided me to the tent. "Let's see to you," she purred.

Chapter 15

The next day, Eliza's skin was blistered but otherwise fine. She knew that in some way she wanted to address Captain McFerrin's extraordinary deed. She said to Molly Evangeline, "I'd like to go into town for a bit. Can you spare me?"

"Aye, after yesterday, no doubt your nerves are frayed. Get yourself a new skirt. And while you're there, bring us a bag of rice for supper."

In the morning, Eliza sets off riding Worthless. But instead of to town, she rides toward the field where the cavalry is drilling. She is not looking for Captain McFerrin exactly. Instead, she is looking for his manservant, the one who, at the former camp, had taken care of Worthless and apparently also Captain McFerrin's wife. She catches sight of Captain McFerrin in the midst of the cavalry exercises, but no sign of his manservant, so she turns. And as she crosses the road across from the camp, she notices him coming from the Tishomingo Hotel.

"Wait, please," she calls. He turns, clearly doubting that she is speaking to him. "Yes, you." Her speech is clear, her mouth feels alive with movement. She dismounts from Worthless and leads the mare closer.

"Ma'am?" His deference is cloying and also insincere, for Eliza notes in his stance that he is reluctant to stand here with her. Clearly he is aware of her station—and scandal—at the other camp. Perhaps too he is suspicious; maybe he believes the rumors of her being a witch.

She takes care to say forthrightly: "I want to take something of use to your mistress. I hear she is ill. I have knowledge of wildcrafting. If you could tell me her malady, I could prepare something to be helpful."

His eyes never meet hers. Instead, he looks beyond her, holding his hat. For a moment he hesitates, then he looks at her in a long glance. Their eyes meet and exchange a deep recognition.

Instantly I knew—could read a change of feeling in him— that we shared knowledge of one thing: survival. His stance of reluctance melted. "They never speak of it," he said. "Him and Miss Rissa pretend it is not there."

"Miss Rissa? What a charming name! So you have no knowledge of her illness?"

"O, I know all about it. I went with 'em—three months back—all the way to Pennsylvania. Famous doctors looked at her there. Now they pretend they never been."

"So you do know?"

He nods, and now for the second time he looks straight at her. "Maybe you would know of a remedy?" He trails off, then averts his eyes once again. "I heard her Mama telling a lady friend, saying her sweet girl has a growth, deep inside, and no way to mend it. She is that too, Miss Rissa—a sweet girl, though she has a playful side like a bad child. That's how come she got to go with the captain now—said she wasn't about to let him go off without her—was going to be with him every minute, stamped her foot and got her way. Yes, I've known her and Mr. Ben since they were children. Mr. Ben chose me to go to this war with him."

"What's your name?"

"Lawrence. Mr. Ben's daddy named me. I was born at his place."

"Where?"

"Brookhaven. Never been anyplace else. It's down past where

we went for Mr. Ben to pick up more riders for his cavalry. That camp where he mustered was where I first met you—remember? Miss ...?"

"Goode. Eliza Goode."

"You been hurt bad."

"But I'm on the mend. And today, I plan to pay a visit to your mistress. All you have told me will help."

She puts her foot in the stirrup and remounts Worthless and rides off, noting Lawrence walking toward the field where the cavalry drills. In the surrounding fields, she hunts for uva ursi leaf. It is a guess as to what ails Rissa McFerrin. Yet a tea made from uva ursi, which is a prescription always used at Madam Francine's for any female ailment, is a safe choice. When she finds it, she dismounts and picks it in abundance.

She then rides into town, buys new clothes, and wearing them, comes back to tie Worthless outside the Tishomingo Hotel.

Inside, she asks for the room of Rissa McFerrin. She climbs the steps, knocks on the door, and when it is opened, she stands looking at the woman whom she first saw two months before. Rissa returns the stare, at first wearing an astonished expression, then an uneasy one, as no doubt the South's caste culture goes to work on her. She quickly darts her eyes away, uneasy with the fact of Eliza's calling on her.

I had seen such women—planters' wives at a distance—but never so close and so intimately as now, knowing what I planned to offer. As she put her hand on the doorframe in a gentle block, I admired everything about her: her stature, her dress, her refined beauty. Here, I thought, would be one I would most like to emulate, though my background had already given me some of this polish, yet here was the real thing. Meanwhile, each of us was allowing seeds of recognition to supply answers, and then I jumped in with my reason.

"I brought you something you might enjoy." Eliza holds out her bouquet of uva ursi leaves. "These make a wonderful tea. Might I make you some?"

Eliza waits. Glancing into the room behind Rissa, she sees *Godey's Lady's Book* spread on the bedcovers—the popular magazine often consulted for the latest fashions by almost everyone at Madam Francine's. Rissa does not step back for Eliza to walk in and also makes a point not to stare at Eliza's face.

"That's kind, but no. I was just about to *leave*. Yes, *leave,* you see." Rissa picks up a blue shawl and drapes it on her shoulders. She wears a gray day dress with pink trim on the collar. Her hair is swept up under a wide-brimmed hat, hair the color of cinnamon. And while she is stately in an overall impression of cream and quality, she does not convey quite the sweetness that Lawrence claimed for her. Instead, Eliza senses an argent tint on Rissa McFerrin's shoulders: a wrapping of palpable stubbornness. She is a few inches taller than Eliza. Her skin looks as thin as a wafer and as pale. Otherwise she seems to hint not at all of a serious illness. In fact, she looks so vigorous that Eliza doubts what Lawrence has told her, and even Captain McFerrin himself.

Suddenly Rissa turns and picks up a parasol. "I don't know your name, but I know you. Most *certainly*. My husband told me you almost became the next *tragedy* in camp, catching on fire. And now until this morning when Lawrence informed me, I didn't know that my husband saved you." She laughs. "Lawrence is always quick to brag of Captain McFerrin's deeds. Yes, most certainly. And now I don't doubt that you have good intentions, but I don't need what you have brought me." Her voice, soft in the Southern rhythm of slow delivery, is also unique in that Rissa emphasizes every few words. It is as though she so loves the sound of them, she holds on for a lingering taste.

"I understand." Eliza turns to leave. But then adds, "I don't think anyone saw me come here. I'm sorry if my visit embarrasses you. Simply, I wanted to thank your husband for what he did for me, and since I know he values you more than anything, I thought a gesture of aid on your behalf is what he would most like."

"Oh, for *goodness* sakes. Don't take what I said like *that*! *Here*. Let me have the leaves you picked. My *goodness*, you were kind to think of this. And these smell very interesting. What did you say they are?"

"Uva ursi."

"Oh, I know about *those*." She smiles. "For female ailments, *right*? Oh, yes, *most* certainly. My mother grew up using *them*. But I *assure* you, *they* are of no use to me. *No*, absolutely." She then laughs loudly, an astonishingly bold laugh. "My father named me Rissa. It's Latin for laughter. So it seems only fitting that I should have a hearty laugh, don't you think?"

Eliza agrees, smiling, admiring Rissa's unexpected blend of boldness, beauty and refinement. She thinks Rissa is the most enchanting woman she has ever met. "Steep them ten minutes, add honey."

"I will. Thank you." She runs her fingers through the bouquet of leaves. "No doubt we'll need every calming tea to make it through this. This separation *à l'agréable*, I mean." She raises a shoulder and twists her mouth. "Oh, it was bound to happen. We have hated each other so—the North and South. We have an incompatibility of temper, most definitely. But that is not worth a fight, is it? We should sulk awhile, then declare the divorce over. This war shouldn't last more than a few weeks."

"I hope not." And then, "*Absolument. Mais malheureusement c'est impossible.*" Eliza uses the best French accent she learned at Madam Francine's.

Rissa looks at her with a clear expression of surprise. Obviously she did not think Eliza capable of knowing French, or at least not such polished French. "I too am afraid it is very much impossible! Ben says for me to *hold* my tongue and not talk about politics. But how can I? If hardheaded Lincoln would have just let us solve this the way some of us want—*Why!* To free slaves in every Southerner's will. I *assure* you, I'm loyal to my Southern roots, but frankly I'll be as happy as a dog ridded of fleas to have slavery lifted from *my* future!" She laughs again boldly, then adds, "When I married Ben I had no idea his father would give us eight slaves as a wedding present—eight! Who then would be my job to clothe, nurse and in every other way take care of. Can you imagine sewing for all eight and attending to the coughs and fevers of their children every day! I couldn't keep up!" She whips her hands around theatrically and sighs. "But then we all know this war is not just about that. In Ben's opinion, we should have freed the slaves before Sumter, then we could have made a clear statement that this is really about states having the right to decide their own futures. He thinks too that would make us on better terms with the former slaves. We must free them ourselves, not let someone else do it! But I ask you, Miss ...”

“Goode.”

“Goode?”

“Yes. *Eliza* Goode.”

“Oh, yes, I remember now your name, Eliza. Well, I ask you, Eliza, have you ever thought how strange it is that abolitionists want to free our slaves and yet would rather muck a thousand stables than give us women the vote? You and me! Ahhhh! In their opinion we are silly, stupid playthings meant only for populating the earth. Rubbish! And if you really want to know what I think, well, Eliza Goode, I'm going to tell you whether you want to know or not! I'm quite sure that Old Abe is really an abolitionist in a compromiser's clothing. He says he cares only about the spread of slavery into the Border States. Fiddlesticks! He will free them all soon. And I predict Jeff Davis will have this whole thing blown over by next month. I'm betting that Ben and I will be home for harvest.”

She adjusts her hat over her forehead and lowers her voice to almost a whisper. “Have you noticed how quiet they all are about this? Like Lawrence, I mean. We haven't a clue about what they are thinking. No doubt they are considering running off to the other side. Lawrence keeps his bronze face as still as a statue. Yet the other night I caught him singing, ‘*Yankee Doodle went to town.*’ I pointed out that he better keep the Yankee out and stick with the doodle, since the Yankee part no longer suits our dispositions. He didn't so much as smile, just kept on singing.”

How charming, Eliza thinks, and she is also reminded of how she herself only months before had a tendency to chatter. Well lately, her travels have more or less thumped the girlishness out of her. “Well, I must be going. I hope the tea will be of help.”

“Oh, here, I apologize. I didn't offer you water. I bet you're sweltering in this heat.”

“No, thank you. I really must go. I don't have permission to be gone long.”

“I see.” Rissa smiles kindly and nods.

Eliza walks down the stairs and goes to untie Worthless. It is a long while after she leaves before Rissa appears at the door of the hotel, which makes it very clear that Rissa spaced the timing so that she would not be seen with Eliza.

Dear One,

It was true: I had never met anyone like her. Over time, I will give you a portrait born of not one day, not one time, but from the long months that Rissa and I would share, for on that day neither she nor I knew what the war would do to us.

PART II

BEN

Chapter 16

Looking out of the upstairs window of my study in Cambridge, Massachusetts, in 2004, so distant in years from Eliza's world, I imagined her walking into Camp Corinth from her first meeting with Rissa. There was the sound of men's voices at drill, the clank of horseshoeing, the chatter, the distant sound of banjos. I was haunted by Eliza's words: "Neither she nor I knew what the war would do to us." Yet while Eliza's life seemed alive and present in my mind, it was Hadley's life that eluded me. It was as if Hadley had timed this—that I should write up to here and have no more letters to draw from.

Then, in a bizarre coincidence, Caleb called from downstairs: "Hadley's on the phone."

Stunned, I stopped and quickly picked up the phone, afraid she might disappear as mysteriously as before. "Hadley, is it really you?"

"Yep, cuz. Just thought we ought to touch base. I'm in Costa Rica already. Got in last night. Sorry I can't meet you at the airport. It's dawn to dusk work here."

"Yes?" I was trying to read her mood to assess what I could say or not say.

"You won't believe the number of cases we've got lined up here. Kids with cleft palates, old ladies with skin tumors, men with broken jaws that were never set. It's outrageous. Anyway, check in, I'll meet you in the dining room at eight. I promise. Or I'll call."

"Okay. But Hadley—"

"Yes?"

"I've been trying for weeks to get in touch with you. Where have you been?"

"Around. In work up to my eyeballs, really. Besides, I don't want to get in your way. I'm scared to ask. How's it going?"

"With Eliza Goode, you mean?"

"Yes."

I was quiet. I let her listen to my breathing. She deserved this silence from me, and I couldn't resist. I had to give in to my own meanness. My desire to get back at her was too great to do otherwise. "I'll let you know when I get there. I've run into some trouble."

"What trouble?"

"I can't talk about it now. You'll see."

Late that afternoon, Caleb drove me to Logan to catch the plane that weeks before Hadley had booked me on. I was determined that she would not drive this whole show so completely anymore. But I also didn't have the nerve to let my bag with the pages in it of Eliza Goode's story be checked as baggage, out of reach in the belly of a plane. Instead, I held them in my lap, flying across the country, changing planes in Miami, hurtling down to San Jose, just as Hadley expected me to.

Landing at the San Jose airport, I watched the plane set down in the midst of dense foliage, and then I walked down the steps to be hit with a humidity that felt as if I were breathing through cotton. I sweated through my blouse just on the way to the cabstand. In the backseat, being driven to the hotel, I guarded Eliza Goode on paper as if she were a small child. I was determined that this time with Hadley, I would make her tell me all the missing parts. I was determined to unearth the real reasons feeding her obsession with Eliza Goode.

My room was on the third floor. The Crowne Plaza was spiffy, if not five-star, certainly comfortable and not what I expected, considering that Hadley was here to do volunteer good-Samaritan work. Why was she not staying with a family? With one of those who had arranged the trip? Was having me here affecting her decisions? A part of me even wondered if she were making all this up. I hated feeling suspicious, but was it possible that she could even be pretending to work at a clinic here, administering anesthesia for surgeries as a cover; but if so, a cover for what?

****

The window of my room looked down on a park with running trails and tennis courts amid the lush foliage that is Costa Rica. I had three hours to wait before meeting Hadley in the dining room, and it would be much better to keep busy than to let my suspicions run wild. I went for a walk on the park trails. I sat awhile and watched a young married couple play tennis—happily married, for they teased each other, and the husband occasionally dropped his racket as though he couldn't help it and watched his wife's winning shot fly by.

I looked up, sensing something moving in the hotel window above me. It was seven o'clock now. But I saw no one in the window that looked like Hadley, only a man's arm and a moving curtain.

Showered and rested, I walked into the dining room with its red and gold tablecloths, a bright setting with Japanese fare. Hadley was not there. I was shown to a table near the window, where the waiter handed me a menu and set one on the table for Hadley. I pretended to study mine while glancing over the top at the entrance. Would Hadley not even appear?

It was nearly eight-thirty when she walked in. At first, my eyes slid off her and then back again as I realized what she had done. Her hair was no longer short and blond, but was now mahogany-dark with, obviously, extensions added, so it could be pulled up and pinned. Her face was illuminated with some sort of shimmering powder, and though the dining room was now filled and busy, everyone seemed to watch her walk across the room toward me. She was simply stunning, more beautiful than I remembered. She was thinner, and when she got closer,

I saw a hollowness to her eyes, a grayness in the surrounding skin. They made me think of photos I had seen during much of my research, the eyes of soldiers, even Lincoln's eyes that became wells of grief. She raised her hand, smiling, tilting her head with affection as our eyes met, mouthing *Susan* in her flirtatious way. She was wearing a red silk ruana, dripping fringe over a long tight skirt, and had abandoned her glasses. As she slipped into the chair opposite me, I saw the mole she had drawn on her cheek and heard myself gasp, even though I am far from the gasping kind. Hadley had so skillfully imitated the one photograph we had of Eliza Hamilton that I was rattled.

"Startled you, didn't I?" She sipped water, looking at me.

"Hadley, you look so much like her, I feel I'm with a ghost."

She laughed. "Got it right, then, didn't I? So tell me, how's it going? You said you had a problem."

"I do."

"Wait, don't tell me. Tell me instead where you are—how far have you gotten?"

"She's at the camp in Corinth, Mississippi."

"Has she told you yet about how she was forced out of the first one?"

"Yes, about Major Morgan and how he died. And the one who—"

"Yeah, raped her, then broke her eardrum. And her facial nerve was damaged, so she set off into the Mississippi woods, partly deaf. And one side of her face was paralyzed."

"Does it come back?"

"Her next letters will tell you. No smile, having to turn her head to hear, her eye fixed open, her eyelid paralyzed. And she drooled, drooled like a freak. She feels like a witch for sure now." Hadley laughed. "I can't wait to read all you have. Is it upstairs—the pages?"

"Yes. But, Hadley, there's so much I don't understand."

"Like what?"

"Why did you split the letters up? Why give me only so many and store the rest? You told me you were at a conference and had time to copy only the first half. But you could have gotten someone else to copy them for you. You could have gotten them all together before you met me. I don't understand."

"I found them that way, in two separate cloths, sewed closed. And frankly, I didn't want you to read all the way through because I didn't want you to make up your mind about her too quickly. I told you how she died, the fact of what she did—all those parts are in the second batch of letters. But I wanted you to capture who she was before she became what she did. Does that make any sense?"

"Some."

"Susan, the point is, I basically know what happened to her. But I even lack the chronology of her letters—some of them are out of place, so they skip around, as no doubt you've discovered. And remember when we met in Boston what I said? All day I read medical files. I can pick out facts and complications at warp speed. But I don't *feel* what happened to Eliza. I need ..." Hadley stopped, waylaid by a fit of coughing. As she raised her hand to her mouth, I noticed the skin on her arm had long streaks of red. She scratched at them again then pulled cloth over her arm when she saw me seeing them.

I wouldn't let her off my hook now. I pushed. "You need what, Hadley?" She shook her head, stifling her cough. I prompted again, "You've got to be honest with me. You've been so out of reach, I've nearly lost my patience. At times I've even wanted to throttle you, or throw all the letters at you. I feel manipulated. And your silence has made me think up all sorts of reasons why I must do this so quickly, and why you're so obsessed with Eliza."

"And so you think that I must be sick and dying?"

"Well, that has occurred to me."

"I knew it would. I know you can't do what you do without a fertile imagination. But you're right about that part." Her voice sounded clinical, detached.

"You have an illness which ...?"

"Mmhmm, terminal, unless ..."

I sat dumb in my own silence. "Hadley ..."

"About a month ago, I was diagnosed with Hodgkin's— you know, that sweet, simple cancer where tumor cells replace normal cells in bone marrow so platelets that prevent bleeding are wiped out and lumps can pop up all over—like here," she said, placing her hand on her chest, "where I have three tumors the size of golf balls." She smiled. "I learned this only a short while after I found Eliza's letters. And that made me think that finding them and finding out about the cancer were connected somehow—mysteriously or otherwise. Think what you want. But I feel sure her life can be a blueprint. I know that sounds creepy and as nutty as hell, but—"

The waiter interrupted to take our order. When he finished, I scrambled to prompt her. I was afraid she'd slip off in another direction. "But Hadley, isn't Hodgkin's one of the most treatable—completely curable with radiation and chemo—or is that non-Hodgkin's? I get them mixed up."

"Smart, cuz. I guess living with Caleb you can't help picking up all sorts of things medical. The catch is, you have to start treatment within six months, or you get past the point of, well, no return, if you want to call it that. And that's what I'm trying to decide."

"Decide!"

"Dammit, Susan, this isn't simple! And it's freaking painful. I'm not sure I want to be treated. I'm stage II now. I have a little time. In stage III and IV, the cure rate goes down to about eighty percent. At this point, I'm opting out of all treatment."

She put her napkin up to her face. Her nose began bleeding through it. "Damn!" She stood up. "At least I'm wearing red. Sorry, I have to leave." I quickly walked behind her across the restaurant. On our way out, I gestured to our waiter and before he even had time to answer, I told him to send our dinners up to Hadley's room.

In the elevator, she added to the napkin the tip of her own ruana, all the while pinching her nose and whispering, "Damn, damn." Her arms, exposed now, were streaked from scratching. Seeing me seeing them, she smiled sardonically, her voice nasal from the pinching. "Pruritis. I itch all over. One of the first signs of cancer."

In her room, she went to the sink and leaned over it. I gave her wet washrags. We worked at it for at least fifteen minutes then the flow almost stopped. She sat down on the bed and kicked off her shoes, casually.

"Hadley, you can't be serious. You don't mean you are opting out of all treatment. Or worse, that you're looking for something from a long-dead relative that will affect your decision?"

She looked at me, a towel to her nose. She laughed. It was a harsh laugh. There was a raw, ironic edge to it.

"Oh, yes I can! And why not? It's no different from how someone gambles—using an answer that appears, unpremeditated, as random as my own birth."

We stared at each other a moment in silence. And then softer, she asked me, "How did she live with it, Susan? How did she live with her past? The way people thought of her? Was she at peace when she died? Was she?"

"Hadley. Don't do this. You can't possibly expect me—"

"Oh, yes I can. You know how to do this. You can put her life down. I know you can. Then I can see it and feel it, and in a sense live it. I'm looking for an answer." She clutched her fist at her chest. "It'll come."

She was being so coldly dramatic, I was flustered. This was the craziest, least rational behavior I had ever come across. I couldn't believe what she was telling me. I wanted to yell, *Yes, you ARE certifiable!* I wanted to call Caleb, to hogtie her and fly her back with me, get a court order if necessary, rush her to a hospital in Boston. Instead, I held my voice in check, though I did hear an edge to it, asking, "But what else won't you tell me? What's the real reason behind all this, Hadley?" When she wouldn't answer, I said, "Two weeks ago, I talked to your mother. I called her."

Hadley laughed louder. "And no doubt she said 'Hadley's dead to me.' It's that great old Southern standby that means you're pissed as hell at your daughter. And even worse, she means it."

"But why?"

"I can't tell you, Susan. Don't ask me to. Just accept that living the way I am is not something I can do any longer, or want to. If Eliza Goode can teach me something that changes the way I feel—well, *that* might make a difference. But now, Susan, I need to get some sleep. I'm scheduled for four cases tomorrow. And I really don't want to talk about this anymore. I feel like I have an elephant on my chest."

She closed her eyes and coughed.

The waiter knocked on our door and wheeled our dinners in. But Hadley refused and said she would eat later. I sat silently, eating my own dinner to spite her. She lay with a washcloth on her face, and soon it seemed she was asleep.

Later, in my room, numerous times I went over all she had said. As crazy as it had sounded, I kept hearing my own voice answer with the simple question, *Why not?* Looking for an answer in some other life—in a life long past, yet lived with a similar haunting—was it so unreasonable? Religions did it all the time. But what could Hadley be so afraid of that she would rather not live than to feel it? Besides, could Eliza Goode's life offer anything other than her own horrendous death?

****

The next morning at five, the phone rang in my room, jarring me awake. "Let's meet at the beach. Two of my cases were canceled. I get finished at noon. I'll bring us a lunch. Want to?"

"Well, yes, Hadley. But—"

"Don't worry. I feel up to it. And I promise, I won't let my nose bleed all over you. I have only quick cases this morning—two kids with cleft palates. It won't take long. So, see you then?"

"Sure, Hadley." I wasn't prepared to do anything like this. I hadn't brought a bathing suit. And even though I felt like a pack mule following Hadley's lead, I also knew that I had no other recourse than to follow, to try to understand more. In the hotel gift shop, I bought a swimsuit with dolphins all over it, and, by noon, was sitting under a beach umbrella watching Hadley walk toward me. She wore a gauzy azalea-pink coverup that flew about her, lifting up enough to show the turquoise bikini underneath, but not enough to show the disturbing scratches on her skin. Laughingly, she held down the hat she wore—as big as a Mexican sombrero—while the ocean breeze toyed with it.

"Thought I might as well see if I could turn a few heads." She chuckled, putting down a beach bag and popping a beer and handing it to me. "Do I look as hot as I feel."

"Definitely." I thumped my midriff where the bathing suit dolphins were downright cartoonish. "Sorry I can't compete." Her gaiety was contagious, and I couldn't help laughing when two young studs jogging down the beach tripped and were swept off their feet by an ocean wave because they were staring so intently at Hadley. She waved at them coquettishly, and we laughed even louder when we saw that they realized she was not anywhere near their age.

"At least I can still fool 'em." She lay down on a beach towel.

Silently for a while, we listened to the North Pacific and to the sounds of people chattering and laughing and the high-pitched babbling of children playing on the beach. I was filled with such a complex mix of emotions: frustration, sorrow, anxiety and a gnawing sense of my own ineffectiveness. Maybe Hadley sensed this. She jumped up and headed for the outdoor bar where loud reggae music was playing. I stood at the edge of the crowd as it gathered quickly around her, watching her dance, watching her teasingly pull others into the space with her, pulling even me, until we were all a ragtag collection of strangers, dancing our heads off, losing ourselves in the music with wild abandon.

Laughing and exhausted, we made our way to lounge chairs on the beach. We ordered piña coladas and sipped them while watching the sun set. Hadley pulled her huge hat down over her face, signaling that she didn't want to talk. By now, I knew that simply being with me, feeling the connection with me, was an essential part of what she was seeking. So I kept quiet, while studying her out of the corner of my eye. Every time the breeze lifted her wrap to reveal her body, she replaced it, buttoning it down, holding it with her hand, while her other held her hat covering her face.

Later that night in the dining room, I watched Hadley reach into her purse and pull out a key and put it on the table. "To the rest of Eliza's letters. It will fit a lockbox at the main Hancock Bank in Jackson, Mississippi. Now tell me, Susan. You said you were having some trouble. What trouble?"

I leaned forward and said bluntly, "I doubt the way Eliza died. I've come to know her so well that now I doubt what you told me: that she died as a spy. A spy? I can't see it, Hadley. She seemed even nonresponsive to the political views of Rissa. I just can't see her becoming embroiled in political issues—not for either side—and certainly not to the extent that she could have been accused of what you say."

Hadley sipped her wine and looked steadily at me. "The new letters will explain."

I pressed on, wound up with all I'd learned.

"So was it the Emancipation Proclamation that changed her? Was it her closeness to Delia and her feelings at Preston Cummings's having 'bought' her? I certainly can't see her becoming an informant before then. Not before the so-called War for Southern Independence became a different war after the Emancipation Proclamation."

I then talked on at my own fevered pace, driven by the history I'd learned in putting Eliza's life on a canvas. I had read enough about Lincoln to understand that from his own experience with the harsh treatment from his father, he felt an enormous empathy for those who suffered the effects of slavery. But with his genius for feeling the pulse of public opinion, he knew he could not ascend to the presidency and push those beliefs. He knew that Northern volunteers would not come into the army to free the black man; the war would have to be fought to preserve the Union. Only later could he turn the war toward the issue of slavery.

"No," Hadley said, smiling ruefully. "Eliza met her end before then, the day before actually."

"Before January 1, 1863?"

Hadley nodded.

"But Lincoln released a preliminary proclamation in September, right after the Battle of Antietam—the battle he could claim as a Union victory, even though it was really a draw. So Eliza would have known slaves would be freed before she died. Is that what ignited her political feelings? Or did it have something to do with Rissa?" My voice was rising.

Hadley took another drink, slowing our discussion.

"There's a newspaper article in the lockbox. And the letters will tell you that while she was in Clarksville during the Union occupation, she became close to a Union supply officer. Too close. You'll see. All along, she did unsavory things—like, she practically ran a soup kitchen for slaves who poured into the protection of Grant's army."

Hadley then looked at me with a pleading expression. "Susan, please don't overthink this. Eliza's story is Eliza's story. Was she at peace when she died?"

The waiter brought our dinners. As Hadley began to eat,

she looked over at me and smiled wistfully. "You know, Susan, you're the only family I have now. Or maybe the only one who will have me?" Her voice lilted upward; she looked at me with a longing expression. "I wonder too if you've ever thought about what I do?"

Our conversation was veering off in a direction that I did not understand.

"I admire you immensely, Hadley. I'm sure I don't know all the elements in what you do. But I'm certainly in awe at what you've accomplished in your life."

"I put people to sleep. It sounds so simple. I put them as close to death as possible. I prevent them from feeling unbearable pain. And then I bring them back to life. All that trust they place in me! I consider it a privilege. But make one little misstep and I'm a prime target for a lawsuit, not to mention self-hatred and shame." Her eyes were misting. Her voice trembled with emotion. "And yet, I wouldn't want to live without doing something as meaningful. Does that make any sense?"

"Of course." I nodded, though I sensed a hidden reason for her telling me all this.

She then laughed her manic laugh, splintering our mood.

"So now, let's talk about something else, Susan. Since you know now how sick I am, you have to doubly indulge me. How is Caleb? How are all those children. Tell me about you."

The next day, we stood on the airport tarmac with the tropical wind blowing our hair. Hadley held the large fastened envelope that contained the pages I had written, holding them as carefully as I had held them on the way down. She then reached over and kissed me. I squeezed her arm.

She asked, "Will you meet me at Clarksville after Thanksgiving? I need to see where she was."

I nodded. She tilted her head and smiled.

"You know I think you're crazy," I said. "Totally out of your brilliant mind. You must seek treatment! You must come to your senses."

"Okay." She grinned. "Make me. Give me Eliza Goode's life."

She walked off, holding the pages I had given her.

Chapter 17

The promise of Eliza's letters burned in my mind from the moment that Hadley gave me the key to the lockbox in the Mississippi bank. As soon as I got home from Costa Rica, I asked for Caleb's help. I simply felt panicked from all that Hadley had told me. And too, I was feeling differently about Eliza's story. No longer was it a set of letters that I could analyze and transpose into a set of actions; it had begun leading me to wildly imagine where it was heading rather than accepting where it was heading. "Can you ..." I slipped up behind Caleb to put my arms around his waist, "go with me down to Jackson?"

He opened a beer and put a peanut near the sink drain. "Do I have a choice?"

I smiled and squeezed harder. "No."

"How is it you know all my weaknesses?"

"Maybe I inherited some of Eliza's magic."

He poured a swallow of beer next to the nut in the sink. "For Rufus," he said.

The roach we'd named Rufus still made nighttime visits to the sink, and we were taking care not to turn on the disposal until we were sure he was not in it.

****

That next week we were on our way to the airport to retrieve the rest of Eliza's letters. Of course right after my meeting with Hadley in Costa Rica, Caleb had immediately called her. And as usual, she would not answer the phone. He left her a message at her home and at her office. He wrote her a letter. He detailed the treatment she needed and the timeline she could not afford to ignore.

Again, her mother was no help. Her brothers said they would talk to her. But we feared what would be the outcome of that: If she indeed listened to them, they would most likely have no influence over her. And, as before, Hadley seemed to just disappear. She refused all contact with us. The weight of what she had placed on me pressed with more insistence than I could almost bear. It was now even more clear: The only power I had over her was to write Eliza's story and give it to her—and even that might turn out to be the final shove into darkness from which Hadley could never emerge.

"Tell me again," I said to Caleb as we parked the car at the airport and walked toward our departure gate, "what you think about Eliza's injuries. Will she fully recover?"

It was fascinating and strange how we talked of her in the present.

"More than likely. Though with facial nerve damage, she could end up with a tearing eye. She would have no control over that."

I contemplated the irony of her having an eye weeping not from emotion but from injury, and on its own, and how amusingly that fit her declaration to keep her heart in its "ice bucket." At first, I'd been suspicious of the letter in which Eliza told of the doctor who treated her in Crystal Springs, saying that she had a "damaged nerve." I wondered if a doctor in 1861 would even know the word "nerve." Nineteenth-century medicine was unaware of germ theory, so why would a physician be knowledgeable of nerves? But Caleb assured me that since the mid-seventeen hundreds, physicians had known of the nervous system. So Eliza was off the hook on that one.

There in Jackson, Mississippi, we walked together into the

Hancock Bank, and I think Caleb was as entranced as I was as I pulled out the box from the bank vault, put it on a table in a private room and slid open its cover. Inside was the same gauze covering over a stack of letters. I gingerly lifted them up.

"Amazing," Caleb whispered.

Yes, it was otherworldly—the feeling of seeing the handwriting of this woman, the history it told. "Hadley assured me this was the rest of the letters. If I find out she has tricked me, I'll kill her."

"I'll help you." Caleb smiled and cautiously lifted the first few letters.

Near the top was the newspaper article that I was most eager to see: what Hadley referred to as "Eliza's end."

Spy Dies in Fire.

Woman Known To Aid Union Forces Succumbs to Fire

Cause Of Fire Unknown.
January 1, 1863.

The body of a woman known as Eliza H. Goode was found burned to death in the house she inhabited from the first day of the Occupation of Clarksville. All efforts to extinguish the fire failed, and to date there is no knowledge of its origin.

Mrs. Goode, allegedly the wife of an imprisoned Confederate officer, aided the Occupying Force in informing them of a plot to free the city by Confederate guerillas, resulting in the deaths of four men who were raising a force to reclaim the city for the secessionists.

The house, once the property of Colonel William Clayton, is now a burned shell. Few of the Clayton Family's possessions survived.

I turned to Caleb, thinking out loud, "How did this get with the letters?"

"Someone had to put it there."

"Yes, clearly. But who?"

"A relative, a friend? From what you know so far, what are the possibilities?"

"I have no idea." I rewrapped the letters. "Maybe these will tell of someone who would have been a friend. Or an accomplice." Always, I was mulling over the possibility that Eliza was manipulating *Dear One*. Or, even worse, that the letters were a hoax, that Hadley herself had written them and was playing with me as she once had as a child.

Aside from those disturbing thoughts were my own doubts that Eliza would have been so political as to be branded a spy, especially to die as the article described. But if so, could she have made someone promise to pass her letters to another who would protect them, then that one add the article and pass the letters on, finally to the hands of the relative in whose attic they were found? *That* would certainly be a way to live forever, in a sense.

"What if she put this here herself?" Caleb asked.

I stared at him, pondering the possibility of that and what it would mean.

I picked up the gauze-wrapped letters to take them with me. Previously, Hadley had written a letter to the bank giving permission for me to remove the contents from the lockbox. And as I walked with Eliza Goode's letters to the car, Caleb and I discussed again Hadley's strange behavior: placing herself in a dangerous situation by refusing treatment while thinking that Eliza Goode's letters would, in some way, hold a sign to affect her decision. Clearly, whatever was eating away at her life was too painful for her to even tell me.

I stared out the car window at Mississippi pine trees, pavement, a Southern autumn where green would never quite disappear. In seven weeks, I was due to meet Hadley in Clarksville. In my lap, Eliza Goode's letters were heavier than their measure in ounces. I could hardly wait to lift one from the other, piecing together her summer of 1861. How would she get from Corinth to Clarksville? Why had she so mysteriously alluded to the long months that she and Rissa McFerrin would spend together?

Even before I got home to Cambridge, I began inhaling the letters, reading the first of them during our trip back, sometimes even reading them aloud to Caleb.

Dear One,

Just as if they were a flock of birds, women descended on the camp at Corinth—setting up shop in nearby houses and tents, setting about to make their living, just as I had once. From a distance, I saw Ellen and Amalee. I hid from them, ducking my head into my laundry duties. Shortly after, sickness broke out across the camp, born of those nights avec les femmes à la Venus—"horizontal refreshment" the men called it. And with it, a most unexpected boon for me. Why! It happened when Molly's husband came to visit her one afternoon. While at my chores, I overheard his exclaiming to Molly: How in the world would his army be fit to fight, what with the clap running wild through camp! Every fifth man lay out of drill with a fever, soreness, or a rash. The camp medical officers couldn't keep up. Remedies of mercury, pokeroots, sassafras, prickly ash and whiskey were in such demand. And of course worst of all were a few beginning signs of the most horrible of all—that which my mother herself constantly checked for: scabs, blisters, the early signs of syphilis that could move into vital organs, eating away the whole of them. My mind reeled backward, remembering hearing Madam Francine quoting from the biographer of Samuel Johnson, who came upon scribbling on the wall of a London men's toilet: "A night with Venus, a lifetime with Mercury." That would have closed up her shop, so frequently Madam Francine quoted the warning to her veshyas to stay clean at all costs.

"Come tomorrow," I said to Molly's husband, "I'll have a remedy your men can try." He looked at me in stark astonishment. "Yes," I said, and lied. "I once had a relative who suffered from such as you describe. And he came upon a remedy that relieved his suffering considerably."

He shook his head. He laughed. "Well, I've never been one to say you can't trip over knowledge in unexpected places."

The next day, I had my syrup ready. Why! I held a wealth of knowledge from growing up where I did! Look at me! I had a means to an income by simply wildcrafting the treatment for what the men suffered. I found silkweed root, mixed it with whiskey, resin and blue vitriol and sold it for a dollar. Soon

throughout the day, men secretly came to me to purchase the
reputed cure for a simple case of clap. At first, Molly regarded
me askance, but then allowed what she saw was a fine resource
toward securing my own financial independence—which any
woman would endorse. Even if she were a mite jealous of my
wildcrafting skill as well as of her husband's admiration for
me, she looked the other way, as long as my laundry duties
were met. Aha! How totally surprising: my past providing a
fine unexpected business!

Toward the middle of that June, another crisis—an outbreak
of measles. I had had rubeola myself as a child—Ned and I holed
up in a room at Madam Francine's with our mothers nursing
us hourly. Fortunate moi!

With scarcely enough tents for the troops, and few for
hospital purposes, houses in town were taken over. Since Eliza
declared, "I'm at no risk," she began offering to take clean linens
to the infirmaries.

"Well, go then." Molly Evangeline agreed, handing Eliza a
basket and adding, "But when you bring the old sheets out, we
are to boil them."

"And with extra care, I know," Eliza concurred.

Molly studied her carefully. "But dear, Eliza, you are sure—
absolutely certain—you are at no risk? You do remember having
these measles as a child?"

"Yes, completely, Molly. I'm as likely to fall sick as our larder
rat. And with one good look at my face while delivering linens,
men will think having measles seems slight."

"Don't treat yourself so meanly. Your blush has only been
nicked. It'll circle back."

Daily, near where Worthless grazed, Eliza hung extra sheets
between trees. At dusk she took them off with their sunbaked
smell and stacked them in a basket. It was there when she was
folding them that she heard behind her: "How do you get them
so *white*?"

Eliza turned to see Rissa, her hand on Captain McFerrin's
arm, both of them walking toward her, obviously taking a late-
day stroll.

Playfully, Eliza replied, "It's the lye soap, I think. I've taken to dissolving it in water like a soup."

Rissa chuckled. "How *clever*! How did you think of *that*?"

"By imagining being the soap with a large job to cover."

"Grand idea." Captain McFerrin laughed too. At the sound, Worthless looked up. Shoots of leaves stuck out from the mare's mouth.

Eliza sensed that it was not the details of her duties, nor the desire to talk to her, that prompted Rissa and her husband to stop by her basket and look inside. Simply, they wanted to spend time with anything that would permit them to linger, and she was merely the excuse they came upon.

"Do you think it will rain?" But Rissa was not asking her. She looked at her husband. It was then that Eliza lifted her hat to see more clearly the look on his face.

As he returned Rissa's gaze, I could not look away. Never had I seen anyone convey such feeling: the expression on his face was completely foreign to me. "No, I don't think there is the least chance of rain," he said, then looked out over the field. His arm, around his wife's waist, tightened, touching her with so much feeling that I could not look away. The affection between them was incandescent, a circle of soft amber. "Your mare seems well," he offhandedly remarked to me.

"Yes." I nodded. "She's grown fat on summer grass."

When he looked at me then, I realized my cue. For my eye was tearing. Recently it had taken to weeping for no reason. And quickly, I wiped it. Noticing, he asked, "Is there something we could help you with?"

"This is not what it seems," I said. "Field grass causes this. I can't seem to stop this eye from weeping. I'm like a Greek mask with duel expressions."

But I suspected I lied. For I was so full of the emotion of seeing him and Rissa exchange strong feelings, I touched my right eye thinking it ready to overflow too, and found it wet.

"Are you at risk from this measles outbreak?"

"No. I had them as a child."

"Rissa and I too. Thank goodness."

"Yes," Rissa added. "Thank almighty goodness." Her hand squeezed his arm. And then, "I think we should go on now, Ben. If we are to walk across this field before dark, we need to step

it up a bit."

They moved beyond Eliza, and he looked back. She lifted her basket. Rissa glanced back too, then said something to him that took his attention.

I carried the basket of fresh linens into an infirmary tent where I had not delivered them before. Inside were cots placed in rows, almost touching. The sick men looked up as I went to the corner to set down the basket. "Eliza," I heard, "is that you?"

There on a cot, so sick he could not lift his head, was Lem. My dear Lem Polk, who had saved me multiple times, it seemed.

"And how's that mare?" he asked. "Still worthless?"

"Twice so," I replied, teasingly. "How long have you been here?"

"Three days, I think. I've lost count."

"Here." I gave him water. But he could not lift his head. His neck was so stiff, it was as rigid as a rake on the pillow. I wiped the sweat from his face. His mind wandered then, speaking of his mother, next calling out for his brother as if in the midst of a boy's game. He was blistered all over with the rash. Then as suddenly, his delirium lifted, and he was back recognizing me.

He took my hand. "Have you heard, Eliza? Companies are being sent to Virginia. To Manassas Junction. General Beauregard is drilling men there. They're asking for a force of twenty-five thousand. I don't have long to get well. Do you have any secret cures?"

"I'll search the fields for something, some remedy."

"Hurry." His breath came short.

"I will, Lem. Give me an hour. I'll be back as soon as I can. Don't worry."

With his ailment—the horrible itching and soreness, his eyes swollen as if by wasp stings, and his breath labored—I knew an hour to him would feel like weeks. I went to the field that stretched out beyond the camp. Time and good luck had cured my rubeola, mine and Ned Tatum's. We had been children; the illness could not grab so tight a hold on us as it did on a grown man who had walked straight off his farm where he'd been isolated from the illnesses that I, as a child, had battled against and won, in crowded New Orleans.

It was dark when I returned with a salve made from aloe

leaves and a mint tea to clear his lungs. The lanterns were lit inside the tent. Shadows against the white canvas were otherworldly like long-dead creatures arisen to again walk the earth. From outside the door, I heard moans. As I stepped inside, a few men began calling, "Here, pretty one. You. Yes. Look what we have here. A beauty with tea. Is that for me?"

On Lem's cot, the blanket was pulled up over his face. I moved close, disbelieving. I had been gone such a short while! And now this! It was as if his life had simply gotten up and walked away, leaving him behind. I pulled back the cover. His eyes were open. His mouth was slack; his expression was puzzled as if he were about to speak but couldn't remember the words. Two men came to lift him up and carry him out. I was too stunned to speak or move. My face was fully wet now, both eyes with a reason. I handed the tea and salve to the closest hand that reached for it and walked out.

I stood a long while in the dark, trying to collect my thoughts. Not the first time would death take me unexpectedly like this. But it was the first as if a grinning Mr. Preston had jumped from the shadows whispering, "Just you wait. This will get easier with practice."

Chapter 18

Part of the camp packed up, preparing to ride the train to Camp Pickens near Manassas Junction. On July 15, Eliza awoke early to the sound of men's voices, the clanking of spurs, the noise of carts and caissons heading to the railway. She was glad the company for whom she was a laundress was among the first to move out. She needed to leave. Lem's dead face was haunting.

She leads Worthless beside Molly, who leads King Charles hooked to the mule cart, all their supplies packed inside, the washpots clanking.

"They're gonna love this," Molly says, meaning King Charles and Worthless, "being tied next to each other in the same car." She patted the mule's nose. "He don't care if he's sterile as a stone; he's in love all the same."

Eliza pats Worthless and joins Molly's joke. "I've never heard Worthless utter a word to make fun of him. We think he's quite handsome."

The train engine, like a panting animal, sits on the rail with men inside feeding the boiler. The walkway, crowded with soldiers calling to each other, is barely passable. In the jumble, Eliza accidentally is bumped square on the shoulder and turns.

"Oh, Miss Eliza!" Lawrence exclaims. "Excuse me." He tips his hat. "Are you coming with us? Hope you bring your mystery medicines. Miss Rissa won't admit it, but that tea made from the leaves you brought helped her mighty much."

"I'm glad to hear it." Then the crowd bumps them apart, and she stands on tiptoe to call back, "So Lawrence, you are going to Virginia too?"

"I am! And ..." But the rest of what he says is swallowed in the noise of the crowd. Quickly, Eliza catches up with Molly, who is unhooking the mule cart near the railcar where the men loading it will pull it inside. "Up, now up," she coaches, popping King Charles with a stick to get him up the ramp to the horses' car. Eliza follows, leading Worthless, and together they tie the mule and mare in the railway car among the cavalry horses, smelling of straw and manure and sweat. Instinctively, Eliza looks around for Captain McFerrin.

There is no sign of him, but she sees his tall sorrel tied near the back of the railcar.

"Did you have breakfast, Eliza?" Molly carries a food bag. She leads the way out of the car onto the walkway.

"No. I didn't have time. Besides, I'm too excited to eat."

"Pshaw! Let's get to our car. I'll share these ham and biscuits."

"Biscuits?" a man's voice calls loudly. "Did I hear biscuits?" The crowd of men on the walkway is so thick that Eliza cannot tell where the voice is coming from.

"No, you didn't hear biscuits!" Molly calls back teasingly. "You heard biscuits for Lieutenant McCarthy. My husband has his name on these!"

In a flash of red, Eliza sees near the back of the walkway a group of Zouaves, the Louisiana company that was obviously being sent to Virginia. A large man among several, all similar in girth and uniform, calls to Molly again, teasing for a biscuit. She turns to one of them whom she knows, and then "Eliza!" another voice calls—a voice Eliza recognizes as well as her own. From the mass of red Zouaves' caps, Ned Tatum bursts toward her.

"Neddy!" He stands close, the same height so that they are looking squarely at each other. His Louisiana Zouaves uniform, unique with its fez cap of soft flannel, is more like an old-fashioned nightcap than the tall French version. And its blue tassel, attached to the side rather than the back, swings across his grinning face. He catches it and holds it, his dark eyes glittering strangely.

"Yes, arrived last night. And now on to Virginia. But oh, my Eliza! You look like dried shit. Fell to the bottom, did you? Just like Hattie Louise said you would. And to think, rich Preston Cummings might have died in his duel and never lived to know how far you've sunk." Stepping closer, he smiles meanly. "I suppose now it's my job to tell him." The crowd noise muffles his words, but she leans with her good ear and reads his lips.

"Oh, Neddy, no! I don't want anyone to know where I am."

"And on to Virginia too, I see. A camp follower for sure, of the lowest type."

"I'm a laundress."

"Oh, sure you are. I heard of a girl causing the suicide of an officer at one of the camps. The description of her traveled: dark hair, an angel face, a mole on the side of her china-white cheek, a sapling waist, a bosom reminiscent of ripe, dangling pears. Ah, I said. This has to be Eliza. Who else could fit those adjectives?"

"Ned, please. I hate to hear you talk like this. We're practically brother and sister."

"More like husband and wife—parted by circumstance. Once, I could have saved you, my darling Eliza, from your dreaded Preston Cummings ... had you let me. We could have run away together, if you had not refused me."

O, what was this! Had he concocted a fantasy, made up his own story? Had he imagined once having proposed to me as a man would? I stood frozen, struggling to comprehend what all this meant. And suspecting too that his mind might have come loose so that his memories had become as shards of glass, spun and whirled in his own mind's kaleidoscope, creating a torturous design. At the color of his simmering hatred, I shivered. He was writing his own story of us, and I would have no say in the plot.

The train whistles. Hastily men begin boarding. One of the Zouaves clamps Ned on the shoulder.

"Get a move on, Tatum, don't hold up the works."

Molly calls from the steps of the camp followers' car, a good distance away.

"Hurry, Eliza! Eleanor and Colleen are already aboard!"

Lifting her skirts, Eliza trots and Ned follows. Her cloth bag is over her shoulder—two other dresses in it and her secret treasure that Amalee had gifted her to deny pregnancy, should she ever again need it. And also her growing collection of herbs and wildcrafted remedies for which she is becoming known.

Ned grabs her by the shoulder, whispering roughly, "Next time when I ask you, Eliza, you won't say no. You'll see." He clamps her shoulder so hard, she flinches. And then he lets go, and leaves her, turning in the opposite direction to the Zouaves' car.

Trotting, she passes one railcar and another, hurrying to where Molly had been waving for her. She glances up to see Rissa sitting beside the window of the car for the officers' wives, looking out. Their eyes meet in recognition and part. The train whistles again. Eliza leaps up the steps into the car.

"Here, my pretty. I saved you a place." Molly pats the seat beside her.

Eliza slips in over Molly's wide knees and sits by the window. As the train starts up, she looks into the window glass and sees her face reflected back. She reaches up and touches it, letting her fingers explore the flesh that seems totally awake now. But more than the reflection of what she sees is the realization that Ned had recognized her with no trouble at all. If her mouth is a bit crooked and her eye tearing often with no cause, they are of no obvious hindrance to how she is now.

Ah! Beauty returned. Well, then, welcome back, you, for whatever your worth in all your treasure and complications. Dear One, the chrysalis was halfway out of its womb.

All day and all night the train steams toward Manassas Junction. Amid the clacking of the wheels and the swaying of motion, she chats with Molly, and plays cards with Eleanor, and tells stories with Colleen. Then as the train is swallowed in darkness, the car grows quiet, the female chatter easing into only an occasional whisper, and she puts her head back on the seat, listening to the heavy, long breathing rhythm of many women sleeping.

Molly, being so large that she craves more room, slips across the aisle into an open seat. Eliza closes her eyes and drifts into sleep. At some time past midnight, a hand on her cheek jolts her into consciousness—the cheek that can move once again. Opening her eyes, she looks straight into Ned's face, so close she feels his breathing on her skin as he bends over her, whispering. "Shhhh, my sweet. Shhhh, Eliza. Listen. I have it all arranged. Tomorrow night, horses will be waiting at the east end of Camp Pickens. We will go off into the mountains, into a new life, you and I, man and wife, and—"

"Ned." Instead of pushing his hand away, she shrinks from it. She senses something very strange and different about him now, and is afraid of him. The sisterly way she would have quarreled with him as before no longer fits. "You can't be here. You'll wake everyone. Go, please. Go now."

"No. I will stay with you the rest of the night. I have to make sure you are safe. Preston Cummings may be at the next stop. The least you could do is give me a kiss to seal our promise." He pushes down on her.

With her arms braced against his shoulders, she hisses a whisper, "Ned, please. It's the middle of the night. You have to go."

"What's this now?" Molly is standing in the aisle, three times bigger than Ned. Shaking off sleep, she grabs him by the collar and pulls. He fights back, elbowing her. The whole car comes awake with the commotion, filling with women's voices, hissing loudly, "What the ...?" "Shhh."

"Outta here. Now!" Half-carrying him, half-prodding him with her knee, Molly pulls Ned, holding him by his neck, to the end of the car. Through the car door, a soldier comes quickly to help. "All right, now. Out with you. What do you think you're doing!" And in a scuffling commotion, Ned is forced out. The door is closed behind him but not before he screams out, "Stop them, Eliza. Tell them who I am, you no good swine of a bitch!"

The swift change in language and mood is so startling that Eliza is alarmed even more at what is happening to him. She closes her eyes and catches her breath.

"You know him?" Molly sits down beside her.

"Yes."

"Well, he won't bother you anymore this night. Get some sleep. We've a busy day tomorrow. No telling what it will hold."

Eliza nods yes, but she cannot let go into sleep, for there beneath her eyelids as she closes them is Ned's face, railing at her. Her body draws up, her hands crossed over her chest, her legs tucked up under the train seat, her muscles contracted as if she were knitting herself into a knot.

****

At daybreak, the train pulls into the station. Sitting on the rails, puffing, it seems to deposit a multitude of offspring as hundreds of men disembark down the ramps. Eliza stands, stretching, uncorking her muscles to collect her bag and move to the station walkway. "I'll get the horses and cart." Molly hurries ahead of her. "You take your time. You had a hard night." Molly moves briskly away. And as Eliza walks slowly behind her, she sees coming from the next car Amalee and Fanny, and Ellen now too. All three have joined up once again. They are among the many women following the great numbers of men called to Virginia.

I shielded myself among all those women in case Ned would be coming for me, though I supposed his officers would be in complete control of him now, for certainly the feel of the army was different that morning. The distant firing of cannons could be heard, practicing I supposed. And also word had traveled that thousands of men were already forming lines along a creek called Bull Run. Being now where all these men had been called with great purpose was palpable: the revelry of a hunting camp, overlaid with an air of apprehension as if disembarking in a foreign country. Certainly we all felt the rising fear-tinged excitement born of the unknown.

I moved with the crowd. And with some objectivity as I watched Ellen and Fanny and Amalee walking ahead of me on the station walkway, I was struck with how much they could be mistaken for officers' wives, who were themselves disembarking from another car. There was Rissa, as elegant as ever, and Lawrence rushing from another car to meet her. The only difference between all the women, really, was a bearing of sorts and an extravagance of dress. If anything the public women of Amalee and Fanny and Ellen's station were more well dressed. Eye-catching to say the least, even with the challenge of travel. Ironically, I felt proud of how well they managed this. The other public women of lesser rank were disembarking nosily, crassly, already trying to attract the soldiers' attention.

There near the railway, riding at a distance, Eliza saw the one who was in charge: the dark-haired Creole brigadier general who had won Sumter and now, as second in command under General Joe Johnston, had called for these thousands of troops to what was hoped to be the first and last great battle that the secessionists called the Second Revolution. General Beauregard sat astride a bay horse, surrounded by staff, his waxed mustache impeccable, his face so high-boned and chiseled, his eyes seemed to disappear in shadow; his bearing was so clearly a product of a military education. He rode up and down the railway, basking in the numbers of men the train had brought him. And as he did, Eliza studied his satisfied expression, noting that it was the exact expression men wore when relieved from agonizing worry. Yes, he had gotten his wish for now—thousands and thousands of men.

It was the 19th of July. I did not then know—indeed, it would soon be in all the papers, and we women too would soon pass the story among ourselves, so proud of it we were—of how Beauregard's battle plans had been changed that very week when a Washington socialite, Rose Greenhow, who, while entertaining Union men, learned that the Union Army would be advancing that very night on Beauregard's men stationed just outside of Washington, and had warned him. She sent a note concealed in the hair of a young woman named Betty Duvall, who dressed up as a country girl, and that very night rode out of Washington, and crossed the Chain Bridge until she was stopped by one of Beauregard's guards at the Fairfax County Courthouse. There, she took the tucking comb out of her long black hair and let it fall—mesmerizing the officer into silence—then handed him a note rolled up in silk with nine simple words: "Order issued for McDowell to march upon Manassas tonight."

Immediately Beauregard fell back to the railway center and called for more troops.

We, the women following the troops, were so proud of this

woman named Betty Duvall that we passed the story among us for months!

By early afternoon, Eliza settled at Camp Pickens with Molly and the other laundresses—their tent set up, their washpots in place. The numbers of men in the camp were beyond comprehension. In a jumble of sounds and dust, she could see men and tents stretching for miles. Eliza, near the laundresses' tent, tied Worthless and King Charles to a picket line while Molly and the other laundresses unpacked the mule cart amid coughs, the neighing of horses, men's voices, the sounds of drill. If it were true that thousands of men had already formed an eight-mile line along one side of the Bull Run Creek, thousands more were waiting to play their parts. And the news spread too— amusing but alarming—that General Beauregard had quickly moved his headquarters the day before because in the house he requisitioned from a Mr. Wilmer McLean, a cannonball came whizzing down the chimney and exploded in his dinner stew.

That evening, Eliza, in the laundresses' tent, was halfway undressed, changing into her sleeping gown.

Like the breath of a preying animal crouched at the outskirts, the threat of a great battle lay across the camp. And then, seemingly out of a story writ by someone far from myself, an officer rode through the camp calling my name. Never would I have predicted my reputation would take such a precipitous, magical turn.

Chapter 19

Eliza Goode, is there an Eliza Goode among you?"
The sound of the officer's voice traveled through the camp. A voice called, "There." And another, "She's there," until the officer stopped his horse in front of her tent, and she came out, fully dressed. Dismounting, he doffed his hat—a short muscular man with a full, dark beard and deep-set eyes. The blade of his sword gleamed in the firelight.

"Eliza Goode?"

"I am."

"Lieutenant Stiles." He lifts the lantern to look at her face. "Through Captain McFerrin's man, Lawrence, I've heard you know how to treat maladies in unconventional ways."

"Sometimes."

"I wonder if you ... You see, our division's medical officer is far down the camp, occupied with an outbreak of measles. He cannot come just now. And last week our sergeant was accidentally gouged by a spur in a drill accident. He's taken a turn for the worst. Would you be willing to look at him?"

"Let me get my things." She hurries into the tent for her wildcrafting bag and returns.

"Let me take you, if you don't mind." He pats the saddle.

When she nods, he lifts her and sets her sideways on his horse. Leading it quickly, trotting at times, so that she grabs the edge of the saddle in quiet desperation, he leads her through the rows of tents speckled with campfires, smelling of recently cooked meat. After a good half-mile, he leads the horse among the tents where a cavalry division is encamped. "Over here." He points.

In front of a tent, he lifts the flap. She slides from the horse and steps inside. In the shadowy candlelight, a man lies with his jaw hideously clenched, his neck arched on the pillow and a grimace on his face with his teeth exposed. The tent smells of sickness and sweat. Beside him, she kneels and whispers, "How long have you been like this?" But he cannot answer; he can give her only a frightened, pained glance. His eyes flicker with panic, and the yellow shine of sickness glows from his face. Behind him a manservant answers, "Been like this a few hours now. I seen this before; going to kill him."

"Shhh. Where's the wound?" Eliza asks impatiently.

The manservant lifts the sheet. Quickly, Eliza unwraps the cloth bandage above his knee and exposes a gash. Though it is not deep, it is an ugly wound with puffed flesh, and she quickly sees remnants of debris in the edges of the slashed skin. She holds up the bandage. "Throw this away. And can you bring me water?"

The manservant leaves, and soon the tent flap opens again. She feels someone behind her. She feels the heat and bulk of his presence, and then his voice:

"It's good of you to come." Ben leans to her and speaks softly. Lawrence is with him.

She looks up, nodding. "I've seen this before. Once. I was a child. But I saw it treated effectively."

"Then you might know—"

"Possibly. I can't promise. But I might can treat this with some success."

What I didn't tell him was where my mind was taking me: back to the time my mother tended to poor Rosemary McNeil, who was mistreated by a customer so inebriated that he never should have been let upstairs with her in the first place, and he slashed her. O! It had been a terrible uproar—his piercing Rosemary's hand with his rusty Arkansas toothpick in a drunken fit, yelling that she had not satisfied him to the amount he had paid. And Madam Francine had called for help to throw him out, which Sabine, our hired protector, did, then barred him from ever coming back—which took some doing. It was about two weeks later that poor Rosemary rose like a bow in her bed and grimaced, just as this poor sergeant lying here at Camp Pickens. So with some thought, I recalled the remedy my mother applied to unclamp poor Rosemary. Only in the dark, I would not be able to find what I needed.

"I'll have to wait for daylight," she explained.

"You can do nothing now?" Ben whispered, bending, almost kneeling beside her.

"I need to find a white oak and witch hazel shrub."

"Then I'll have Lawrence help you."

The wounded man moans. Lawrence speaks up. "I saw a stand of trees near the horse picket line, and I'm willing to take you by way of a lantern."

Captain McFerrin stands up and nods to Lawrence. "Use Sergeant Stiles's horse. I'll go get my second. Eliza, are you willing to ride my horse? He's gentle—I guarantee it."

She nods. "I'll need a cup of lye soap too."

"Yes, I'll go to our laundress."

By then the other manservant returns with a bucket of water. Looking into the bucket, Eliza exclaims, "From the horse watering trough?"

The man nods.

"Well, this won't do. Pour it in a coffeepot, heat it over the fire. Let it boil. Add a handful of salt, then bring it to me."

Quickly she leaves the tent, and when Ben McFerrin brings his backup horse—not the sorrel but a dark bay that was a shadow in the moonlight—she holds her breath at the fear of him. "Don't worry, he's safe." Then, "Here." He holds out the stirrup. She puts her foot in, but slips and falls. Catching her, he chuckles. "I promise, he'll follow Lawrence like a kitten. You won't have to do a thing." In silent agreement, she lets him hold her knee and give her a leg up into the saddle. With no side pommel, she rides astride, breaking every tradition in the proper way a woman should be on a horse, yet finding the extra security comforting—and somewhat amusing. As the horse obediently turns and follows Lawrence on Officer Stiles's horse, she breathes out, finally, and eases into taking more normal breaths. At least in the dark, no one will see her clearly enough to notice her astride.

"This way," Lawrence calls.

Early on, we didn't need a lantern, for the horses could see in the dark, and the moonlight was sufficient to find the way that Lawrence had in mind. We must have ridden nearly an hour into the woods, and there Lawrence dismounted and lighted the lantern. I too dismounted and began hunting obsessively, for I knew the witch hazel shrub would be the hardest to find. We must have searched a good hour, but with Lawrence's help I secured a sliver of white oak bark and the leaves of witch hazel. I then remounted with Lawrence's assistance and together we rode quickly back—me holding on for dear life and thankful for the security of being astride.

Dear One, my recipe was so simple. And, once again, provided by my past. I poured the boiled salted water in the poor man's wound, then made a potion of white oak bark, witch hazel, and lye soap to rub into the slashed skin. I refused to let anyone cover the wound but insisted they leave off all dressing to expose the gash to the air.

On the second day after my treatment, Captain Stiles rode to where I was at work doing laundry. He arrived all smiling and bright. The poor man had been released from his sick prison, he reported. He was not yet completely well, but greatly recovered.

And, Dear One, as you might imagine, word of what I had done sped through camp as quickly as months before my supposed part in killing poor Major Morgan had traveled. If not quite a miracle, the man's recovery seemed close to being one—and me the handmaiden to deliver it. The truth is, if it were seen as a miracle, it was mostly luck. It was then on the dawn of that Sunday, July 21, not yet six o' clock, and with the sounds of rifle fire at a distance, a freed slave by the name of Lucy came to my tent and asked for me.

The battle actually began earlier, at two that Sunday night, in the cool of what would become a stifling, humid heat, when the last of the thirty-five thousand men that Union General

McDowell marched toward Manassas Junction—in what was the largest army ever amassed on the North American continent— took positions near the Bull Run Creek. For nearly a week the Union general had been marching his army there, men who were green and naïve as to the cost of war, moving in an air of feverish excitement. All of them were untried soldiers and undisciplined. Along the way they had so often stopped to pick berries, it was said that they moved like an accordion, stretching out, pulling together. McDowell, weeks before, had complained to Lincoln that their army was not ready for battle, to which Lincoln replied, "You are green; they are green. You are green alike," which was prompted by Lincoln's desperate need for a battle. With the Union soldiers' enlistment expiring in only a few weeks, he feared being left with barely any army at all.

Even before Betty Duvall had warned Rebel General Beauregard that the Union troops were moving, the secessionists had been barely twenty-five miles from Washington. There they breathed down the capital's neck, easily within striking range to take the city and demand a formal recognition of the Confederate States as a separate nation, which Lincoln strived to prevent above all else.

****

Near dawn Eliza steps through her tent flap. She has been hearing, "Eliza, Eliza Goode ..." in a woman's voice, calling, coming closer. Eliza's hair is wound into a bun, slick and neat. Her brown-patterned dress is cotton. It is her favorite laundress dress for its cool looseness. In the distance, gunfire comes more rapidly. Apparently skirmishes are breaking out with Confederate troops stationed along the creek to defend it. But Eliza has been hearing distant gunfire for days now and thinks of it as no more threatening than the day before.

"You are calling for me?" She looks at the dark-skinned woman running to stop in front of her.

"If you're Eliza Goode, I am. I'm Lucy. Lucy Griffith." The dark-skinned woman pants, her breath lost to running. She wears a head wrap and looks squarely at Eliza. "I'm free. Hired by my mistress for a long while now." She is short, with an impish face, but a regal bearing, and she wipes sweat from her face, talking between pants. "My mistress, Miz Henry, is bad, very bad ... stove up ... this morn ... and her heart's beating fast. So fast you see it, all up under her dress like a bird, catched. I've come, 'cause I hear, you might could ease her. Would you?"

"Of course. If I can." Eliza returns to her tent, grabs her wildcrafting bag, and then, "I'll ride my mare. I can go faster. Tell me the way." She also knows that on horseback she can move quicker out of harm's way, if need be.

She hurries to saddle the mare.

"There. That road." Lucy points. "I'll run now, and you catch up. You'll see. Her house is a good hour from here. But I'll run. Running's my pleasure."

Soon, Eliza, riding sidesaddle, catches up.

"This is silly." Eliza guides Worthless beside Lucy and stops. "Here." She reaches down, takes Lucy by the hand, and kicking her own foot out of the stirrup so Lucy can use it, she then pulls Lucy up behind her. Lucy tucks her fingers around the edges of the saddle, holding on for dear life.

Yes, she may have been free, but the bonds on her freedom were still mightily there. She was going to great pains not to cross the line of my whiteness to hold on to my waist.

Then soon, "Lord, what?" Lucy exclaims as a great balloon rises above the earth. Lucy sways, leaning, then, "Is it alive?"

"I have no idea!"

Eliza urges Worthless on, holding tightly since the mare is now prancing at the fear of the great monster that seems to even breathe. Indeed, the flame below the hot air in the balloon imitates the sounds of breath. "Suppose it has to do with the army?"

"If so, that balloon's getting a good look at everything."

"I bet that's what it's for." Eliza forces a laugh, hoping to lighten their alarm. "Unless it's a carnival setting up."

"Carnival of fools." Lucy jiggles, urging Worthless to pay a mind to where she is going and go there faster. "Men fighting is one thing. Men fighting to set my people free is another. I'll pray the Lord'll pull that balloon higher, if it'll help. But I don't want to get caught in between." Then, "There." She points to the white clapboard house on a hill.

In a ravine near the house is a small springhouse. Outside it, Eliza ties Worthless and then rushes to the main house where Lucy is running.

Inside, the hall opens into several rooms. "Lucy?" Eliza calls. The house smells of liniment and bacon. The remnant scent of a fine breakfast wafts through the hall. July sun streams in the windows and shoots blades of light. The summer day promises to be stifling. "Here, up here." Lucy stands at the top of the stairs.

Eliza quickly goes up, carrying her wildcrafting bag, holding her skirt so as not to trip. She follows Lucy into a bedroom. There Mrs. Henry lies on a rumpled bed, her face lined as intricately as lace, her hair lying about the pillow in the ephemeral texture of a spiderweb. Her daughter, Ellen, sits beside her.

It is now nearly nine o'clock.

Eliza bends over Mrs. Henry, who looks up and studies Eliza. She whispers: "This is not a good day to die. Not a good day,"

"Who said anything about dying?" Eliza opens her wildcrafting bag. "Now, Mrs. Henry, what would you say is your most pressing complaint?"

"Eighty-five. Being eighty-five."

Eliza smiles. "So shall we call it rheumatism, chills, a wobbling heart, a slight fever and too much dancing last night?"

"Look at my knee." She lifts the sheets. "It's swolled up, and not from dancing."

Eliza takes leaves out of her bag for a tea, also for a salve, and a calming agent for the heart. Before she lays them on the table beside the bed, a great boom shakes the house. Plaster falls from the ceiling. A cloud of dust rises from the plaster crumbs on the floor. Mrs. Henry screams. Another cannon booms. A brick falls from the chimney. Lucy and Ellen duck down and cover their heads.

Eliza puts her hands over the old woman's ears as one cannon's fire is followed by another, and another.

It is now a little after nine o'clock. At the Bull Run Creek, the Union general, McDowell, has begun sending his men across.

"We've got to get out of here." Ellen stands up and grabs a blanket.

"God-a-mighty!" Lucy wraps Mrs. Henry in the bedsheets.

"The springhouse!" Eliza yells over the cannon roar, helping to lift Mrs. Henry. The three women carry her down the steps and out the door. Ellen, Lucy and Eliza, moving in tandem, shuffle down the hill toward the springhouse, carrying Mrs. Henry. Ellen supports her mother's head and neck, Lucy, the middle, and Eliza, her feet. Mrs. Henry's scratchy, age-worn voice calls in the rhythm of a chant, "Don't forsake us now, Lord. Not now, Lord. Help us, Lord God Almighty." And then a scream flies as a shell explodes on the ground near the house and the earth is rocked as if someone has clutched the soil to pull it out from under them.

Still shuffling, Lucy prays her own chant: "Surely, Lord God Great One Above Us, you won't leave us poor souls in such need. I'm asking you, Lord, sure enough. You aren't going to sit through this, are you? Please come down. Down, Lord! Put your hands around us. Keep us safe. You hear me, Lord?!" Another cannon fires. The ball lands near the house, shaking the earth. Lucy screams: "Lord, if I'd known you were sending the Union men to set us all free, I'd have saved my money!"

"Quick, Lucy!" Eliza kicks open the springhouse door. Worthless, tied to a pole, dances in fear. Another cannon boom splits the air. The mare rears. Eliza speaks soothingly to her, "There now, there now, it's all right." With her back propping open the door, they carry Mrs. Henry inside.

They set Mrs. Henry on the damp dirt floor, and then the three women crouch and exchange panicked stares. Between cannon booms, Eliza yells, "Mrs. Henry, I'm going to bring my horse in here, if you don't mind! I can't stand leaving her out there to be frightened to death."

Mrs. Henry nods. Her eyes are closed. Her hands tremble.

The cannon fire is constant now. At each explosion, the springhouse shakes. Eliza rushes out the door to untie Worthless. She sees smoke spreading like a fog over the fields. She pulls on Worthless's lead rope, and as the mare almost jumps over her into the springhouse, Eliza sees through the smoke the pink burst of rifle fire farther up the hill. The firing mixes with the yelling of men, and, with the thunder of more artillery fire, rifles pop in steady claps.

Eliza ties Worthless to a metal ring on the wall. She looks down at Judith Henry's face as she now opens her eyes and begs,

"Take me back. Back. Please. I want to die in my own house. Please, please, take me back."

Ellen leans over her. "What, Mother?"

"Please. I want to go back. Take me back to my own house. If I'm going to die, I want to die there."

Ellen looks at Eliza. Lucy is staring at the door as if someone might burst through it. Ellen whispers, "Yes. Okay, Mother. Okay." Then she looks at Eliza again. "Here is no better than there. Indeed, this springhouse is less protection. Will you help me?"

Eliza nods. Lucy cries, tears glazing the dust on her face. She shakes her head back and forth, trembling in panic and frustration. "I don't want to die anywhere. Not today. Not today."

All three women lift Judith Henry again, and while shuffling around the bulk of Worthless, who skitters near the door, Eliza pushes it open. They run, hunched over as if scurrying forest animals, to burst into the house. There, standing in the hall blocking it, is a Union soldier firing into the back room. A Confederate peeks around the doorframe and fires back. More rifle fire in quick earsplitting bursts comes from upstairs.

The Union soldier turns. His face is blackened from the cartridge powder he has bitten open. His eyes alight on Eliza, who stands holding Mrs. Henry's feet. She looks back at him, their eyes lock, and she watches in horror as a bullet goes through his neck. He falls, gasping, blocking the hallway even more.

Ellen orders: "Into the dining room."

"Yes, yes, there. Let's go there!" Eliza yells.

They step over the man's arms and legs, splayed. Eliza, carrying Mrs. Henry's feet, leads the way.

They lay Mrs. Henry on the table there and wrap a blanket around her ears to dampen the cannon fire.

Eliza looks into the hall. Two Confederates are now pulling the Union soldier out the door. A trail of blood is smeared across the wood floor like a paint stain.

Once again the house seems empty except for the three women. They stand, leaning over the table, over Mrs. Henry, and share their terror in exchanged stares. The Confederates seem not to be firing from the sides of the house, nor from anywhere that Eliza can place. There is only cannon fire, intermittent but constant, as if two great orchestras were dueling in a mad concert.

It is now nearly noon. For a short while, Eliza and the two other women continue to huddle over Judith Henry, their breaths coming in short pants, fear and heat drenching them with sweat that they wipe with their hands and dress sleeves. Suddenly, a great stampeding seems to be coming toward the house. Eliza, fearing that again the house is to be overtaken with either Confederate or Union soldiers, or both, looks carefully out a window. Confederates are running toward her, streaming past the house to the back of the hill. Is it a retreat of some kind? The confusion and mania are evident.

Now officers on horseback ride across the hill, shouting orders. Troops are regrouping, clearly taking up positions on the downside of the hill past the house.

Instinctively, Eliza knows that she and the Henry House are in the exact center of a great X, caught in the two armies' crossfire. Smoke now fills the house like a blocked chimney fire, and there is such a rising sense of confusion that she looks at Ellen holding the blanket over her mother's ears, and then at Lucy, crouched by the chimney as though about to crawl inside it. Abruptly, with great exploding force, an artillery shell crashes through the wall. The room lights up in screams and smoke. The force knocks Eliza to the floor.

After a moment when she opens her eyes and looks up, coughing, squinting through the smoke, she sees Judith Henry's body twitching, her foot missing, other parts of her body bleeding.

Truly panicked now, Eliza rushes out the front door. She crouches and runs down the hill to the springhouse, oblivious of the horrific cannon pounding and the stinging smoke. Inside, she grabs Worthless and holds the mare to her while they tremble together. As each artillery shell passes over, Worthless whirls and Eliza hangs on in a frantic dance. All across the hill, the cannon fire leaves smoke as if the earth itself is on fire.

I wanted so badly to jump onto the poor terrified mare and let her fly. It seemed the most natural of all things to do, but I also knew the sight of me fleeing would have stopped not one moment of firing. I would be as much in the heat of that battle as any soldier fighting on either side. The fight itself now was a rabid animal no one could restrain. My good sense told me to hang on to the mad war beast until it spent its fury and collapsed.

But the shelling became louder. Harder. Quicker. I could be still no longer. In a panic, I ran out the door and down deeper into the ravine, leaving poor Worthless to fend for herself, yet closing the door behind me so that the mare might have cover, if, indeed, the springhouse could offer that. The smell of sulfur and smoke was suffocating. The noise was deafening with shells shrieking overhead. Hell itself could not be worse. There in the ravine, I crouched in an indentation in the slope, pulled my knees to my chin in the same posture in which I had come into the world, and grabbed grass and dirt to put over me, and waited, breathing shallowly against the sulfur smell. My only hope of surviving was to melt into the earth.

Chapter 20

What Eliza could not see or know—until she read it in the paper or heard—was that at noon, a Virginia brigade came to the top of the hill behind her, set up thirteen cannons, which then would fire, roll down the slope to reload in cover, and roll back up to fire again. Opposite on the other side of the Henry House were eleven Union guns. So the Henry House was in the middle of the first great artillery duel of the war.

When Confederate sharpshooters ran into the house to fire at the Union Artillery, and the Union sent their own sharpshooters in retaliation, the shootout, which Eliza witnessed, ended in the Confederates winning the occupation of the house. This so infuriated the Union Artillery commander that he turned his cannon on the house, and poor Judith Henry and the two other women were caught in the fury. And Eliza ran.

Late in the afternoon, I saw men in blue running by my ravine toward the opposite side of the hill, storming the source of the Union cannon fire. Most confusing it was, for in blue uniforms, who was who? I lay, crouched, then turned on my back, and looked up to see at some distance an officer on a small sorrel horse, both man and animal as still as garnet brooches.

And behind him, swarming, as the cavalry always drilled to "swarm" as a hive of released bees, was Captain McFerrin galloping on his tall sorrel, hat plume fluttering, saber drawn, his horse skittish at the sound of the cannon booms. I lay and watched as if in a dream, and now I realized I was breathing quite normally, no longer holding my breath, nor panting, but watching all as if removed from it. How I escaped death, I'll never quite know, except that no one was interested in shooting any poor laundry girl in a ravine, and I was spared a stray shot doing me in at random. No one would hunt me here either. Why should they? Searching for a soldier here would mean only that he would be a coward, a deserter, or dead. Alas, I was the only one breathing when someone dead or dying rolled down the ravine's slope at a distance from me. I watched as if detached. I was a forest animal in its hole. I was as wildly set on survival as a rat. The battle was all topside. And then I heard the most hair-raising howling.

It was true: The blue uniforms of the charging Confederates had so confused the Union Artillery force, thinking they were their own, they did not fire on the charging infantry until too late. And the Artillery Duel became a Confederate victory, while the Virginia infantry stormed the field in the first unleashing of the rebel yell—part Indian war cry, part foxhunter, all-the-way crazed warrior.

Union forces retreated in panic when the train brought Confederate reinforcements, and even more on horseback, so that by four p.m. the last Union troops were pushed off Henry House Hill, and they began skedaddling back to Washington. In panic they splashed back over Bull Run Creek and bungled up the roads as the Washington citizenry—who had driven out to watch the battle like a sporting event—whipped their carriage horses into flight.

When Eliza realized that the sounds of gun and cannon fire were dwindling, and she could hear only desperate dying calls and moans, she crawled out of the ravine, intending to run to the Henry House.

On top of the hill, she stood, staring. Around her was a sea of wounded and dead and dying men. The house was not standing. Only a chimney rose from the rubble. The springhouse was battered—one wall missing, the others, leaning slats.

Eliza walked toward the house, stiff and slow, in shock. The scope of the destruction was beyond her ability to take it in. Making her way over the dead men and fallen timbers and debris in what was once the house, she looked toward the chimney and heard a pitiful cry. Leaning down, she spied Ellen squatting in the chimney, crying hysterically. Her hands were over her ears, her face blackened from smoke and ash. Eliza gave Ellen her hand to help crawl out

"Lucy?" Eliza asked.

Ellen shook her head, deaf from cannon fire. "Ran off. Thought the Union soldiers would take care of her."

"Did she make it?'

"I don't know."

Eliza knew it was of no use to ask about Ellen's mother. She herself had witnessed Judith Henry's horrifying end. Yet Ellen said, as if in need to announce, "Mother died this afternoon. About three, I think. They have killed my mother."

Eliza touched Ellen's shoulder. She put her arm around her. She rubbed her ears, trying to ease a deafness that she herself could understand. *And then quite suddenly, a strange feeling came over me. It was like a first morning awakening when sun pours over my face. And I saw myself as two: an ice-locked seventeen-year-old girl whispering to Preston Cummings, "I hope you die, die," and now someone of more than years could measure, deeply tender in consoling another who had just lost a precious part of her life. Yes, I was meant to beat death and to give solace to the living. Perseverance was stitched into my very bones. More than merely surviving, I would prevail—and alight as someone whose acquaintance I was just now making. Yes, I was crawling topside into a world I could not yet imagine, so foreign it was to me. And beckoning.*

"Come," I said, leading Ellen to the springhouse to find Worthless. For I had this fanciful vision: I imagined the two of us riding off across the battlefield, victors in our survival. But my wish was sorely revised when we found Worthless's mangled body in the ruins of the springhouse. O! My dear honest companion! With a name I never should have given her! I touched her. I whispered thank you once and then again.

Ellen turned, nodded with a feeling that we both shared, and she silently walked to an ambulance cart in hopes of their helping her find her mother's remains.

So yes, Dear One, I witnessed the first great battle of that war, saw from a distance on the ridge behind my ravine what must have been General Thomas Jackson, to be called afterward into eternity Stonewall. And walking back toward Manassas, passing foot soldiers either celebrating or crying, hobbling, bleeding, all with their faces blackened from biting open their cartridge rounds, I saw what could have been Jefferson Davis—an elegant man with fine, cultured features riding a horse across the field. For later I learned he had frantically taken the train from Richmond to rally the troops and witness the battle and had borrowed a horse to ride to the battleground.

Walking as I was, a wagonload of wounded pulled alongside, and the driver called, offering me a ride. It was miles yet back to Manassas. I climbed inside, and soon found myself frustrated to the point of my own suffering. For I was of little use to those poor men with my wildcrafting bag destroyed in the Henry House. Blood dripped through the wagon slats, and men cried for their mothers. I could have at least used ragwort, wood sage and goldenseal for swelling and ragged flesh. Instead, I applied tourniquets by tearing my hem and wrapping the strips around arms and legs where needed.

As night fell, a full moon opened in the sky. And then clouds moved across it, stippling the glow with a lacelike lobo gris. As we drew near to a house designated as a hospital, I heard a voice coming above the rumble of the wagon wheels to catch my attention. It was Captain McFerrin, riding next to us, calling my name, "Eliza!" and then, "Are you all right?"

"I am, yes." From the lantern light in the wagon, I could see he was covered with gunpowder and dirt. His horse was lathered and exhausted, walking slowly with its head low to the ground. The captain's face was weary if not haggard. Lines of worry, long embedded in short, curved lines on his forehead, now seemed to loosen as we looked at each other. His hat was torn, his pheasant feather missing. And now it began raining, a light drizzle that fell from his hat onto his face.

"Where is Rissa?" I held on to the wagon, looking up at him, one hand shielding the mist from my eyes. I spoke loudly so as to be heard above the sound of the wagon's movement and the moans of the wounded men.

"With Lawrence. I sent them to a hotel at Warrenton Junction. She doesn't need to be anywhere near here. She shouldn't see any of this."

"No." I ducked my head, for the rain began coming harder now.

"So, you are fine, then?" His eyes studied me with concern.

"Yes. Fine and survived." I smiled and wiped the wet hair from my forehead.

"I am glad to hear of it."

How strange it was and yet how perfectly natural it felt in how we looked at each other in silence with no other words exchanged between us but a lingering desire to not end our conversation. After a few minutes, he turned his horse and rode in another direction.

Over to my left, I heard another voice calling: "Eliza, Eliza!" It was poor Molly hurrying to the hospital building. Her husband, dear Lieutenant McCarthy, would die that very night.

The wagon pulled close. The poor men beside me were carried across the mud into the dressing station. Streams of rainwater were now flowing in the ruts of the road, and everything seemed to smell of blood. I hurried to be with Molly and do whatever I could.

Dear One, I tell you all this not so that you might eventually regard me in a sympathetic light but to know of how life can wind you into a history that you cannot see for living it. And in the winding, you become someone other than who you thought you were. Even a misguided people found themselves struggling toward a statement of new identity: for after that first great battle, the uniforms of the secessionists became gray or butternut, anything but Federal blue, and their flag too— found to be too similar in battle to the Union one—took on the crossed stripes that still rein as a symbol of the Confederacy. It was driven home for certain that this would be no three months war born of feverish dreams of glory. O, no, this was insanity *unleashed.*

That night, Eliza could not sleep. Every time she closed her eyes, scenes from the day filled her mind. Her hearing was muffled from the cannon fire. Her left ear, half-deaf anyway, seemed even more so. But she had grown so agile in reading lips and deciphering words that it seemed of little consequence.

Molly did not come back to the tent, and Eleanor and Colleen were so unstrung by the day's events—even though they had not ventured outside camp—that they talked incessantly about them, which gave Eliza an amused appreciation for her muffled hearing. She lay on her cot and drifted into a broken sleep, then sat up, wakened at the sound of her own voice. She had been calling out Ned's name. And calling his name as she had sometimes called as a child, especially when they had lain sick in the same room, high up on the third floor in Madam Francine's house. *Ned, Neddy. What had become of Neddy?* Her apprehension and fear from their last meeting were overcome by a realization that she had to know where he was. Had he survived? Was he wounded? Had he fled? Had he distinguished himself in some way that might heal his self-regard? Had battle dampened his inward rage?

Through the night, the rain fell harder, washing against the tent canvas, howling in wind gusts. Passing by were the sounds of men returning—the splash of wagon wheels, the clink of sabers and guns, the sound of hacking coughs, the clanking of canteens and rifles, the creaking roll of caissons bearing artillery.

At daybreak Eliza dresses with Eleanor and Colleen, who are rising from their cots and pulling on day dresses.

"I will be back at noon," she says. "Put my share of the wash aside; I'll do twice as much tomorrow."

Eleanor twists her mouth. "Without Molly that makes twice as much for us."

Colleen buttons her dress, turning her head so Eleanor can hear. "Be kind, El. Poor Molly needs to be with her husband. We can take over for her for a while. It's the least we can do."

"But what about this one?" Eleanor points at Eliza, who is now pinning up her hair that is still thick and lovely, as rich in color as whiskey satin or a raven. Tendrils escape and twirl down her neck. Eliza does not know if they know of her past, but if so, Eleanor takes it as a point where a worded dagger might enter, whereas Colleen sees it as a bygone to be stepped around and pitied.

"Eliza's due a leave after what she went through yesterday. Did you not hear of the old woman's foot being blown off? Have mercy, Eleanor. For God's sake. Besides, it's still raining; we can't do any laundry, much less dry it."

Eleanor does not answer, but turns away in silence, tying her shoes.

Dressed now, Eliza walks from the tent. She holds an umbrella to shield most of herself from the rain. She lets her hem trail in the mud and strikes off in the direction of the road, asking along the way, "Have you seen Zouaves? Any knowledge of the Zouaves?"

"No." "No." "Not since yesterday." "Can't say I do, miss." And more than once an answer similar to, "No, miss, but for a kiss, I'll find 'em for ya."

Their stares or suggestive teasing are of no matter, for they all look so worn and haunted. Once she overhears a private telling a blacksmith as he passes, "I've been to the monkey show and care never again to go."

She walks against the steady flow of stragglers still coming back from the battlefield. Wagons are carrying out the dead and more wounded. Worse than seeing Ned mangled and dead on the battlefield is not knowing if he is mangled and dead. Behind her she hears the rattle of a wagon. It is empty, on its way to the field again. As it passes, she waves and calls, "Can I ride?"

The grizzled wagoner stops. The horse's feet, as wide as pancakes, disappear into the mud. "A battlefield's no place for you."

"I'm looking for someone. I have to know."

His face is as careworn as used yarn. "I know about knowing." He waves her on. As she climbs in the back of the wagon, she asks, "Have you seen Zouaves?"

"No. Not since yesterday morning. I ain't heard nothing about 'em neither."

She sits, holding her umbrella, looking back through the rain at the muddy road and the backs of the exhausted men.

At the battlefield, the wagon bumps over muddy grass.

Officers ride on horseback across it, identifying dead. They are dressed in black rain gear, giving them an otherworldly appearance like medieval armored knights. Across the field, soldiers are laying the dead in rows. In the distance Eliza sees mass graves with legs of horses sticking up through the mud. Almost everywhere on the ground are articles of soldiers' uniforms and parts of equipment. The trees are checkered by minie balls, their bark split and sometimes even whole tops felled. Fencing is leveled as if by a hurricane.

The wagon stops. Two privates lift dead bodies and load them on as Eliza moves to a corner, thinking how strange that the dead men's faces are black and bloated, as akin in skin color to slaves. "Have you seen Zouaves?" she asks.

The task at hand is so gruesome, and the privates have clearly been at it from the first sickening hours to now, when numbness has set in. One answers: "Sure, miss. Saw 'em square dancing over there near that hill." His face contorts in bitter humor. "Choose you a partner. Do-se-do."

"Hush, man!" the other snarls. "You're among the dead."

"Aw ... I thought I was at a soiree!"

"Forgive him, miss. My friend says what he can in the worst way he knows. Ah, yes ... this battle has changed the living into the dead. And us into animals, and we're doing the best we can to come out the other end."

"Yes," she whispers, "I know."

The wagon turns to head back. Lying there with her, the dead men's arms and legs jiggle in the rutted road as they move over it. The rain washes their black faces and soaks their clothes. Eliza holds her sleeve over her nose, pulling the umbrella down until it touches her hair. She thinks that gazing at the dead faces is the least she can do in respect for them, and then yes, there is one—one she knows. Crouching on her knees to see better, the realization is like a fist punch. *For it was Jesse Marks—poor Jesse Marks, whom I met seemingly so long ago in the woods near the pond when Lem Polk sold me Mama Mean.* Gasping, she lets go a little cry, putting her hand over her mouth while reaching across the other bodies to touch his blackened face.

The wagon stops at a makeshift graveyard. Men come to unload the dead. She climbs from the wagon and watches them lift Jesse to lie on the ground beside a grave filling with rainwater. She walks among the dead, stretched out, waiting for their graves, disbelieving that there are so many, that they are so mangled. Along the long row, another face registers in her memory, jolting her to stand staring. For it is Jim Lukens, who, in revenge for Major Morgan, had raped and beat her, his chest now blown open, his clothes blood-soaked, his face frozen in a grimace. *So it was that good and evil lay side by side. If what the nuns told me had any truth in it, the one whose face I stood over and stared at was already now several hours in Hell.*

She feels even more frantic now to find out about Ned. Walking briskly among the gravediggers, she keeps asking, "Have you seen Zouaves?"

"Can't say I have," one replies, then another.

Finally, "I have," one calls back while carrying the feet of a fellow dead Confederate as his partner holds the head, " 'bout a quarter-mile, over near the woods—there." He points with his chin, since his hands can't be free.

"Thank you." She begins walking to where he points.

"Good luck, miss."

Near the edge of the woods, she sees a camp of Zouaves under makeshift canopies of canvas, pots of coffee resting on coals of a fire sputtering in the rain. She draws near and says, "I'm looking for Ned Tatum. He's one of you from New Orleans. We grew up together. Have you seen him?"

Two of the Zouaves laugh. Another says, "Yeah, old Ned. Look over yonder." He points to the woods.

Another adds, "Our major put him there to sober up. Can't say old Ned shot a Yankee yesterday. He took to the bottle too soon to do us much good."

As she walks in the direction where he points, she hears behind her, "Lucky devil he is to have you come looking for him." And, "Oh, yeah ... I'm a better find for you, miss. Won't you come back ... stay awhile?"

She walks on, ignoring the remark. And at the edge of the woods, she hears Ned's voice chattering, babbling in an incoherent way.

A few steps into the trees, and there was poor Neddy—tied to the trunk of an oak, his face spattered with mud, the beautiful red of his Zouaves shirt soaked, his pantaloons so wet the cloth was stuck to his legs. He didn't recognize me. As I stood before him, he kept railing at the sky as if in the midst of a battle, yelling, cursing, calling Yankees' names with threats of what he would do to them in only a minute. "In only a minute, now, you vile snakes. Cover your head! You Yankee Rotten ... To Hell with you. Get ready now! Prepare to meet your maker ... Bam, bam, cover your head, idiot-man!"

"Ned," I said. "Neddy." I went close to touch his face, hoping to interrupt wherever his mind was taking him. So similar to drunkenness his insanity seemed, it was indeed an easy mistake to make. Yet no amount of time tied to a tree would bring the sobriety his superiors counted on. And perhaps they decided they would take no action against him for behaving so badly in battle; perhaps tying him to a tree was enough discipline for now. It was a most terrible bind. For should I try to explain this to his major? What then would be the outcome? Would they then send poor Neddy to one of those houses of bedlam? A worse fate I could not imagine. Better to let him rail like this on the chance that patches of lucidity would return. My greatest temptation was to untie him, and I seriously contemplated doing so, when just then he recognized me and softly said, "Eliza."

"Yes."

"You are here!"

"Yes, Neddy. I needed to see if you are all right. I needed to see if you were wounded in the battle."

"I was."

"You were?"

"Yes, here." He nodded with this chin to his chest.

But there was no blood, no wound. I stepped close and opened his shirt enough to see for sure, and then realized his idea of a wound was fantasy. It occurred to me that he may have hid during the battle and that the violence of it unhinged his mind.

"Eliza." He said it so piteously, I stayed close. "Please love me. Please give me what I ask. Accept my proposal. Be my wife. If you would only say yes, we could go away. We would be fine. All fine."

"I do love you, Ned. But I can't do what you ask—not love

you as a wife. You and I are brother and sister. You know that. Remember how as children we—"

"*I am not your brother! Admit what you know, you vile strumpet. I have been your lover! LOVER! Coldhearted slut— just as Hattie Louise said you were. An icepick for a heart." He railed for quite a while in the most hateful language imaginable. Then he spat at me and kicked mud with his boot, straining the ropes around his chest and thighs.*

I stepped back, startled. I could do nothing except stare. I had never felt such a torment, such a crucifying crossroad. If only I could have given what he believed could heal his life. And O! How desperately I wanted to! But even if I could, we both knew it would be no elixir for what ailed him. I walked away, looking back once, twice, hating myself and the moment and hearing his voice calling for me, even today. My fervent wish is that I am never again asked for what is impossible to give.

I walked back to the mud road. I walked among the traffic toward camp, until again a wagoner gave me a ride. My heart was broken with no chance for recovery.

Chapter 21

For weeks, she would not have the heart to leave Molly, not until after Molly packed up and headed home as a widow with a widow's pension to sustain her. And then three months later, Eliza found herself far north, thirty miles west of Washington, still following the Mississippi regiment that she had joined in Corinth. Eleanor was in charge of their little group of laundresses now. And a fourth had been added to take Molly's place. She was a talkative older woman with a love of *Godey's Lady's Books*, a sergeant's wife who had caught the train up from Memphis.

I still felt like a new species of creature, emerging and unfinished, aimed for some transformation yet unnamed. Except that, every time someone called "Eliza Goode," I answered.

Ha! "Eliza Goode." That was stuck for good!

Quickly newspapers heralded the Rebel victory. And in time I learned that Lincoln, unhinged by the loss of the battle, was even seen riding his carriage near the battlefield, distraught and in sorrow. He called the next day for five hundred thousand men recruited for three years. Then four days later, he put General George McClellan, the young Napoleon, in charge.

Although about the same number were killed at Manassas in each army, the salt in the wound for the Union was the one thousand sent as prisoners to Richmond where the Confederate capital was moved when Montgomery was thought to be too remote. And not one, not a single Rebel had been captured! Yet twenty-eight Union cannon were taken, five hundred muskets and nine flags!

The company I was with was ordered to encamp up near Leesburg, and it was there, where, in only a matter of days, I heard the story of General Bee, the one who pointed to Thomas Jackson on the battlefield and yelled, "There is Jackson standing like a stone wall! Let us determine to die here, and we will conquer." Like hot lava spilling down a mountain, the rumor spread that he had not said what he said in admiration of Jackson but sarcastically in retaliation for Jackson's not coming to his aid in the heated attack he was under. Since Bee was wounded and died the next day, there was no way to clear up the matter. Yet I myself had seen Jackson. And how well I know of the love of a rumor! Besides, I saw the glow in the general's eyes of his sheer love of battle, his sense of invincibility. I doubt he would refuse a fellow soldier's call for help.

That next week, it was so strange and amusing when I watched a company of Rebels peel logs and paint them black and put them on pairs of rickety wheels. They moved them to where they could point toward Washington as if they were cannon. As hoped, General McClellan took the bait and was quoted in a newspaper as saying he could see for himself that the Confederates were encamped in huge numbers all along the Potomac.

In that late September, General Joe Johnston ordered us to evacuate Leesburg. I packed up to follow the army farther north. In a matter of days, a Union cavalry rode close enough to our abandoned camp to figure out that the Rebel cannons were only painted logs, and the report, spread by a newspaper, infiltrated the capital like a bad smell. Apparently the Union generals were so irked at being the butt of a Confederate joke, they were blinded in seeing that having painted log cannon could also mean the Confederates had less artillery than was believed, and also that leaving a painted log behind could have been simply a mistake—left unintentionally. The fact was, McClellan was bound to feel enormous pressure since there had been no Union victory as yet. That past August a bloody battle at Wilson's Creek, Missouri, gave another Confederate victory. So everyone knew it was only a matter of time before McClellan moved against us.

Six in the morning, October 21, Eliza is stoking fires under the laundry pots to heat water. The morning mist is damp and cold. She picks up a bucket of feed and carries it to King Charles, whom Molly left behind. Suddenly, coming from near the river, she hears the nervous popping of rifle fire like fat pine catching ablaze. King Charles flinches and whirls. Eliza puts her hand against the mule's shaggy neck, speaking calmly to him, then stands, listening. Yes, rifle fire is coming from the glade near the cliff that overlooks the river. Earlier she heard men talking of the land there: about ten acres of open ground that ended at a steep cliff overlooking the river, a cliff they call Ball's Bluff. It is said to be a mean-looking rise of over a hundred feet. Days ago sharpshooters were sent to watch in the event the Union Army might choose to cross to it from Harrison's Island. And apparently they have.

Colleen and Eleanor, and the new laundress, Shirley from Memphis, are frying sausage and eggs on their cooking fire, surrounded by dirty shirts and other laundry. "I am sick of bloody shirts and pants tearing apart." Colleen throws a load into Eliza's tub to be worked on her scrub board.

"No sense complaining." Eleanor sips from a coffee cup, her hair halfway tied up, disheveled. "I see no chance of that changing."

"What about these?" Shirley holds up a pair of pants with holes in the knees. Short and stout with a husky voice, the new laundress has her brown hair covered with a plaid wool scarf and wears a purple stain on her lips in imitation of pictures she has studied in her *Godey's Lady's Books*.

"I can mend them." Eliza holds out her hand. "Give them to me."

"No, I'll do it. You get too much credit for fixing things. Besides, I can do them better." Eleanor grabs the worn pants and carries them inside their tent.

"Listen!" Colleen stands in a paralyzed moment, her plate of sausage and eggs in her hand, her fork suspended.

All four women lean to listen. From the woods surrounding them, they hear the dull thunder of running. Suddenly, a herd of deer burst through, stampeding near their campsite, jumping logs and tall grass. Now the sound of the rifle fire is coming in sharper bursts. Shots seem to ricochet in twangs as if hitting the cliff rocks.

And then the thunderous sound of artillery fire comes from the river. It is as if the heavens have opened and great claps of thunder roll over the earth.

The rhythm of musket fire increases now too, popping like sticks striking drums. It is obvious: A ferocious battle is underway, and to handle their nervousness, the four women clean the campsite of foul laundry, tossing it into the heated tubs. "Here, take this now." "No! Use the soap there. There!" They begin scrubbing and chattering, arguing over who will do which laundry.

All morning, they, just as Eliza, stop often to listen—suds dripping from their hands, their heads turned in the direction of the gunfire. The battle rages at a distance, but its sounds needle every thought. And Eliza thinks how in these moments, lives were changing; the sense of life and its finality would never be more clearly felt. By nightfall, they all will see suffering wounded, faces dead and blackened, blood dripping and pooling.

No, I would never get used to this.

No—her heart like a kneading fist in her chest and her breath stunted by nervousness. Reflexively her thoughts turn to Ned and to Captain McFerrin. Over the weeks, she has seen them both, for they, as well as she, were sent here just beyond Leesburg, though she knows that Rissa probably stayed with Lawrence in the town where Captain McFerrin sent them.

****

Weeks ago, when Eliza went into town for supplies, she saw Ned in front of a store, holding forth with a group of Zouaves, talking loudly, no doubt entertaining them with some drama he was concocting. She ducked behind a wagon and slipped away, unseen, but was relieved to learn that he was all right or at least reunited with his company, and for the moment, lucid enough to function.

She also knew that Captain McFerrin's cavalry was bivouacked down the river. Once, she had seen him ride by the camp where she was, and she had simply stood and admired his strength—tall astride his sorrel, both he and his horse fully recovered from the ordeal of Manassas, about which she had overheard talk of his company being joined at Manassas with others under the command of Colonel Jeb Stuart and of how they had captured several cannon by cutting loose the Union horses pulling them. More than several in his company had been accidentally killed by Confederate infantry because their uniforms were so similar to the dark blue of the Union. But on the day she had seen him riding across the field near her in their new camp, he wore gray, now the official Confederate dress for a cavalry officer: short coat, brass buttons and a vest for warmth beneath. Sun glinted off his horse's copper coat that was growing thick now for winter. And when he recognized her, he had ridden closer and taken off his hat in salute. She had laughed as he pointed to the new feather adorning his hatband— "I now have a new one," he called. It was a duck feather this time, short and thin, brown with a white-and-green tip. Probably no pheasant had been at hand for a replacement, and the duck feather seemed fitting if not grand. Besides it was short, less of a target, considering the reality of where it would be going.

"How are you?" he asked, riding closer.

"Fine. Still fine."

"I am glad to hear it."

"So am I!"

He halted his horse and sat looking at her. "And so you are again at work with much to do?"

"Yes, always much to do. And Rissa?"

"Still with Lawrence. When we leave here I hope to have her join us."

"Good. I hope she is fine."

His horse stomped. He reached down to stroke its neck, softly asking for patience. "Yes. Well, then, good day. Continue to stay well. Continue to stay fine. I hope to see you later."

"Yes. Later."

Their exchange had been quick. And despite its few words and little information, it had contained a familiarity that only the events they had lived through together would have given it. And then, he had replaced his hat and ridden on.

Now, standing in camp, hearing sounds of the battle down the river, she worries about him, not in words but in pictures. She imagines him leading a charge on the open ground at Ball's Bluff, riding, saber drawn, through cannon smoke and past rifle fire, and coming out to be at the end of the day once again battle-worn but survived and fine. She also thinks of Rissa and realizes that if it is indeed true that she is seriously ill, losing her husband in battle would be what she could not survive.

No, Captain McFerrin must not be lost—not ever be lost; the effect would be too horrible for Rissa. If imagining can be a kind of rehearsal, if not an out-and-out wish, I ran it over and over in my mind—Captain McFerrin riding back into camp on his same fine sun-colored horse, battle-worn but fine. And Ned too, perhaps this time he would perform in battle and his reputation be back intact. Perhaps he would even be decorated at war's end, if there were soon an end, which I still believed in and hoped for.

Yes, we will all be fine. Changed and wounded by what we see, but fine, still fine.

The word takes on a single line in her mind in much the same way that a light beam crosses a landscape.

Fine. Fine. We will all come out of this fine.

The wash is hung on lines. The afternoon moves into the need for more food. Eleanor begins cooking bacon and hominy, baked biscuits and succotash. Soon the smell of cooking wafts from their campfire. And when the horrifying boom of cannon, followed by a great terrifying crash, comes from the river, they stand paralyzed to listen, not understanding, not even able to imagine what has happened.

Not until the next morning—and a week more when I could read in the papers and mix with what I read there with what I heard—would I know that one of the Union regiments, led by the senator from Oregon, a Colonel Edward Baker—an intimate friend of Lincoln's, in fact, the namesake of Lincoln's first son, who had also even introduced Lincoln at his Inaugural— placed his two cannons near the edge of Ball's Bluff. His lack of military experience apparently blinded him to the danger of his position, and all afternoon the Confederate sharpshooters in the glade near the bluff had simply been picking off Baker's regiment as if they were in a turkey shoot. Suddenly after one cannon fired, it recoiled sharply and fell backward from the cliff. In stark reality of what could happen next, a shiver was said to run through every man there, and then as feared, the soil gave way, unleashing an avalanche. General Baker, rallying his men, moved up and down the line, yelling for them to stand fast. He was not even aware of the moment when a bullet went through his brain, killing him instantly. As then the Rebels charged, yipping their furious war cry, the panicked Union soldiers either tumbled off the cliff or jumped against the jagged rocks onto the bayonets of the waiting Rebels below. Some pulled the flatboat out of a nearby canal that had brought the cannon across the river and climbed on to ride it to the opposite bank. But it capsized, drowning nearly all.

It was such a horrifying event, I shiver now myself even writing of it.

At dusk, gray gunsmoke trailed over the river like a fog, and an unnatural silence echoed from the rocks. Baker was dead; two hundred of the Union were wounded or killed. And seven hundred were taken prisoner, among them, Paul Revere's grandson.

The defeat was so horrifying that a Joint Committee on the Conduct of the War was quickly formed, soon accusing General Stone, who led the Union regiment, of the horrifying defeat. In quick order, he was sent to a cell in New York Harbor.

The night of the battle, Eliza walks to the camp medical tent. By now she has replaced her wildcrafting bag, and the company's physician knows her. Robert Drury has made sure of that—after all, it is he who brought her on as a hired laundress, and when he learned of her wildcrafting skills, he found many in his company to treat.

The wounded are now being brought in. She walks in between the clink of wheels and the creak of harnesses with draft horses pulling the ambulance wagons toward the medical tents. The moans from the wagons mix with the clank of the wheels on the hilly road, and as she nears the tents, she sees more wounded lying on the ground; others are being rushed from wagons to inside the dressing station. Campfires speckle the open ground, and lanterns on trees throw blades of light that dapple the ground. There seems more than fifty wounded. Eliza knows the night will be long. Under trees are rows of dead. Tent lanterns turn the white canvas into a gray glow.

For hours, it seems, she assists the surgeon, bringing him dressings, holding instruments for him, then making teas for those moved from the operating table to the recovery tent. She boils water and stirs in astragalus herbs for teas, mixing the concoction with whiskey, knowing the astragalus herb cannot be used except before a fever starts. So she must use it now, when its strength will fortify a body weakened by shock. She also knows that in a day—if the wounded one does not die—she will follow the tea with goldenseal to cleanse the body and help prevent a fever.

After midnight, she hears outside the tent: "Is there an Eliza Hamilton here? Eliza Hamilton." The name stuns her. She has to remember: That too is she, the real she.

Whoever is calling steps inside. "Are you ...?" He is small, a grizzled man, a private with whiskers blooded by a cut across his cheek. He has one arm in a sling. "Eliza Hamilton?" he asks again.

"Yes." She pulls a cover up over the chest of the man she has been attending and turns to listen.

"Sergeant Drury is asking for you."

"Robert?"

"Yes, Sergeant Robert Drury. Can you come?"

"Where?"

"In the next tent over."

She grabs her wildcrafting bag and hurries. She doesn't wait for the private's guidance. She runs to the next tent. There inside, where candlelight illuminates a nightmare of suffering, she hears Robert's voice.

"Eliza, here. Eliza." He is calling from a cot on the far side.

She kneels beside him. "Robert. Yes, it's me. Let me see ..."

"Yes, I want you to see. And tell me. They say my legs is gone, but I feel them. I'm too weak to sit up. Can you please take a look and tell me."

For a moment, she hesitates. Then carefully she lifts the blanket that covers him from his chest down. Below the wool that she holds up are the bloody stumps of what are left of his legs from above the knees.

"All I remember is the artillery fire." Robert looks blurrily into her eyes as she lifts the blanket. He then chatters on, fuzzy-brained, his mind still clouded from chloroform. His hair, in its fox-coat color, is sweated through and browned with dirt.

"They are not here, Robert. What they have told you is real."

He looks at her in a long silence, his eyes becoming momentarily clear. "Gone then. You can see that for sure?"

"Yes." She lays the blanket back over him and opens her bag. She nervously sorts through the herbs. "I will make you something that will help you sleep. You will be fine, Robert, fine."

In the candlelight beside his cot, she makes the tea and holds the cup as he drinks. He looks up and smiles. "I suspect I'll be a good bit shorter." His eyes meet hers. "Wonder why I can still feel them, though?"

"Count your blessings that you are not in much pain, for later I fear you will be."

"Yes, later. Later." His mind is lucid in short moments, and he asks, "Do you remember where we met? Back in the woods by that pond in the lovely country. Mississippi. Home?"

"I remember. I remember that day very well."

"And we thought—"

"Yes, that I was on the way to see my aunt just as I said I was."

"That's what you said. And you was so believable—so pretty and refined. That's what my mother says when she talks about girls—whether they is refined or not. And you was."

"I at least knew how to look like I was."

"Oh, yes, you was looking fine."

"I didn't tell you all the truth, because I was ashamed of the truth. I was running away from who I was."

"I figured that out. Later, I figured it out. We heard—me and Lem and Jesse. Major Morgan and ... There's just something about you one never forgets. And stories of you travel. But I hear now people call you something else."

"Yes, they've called me all sorts of things."

"No. I wasn't meaning that. I was meaning they call you Eliza Goode."

"Well, if the name doesn't exactly fit, it at least covers up my real one. It's like jasmine, smelling sweet. It can cover up what otherwise might seep through." She laughs ironically. "I don't know if you know, but Molly Evangeline hired me because she misheard what you said about me. She thought you said my name was good, when only you were saying that as a laundress I'd be good. A good worker for her. And you didn't even know if I knew how to wash anything!"

"I figured you'd learn. I didn't know that—what you just told me. So I named you? And by accident?" He laughs, coughs and chokes. She lifts him, then squeezes water from a rag into his mouth, so it will trickle slowly.

His voice now goes on, scratchy, his tongue loosened by whiskey and herbs. "But you *is* good, Eliza. I've never told anyone it was a made-up name. I've been glad to be the one to bring you on as what you are now. Poor Lem. He was the one talked me into it."

"Yes. I know."

"And Jesse, dead at Manassas. His sweetheart back in Mississippi, sore-hearted for sure. Will you ...," he mumbles and closes his eyes.

"Yes, I will. I'll be back again tomorrow." She then leaves, glancing back and feeling relieved that he is sleeping.

Toward morning, as she is at the surgeon's station helping to clean up, the company's medical officer comes to her. He is a big burly man untying what seems to be a butcher's apron, and he thanks her. "You bring comfort to them, if comfort can be had." He scowls. "If none of these die, this will be recorded as a slight battle with few losses. Insane mathematics keeps count of the war now."

She turns to see if one of the privates might ride her back to the laundresses' campsite. She is so tired, she feels sick.

When a wagoner offers, she climbs up, and he aims the team of horses to her laundress tent. The sun is up, and rose rays of light filter through trees. The smell of campsite embers trail in the air, pungent and comforting.

Wearily she goes into the tent she shares with the other laundresses, and as she is undressing, taking off her dirty blood-smelling clothes, Eleanor rises from her cot and begins taking off her nightgown. Eleanor says, "I'll do your wash today. You've done your part. But if you're going to continue nursing, we're going to have to swap you out."

Eliza nods, too tired to worry about any of that now.

Colleen and Shirley are gathering kindling for the laundry fires. Eliza can hear them chattering outside the tent. She lies down on her cot and falls deeply asleep.

At noon, Eleanor is shaking her shoulder. Eliza opens her eyes and sees Eleanor pointing. "Someone out here says he heard you know someone by the name of Ted Tatum. S'right?"

Sitting bolt upright, Eliza's head swims with the sudden movement. "Ned?"

"I guess. Anyway, he says he needs to talk to you, and it can't wait."

She stands up and sweeps her loose hair over her shoulder. "He will have to wait, though, while I wash and dress."

Eleanor nods. Then from outside the tent, Eliza hears Eleanor's voice offering the man a cup of coffee. His voice is deep and husky as if from an older soldier, not a young one—an officer probably.

She splashes water over her arms and neck, running a washcloth over the rest of her, trailing water from the basin. She puts on a clean green-and-tan plaid dress. Quickly she spins up her hair and fastens it with a comb. Tendrils trail down her neck, but she can take no longer to make it neater. She must go, dreading what she is bound to learn, dreading what she might be asked to do.

What if Ned is dead, or passed again into an insane cloud, placing him in trouble with his superiors? What would I do?

Outside the tent, a Zouaves lieutenant holds a horse, harnessed to a mess cart. "Would you be willing to come with me? I saw you before, after Manassas, coming to look for Ned Tatum. I remember you talking to him that time we were waiting for him to sober up. That was you, wasn't it?"

She nods yes. "And now has Ned done it again?"

"No. Well, we don't know. But sober he is not. Though not exactly drunk either. We thought you could help sort it out."

"Quick, take me to him. Is he all right—I mean not wounded?"

"No. Not wounded."

Together they ride the mess cart down the road, a small black horse pulling it, its coat fuzzy and dull. Eliza fears imagining what state Ned might be in. She blocks her mind from rehearsing the possibilities. And she asks no more questions. Instead she wills her eyes to close and rest, rocking on the wood seat of the cart beside the Zouaves lieutenant in his colorful uniform that has been freshly laundered.

They pull up to a clearing near the Zouaves' camp. "Come with me." The lieutenant leads her to a tent. He holds open the flap, letting her enter first.

There inside, standing against a framing pole, is Ned. His face is blank, his eyes staring, his right arm up over his head, his other reaching out as if for something, but frozen, his fingers spread. She can hear that strange way he has of breathing, the long rasping pull of air. The sort of breathing she had heard so much, growing up, and that she has associated with him for as long as she can remember. But now he looks as if he is held captive in a dream. He is stiff, as stiff as whittled wood, and his eyes stare like fish eyes, like a fish at a market on a New Orleans street. "What?" she whispers. She can see his shirt lifting with his breathing.

"We think," the lieutenant says, "he is in a stupor. The medical officer has had time for only a quick look. He says it is a mental disorder. He calls it a cataleptic trance."

"Meaning what?"

"Only this. That's all we know. Before, he sobered up fine; it took a few days, but he was back as he was. I mean, he's always been a little odd—loud and fanciful. And it's only natural for a young man to be scared out of his wits in a first battle. But now, I don't know. We're thinking when he comes out of this, we'll send him home. That's what we need to know. Who should we send him to? His sign-up papers don't say. He wrote only that if anything happens to him, notify the New Orleans newspaper and Eliza Hamilton. I hear that is you."

"Yes. It is me. But ..."

She walks up and touches Ned's face. He doesn't respond. His eyes look past her. "Ned. Neddy, do you hear me? Are you thinking of any of us: of your mother, Madam Francine, Zapa? The pretty rings you had. And Delia who made the sweetest, hottest cornbread?"

She is thinking that perhaps some memory can jolt him back from wherever he is. But he makes no signs of hearing her.

At least he was not railing as before. No, not as before, which was so terrifying, though this was another sort of terrifying: the lifeless form he had taken. O, what should I do? What could I do? I had no place of my own to take him, even if I could have nursed him back to health. And what if I did? Would he turn on me as he had before? O, it was a terrible place to be, in such a fitful squeezing of my heart and mind. "I have no way ....," I heard myself saying.

"I have no way to take care of him." She looks at the Zouaves in the tent who are watching her. She feels a need to say, "Yes, it is true, we grew up together. Like brother and sister. But Ned's mother is dead. She died shortly before the war broke out. And he does not have a home to go home to ... unless." She bites her lip and says it now with an apologetic tone, for she knows they will quickly realize its purpose: "Madam Francine's establishment on South Basin Street in New Orleans."

"I better write that down," the lieutenant says, doing so. Twice he asks her to repeat it and to give its correct spelling. His eyes flicker with the realization of what "Madam Francine's establishment" means. She turns away in embarrassment, not wanting to meet his eyes, nor see a possible smirk.

The lieutenant then stands up from his writing desk and says behind her back, "I think now, though, the plan is to put him on the train back to Corinth. If he is not better by then, the army will find a place to send him. If he is well enough to set loose, he will be released from duty. We obviously have no place for him with his troubles. A shame, though, for I've rarely seen a man so burning to fight."

She turns to glance at him. "I'm sorry. I'm sorry I cannot be of more help."

And then she slips past him and goes out.

Walking across the grounds, she smells ham frying over campfires. Coffee wafts its roasted smell as she walks to the wagoner, who now offers her a ride back to her campsite.

O yes, I knew so well now. Knew all the sounds and the feel. The purple gray of a morning after a battle when every sound is of pain, diluted only by the fact of a victory. And my heart, sorrow-drowned over Ned.

Chapter 22

The next day, she went back to see Robert. He was in great pain, both physically and in his soul, but he had longer moments of mental clarity. Looking up as she walks close, he pulls himself up to sit taller.

Straightening the blanket over him, she smiles. He nods. "I'm being sent back to Corinth, Eliza, and from there to Crystal Springs. My family will come for me." He squints, holding off emotions. "I'm of no use to the army now. And there is a supply officer's wife who has long—"

"Yes ..., " she finishes for him, "I imagine she has long wanted to join him, which means she will take my place."

He nods.

I made him a goldenseal tea, heartened to see he had no fever. How strange that he and I, once strangers, had so joined our lives that what happened to him, happened to me. We were both now set off beyond the army that we had been with for these months.

It was time for me to think about what I would do. I could, I thought, continue following the army as a wildcrafter. Probably I would be tolerated to be there that way. But something in me was sore and used up. I had money to spare for collecting pay as a laundress and from my wildcrafting on the side. For the first time in my life, I had choices. I toyed with the idea of catching the train at Manassas and riding it back toward the climate and ways I was familiar with. But I was too fearful of the nightmare that pushed me to flee—Preston Cummings at any train stop. The thought too that Ned might be put on a train that I might happen to be on—O! All that gave me more than second thoughts.

Unexpectedly, when I asked myself what I really wanted to do, I answered: Why! I had an itch to see the capital city. Why not? It was heavily a secessionist town; I would not be among enemies or hostilities in that sense. It was merely a few miles away; I had only to cross one of the bridges to be there. If Betty Duvall had done it, carrying her spy message to General Beauregard, I could too.

For most of that morning, I stayed with Robert, making him as comfortable as I was able. And also administering to those poor men lying on cots around him.

I went back to my campsite. I began packing my things. Eleanor was happy to see me go. Colleen did not much mind. I was a thorn in their sides, especially as I was called off so often for my wildcrafted remedies, which they envied me for.

How little I had to put into my bag now in the way of personal things: two dresses, one pair of shoes, no hat, a scarf, the birthing beads that I had worn under my clothes on the day Jim Lukens raped me—the ones I had been given that day, seemingly so long ago now—on that Mississippi plantation where Quashi had led me and, also, still, my prized beeswax cervical cap which would always remind me of the occupation I had been intended for, as well as the day Amalee had given me it to protect me, in one sense, from the father-devil who thought he owned me.

On the morning the supply officer's wife was to arrive from the train station in Manassas, I paid a wagoner to drive me to the nearest town. The delight of having my own money I cannot state too often. I hid it in my underclothes, fearful of robbery, for many knew I had it, so much had I collected selling my treatments for the illness born from public women who always followed the army. Also often for agues, boils, sore throats, coughs, dysentery.

O! How full I felt of my own power!

She pays the wagoner at a village named Chantilly, stepping down from the wagon and opening her coin purse. She is only about twelve miles now from the Potomac River and Washington. She likes the name Chantilly.

There she catches a coach to take her into the city. It is full of other passengers, and she sits wedged between two men who carry salesmen's satchels. They each glance and then glance again. And soon she feels the heat from their bodies and, with it, their desire, which tells her unequivocally that the power she once had she still has—a physical effect of not only her beauty but a certain instinctual message: Here is one who knows of and understands sex in its most feral sense.

The coach passes through the Chain Bridge. And on the dirt road into the city, it moves through flocks of wandering ducks, past soldiers on guard, past bystanders, on and on rolling through mud and manure. The city is as busy as New Orleans, and she breathes deeply, taking comfort in the familiarity of a city's pace. Everywhere are soldiers, either bivouacked or standing guard.

Stepping down from the coach where it stops on the corner of Pennsylvania Avenue, she looks across at the Willard Hotel. Even though it is very grand, she has the funds to secure a room. So why not? She walks up to the desk, and the reservation clerk looks up, holding his pen suspended in air. Tall and thin with scarecrow bones that seem tethered by string, he tilts his head, then scowls. So now she realizes that a woman traveling alone seems strange, if not suspect. The war is too new for women's roles to have been relaxed as yet. He repeats her request as if he hopes she will have another answer. "One room, single?" She nods yes. "Well then." She catches him studying more closely her way of dress, the plainness of it. Not missing, though, is his admiration of her beauty, nor his reading of the subliminal message she cannot help but carry, having been raised as she was. "I wonder," he starts. "You wouldn't be in need of a job, would you?"

"What kind?"

"Down the street. My cousin and I opened a new tearoom there last week. We have only one server at the moment, and she is overwhelmed."

"Perhaps. I'll think on it."

"Oh, but let me show you!" He calls someone to cover the desk for him, and then he leads her to the door. Ordinarily she would be suspicious of his intentions if he were not an employee who couldn't be absent from his duties for long. He leads her down the block to a rooming house. The bottom floor has been converted to a tearoom. He opens the door and they go in: a big room, empty now in the sunshine that streams through big windows.

A small bar is across one wall; but overall, the room has been disguised as a tearoom since it would be unacceptable for a woman to serve alcohol. The tables sport white tablecloths, and no doubt a bit of liqueur will be quickly added to any tea ordered.

He looks at her as she walks in for a closer look.

"We open at two. You would serve until ten, and we can give you a room upstairs for half-price, less so if you room with the girl already hired. Indeed, you could stay here tonight."

She does not look back at him. She catches his meaning—that he would rather she be here and not in the Willard Hotel where her plain dress and single status would not be of their standards. She walks into the newly disguised tavern for a closer look. It has a low ceiling with huge wooden beams. A large fireplace with old Dutch tiles centers the room, and silhouettes of various women are hung over it. On the mantelshelf are candlesticks and an Old English clock in a tall mahogany case. On the opposite wall is a large mirror in a heavy wood frame. It is indeed an elegant room. The idea of working here is intriguing.

"I'll think on it," she says, "and give you an answer tomorrow. How much?"

He mentions the salary: five dollars a week.

Upstairs, she finds her room and unpacks. For a long while she looks excitedly out the window. The street is heavily traveled by carriages and horses, some men on horseback. There is the clang of street sounds. No doubt there is a mix of Union sympathizers with secessionists—a good place to be where not too many questions would be asked of anyone.

The next day she accepts the job. Her new boss gives her

money for a proper serving wardrobe—two silk dresses that he says must be highly colored with small hoops so she can move easily between tables.

"Do yourself up," he says. "Do yourself up fine." With his scarecrowlike fingers, he hands her Union money.

It was at noon when I was just leaving my room, dressed in a blue silk, ready for my first day of work, that I stepped outside my door and nearly collided with a young woman in a raspberry silk, a white lace apron over it, coming from down the hall. Bright gold hair, a face painted in high color, a quick smile and husky voice as if she were nursing a cold, she stepped back at arm's length and exclaimed, "Why I know you! Don't I? Don't I know you?'

"I think not," I said.

Annie Fisk she said she was, and didn't stop talking—it was clear she'd kissed the Blarney Stone—as together we walked down the stairs. And then, "O, but somewhere I have seen you! That is unmistakable. O, my! You are very pretty indeed. Heart-shaped face. The look of an angel. And your hair, so thick and dark. Let me see how you have put it up! O yes, quite wonderful, that style."

I was overwhelmed and baffled at her studying me. Then as we reached the end of the stair, while still studying me with that obsession to fix in her memory an image with a fact, she suddenly stopped and exclaimed, "O, I know now. I know. That mole on your cheek there. That's what I realize now."

I stood, taken aback. Was she crazy or what? Quickly, she began whispering,"You see, I used to be on the other side of the city. I just came from there last week, and back where I was, a gentleman who I met had a picture of you. I'm certain now. He was showing it around, asking if anyone had seen you. Yes, that's where I saw you!"

My heart flew up, clogging my throat. My breath stalled midair. "Who? Do you know his name?"

"Of course. I—" and then she caught herself.

Believe me, it did not take more than a second more for me to affirm what I was thinking. You see, it takes one to know one, you might say. She was indeed a "boarder" at Sal Austin's. She knew Lotty's cousin, when I mentioned her name. Yes, she had worked at Mrs. Wolf's too. And after only a few more of my probing questions, I knew the rest. The week before she had serviced Preston Cummings himself, who had been there conducting business in the city of Washington, so he had said. After a bit of drink, he could not contain the plans he was so happy to boast of: supplying money to a secret few with the intention of harming President Lincoln, as well as the whole city, by unleashing a yellow fever epidemic. He had concocted an elaborate plan: packing clothes stripped from dead yellow fever victims whenever an epidemic would break out, most likely in the Bahamas islands or somewhere like that, soon. Then sending the dead victims' clothes to Lincoln in a trunk, which when opened would seed a yellow fever epidemic, infecting the President first, then spreading throughout the city. Preston Cummings was so proud of his devious plan—for indeed it was a clever idea, if you were of that mindset, to rip Lincoln from power and give the war's victory to the government in Richmond—that is, if the plan had not been so stupid. For no one knew that clothes could not carry the infection. Mosquitoes were suspected as the bearer of Bronze John, but no one knew for sure. Only that cold weather seemed paired with the end of an epidemic.

Making Preston Cummings's tongue so loose with Annie Fisk, and perhaps others, was his need to find those who could infiltrate the city with his fever-infected clothes, once he had them.

Then, in the midst of his stay at Sal Austin's, he had begun showing my photograph around. "Have you seen her? Yes, this one. Seventeen, a face like an angel. Look at that hair. Look at that mark of beauty there, on her cheek. Skin. Soft as a fawn. As beautiful as a girl can ever be. I must find her." He even added that money was involved.

"And so?" Annie asked. "Are you eager to find him to collect what you must have inherited and not yet know of?"

I laughed. I laughed raucously and wildly. "No. It's the other way around," I said. "I owe him money!" I laughed even louder. After all, wasn't I the debt he was determined to collect?

"Look," Annie whispered, entering the tavern tearoom to set up tables, to serve the spiked tea. Already three men were

sitting at tables, waiting. "I'm so glad you're working with me.
We'll have a grand time!"

Right away, Eliza had wanted to flee—get back on a coach
and out of the city, fearing *he* was still there. But she had just
"landed." *Think, think. Don't fly off, crazy bird.* And she was
intrigued with this new city life. So she latched onto the logic
that probably he had already left Washington. She was in an
unlikely place, after all, and he was also unlikely to come looking
for Annie Fisk, if indeed he had developed a particular taste for
her. To verify what she suspected, Eliza asked, at the end of that
first week, while they were in the room that they now shared,
"Annie, were you asked to leave Sal Austin's?"

Annie looks up, stunned, dropping the shoe she has been
cleaning."Why do you ask?"

Gently Eliza says, "Were you ...? Are you ... well sick—a little
infected?" As though there is such a thing as *little*.

"God! Does it show?"

Eliza shakes her head, tempted to smile. "No. I made a
guess."

Annie covers her face. "Yes. I had to leave. And leave everyone
I know. It's been so lonely here. Until you ... I didn't know how
I would ... But it's been good, so far, good. I didn't know I could
work at anything else ... and feel so bad about—"

"Are you favoring Mr. Scarecrow too?"

Annie peeks through her fingers and guffaws. Both of them
laugh big, whooping laughs. And then Annie nods yes.

"I know a remedy that sometimes helps." Eliza goes to her
wildcrafting bag.

Annie looks at Eliza in a puzzled stare. "How do you know
all about this?"

Eliza smiles. Their eyes meet. "I grew up somewhere like Sal
Austin's. The one who showed you my picture. I thought of him
as ... well, until ..."

Annie stares.

In silence we understood what did not have to be said.

"Oh, God!" Annie exclaims."To look at you I would never
know!"

I laughed loudly, raucously, ending with a sound cut off
in my throat. I told her that was my special gift: I could be

anything. Anyone. I'd been wonderfully taught.

Our friendship was sealed; our pasts were glue of our own brand. The next two months Annie and I spent working together as friends. And spending time together as friends, talking, jabbering like the young girls we were. Sometimes I'm sure our room sounded like magpies at roost. We swapped stories. Mine in New Orleans for hers in Illinois. She told me of growing up, the child of six from a family so poor she was given away to neighbors. And then ran away, driven by their mistreatment and her taste for adventure that eventually landed her in the capital city. Destitute, she met up with one of Sal Austin's boarders, which then made it an old story that I'd heard many times.

Yes, Annie and I were bonded. We spent Christmas Day together, first serving tea in the tearoom, then celebrating, just the two of us—eating cake, exchanging hats as gifts. Mine to her, a rich strawberry with a matching veil; hers to me, blue-gray felt with a black veil. We put them on and danced, holding on to each other, taking turns pretending to be certain kinds of men, rough or phony sweet, but each bulging with lust.

December passed. The weather was brutally cold and wet. I was satisfied and moderately happy, making out on my own with Annie as the only family I needed. Then, one afternoon as I was walking on the street, my hem caught on my shoe, and as I looked up from freeing it, I saw President Lincoln coming down the sidewalk toward me. Instantly, I knew it was he: so tall, with a shock of hair fit for a fireplace broom. Who else could it be? He looked my way, then beyond, took off his hat, put a piece of paper in the bowl of it, then put it back on. Obviously he had his own filing system! Seeing up close how singular his appearance was, I remembered Madam Francine telling me that she thought she had seen him in New Orleans when she was young. She had been on the wharf and saw him disembark from a flatboat—a young man of only about nineteen, so tall and singular in his looks that her memory became an echo to come back to her when she saw his picture as president.

Looking now at Mr. Lincoln, I thought of Preston Cummings's plan, and recalled the sound of his voice denouncing him as a tyrant. Quickly, I took paper from my bag and wrote: BEWARE

OF STRANGE TRUNKS. DON'T OPEN A ONE. Which sounded so childish, I nearly tore it up. Instead on impulse, I left it on the sidewalk where I thought he might find it on his way back.

Another day, I thought I saw him look into the tearoom window as he walked by. When I told Annie, she sucked in her breath in a thrilled moment, her eyes growing big as she cried, "O, I have to tell you!" We were sitting on her bed, folding napkins for the tearoom. "I saw him once, back in Illinois, when I was fifteen. He was climbing up on a platform to speak and wearing the eye of an opponent—that's how I like him best. He was taking on Mr. Douglas. After one look, anyone who'd never heard of him would want to know more. Why! He was as awkward as a newborn calf, all bony and angles. And something about that, plus his homely face, would have made anyone passing him in the street or seeing him sitting on a platform remember him. I heard a farmer say, 'There ain't no one else, and there never will be, jest like Abe Lincoln.' I think that awkwardness was a good thing. It made him more appealing once you heard him start speaking. He talked straight, simple, brushing away all silly subjects. Yes, the ungainly body, the bony face, the strong mouth and quiet, kindly eyes took you out of yourself. If I could have voted, I would have—for him by God. Though I guess you wouldn't 'av."

"O, probably," I said, adding, "just for spite if nothing else. Because all I heard was hatred of him. Surely too I don't want him or anybody to die of Bronze John because of some stupid scheme." Often Annie and I talked of him, feeling his presence all over the city and hoping to hear him declare that the war was over. I recalled Delia once secretly calling him Father Abraham after his election.

In the last week of that December, on the night of a vicious thunderstorm, Annie came rushing into the tearoom kitchen where I was washing plates. "He's here," she whisper-cried.

"President Lincoln?" I blurted as my first guess.

"God no. Though I wish."

From the look on her face, I didn't have to ask who again. Preston Cummings.

I looked through the curtain between the kitchen and main room. I caught the scent of cherry smoking tobacco. His face was reflected in the mirror on the wall across from him. There were the same features I had adored as a child, only now they were travel-worn and gaunt and tainted with my new, vile memories. He was sitting at a table with two other men, drinking, smoking, his back to me and the dark wideness of his head so familiar—the turned-down skin on the top of his ear. He looked up. I saw his eyes reflected in the mirror—cold, glittery black—that I did not realize as a child often wore an animal's predatory stare. I ducked.

"Here!" Annie held a pot under my chin, as though I might vomit. I grabbed it and went to the back of the kitchen to sit on a stool, a wet towel over my face, the pot under my chin.

I stayed there long after he walked out the door. Annie helped me up the stairs; I seemed so weak with fear. In an hour flat, I was packed and ready to flee. But Annie made me wait until daylight. Again I was a bird teetering on a leaf, nearly frightened out of good sense. All I could think about was that I had to go. Go anywhere but away, and quickly.

I told Annie to give my notice to "Mr. Tearoom Scarecrow," and in a matter of hours, Annie walked me to the corner where I caught a horsecar across the river.

Chapter 23

Taking a coach back to Chantilly, Eliza got off there and set about to find the Mississippi regiment that Captain McFerrin's company had been swept into. Pulling a shawl up over her shoulders, she stepped from the coach and headed quickly into the store across the street. She filled her lungs with the sweet, crisp air that seemed to even have a taste. She could let her guard down here; she could, here, at least for a short while, be surrounded by the safety of the little town. Chantilly, Chantilly—so small but with the promise that something totally good and delightful would be around the next corner. Yes, here she would find *him*.

She buys something to eat, listening to the townspeople chatting, learning that Jeb Stuart's cavalry is bivouacked close by. Indeed the whole Rebel line is stretched out along the Potomac down to Richmond.

But when she asks several soldiers if they know of Captain McFerrin, she unearths no news, until finally, a private on the street stops, and in a heavy Irish brogue tells: "Oh, that company. Headed down to Nashville. Or was it Kentucky with Bedford Forrest? Forrest, we hear, was given a regiment early in October. Can't rightly say where your Captain McFerrin is.

Probably Nashville. Cavalry's always being scratched together."

"Nashville?"

"Mmhmm. Supply base for 'bout everything. Close to the ironworks in Clarksville. Have to keep an eye on it, you know. Only other one we's got's in Richmond. Without 'em, we'd be cannon and minie ball poor."

He grins, showing blackened teeth and a liking for her.

"Thank you and here, put this salve on your face burns."

The next day she is on a steamer headed for the Cumberland River. In the night, snow falls, and looking out from the rail at the passing bank with leafless trees and snow-dusted roofs, she shivers as much from uncertainty as cold.

I was set on my plan, but uneasy underneath, for I could not deny that there was something between us, Ben and me— born as much from curiosity as from physical awareness, going back to the moment we first knew of the other. And I feared Rissa's sensing that. I never had a desire to unbalance them, no never—only to find a way to exist and be safe.

Now in the middle of January 1862, Eliza stands on the steamboat deck watching the city of Nashville come into view. People range over the wharf in antlike busyness. In a year, some one hundred steamboats come and go to what is now the major supply base for the Confederacy. A new suspension bridge crosses over the river. Along the bank, trees hang a patchwork of icy limbs like lines scratched in ink.

She walks down the boat ramp, surrounded by the river smell and lap of water. The musty odor of manure comes from the snow-melted mud. Lifting her hem, she steps onto the wooden walkway amid the clang and chatter of farmers and merchants bringing wares to ship to other Confederate cities. She carries her bag and wears one of her tearoom dresses: sapphire taffeta, along with the hat that Annie Fisk gave her.

Carriages pass up and down, ferrying businessmen in beaver felt hats, women in fine dress. Obviously it is a prosperous city. Seemingly everywhere she looks is a church steeple. In the distance, the spire of the state capitol rises above the rooftops. It's a city of fourteen thousand non-slave residents, bulging now with part of the army of General Albert Sidney Johnston.

Aimlessly she walks, searching for a hotel. Passing

businessmen and soldiers, their canteens and sabers clanking, she often stops to ask, "Would you know of Captain McFerrin? Is there a cavalry encamped nearby?" More often than not, she hears, "No'm, can't say I do. But a cavalry is bivouacked a few miles west of here."

Walking toward Tennessee's capitol, she assumes that a good Nashville hotel will be nearby. Men step aside, then linger to steal a longer look, their notice making her nervous. She plans that as soon as she finds a place to stay, she will take a horsecar to the west of the city and ask for Captain McFerrin.

Down the hill from the capitol, closer to the river, she walks on Spring Street, where after a short distance, she instinctively knows where she is. Houses line each side of the street that, in daylight, are unnaturally quiet and shuttered. In a few windows, she glimpses girls. Changing the weight of her bag from her right arm to her left, she lowers the veil on her hat and pretends to be the widow of an officer. *Straight now. Dignity. Prim steps. That's right.* If in the next block she does not come upon a hotel, she will turn around.

After the first full block, she sees that there are only blocks and blocks more and that it is, indeed, a whole district: a district of brothels and parlor houses. *Smokey Row—only later would I know the name of where I was: a district much like the one near Constitution Avenue in Washington, which took on the name of Hooker's Division because of that general's proclivities. By nightfall, this Nasvhille street would be teeming with activity, and I was not about to stay anywhere near there, so I turned to head to the other side of the city. But after a few blocks, a cavalry officer came toward me—obviously cavalry: spurs, saber, sash, plumed hat. Dark-haired, warm-eyed, whiskered past his collar. O, he was quite fancily dressed. Abruptly I stopped him to ask, "Excuse me. Do you happen to know of Captain McFerrin? Bennett McFerrin?"*

Doffing his hat, he bowed. Dressed as I was, I looked similar to someone who lived in Smokey Row, but I was carrying my bag and consciously walking with my pretense of being an officer's widow. The dignity of that infused my mind.

"I do," he said. "And quite well at one time. He and I were classmates at VMI. I saw him not long ago."

"Here? In Nashville?" I asked eagerly.

He smiled, jauntily fingering his hat. "Yes, he was here not long ago. He'd been up in Kentucky riding with Bedford Forrest, much to his dislike. Do you know McFerrin well?"

"Yes. We grew up together." The lie just flew off my tongue.

"Well, then you know how stubbornly principled he is—no tolerance for unnecessary talk or action." He laughed.

"O, yes," I prompted. "I suppose you have many stories from the days at VMI." Actually, I was eager to learn more about Ben, for the reality was that even though we had shared pivotal moments, I knew very little about him.

Playfully, his dark eyes looked at me. "I don't have many good stories, I'm sorry to say. We never could get Ben off the path long enough for much mischief. Had two demerits in four years, I think. Too good at everything in my opinion. We called him Prim Ben. It was his father who insisted he go to VMI. He simply made himself be good at it."

He then looked at me with an amused stare.

"So where might I find him? Encamped west of here?"

"Not since Tuesday. Apparently in a skirmish in Kentucky, Forrest went mad after his brother was killed. Wiped out a company with unnecessary force, in Ben's mind, so he asked to be assigned to another division. Now's in Clarksville under Gideon Pillow's command. His wife is quite ill, you know."

"Yes. Rissa. But when last I saw her, she was doing fine. You say they are no longer here?"

"No, I'm sorry to say. Is there anything else I can help you with?"

"No, and thank you." Watching him bow and walk off, looking back several times, I quickly headed to the river.

The wharf now was even busier than in the morning. Eliza made her way through the crowd to the ticket office and learned that a transport was leaving that very hour for Clarksville. But it was full. Slaves were carrying boxes on board. Soldiers were lined up on the ramp.

It will be two days before another steamer can take her. *Well, then, go now, find a place to stay.* She buys a ticket for future use, and, leaving the wharf, she suddenly cries out, "Quashi!" For there he is, with two soldiers, his farrier bag over his shoulder, walking toward the wharf. Grinning, he stops, murmuring, "Miss Eliza."

"Quashi! It is really you!"

"Yes."

"Yes?" She nods, encouraging him on.

"Got leased to a general. Been keeping up Jeb Stuart's horses. And now they got me going to keep up Colonel Forrest's horses. He's up at Fort Donelson."

"You been here long?"

"A day. Had to get supplies. You lookin' healthy."

"Yes, I am fine. What do you hear of Delia?"

"Good as ever. You heard? Mr. Ned came home."

"Ned is back?!"

"Several months ago. Not in the army no more. But still burning with the fight fever."

"Oh, Quashi, I saw him in Virginia. He was not well."

"No. Outta his mind. But then he straightened out. Went off again. He kept asking 'bout you. None of us knew where you was. Yesterday, though, I thought I saw him here—getting on one of these boats. Your mama and Madam Francine—they sure miss you. When you left, your mother took sick outta grief. Madam Francine pumped me for days about where I'd left you off. I think she sent folks looking for you. She didn't think you'd stay gone this long."

"No. She didn't give me enough money to make it far. I think that's what she counted on."

"Quashi! Come up!"

Quashi looks over his shoulder. A soldier now yells for him to catch up. He looks back at her, his eyes swimming with emotion. "Miss Eliza, you think you could spare me a dollar? The general I'm leased to cuts me short. And I can't say nothing."

"Of course." She opens her bag and gives him a Confederate dollar left over from her wildcrafting days. "I owe you more than this."

"I'll pay you back. I promise you that. And now, Miss Eliza, you still got that mare?"

"Oh, Quashi. No. She died. I miss her terribly. And we were both so wrong. She was never worthless."

He readjusts the bag on his shoulder and smiles. "Yeah, she

was one you had to know to know she was good."

"Quashi, get a move on! Hurry!"

The soldiers are walking up the boarding ramp. The steamboat whistles; a blast of smoke shoots into the air.

Now there is no other recourse; she has to find a place to stay. And there is another new worry: The months she was in Washington city, she was paid in Union money. She has hardly any Confederate dollars.

Finding a small hotel near the center of the city, she undresses and sleeps. And in the morning, as if her feet know where to take her, she walks to Spring Street, where she searches out the most luxurious parlor house in the district. At 101-103 North Front Street, she knocks on the door, holding her wildcrafting bag, wearing her other tearoom dress, a raspberry silk with a hoop. And when the door opens, she learns it is the owner herself, Rebecca Higgins, who holds open the door while Eliza easily explains of her wildcrafting skills, the means to treat the illnesses that many of those who live there might have. She even mentions Madam Francine and the address in New Orleans.

"Humph." Rebecca Higgins furrows her brow. As wide as she is tall, in cranberry silk ruffles fluttering at her drooping breasts, she studies Eliza, then asks more questions and invites her in. "Let's see what you got."

Stepping inside, I instantly saw how elegant it was—a natural rival to Madam Francine's: twelve-foot ceilings, heavy cornices, elaborate chandeliers, a dark rug with a leaf pattern twining busily over it, covering soil and hundreds of boot marks.

Rebecca leads her to one of the parlor rooms, smelling musty, its walls painted dark mauve, trimmed in white. "Wait here," she says, pointing to a heavy mahogany couch with an arched back, its arms reminiscent of the curves on a sled.

Eliza walks to it. The floors creak, and sitting down, she reads a smoky tint of *violeta azulado* while seemingly hearing a million whispered exchanges of erotic desires. *Yes, memory, yes, the home I had known.*

Soon Eliza is taken to a room upstairs where, on a tester bed, a group of women sit, waiting to be treated with Eliza's wildcrafted cures for rashes, ague, flux and "private diseases," then the talk moves into "sheathing the spear," which prompts giggles and jokes as the women tell that since the war, newspapers now advertise both "skins" and "India rubber"—the "skins" being lamb caeca, expensive and most unpopular with customers.

In all, there were seventeen there, mostly thirty years old, mostly widowed. In total six schoolchildren, two preschool children, a carpenter, a brick mason, and a twenty-two-year-old black man named Tom Trimble.

And then there was that other talk, infused with terror, of failed abortions and horrible deaths.

I told them to beware of "taking the cold"—a common remedy for what we called missed periods—since commonly savin, extracted from juniper bushes, was known to bring about an abortion. But many overdid it and died. This, I said, is better, to avoid that trouble in the first place—and I took from my bag the gift from Amalee, my prized beeswax cervical cap. The rest of that afternoon until late, I stayed there—even having tea and a light supper—feeling so at home and explaining how the "cap" was used, that I had learned of it at Madam Francine's, who brought it from France. And we set about in an experiment to make our own, bustling about the kitchen, laughing, burning down candles to collect the wax and trying to mold it into a shape like the one I had, without it cracking and crumbling. Simply I did not realize I was staying so late, it being winter, the light outside fading early and fast. I was so at home there, splitting the loneliness I had felt for some time. (And O! How I missed Annie Fisk!) I overstayed until one by one, the kitchen cleared, as each went to her room to ready herself for the evening's work.

Realizing I would need to get back to my hotel before total dark, I grabbed my bag, hurrying to put herbs and treatments quickly back in, as well as all I had collected in Confederate money, and rushed to the front door. By then, Rebecca and her sister had grown fond of me, and protective, for as soon as I opened the door and gasped—an animal shriek came from deep within me—they hurried to see what had caused me such alarm. There on the first step stood Preston Cummings, obviously ready to frequent their house as he had before, and startled to see me as I was to see him.

"Ah," he breathed, taking my arm, squeezing it tightly at the shoulder. I tried to pull away, but couldn't.

"Leave her be!" Rebecca growled.

"What do you think you're doing?" Her sister stepped outside to yell at him closer.

"This," he said, shaking me slightly, "is a debt I have been owed." And then he added quickly in a less threatening businesslike tone, "Excuse us."

Forcefully he guided me down the steps and into the street. He had a carriage there that apparently had just dropped him off to come back later, and he thrust me into it. As soon as he sat down, his voice took on the tone I heard growing up—a tone I adored, a tone that said I was the most precious, important thing in his world. With a liquid softness, his eyes swept over me. "And how are you, my sweet. So glad to have found you. And now, where all have you been? I've looked everywhere!"

He reached into his inside coat pocket while his eyes, glittery and moist, moved up and down my face, tasting me, drinking every bit of me. "What is this?" His finger roamed my cheek and my eye, which I could feel was drooping from tiredness. "Have you been sick?" I nodded. He closed my eyelid with the tip of his finger, then nuzzled my face, painting my cheeks and mouth with his mustache and kissing me where the mole on my cheek was my signature. "How I adore you," he whispered as his hand came up from his pocket, and he placed a small pistol on the seat beside us then handed me a piece of candy.

Chapter 24

*H*is carriage let us off at a hotel, and holding my arm tightly, sensing that I'd fly off at any chance, he forced me, pistol at the ready, up the stairs into the room where he had been staying, murmuring, "My sweet, my pretty." Then peeling away my tearoom dress, whispering, "Tes jolis yeux bleus, bleus comme les cieux, tes jolis yeux bleus on ravi mon âme," he raped me once, quickly, then again, slowly. My mind stiffened, disgusted, and then morphed into a cold-eyed slant, vowing a plan of escape. Remembering my vow of so many months ago: My holy of holies, at least this part of me could never be sold. I chanted the promise to myself over and over.

In the evening, he took me to dine to a place of fine food and dance and talk, but he would not let me be alone for even one second or be at any distance from him. He held me by the top of my arm, squeezing it in a silent message, while at the same time speaking in a civil tone: "Yes, thank you, that table there. That would be fine. And my young friend here would like Châteauneuf-du-Pape and pâté de foie gras."

He even paid a coat-check girl to go with me to the powder room and then escort me back, straight to him. And such noticeable pride he took in the admiring eyes that followed me across the room.

That night, if he slept, I couldn't sense it. He kept his fingers around my arm or his arm across me. And every time I rose to stand up, he sat up. "Quelle heure est-il?"

And I answered him, telling the time of night, as though I had no other intention.

I have never been so gripped with terror: never sleeping, listening only to his breathing, hoping to hear it take on the rhythm of deep sleep. And keeping my good ear tuned to his every movement, I turned away from him, pretending to be asleep myself, even breathing in long intakes as though I were deeply sleeping, exhausted, with my hands spread over the edge of the mattress, gripping the bed linen with my fingers while the smell of his skin now rose from my own arm and thigh and breast where it had been rubbed in. Hanging on, I lay coldly, sweating lest he think I was awake and he would become aroused again. Fear ate me from the inside. I was like an animal, caged, lying without moving, listening to carriages passing in the street, the whistle of a train, the sound of conversation under our window: "Tomorrow then," "Yes. Take care of yourself," "Until then, adieu and good-night"—voices in a normal world as remote now as in a foreign place.

The next morning, as I was dressing, he came to pet me, moving his tongue up the back of my neck and touching my dress. "This won't do. First thing, we'll get something else made for you." He then told me he had eight more days there doing business—apparently selling war bonds and arranging to slip the Union's blockade to deliver cotton to Europe. And then, "We will go back by train. O, little Eliza, I will find you the most beautiful house in New Orleans. And it will be ours. Ours alone. Tell me about this. Tell me how you were hurt here?" He ran his finger over my eye, still drooping slightly from the fatigue of no sleep.

"Nothing really," I explained. "It does this only when I am tired. Very tired."

"Ah, then, you sleep, and I will watch."

As much as I feared to, I did; and upon waking, I saw him sitting in a chair watching me.

It was a few hours later as I was standing in the dress-maker's shop, being measured, while he sat a short distance away, his eyes licking me, that I talked my shoulders into easing back and, by steely determination, melted the ramrod stance in my spine, and I said as softly and normally as I could, "I'm looking so forward to going back." And then I forced my eyes to meet his, and smiled.

Through that day, that first day of the next seven, he never let me out of his sight. I went to every business meeting with him, sat through hours of bankers and cotton brokers talking with him, and to make it seem normal that I could be with him, he transferred his business meetings from offices to cafés where I could be at the table with him and others without it seeming a strange arrangement. Elsewhere a woman would be out of place at a business meeting.

We rode through the parks in his carriage, and he bought me a fur coat for the sudden chill that fell over the city, dropping a light snow. And jewelry. He plied me with flowers and gifts, but back in our hotel room, he was too much onto my skills to accept a tea that I made for him. Instead, he called for tea to be sent up. Even though he did not have full knowledge of my wildcrafting skills for which I had become renowned during the early months of the war, he knew of my mother's skills, enough to distrust my fixing anything for him to eat.

Alas, my wildcrafting bag was of no use. And much to my horror, I discovered that my prized protection against him had been left at the Higgins's house, back in the kitchen when I had been trying to duplicate it for those poor girls so at risk there. And in my haste, I had not repacked it.

I was horrified at the thought. Even more so when I counted up and realized that I was at my most susceptible time. I recalled the scratching of dates on the walls of the closets back at Madam Francine's as my mother and others kept count of their times of when they were most susceptible, writing dates in their dressing rooms of the days they bled and the days two weeks afterward, as though keeping track might keep at bay the most feared result. I calmed myself only by thinking that if the worst of the worst happened, I would resort to my remedies. My belief in my remedies was the only way I could keep sensibly calm.

And then on the 3rd day and the 4th and the 5th, I saw him relaxing his hold. Not that he stopped gripping my arm when we went out, or that he left me in the room alone, but that he would tilt his head when I talked sweetly, as if he were beginning to believe that I might indeed have had a change of heart. And that the one whose lips he had read at the St. Louis Cathedral on the day he killed the poor man from Savannah might not have been me. Not this me. Not this one who stood before him in my new azure velvet with fur cuffs, so widely hooped that he had trouble getting close (the exact intention). That perhaps I no longer wished him to die, die, die, but to actually take me to New Orleans to live with him. "To be his only," as my mother had said.

On the 8th day, we went to the park. It was a fine, mild February afternoon. And as there was a band playing, and I happened to look over and see the cavalry officer who had been a classmate of Bennett McFerrin, I nodded, and the officer looked shocked—obviously wondering if it was really me, the one he had spoken to on the street. And his eyes would not leave me, and I nodded, and seeing him, the father-devil himself took hold of my arm to lead me away. But "O no," I said. "I must speak to him. It is only someone I met on my travels. Just a hello. A brief hello." And before he could hold me tighter, I pulled away and walked sedately to speak to the one who was now walking to meet me.

"You're staying here?" he asked. And "Yes," I said, "my father came on business, but we will leave soon." His eyes were drinking my new state of dress, and I have to admit, I was looking as fine as I had ever looked or could look.

"I still think you have," I said coquettishly, "at least one funny story about Captain McFerrin."

He laughed. "I guess I do. If you see him, ask him about Jackson's fifth lesson, the one we relieved him of." He chuckled.

All the while, I could feel the father-devil's eyes on my back. I turned and nodded at him. And then, as sweet as you please, I walked right back to him as though that was where I wanted to be above all others.

"How fine, my dear. How fine you look," he purred, taking

my arm when I was within a few feet of him.

Yes, it was a fine rehearsal. It was just enough to sweep a clear path through his stranglehold. For when the band struck up, and the crowd moved 'round, I hurried to be in among it, and he loosed his arm, following me. He let me be a few steps from him, and to the loud opening notes of a cheerful marching tune, I slipped into the crowd and was gone.

She hurried to the wharf, scurrying, having planned this, so that into her petticoats she had tied her steamboat ticket, the one she'd bought on the day she'd seen Quashi, and a few herbs to restart wildcrafting.

Thank you, thank you, hoop and all.

She pants and laughs, trying to ease the fear, glancing back, but going on, on as fast as she dares, her feet fairly skipping, so as not to draw attention to herself. She steps onto the ramp of the transport filled with infantry and war goods: ammunition, guns, cannon, cages of chickens, barrels of flour. She gives up her ticket and hurries inside. The boat will not leave for another hour, an hour in which she has to hide, though there are boats docked going to Memphis and farther south. Hopefully, if he begins searching steamboats, he will least suspect the one going to Clarksville. Why in the world would she ever want to go to Clarksville, no doubt he would think.

She finds a corner where she sits down, and puts her hands over her ears to dampen the hum of men's voices and the purring of roosting birds, then lowers her face into her lap and breathes, whispering over and over, *"Please don't find me. Don't. Go off. Go off into your putrid, wicked life, father-devil."*

But a moment later, I was coldly thinking, actually trying to answer myself on how and why it was that I was feeling this: for how strange to be wishing death to one, who at another time I might have said I loved—if indeed love is what I would have called it.

The boat whistles, shoves off, rocks into the center of the river and steams toward Clarksville. She comes up on deck only after a long while, where she sees the sun about to set behind a ridge of pine trees, the tops blushed pink. The evening is unseasonably warm, and she takes off her coat.

She breathes deeply, taking in a delicious taste of air. Putting her arm around her waist and squeezing, she whispers: *My holy of holies, never again but over my dead body will I let this happen.*

Chapter 25

All during the trip, she sits in a corner on the deck, her grand coat pulled up over her, and her arms crossed, dodging the whispers of, "Where you going, miss?" "Mind if I ..." She waves them away, soldiers trying to tease her into conversation, then mumbles, "Sick, sick, go away," and pulls her coat up higher. She tucks her chin against her chest and wraps her arms around herself.

My own skin now had taken on the sweet cherry tobacco smell of his, and I knew it would be there until I could wash. And O! How strangely did I breathe it in, reliving sweet childhood's memories mixing now with the sharp-edged acknowledgment of my own naivety—my girlhood dreaminess. Stupid, dummy girl!

She coughs, pinches her nose, closes her eyes. *My holy of holies ...* And as the steamboat pulls into the Clarksville harbor, she does not get up but instead waits, wanting to be among the last disembarking. Yet unlike she expected, the infantry does not form companies and move off. She realizes they must be going farther up the river, most likely to Fort Donelson. Soon a steamboat employee moves down the deck crying, "Clarksville, Clarksville!" Only then does she put her coat over her arm and walk down the ramp into the small city.

She stiffens, listening. Something is wrong here. Strangely, the streets are empty. There can be no great army here. She rushes into a café to order breakfast and to hear news. When the café owner comes to serve her, she quickly asks, "General Pillow's army—is it close by?"

The café owner scans her dress, his eyes drinking her face, her gray velvet hat, her grand coat, her bright-colored dress. She can read his thoughts as he filters them: *An officer's wife? Or one of those other ones?* Then, *one of those other ones* registers in his glance. And he answers, "What's left of it. All those that ain't sick's gone to the fort."

"Fort Donelson?" She watches his suspicious eyes.

"That's it."

"How do I get there?"

His brow furrows. "Across the river. You'll have to take a ferry. Then a coach to Dover. But I doubt one's running. A few days ago Fort Henry in Kentucky fell. We hear the Union Army's now on the way to Donelson. S'why Pillow went there."

"But where is the rest? The rest, I mean, of Pillow's army?"

"West of town—a good way."

"And many men are sick there?"

"Mmhmm, outbreak of measles. And 'course all the other stuff."

Yes, all the other stuff. Of course he would think that she knows all about the other stuff. Now she eases back in her chair. As soon as she eats, she will walk to wherever the ailing army is encamped, wildcrafting the fields on her way.

As she eats, to keep her eyes down she looks over the town newspaper. While reading the front page she laughs out loud, for the ordinances of the city are listed there in a column, and among them: * *No one shall shoot a pistol or gallop a horse. $1 fine for each. *Unlawful to strip and wash in the Cumberland River in daylight. $1 fine. * No steamboat to unload on Sabbath Day without permission from Mayor. $50 fine. *Persons keeping more than one dog shall pay a tax of $1 for each additional dog. *No negroes shall come to Clarksville on the Sabbath Day. If the constable should find an unusual assemblage of negroes, he should disperse them and punish them by inflicting ten lashes* *on each, if he deems it necessary.*

She stands up, rolls up the paper, pays her bill and heads to the door. Clearly, this is a very proper town, and the paper will make a suitable flyswatter if not a good reminder of how to stay out of trouble.

She breathes deeply, stepping onto the street.

I wanted to just hesitate, to take in the normal world of birdsong, loud and chatty. The day, so unseasonably warm, had fooled even the birds. And how good to be away from the father-devil! To be once again on my own, even with its nagging worries and dangers.

At a nearby store, she buys a bag. And while paying for it, feels the stare of the few townspeople who are there. And then back out on the street, she feels intently how too fine her dress is. It is especially wrong for where she heads now, walking west. Her heels tap on the brick street. Masonry houses line the road— two-story, well kept. Then a tall grand building, an academy for girls. Also a college for men, quiet and nearly empty. No doubt, all of age have enlisted. The city is small—maybe no more than five thousand—and yet so clearly prosperous.

In the distance, she sees the smoke bellowing from the foundry turning out ammunition and cannon, most likely the favorite cannon that the troops affectionately nicknamed Napoleon. The street turns into dirt, and she walks, carrying her heavy coat on one arm, her bag in the other, and now cuts across a field. She stops to pick herbs and grasses, putting them in her new bag, wiping her face with her sleeve in the unusual warmth of the February day.

Leaning over, close to the grass at a juniper bush, she snaps the bark and picks stems of leaves. From these she can extract savin. The thought of that is calming, for she will have now the means to do what she has to, if need be. The fear that she might be pregnant is a torment, flickering in her mind every waking minute. Suddenly behind her, she hears a man's voice saying her name, low and surprised, "Eliza? Eliza Goode?"

She turns. "Yes."

The hooves of the horse coming across the grass field have been muted by the turf, unheard. And now dismounting and walking toward her is Bennett McFerrin, his face wearing a look of curiosity and delight. "Eliza? I didn't expect to see—"

"Yes, me here." She smiles. The warmth of her relief, the feel of her brightening mood are like the swallow of a craved drink. She could almost fool herself: that her desire to find him has made him appear. So now she playfully adds, "I've actually been trying to locate you, thinking that ..."

But she hesitates, noticing that his face is so gaunt. Circles rim his eyes; his full beard now is unkempt, and his uniform is dusty and worn. There is a pink scratch across his left cheek. She pauses. "Have you been ill?"

"No. Just lacking sleep. I've been riding back and forth. One of the generals in command at the fort is my mother's cousin, General Buckner. He's taken to having me on his personal staff. So Pillow is loaning me out, you might say." He smiles and loosens the reins in his hand. His horse reaches down to eat grass. He adds, "But you are looking very well."

She ducks her head, ashamed as though marks of the previous week might be noticeable somehow. Then she looks up to meet his eyes. "Well, I myself ... I ... well; I've been thinking you might could recommend my wildcrafting skills. Because I hear ..."

"Yes. Most of the army is at the Fort. But for the rest ... there's been an outbreak of measles. Several hundred are encamped five miles from here. And Rissa too is unwell."

"Rissa? Where?"

"There. I wanted her to stay behind in Nashville, because I was there for a while. Most of the horses in my company came down with greased heels. We had to lay out for a month. But Rissa insisted on coming here with me." He shakes his head. "She's so stubborn. Once she makes up her mind on something, she won't budge, come rain or come shine." He accomplishes a halfhearted smile. "I've been in town looking for someplace to move her. She's too sick to go just now. She says it's just a slight cold. But—"

"Shall I see if perhaps I have something to ease her?"

"Would you?" His eyes mist. He looks away. Abruptly he pulls the reins of his horse, raising its head, stepping it closer. "May I?" He lowers his hand, gesturing for her to use it as a stirrup.

"Oh, but I can walk."

"But I don't want you to."

He still holds his hand, palm up, for her to step into. He looks at her steadily, silently.

Finally, when she does, he steps forward, leading his horse as she rides.

Rocking with the motion, seated as though on a chair and not a saddle, holding my hoop so it would not flip up the edge of my skirt, I felt as ridiculous as a doll made of glass and thin thread. But I felt safe, truly safe.

Suddenly she slides down, startling him and the horse, and walks beside him. She asks, "How long have you been here?"

"Three weeks. Before that in Kentucky. Rissa stayed there in a hotel in Sacramento. And then in Nashville. Now she and Lawrence are both here."

"And the fort is about to be attacked?"

"Yes. We hear this new general—somebody named Grant—is dead set on taking it, which means the Union would get control of the river. And we can't let that happen. We hear that this Grant has failed at everything in life and now has nothing to lose. Fights like a rabid dog. Won't let go. We hear that at Fort Henry he had a horse shot out from under him, then mounted another and slid it down a cliff and jumped it onto the steamboat to head here."

"When will you be going back?"

"As soon as I check on Rissa. Lawrence is good help, and there are other officers' wives who look in on her. But I want to move her to a hotel where some other wives are. But now ..." He stops and looks at her, his eyes studying her face. "Would you be so inclined as ... would you reconsider now ...?"

She nods yes, adding, "I'll be happy to, until she is well. Maybe it is just a slight cold, and she will soon be strong enough to move to town and be—"

"Eliza ...," he interrupts her. But for a moment he can't finish. "Thank you. I'll make good for your services. You needn't worry about that. As soon as I can come to you, I will. But you should also know, Rissa is ill. Very, very ill."

"Lawrence told me. When we were at Camp Corinth, he confided in me that his mistress was seriously ill."

He studies her face. "He did?"

She nods yes, but stays silent.

He then looks back at the road. "When the war broke out, she wouldn't stay home. She was so insistent on following the army! She was afraid we'd ... that we'd never again see each other."

"I gathered as much," Eliza whispers. Then she looks steadily at him, hoping to lift his spirits. "But then again, right now it could be just a cold."

"Yes. Let's hope you are right." His eyes meet hers.

"Yes. Let's think so."

The camp comes into sight. With his horse between them, he and Eliza walk among the tents where men are cooking. She reads the heavy gloom of sickness—the *lobo gris* of an adversary against which there is only luck and no weapons. Ordinarily, a makeshift band would be playing; men would be immersed in card games and stirring about. But here now, all seems set in slow motion, every tent an infirmary.

He leads her near the back of the camp, next to woods. Three other tents here house officers' wives, their fine furnishings seen through the open flaps. Two of the wives are taking walks, dressed almost as elegantly as Eliza. Outside Rissa's tent, Lawrence has built a cookfire and stands over it, making soup. Silently he and Eliza nod, exchanging greetings, and then Ben holds the tent flap open, leaning inside, calling cheerfully, "Rissa, look who I found!"

Standing beside him, Eliza sees inside: Rissa lying on a cot, white bedclothes and gown swirling around her. The smell of menthol and sickness is heavy. Rissa lifts herself on her elbows and squints at the raised tent flap where a wedge of daylight comes in. "Who?" Her hoarse voice breaks. She grabs at her bedclothes, wet with sweat. She squints harder. "Can you believe this infernal weather? Whoever heard of summer in the month of February?" And then, "Who, Ben? Who is this?"

Ben moves to kneel by her cot. "Eliza, Eliza Goode. You remember Eliza. She has come to help treat the outbreak of measles. She might find a treatment for your cold. And best of all, Rissa, she is willing to stay. She will be here all night, as long as you need her."

Rissa's lips tighten, then she says loudly, "I *don't* need her."

She sits up more, her arms trembling with the effort. Ligaments in her neck strain. "I don't want her! Not in this tent. Not anywhere near. No. Not her. No. Ben, how could you?"

"Shhh." He brushes her hair back from her forehead.

Eliza slips out, closing the tent flap behind her.

There, standing among the tents, I heard first Rissa's hoarse voice, and then Ben's low soothing one, sounding as oddly startling to my ear as if I had come upon a glance of my own face in a mirror, for in their exchange, I could not only hear and see, but feel my life, my whole intended life. "How can you expect ... be with ... what she is. Don't you know?!" *And then the low-toned rebuttal:* "But just a little while, until you are better. And can ... she is steady and knows ...," "Yes! Many and much. A million reasons never to be seen with her. No. No. I won't have it! Never have it! Get her out of here, Ben, far away. And don't ever ask again." *The words disappeared in coughing.*

When Ben came out of the tent, Eliza looked away. She felt his eyes silently avoid her. She saw that he was at a profound loss for words, so quickly, she spoke for him. "Another time, then. I have much to do," she said, sweeping her hand toward the infirmary tents. "And now, excuse me. I must hurry to get to work." She walked away.

That night she slept on a cot in the infirmary's cook tent. The medical officer on duty was more than happy to have her. Her miraculous treatment of the soldier prior to Manassas was still a favorite fireside story, so she was eagerly welcomed.

Yet in the night, a bitter cold blew through. Snow fell, waking her with its wind and damp coldness. She got up and worked throughout the rest of that night and the next day, until three o'clock, when in the afternoon, the sound of cannon firing far down the river stilled everyone—the sick men, the others milling about, the entire camp. They stood, frozen in the first horrifying moments of realizing the battle had begun.

Eliza rushed outside the tent to listen harder.

The trees, covered now in an icy armor, seemed otherworldly. The ground, dusted with snow, seemed to tremble. And then suddenly, she and all those who were able, rushed feverishly, trying to find what they knew they could never find: adequate room for the coming wounded.

At dusk, Eliza stood listening toward the direction of the river. The camp was as ready as it could be to receive the wounded. There must have been many lying on the battlefield. The sound of cannon fire had ceased. With night coming on, it had become a battle of rifle fire. The covering of snow seemed to muffle all, yet amplify the anxiety from lack of news.

The next day, the sounds of battle began again. The thought of what was happening on the other side of the river made her so restless that she paced about the camp, tending to the sick, impatiently.

Why were the wounded not yet coming? What was happening that they had no news? Ben, what was happening to Ben?

Nervously, she glanced at the tent where Rissa lay. Lawrence obediently prepared her meals, going in and out regularly, frantically keeping his cookfire going despite the wet ground and wind. At dusk, unable to bear much longer the lack of news, Eliza saw at the far end of camp a supply wagon pulling out. She ran toward it, waving her bag. "I have tourniquets here. Can I ride with you? You can drop me off where I might can help."

The driver of the team nodded. It was easy to read his thoughts: that she'd be good company, if nothing else.

She climbed up in the back with barrels of water and blankets. The draft horses slipped through the snow, their coats shaggy and thick, steam rising from their wide backs. They pulled the covered supply wagon across the river toward the Confederates' supply base, the little town of Dover. The hotel there was fronted by a swollen stream, its waters almost overflowing its banks, and on the bank closest to the city of Clarksville, a collection of townspeople had gathered, huddling around bonfires, eager to hear news and to see any part of the battle that they might glimpse.

There, where the supply wagon let me off, I sat on a tree stump and listened to the pop of rifle fire. The air was heavy with something ominous, like a mad beast, just beyond where we were. I expected to see, any minute, riders and infantry coming. But dark fell, and I could not bear to leave, fearing for Ben, fearing for all of them, eager too to be where I might help the first of the wounded to be brought out. Why were none coming? What was happening?

Flickers of lanterns were seen going in and out of the hotel. We could see that the Confederate generals had their headquarters there. All the uniforms going in and out were gray. But we were too far away to hear voices.

Townspeople batted about bits of news, one saying that yesterday he had heard the Rebels cheering—that the battle was theirs. But by daybreak, it had raged again in deafening gunfire. "It can't hold." Another declared, "Not against the god-a-mighty force this damn Blue-coat's brought. Enough Yankees to fill an ant nest. Fort's made of crude stockade. Not made to hold." I walked among them, catching bits of what might indeed be the situation. "Pshaw, it's gonna be another Fort Henry. And mark my words, damn Yankees will take over our town and then head toward Nashville quicker than a hound-bitch after a coon." "Shhhh."

Suddenly in the dark, we could hear the splashing of horses coming across the creek. It was close to insane, the way the riders were plunging their horses through the swollen stream, the water so deep that in the meager moonlight and lights from our warming fires, we could see the water sloshing up to the saddles. They were riding two by two, double. It seemed that each cavalry member had pulled up behind him a foot soldier and was now riding furiously across the stream. In the frosty air, the horses' breaths puffed gray-white in the dark. And then I saw who I instinctively knew was Bedford Forrest leading them, so large, bigger than all, riding in controlled fury, hastening his men on. Behind him must have been his own slaves—about eight—riding with bags of oats held high up on their shoulders. As the horses reached the far side of the creek, they slipped and slid up the bank and then onto the icy road. As the last passed near where I was, I heard a high surprised call. "Miz Eliza, Miz Eliza!" I stepped closer, sliding on the snow, and saw that it was Quashi riding double with one of the escaping Confederates. "Quashi!" I called, my voice hanging for only an instant in the dark cold.

Shortly after, white flags appeared at the hotel, and we heard the sound of a bugle. At daybreak we watched, stunned and silent, at both Union and Confederate soldiers mingling across the lines and then at what we realized must be the Union general, the one we'd heard was Ulysses S. Grant, ride toward the hotel, his horse's hooves cracking the icy road. He dismounted and went into the hotel. I, as well as those around me, realized now: The battle was over. The Confederates had surrendered. The dead and wounded lay, waiting. I ran up the bank, knowing soon now an ambulance wagon would come and I would be at work. I would ride the first one that came out of the fort back to the camp.

Inside the fort, some fourteen thousand Confederate soldiers waited chivalrously, waited patiently, to be sent north as prisoners of war. And among them was Ben. Only later would I learn this. Only later would I learn too that my own life was to be captured—but in a most unexpected way. For in my captivity, I would be set free.

Chapter 26

Cold, exhausted, Bennett McFerrin waited for hours near the Dover Hotel as one of Buckner's aides. He put the reins of his horse over his arm and took off his gloves and reached into his saddlebag to pull out a scrap of paper and a pen. *Sir, if you will allow me to ride into Clarksville to find someone to care for my seriously ill wife, I shall report back as your prisoner.*

—Captain Bennett G. McFerrin CSA

When Grant walks by, Ben hands the note to one of the general's staff. The general turns. Perhaps the sorrel horse catches Grant's attention as much as anything else. Bennett nods. Their eyes meet. The general holds out his hand, and the aide puts the note in the palm of Grant's glove.

Ben watches, chewing his lip, pulling his gloves back on, then stands stiffly as a courier comes back with a note.

Request granted.

Now he rides, alone, fast, down past Dover, across the Cumberland, slipping on the ice and jumping muddy frozen ruts, up the bank toward Clarksville, in and among ambulance wagons and spectators walking, who, for three days, have watched the battle from a safe distance. Up the bank onto the street that then turns onto the brick main street, he rides, trotting, where now people are rushing out of their houses, evacuating the city before the Yankees come.

Slaves load belongings onto carts and into carriages. People are frantically rushing from their houses and climbing into buggies and wagons. Goats and fowl skitter loose in the streets. The voices of shouting people and the brays of alarmed animals mix in a tuneless din.

Soldiers from both sides carry wounded up the hillside to the city's hospital, where patients, previously confined, now pitifully hobble or are wheeled out to find care elsewhere. Cobblestones and brick are splash-dotted with blood. Ben rides up and down, stopping people along the way to ask for a place where he might take his wife to be looked after.

Eliza is back at the camp now. Looking up while carrying bandages into one of the infirmaries, she catches sight of the sorrel horse galloping toward the camp, Ben sitting forward to urge for speed. She stands, watching, breathing deeply, then letting go.

He has survived. He is here now.

But instead of going straight to Rissa's tent, he comes straight to her, dismounting at the edge of camp and walking quickly toward her, leading his horse. His eyes wear a frantic look. His clothes and horse are spattered with mud, his beard frozen in twisted clumps and his eyebrows dotted with ice. "You must," he begins, then stops, then starts again. "Please, will you? You must help us now."

"Of course." I nodded and followed him to where he stopped outside Rissa's tent. He motioned Lawrence to him. And there he explained what he had managed to arrange. With such a frantic sense of desperation throughout the city, his desire for a place for Rissa had actually been quickly agreed to, since so many houses were being abandoned.

"I found a place," he began, "the house of a colonel who has been seriously wounded and is being carried back to be nursed there. He has agreed to let Rissa be there too. You will be able to stay and have help. And Lawrence, there's a place for you on the grounds where you can help Eliza as she looks after Rissa. Do you understand?"

"Yes." Lawrence nods.

"Eliza, I will pay you in time. Do you trust me?"

"Of course. Although ... will she let me?"

His face was so tensely held; I could see muscles grind in his jaw. And he never took his eyes from mine. "Please don't hold her recent outburst against her. I sense her objections were just a result of her fever. I know you are steadfast. I feel—I know— that you will be with her until—"

"Shhh. I promise. I won't leave her."

For a moment, neither of us spoke. Then he said, "I'm sure I won't be gone long. It is better that I am hidden away as a prisoner than at risk on a battlefield. I predict that as General Buckner's aide, I'll be sent with him. And he won't be held anywhere for long. The North is paroling prisoners quickly. They're in no mood to build prisons. So now, let's hurry. I can only stay to get Rissa settled. As an officer, I will be hunted down if I don't return according to orders."

I nodded and said, "Let me get my things and tell the medical officer."

He walked to Rissa's tent, calling, "Lawrence, bring up Rissa's carriage. Help me pack her things."

Soon after, Lawrence was driving the carriage, me sitting beside him and a sick and crying Rissa inside, while battle-worn Bennett McFerrin rode his horse alongside. At the thought of Ben's going back as Grant's prisoner, Rissa was inconsolable. His sense of honor she interpreted as abandonment. I could feel the three-way prong pressing on him: caught between her needs, his feelings for her, and his sense of honor. It pricked unrelentingly, bearable only by thinking that she was not herself but a captive of her fever. We pretended not to hear what came from the carriage window: her cries berating him for leaving her, leaving her to die.

She was the first to use the word. And as it escaped from the carriage window, it was like a shard of ice, suspended in air that, strangely, we dismissed as if it had gone unheard. But in that one moment, I think we all silently agreed never to use the word ourselves.

We drove through streets tangled with people fleeing, church bells ringing hysterically in alarm. At the Colonel's house, Ben lifted Rissa out of the carriage. Lawrence drove on to the stables, while I walked behind Ben as he carried Rissa gently up the steps and across the porch. Her white gown and blankets trailed over his arms in plumes of cotton. The hall, in its mix of confusion with the Colonel's wife and daughters hurrying back and forth from the outside kitchen to the Colonel's bedside, was a cacophony of voices. Two slaves rushed bloody bedsheets out the door.

"Here, this room, here. Put her here." The wife motioned to the second room on the second floor. I trailed Ben up the stairs, staying out of sight as Ben carried her so Rissa would not see me. I dreaded his leaving.

"Rissa ..." He lay her on the bed, whispering, and kissed her hair. "I will be back. I'll be back before you can finish reading, you know, the play we used to read together, from front to back, all the way through."

In her fevered delirium she began quoting, "And four nights will quickly dream away the time, and then the moon ..."

He nodded, smiling. "Yes, that's it. Keep thinking of it. By the time you read it and three others, I'll be here. And then, we'll go on, just as we have been."

I stayed back by the doorway. But he now motioned for me to come forward. Rissa's eyes were closed. She was clearly drifting off to sleep. The trip there had exhausted her, and she was so thin, so very thin. I should make her a soup, a hearty soup and quick.

"Do you know it?" he whispered to me, "A Midsummer Night's Dream?" We then listened to Rissa's fading sentence: "Awake the pert and nimble spirit of mirth."

"No," I whispered back, "but I know this one." I launched into the fractured epilogue of As You Like It, which, as children, Ned and I had been made to memorize and perform in the house where we were raised. "For the love you bear to women, Men, I charge you," and then I stopped, realizing and regretting that I knew only the parts that could carry innuendo. "... Like as much of this play as pleases you," I finished, and quickly added, "Sorry, I don't know more."

He raised his eyebrows and smiled. "Use this for now." He then put into my hand Confederate dollars, most likely all he had, and slipped out. My eyes lingered on his back as he went out the door, and I held on to the sound of his boots in the *stairwell as long as I could. I sat down.*

Desiring to stay out of the way of the family, bustling about while the dear, wounded Colonel fought for his life, I watched Rissa sleep. I looked out the window. The city was a mass of confusion, the clank of wagon wheels, the shouts of hundreds abandoning the city before it was occupied. Those Rebel soldiers who had been too sick to be part of the battle were now in danger of being captured and were fleeing with the townspeople.

I aimed my gaze far down the street, searching for a grassy area where might be herbs to strengthen a soup. Soon I would go to the kitchen to figure out how I would feed her. But for the moment, I wanted to savor what I had just witnessed: the sweet, genuine caring of Ben for Rissa, and wondered, what would one call that? What word could name that? When I couldn't alight on one, I focused on a new puzzle. For what would it be like to feel that—to be the object of that?

Wondering kept me occupied. Above all, I needed to steel myself for when she awoke. And as I did, the word for which my mind searched came to me in a bright light, one word, simple: devotion. That is what I knew I had witnessed. It was as foreign to me as a language I could not speak.

That night Eliza slept in a bed she made of two chairs to be near Rissa. At dawn, she was awakened by the sound of Rissa's hiss. "*You,* what are you doing here? How did you ..."

Eliza lit a candle so that she could be fully seen. "How are you? Better?" She felt Rissa's forehead.

"Where is Ben?"

"Gone for a while."

"When, *where?*" Rissa's questions, so blunt, seemed good evidence that her fever had lifted. Perhaps her current illness was, after all, only a cold and fever. It was then that Eliza filled in all that had happened in the last few days: the fall of Donelson, the thousands sent to Northern prisons, the house of the dying Colonel where they were now.

Rissa shook her head, refusing to believe what Eliza had told her. Then the Colonel's wife knocked on the door—a slender woman, a pale, lined face, her fingers twitching against her skirt, telling in a wavering voice that the Colonel had just died, and that she and her daughters were fleeing the city now. They had no desire to be there when the Yankee Army flooded the city, occupying it, as no doubt Grant's army would do in a matter of days. Rissa covered her lower lip with her teeth and sighed so deeply, her chest trembled.

"Go then. *Go!*" Rissa threw back the bedclothes and stood up. Her hair hung limply; her face wore the yellow shine of sickness. "But I ... I cannot go. I must stay here to wait for Ben. Lawrence and I will stay. But Eliza, not *you*. You must go. You are not needed. Go! Go!" Then to the Colonel's wife, "Will you be so *kind* as to *lease* me your house?"

"Stay as long as you like. But excuse us now. We must hurry." The Colonel's wife rushed out the door, leaving it open behind her.

Rissa slumped onto the bed, too weak to stand any longer.

Eliza walked out of the door and shut it loudly.

That was Monday. By the next day, Eliza had taken over the first floor. Alone, she walked the house, taking inventory of what was there that she might need. It was a grand house, a beautiful house, and growing very cold now with fires in every room to tend. A circular window in the front hall faced the street like a faceless clock. In the backyard she found chickens walking and pecking in the melted snow. There was a smokehouse filled with pork. Every few hours, she sent Lawrence up the stairs to check on Rissa, and by way of him, sent eggs and soups.

Tuesday morning, a white flag had been raised over the city. On Wednesday, after sending Rissa up her breakfast, Eliza stood at the window in the main parlor of the grand house and looked out at the street as General Grant rode past on his dark bay horse, his staff around him. By evening, the town was fully occupied, a General C.F. Smith in charge. Union solders now camped in open spaces and stood guard on every corner. Many had come down with pneumonia and typhoid fever and were placed in houses all around the city.

Thursday, Eliza opened the door to the knock of a Union sergeant who announced he was requisitioning the house for eight of Grant's sick officers. "I wouldn't advise it," Eliza said, refusing to step back. "There is a woman upstairs with smallpox. She is the only reason we ourselves have not fled. I can't guarantee that your men won't catch it."

That was enough of a deterrent so that Eliza watched the sergeant quickly turn and walk off, remount his horse and ride away.

But later, he was there again. And Eliza was startled to hear him knocking, standing on the porch. She opened the door only a crack as though there were a dangerous disease inside that she should not let out. "Yes?"

His request was blunt, his eyes blazing a threat. "I want to see this sick lady."

Eliza leaned into the space that she held open and said firmly, "I assure you it is the truth. This would be no house you would want for your sick soldiers. They would die here in quick order, for sure."

"I want to see for myself." He put his hand on the door and pushed against it.

There was nothing now to do but let him in and lead him upstairs. So she walked slowly up ahead of him, feeling the heat and bulk of his presence close behind her. And as she climbed each step, she called out, "Mrs. McFerrin, a Union officer here wants to meet you. I have told him you are a victim of smallpox, but he doubts your diagnosis and needs to see for himself. Are you dressed, dear? Let us know, please."

In that way, Eliza had him stand in the hall outside Rissa's closed door. Not knowing exactly what would be her next move, she suddenly heard Rissa reply, her voice weak but forceful: "Bring him in. Let him see for himself my wretched sores. We tell only the truth in this house."

Eliza whispered: "Her husband was taken prisoner. We haven't heard from him since. She is quite unbalanced with worry, but it is also her fever. If she lives, she will most likely be mad."

That, she thought, would give him hesitation if not provoke fear. But his jaw was set. Clearly, he wanted the house and knew she was lying to keep it. He put his hand on the handle of his saber and pursed his lips. "Open the door."

Eliza pushed open Rissa's door and there Rissa lay, her head resting heavily on the pillow. The look of her indeed made the statement that she was very sick, yet there were no obvious signs of smallpox. For a moment there was a reluctance for any of them to move or speak; the lie spoke for itself. Then suddenly Rissa sat up and pulled a pistol from under the covers and pointed it at the soldier's chest.

"I am ill and don't you doubt it. I have leased this house, and I intend to stay here with no one intruding. I will be here until my husband is released from your damn putrid prison. Furthermore, if you don't get out of here, I'm going to blow your *shitty* head off." As punctuation, she aimed the pistol at the ceiling and fired a shot.

Plaster fell, dribbling across the rug and her bed linens. The soldier flinched. He furrowed his brow. Perhaps to him a wife gone mad was as strong a deterrent as the shot she had fired. Eliza whispered, "I warned you she was out of her head. I assure you, though, this house is contaminated for sure."

He turned. "When she dies, I'll be back. And madam, if there is no good reason you have kept this house from us, you'll be charged with treason."

Startled, but refusing to reveal it, "Yes, of course," Eliza whispered. She then led him downstairs to the door and locked it behind him. Quickly, she ran back up.

Rissa brandished the pistol and put it on the table beside her bed. "Ben gave me this when we left home. I guess now I've pretty much ruined the ceiling. Do you think the Yankees will leave us alone?"

"Probably not. But you play the part of a madwoman so well, I predict we can pull off an encore."

Rissa covered her face with her hands and laughed. Eliza laughed too, picking up pieces of broken plaster. "I'm glad you didn't use French," she said. "I doubt he would have gotten the point if you'd said he had a 'merdeux' head instead of a shitty one."

On Friday, Eliza went into the outdoor kitchen to make breakfast and instantly saw that someone had entered the smokehouse and stable. The stored meats that she counted on had been taken. The horse that had pulled Rissa's carriage was gone. And by the end of the week, so was Lawrence.

Chapter 27

*D*ear One,

    This is where my story changes.

Name it a kind of lust to be who I was not. Name it a desire for power. For when Rissa's and my shared success in rebuking the Yankee Occupier turned out to be so short-lived by dissolving not a whit of the distance between us, I forcefully took charge. She returned to her old impatient, fever-ridden disdain and, in a fit of ill anger, told me to leave, leave! Go away, that she preferred Lawrence to meet her needs, and I said, "All right then, I am gone."

All morning I stayed downstairs, hearing her most desperately call, 'Lawrence, Lawrence! Are you there? I need you!' And I would say nothing—just stand still and say nothing.

I let her hear only the ticking of the hall clock and its chiming. I let her hear the click of my footsteps on the hall floor and not ever answer when she called, "Who is there? Is someone there? Please answer. Please!" Alone, I let her feel what gripped the city, the reality of occupation that spewed strangeness and fear. Outside, there was the movement of Union soldiers, the sound of their horses, the sound of their voices, the clank of their swords. And throughout it all, I said nothing. I let her hear the floors creak, the doors shut, the branches blow against the window glass in winter gusts. I let her feel the abandonment of the grand old house as I walked through it, ghostlike.

When I felt she was asleep, I took the soups I made from potatoes I found in the cellar and left them by her bedside.

And then, as I knew it was likely to happen, she called out one morning, "Lawrence, Lawrence!" in a shrieking so pitiful, I knew it was time. I called back up: "He is gone."

"Gone where?"

"Run off." I said it in a disguised voice that I hoped she would not attribute to me.

I stood at the bottom of the stairs, calling up my answers in a calm, but foreign voice, while I myself did not move.

"Who? Who are you?"

"No one."

I then went to the dining room where there was a tea service. The Yankees had not yet looted inside the house—only the grounds. I was steeping a tea from wildcrafted leaves that I had dug out of a nearby field under melted snow.

And as I predicted she might, she did: She came haltingly down the stairs, afraid to see who she might see. And there I was. I did not say her name. And she did not say mine.

She walked closer to me, across the grand rug to the dining table. And I said only, "I have always heard it is never wise to travel in the early months of a pregnancy." I held out to her a cup of tea.

"Yes. I have heard that too." She then took the tea but did not sit down. She drank, standing up. "Indeed, that is my greatest sadness, that I was never with child." And then the meaning of what I had said seemed to finally strike her. She looked at me, stunned.

I said, using a voice as flat as a rail tie, "Therefore, I have decided it is better for me to stay."

For a long while, she seemed to drink the words that I had said. Then, "You, then?"

"Yes. But I know how to end it." I turned and looked at her, holding her eyes by my own, woman-to-woman, which erased *the most base barrier between us with my next simple question,* "*Should I?*"

She stared at me in silence. She turned, and while she left my question unanswered, she half-crawled, half-pulled herself back upstairs.

For ten days, a potion made of savin sat on the dining room table. Rissa came downstairs for breakfast, then went upstairs to rest, and Eliza went to the outside kitchen, then back to the house, fixing meals, hauling firewood, keeping both Rissa's room and hers as comfortable as possible. The silence between them was like a taut-drawn sheet, yet always they each were glancing at the untouched glass, there on the table, waiting. Eliza knew only that Rissa was well enough to leave her room. To Eliza it seemed that her news had so shocked Rissa that she was jolted into a state of revival—and crisis.

Yet whenever Eliza sat down at the grand dining table, Rissa would not eat with her. The glass of abortifacient sat at the head of the table, passive, hugely present. "I must say, I feel so much *better*!" Rissa said two nights after Eliza told her the news, attired now in a day dress with her hair drawn up and pinned in an elegant twist, its sunlight color like maple wood mixed with ice.

Candlelight played on her face. She stood by the dining table. Eliza was halfway through her dinner of potato soup and biscuits made from a bag of flour she found in the cellar. Both women listened to the clink of spoon on fine china, then, "Where'd you learn to cook?" Rissa's voice was less cold now, with a hint of playfulness.

"Where I grew up."

Eliza lifts a spoonful of soup, then swallows. As the warm liquid makes its way down her throat, it is as if it washes loose a great welling of anger, anger unlike any she has known, rising from childhood, rising from running, rising from being owned and hunted and raped, from being cloistered with this spiteful woman whom she has promised to nurse and never leave. Never leave! How can she stay with one who so clearly despises her presence? Spilling over the rim of her lip, the anger surfaces in a clipped, hard sound that startles even her.

"No, not anything like you. Not like you at all. But still, no less. I may be less wellborn, less well-off, less educated, but I am still no less than you. And from now on, you will treat me with all the respect I am due!"

"Good heavens!" Rissa grabs a chair for balance. "Eliza, if we weren't caught in these extreme circumstances, we would never be *seen* in the same room. We can't erase what you are nor the differences between our stations."

"Stations! God help you, Rissa. There are no stations! Look! Practically the whole town has fled. We are in an occupied city. There are only Blue Coats here—Yankees, some of whom, no doubt, would just as soon shoot or rape you as not. And you're worried about stations! This war—oh God, this damnable, putrid war. This silly argument between men who act as though it were sport while all the rest of us are caught between—it may never be over!"

"There. See. That's exactly what I mean—the coarseness of your speech. That's proof enough. If we have to be here together, that does not mean we have to be anything more than dependent on each other."

"Oh. So that's how you'd like to think of it! Well then, let's see if I fully comprehend your rules. For however long we are here, you will never feel that it is proper to sit down and eat with me? Hmm? What else? That we should never walk side by side. Never be seen together in public. Tell me how, Mrs. Bennett McFerrin, officer's wife, who is now completely dependent on me in this Yankee occupation—how else will you show your station? Shall we announce an open house, throw a party and you dance while I smooth your dress?"

Eliza abruptly stands up, pushing her chair against the table. There is a loud bang of wood against wood. Not since childhood has she had such an outburst, and she does indeed feel childish, even a stranger to herself. Yet the hot flow of anger is so invigorating, she shoves her chair up under the table with an even harder thrust.

Rissa bobbles; her teacup rattles. It falls off its saucer. She then falls too, gripping the edge of the table, unbalancing it. The glass of savin slides, toppling, and both women watch as it falls over the edge and breaks on the floor.

"Oh!" Rissa reaches, grabbing for a chair.

Quickly, Eliza bends to help Rissa up. Holding Eliza's hand, Rissa stands, exclaiming, "Oh, look what I have done! It's broken. It's gone! I'm sorry, Eliza. I'm really sorry." Then she becomes silent, looking at Eliza, keeping her eyes steadily on Eliza's face. "But then again, I'm not. I'm glad. Very glad. All along, I've *wanted* this to happen." She then settles herself in a chair and holds on to the table to steady her balance.

Eliza steps back. She reaches for a napkin and begins wiping up the mess. "It doesn't really matter. I can always make more. It's the decision that is hard to make."

"Eliza." Rissa pats the chair beside her. "Yes, please. Sit here. Don't look at me like that. A lot of what you've said *is* true. At a time like this, it is indeed silly for me to think about stations. What do appearances matter now? Besides," she says, laughing, waving her hand toward the windows, "who will see? As you say, streets full of Yankees? Detestable Blue Coats! What does any of what I said matter? The war changes everything."

Her face contorts with emotion. Light glows through her skin. "And now I want to say something. Something that I've been thinking very hard about. Will you listen?"

"Maybe."

"Well, maybe then you will hear ... " She smiles and her eyes look steadily at Eliza. "I don't care how it came to be ... or whose it is ... I just want to believe that there is a reason that this has come to you and me, here alone as we are now. I want to believe that I will survive. And that Ben will come back. Oh! I do believe this! Yet if it is only a dream, I don't want anyone to wake me. So, as I've been thinking, I'd like to say—if you will have this child, Eliza Goode, I would like to take it as mine; that is, if you would agree. I can't stop thinking that no one asking to be born in a time like this should be denied. No, never denied. We should help this little person, whoever it is. Out of contrariness, if nothing else, help it to be born."

Rissa's offer shocks Eliza, and softens her. She tilts her head in a questioning, playful way. "That last part—I like the way you put that last part. Actually, I've been thinking along the same lines, though not so eloquently. And I have certainly had no thoughts about giving the child away."

She then begins picking up the broken glass. And with

Rissa's admonishments, "Be careful, don't cut yourself," she walks to the back of the house and goes down the steps. Rissa follows, holding on to the wall to steady herself, saying, "I meant everything, Eliza. Everything I said. Ben and I would love that child. If you should ... will you at least think on it?"

Eliza answers back, "I will. And I realize you were generous in offering it. But let me first get used to the idea that I am to have a child."

Between the house and stable, Eliza chooses a muddy patch by a large tree that stretches leafless limbs over the ground. There she buries the broken glass and the last of the savin.

Rissa claps her hands. "Can you imagine! A baby, a baby. When, Eliza, this summer?"

"Fall. October, I think," Eliza replies, having counted up the weeks since Preston Cummings abducted her.

"Harvest time. What better sign that this life should *not* end, that Ben will be fine, that this war will soon be over? Yes, this baby is a good sign. Good."

Eliza takes Rissa's arm to help her back into the house, and as they go up the steps, she says, "I don't think we should pick out a name just yet. But a good-sign baby is something to think about. If it's a girl, I might name it Annie."

"And if it's a boy?" Rissa turns to look into Eliza's eyes.

"Easy."

"Ben?"

"Ben."

****

Over the weeks, all the hens that had been on the grounds around the house and stable had been boiled and eaten. But now Eliza discovers that other fowl are wandering loose over the city. In early morning, she searches out eggs in feed buckets, in flowerpots, in clumps of grass. She puts them in Rissa's soups and eats them herself, all the while moving back and forth from the kitchen to the house. So many chores are to be done that she can never stop, though often she doubles over with morning sickness, then straightens up to go on. Carefully, she and Rissa talk to each other, cradling in silence the sore tracks that their sharp words have cut in their memories. Conversation is filled by Rissa's need to calm herself about Ben, while concerns about herself and fading strength are caged in silence. She is still strong enough to sweep out the fireplaces. But keeping the fires going, doing laundry and feeding the both of them is Eliza's job. From early morning to noon, she walks across town, foraging.

As she walks to the fields to wildcraft herbs and roots, the occupying soldiers' eyes follow on her neck and arms and breast like pinpricks of heat. The owner of the house across the street, who had obviously stayed behind to protect his property, waves often to Eliza. And then, as she turns at the walkway one day, returning to the house, she doubles over with a sudden attack of nausea and hears behind her, "Can I help?" He quickly crosses the road and stands, hesitating to touch her, but his hand is reaching out.

"I'm fine. But thank you," she replies.

His boots, she notices, are shined to a high gloss.

Straightening up, she sees his round boyish face, his ruddy shaved face, his portly middle covered by a plaid wool coat, expensively tailored. He clicks his heels. "We have to keep up appearances, you know. Can't let the Yanks think we're riff-raff." Then, "Irving Lowry." He takes off his derby hat and bows slightly. "I met Captain McFerrin the day he was looking for a house for his wife. I suggested the Colonel's." He shrugs. His hair is dark and splays upward like thistle where his hat has lifted it. His eyebrows are wiry thick, reminiscent of caterpillars, and arch above lively green eyes. "At the time, mine was full of squawking women. You see, I am the elocution teacher at the Female Academy. Or, I was. As you probably know, it was taken over as a hospital—Rebels and Blue Coats lying wounded together. Now I ask you, isn't that the craziest—lying in peace after they've blasted each other half to death, but not before? I had no recourse but to move half the senior class here to my house."

He now holds out a bottle of milk. "But girls in panic. I just can't take girls in panic. So I sent them with my wife and daughters to Richmond. Now it's just me here, and I'm not about to abandon my house to the whims of an occupying army. I intend to watch over my property with all the energy I have. Now, I know you can use this. I should have brought over some before now. But my cow Esther has been put off—totally bumfuzzled. All the gun firing, you know. She's back now, calm and flowing. I wonder, have you heard from the captain?"

Eliza takes the milk. "Thank you. Thank you so much for this. And yes, finally, I can say yes. Mrs. McFerrin heard yesterday. A letter came. She tells me he is in a prison in Boston. That's all I know."

He nods toward the milk. "I have more than that to share. If I give you a slab of salted pork hidden in my cellar, can you make a stew of it and give a share to me? You see, I can't cook. I'm worthless in the kitchen. It's like I have a culinary malformation when it comes to preparing sustenance. In short, I'm not worth squat. But I know that Mrs. McFerrin needs the nourishment of meat."

"Well, I *would* be willing to do that." She nods and laughs, reading signs of good humor all about him.

He carries the side of pork, taking it to Eliza's kitchen, then walks home, reminding her to call him when dinner is ready.

"You needn't worry, Mr. Lowry," she calls behind him. "You'll be the first invited."

The rest of the day in the kitchen behind the grand house, she pulls down pots hanging from the rafters. Herbs, tied to strings, cross over the room, spicy and pungent. She stirs coals in the fireplace, bringing a roaring fire back to life.

How often the truth seemed in need of bending. And how much I seemed to have developed an appetite for feeling what might be new. New to be learned. Insatiable, in fact. For when the letter came that previous afternoon and Rissa read it, saying only in a shrieking voice, "He is in Boston Harbor! In Boston. In a prison where they took him and General Buckner. He is fine, Eliza! He is fine! And will soon come back to us!" I said only, "Yes, good. And thank goodness! Now at least we know."

But afterward, when Rissa was asleep, I pried loose the letter from her hand. Then read for myself: My Dear Rissa, I have just been served an acceptable dinner of boiled ham and Irish potatoes. You see, you needn't worry. I am fine. The ham was not so well seasoned, as Lawrence would serve, but still quite passable. I am being held in Fort Warren in Boston Harbor. Indeed, it is not a prison as you might expect. Colonel Dimick, who is in command, actually cried when he opened the cell for General Buckner to step into. I predict we will be well cared for and I will be back to you quicker than you can sing all the verses of Dixie. Which really is a fine tune, you know.

I miss you so much, my darling Rissa. The sound of your voice in my memory comes to me with the lapping of water against the wall just outside my window. So that I can (with some concentration, in shutting my eyes) fool myself by thinking you are just outside, talking, telling me delightful things as you always do, and it is only that your words are muffled. Do you remember us at seventeen? On the evenings of cornhuskings? You would sit beside me as my chosen partner and then—O, my darling Rissa, if I could only hold you as I did then. I delight in remembering how you would jump and blush when we would come upon an ear of red corn—a sign that then according to the game's rules, I could steal a kiss. Amuse yourself with this, because now that I am in prison, where always one is expected to confess, I may as well disclose that whenever you pretended to be affronted at my stealing a kiss, I could tell that it was willingly given. My darling Rissa, I long always to be your thief.

Ben

Eliza tucks the letter back into Rissa's hand. *So,* she thinks, *he is as good a liar as I.* For no doubt he is suffering hardships that they cannot imagine. And if, when Rissa awakes she asks if she has stolen a glance at Ben's letter, Eliza will not hesitate to answer, "Of course not."

Chapter 28

News ran through town that Nashville had fallen. Newspapers told that the governor had left the statehouse and took the train to Memphis and declared it the new capital. The Nashville mayor met the Union Army marching from Fort Donelson and quickly surrendered the city.

Now there is a Federal line from Clarksville down through Tennessee, and no one can travel to or from the cities without a pass.

Soldiers stand guard at all roads. To Eliza, the feel of occupation is like soaked cotton squeezed between every building in the little city, soaked in whispers of uncertainty and choked threats. Every day the reins are tightened. No one goes outside except when necessary. The only businesses staying open are those whose owners are willing to take the oath of allegiance to the Union. Eliza burns a single candle in Rissa's window all night, thinking it is a sign to the occupiers that the ill woman is still there and a deterrent to taking the house.

A boarding house for Federal officers' wives opened on a side street and was quickly filled. A Colonel Bruce from Kentucky took over, in charge of the city now. Some called him a black-hearted abolitionist. Those sympathetic to the Union kept their mouths shut. Federal troops vandalized the college for young men. As hundreds of soldiers stood guard in and around the city, a teenager would occasionally call the occupiers Blue Snakes and throw a rock and run. Two bawdy houses opened up near the railroad, servicing the occupiers who chose to use them. The women there slept during daytime, and otherwise stayed mostly out of sight. If Eliza passed one on the street, she viewed her sympathetically, once even helping a young woman pick up grocery goods she dropped, hoping no one was nearby to witness her gesture, nor guess at where her kindness came from.

The citizens who were left began to take on a shape of their own, faces and names that Eliza began to know: Thomas, Gertie, Irving, Lucinda, Whitworth, Sarah ... each wearing lined faces of anxiety, swallowing stifled feelings, wondering if they could outsmart illness and starvation, or be accidentally shot. Rarely did any share, or even disclose, what foodstuffs or medicines they hid, for fear of needing them themselves. Sometimes, one would invite Eliza to church, where, since some Union soldiers attended, the tension between the occupied and the occupiers was like a plucked tightwire that felt far from Christian. Always Eliza declined those invitations, saying she couldn't leave Captain McFerrin's ill wife, which conveniently led to the belief that she too was an officer's wife. After all, that lie was one she could comfortably walk in, going to and from the fields to wildcraft, crossing the town for some item at a store. Who was she? Let them guess.

Yes, she was the pregnant wife of some imprisoned officer, especially as her girth expanded with the child inside her. No other time but during war and occupation could a woman in her state be seen out walking, especially alone. Hunger, survival, necessity were her nods of permission.

Near the river, a shantytown grew of slaves who had run away to be under the protection of the occupying army. Contraband, the Union called them. And their numbers grew, banding together with their warming fires like decorations outside their shacks. Dependent on food that the Union soldiers gave them, they soon ventured onto adjacent streets, begging. Along the wharf where the steamboats docked, the Federals took over the warehouses to store their army's supplies. And it is there that Eliza soon found she needed to go. Although her wildcrafting supplied vitamins and minerals, and Irving shared all he could, Eliza is desperate for fruit, flour, soup bones—protein and nutritious foods that she could feed Rissa, who seems to follow a cycle of weakening and reviving every few weeks. All of the Confederate money that Ben had given her is gone. The town is using Union money now, anyway.

Walking along the wharf, Eliza has plans to get those things which she knows her body and Rissa require. Wearing the fur coat that Preston Cummings had bought her, buttoned tightly, and the velvet dress sashed loosely underneath, she walks lightly, quickly. Her hair is coiled on top under one of Rissa's hats with a veil pulled over the upper part of her face.

She notices a supply officer loading a bag of flour onto a cart. And he calls, "Looking for someone?" She sees him studying her with the red-gold tint of lust rising from him.

"No." She lingers. "But looking for something. A side of beef. cornmeal, a bag of flour." She opens her hand. Rissa's sapphire brooch sparkles in her palm. This was one Rissa had chosen, the least of her favorites.

He smiles crookedly. Then winks. Rangy, not more than thirty, he has a handsome face: blue-black mustache, dark liquid eyes, an alluring grin. He takes off his gloves and with long, expressive fingers takes the brooch from Eliza's hand, looking at her face as much as at the gem. "That I can do. I've seen you before. This is a nice piece, but not quite enough for what you ask for. What other way can you pay me?"

His eyes squint suggestively.

"None."

"No?" He tilts his head.

"No," she says firmly.

"Well, then. How much flour do you think that little pin is worth?"

"Two bags. And a side of beef."

"Oh, my! You drive a pretty hard bargain." He draws out the word *pretty,* his eyes licking her. "I can't spare beef. I have an army to feed, or maybe you know."

"A soup bone, then. Two."

"Two?"

"Yes, two and no less."

"I'll have to see if we have two to spare. How big?"

"Big. As big as you've got."

"So, you like it big?" He grins, goes into the warehouse, and she calls after him, "And any newspapers that you can spare."

He comes out with two large soup bones wrapped in butcher paper. He also gives her two newspapers, months old. As she walks off, he calls after her, "Don't you want to know my name? You may need it the next time you come looking for something. Something big."

She glances back, smiling slightly, but does not answer.

"Tom Saxton," he calls after her. "You come asking for Tom Saxton when you need something. Something big for your hunger. Remember me, now. I know you will."

Darting into a nook between buildings, she opens the papers and scans them quickly. Her eyes are stopped first by the headline of the death of President Lincoln's young son, Willie, who had lain deathly ill during the Battle of Fort Donelson. Gasping, she leans over, the news like a fist punch as she thinks back to the day she passed the President on the street in Washington. And now ... oh, what sorrow that poor man had to endure. She closes her eyes to stop imagining the pain. Weeks earlier, she had heard whispered rumors that Willie, the adored son, had become ill, but now the newspaper made it all true. And making it even worse, the adored child had died on February 20, just as she herself was struggling to settle into the occupied Confederate city and keep herself and Rissa alive.

Then there on the next page she finds, just as she hoped, a newspaper article describing Fort Warren in Boston. It tells of how it was converted now into a Union prison. She reads a description of General Buckner and his staff being marched through the streets of Boston while citizens jeered, and also that Buckner and his personal staff were placed in solitary confinement. Fort Warren. Yes, Fort Warren, a fort in Boston Harbor, now a Federal prison for secessionists, where the ocean lapped against its outer walls, where rats as big as cats scurried over the grounds and slid under the walls to crawl over those who lay on the bare ground in their cells.

Back at her borrowed home, she quickly burns the newspaper in the kitchen fire. There will now be no chance that Rissa will ever see the article describing Fort Warren.

For hours she works on the soup, boiling the bones until the marrow floats in the broth like foam, adding wildcrafted herbs of purslane, pigweed, tumbleweed and lotus lily. The intoxicating smell wafts from the kitchen's chimney and travels. Near noon, she spoons up a bowl of the soup and opens the door to carry it to the house for Rissa. But as soon as she steps out, she is frozen by the shock of an unexpected sight: a yard full of ex-slaves, squatting on the cold ground surrounding her, who then stand and move toward her, the round moons of their eyes begging. One even ventures to say, "Just a little taste, please, ole miss." Silently she quickly takes the soup to Rissa, who is in bed and does not get up to look out the window, since the silence of those waiting give no hint that they are there.

Then quickly, Eliza returns to the kitchen, adding large amounts of water to the soup pot and throwing in more carefully chosen herbs and grated roots, as well as handfuls of wild rice. And so she enlarges the soup to a great quantity, which she then spoons into bowls. Watching as the bowls are passed and shared, she holds out her hands to have them returned to her, and she refills them. "Here too," she says, walking among those squatting in the yard, distributing squares of cornbread made from Delia's old recipe, which she discovered she could double by mixing swamp cabbage to the cornmeal.

Dear One, it was as if the soup magically doubled itself, not just because I had the skill to make it seem so, but also because I needed so desperately to not say no.

Over the next weeks, she wildcrafts skunk cabbage, crushed peppercorns, parsley, sprigs of squash berry, grated birch bark— all to go into the soups that grow in quantity as do those who wait outside while Eliza cooks them. She catches turtles, frogs and crayfish at the spring near a place known as Dunbar Cave; herbs, she finds beside streams and in swamps. She seasons the broths, giving them wild and tangy flavors that linger on the tongue, becoming the stuff of rumor and story. And in exchange, she often finds on the kitchen stoop a carved animal or a wooden spoon or a trinket made by one of those she feeds. Moving among them, ladling soup into the bowls that they now bring themselves, she smiles and chats.

"Enjoy this; Yes, O, yes, real corn today and sweet butter beans. What's that? Turtle meat? O, it is surely."

She sees their eyes following her, glittering with wonder and with what must be a timid rekindling of hope. At least, she reads this in the light that brushes their faces as she walks among them.

Despite my original intention to simply feed them, I had become the means for their believing in a new kind of kindness, in the possibility that it could indeed exist in the world. And I was stunned by this. Never had I considered myself capable of this. The power of it swelled inside me. Clearly I was still an unfinished creature, hatching.

Snow melts, then falls again; the ground freezes and thaws, challenging her wildcrafting skills. She scratches out roots to provide as much carbohydrates as potatoes. Certain leaves, which, when boiled, release vitamin C. Cattails, crushed, become starch in boiling water that swells her soups to nutritiously feed twenty-five, thirty, the number growing each day.

"Why are you doing this? You'll have us talked about all over. You put us at risk, having vagabonds hanging about our door." Rissa shuffles weakly from window to window, looking out at the gathering crowd that arrives in late morning and stays until midday.

Eliza never answers. She serves Rissa her soup, asking, "Have I put too much bayberry in it? Is the wild rice at the bottom too firm?" Distracting Rissa is always better than trying to change her views.

Since Eliza had not known Rissa well before, she cannot be certain, but it seems that Rissa's illness is affecting her mind. Perhaps the cancer is invading her brain, for Rissa's moods are becoming as wildly sporadic as storm gusts. Often her thoughts are muddled. Some days Rissa asks Eliza where exactly Ben is. Hadn't he said in his last letter that he would be home next Tuesday?

"No," Eliza says at those times. "He said *some* Tuesday. He would be home on some Tuesday, but not *this* Tuesday next."

"Oh." But while Rissa focuses on Tuesdays, she soon forgets, and her obsessions move to other subjects. Other sources of anger spew out with no restraint.

When Eliza first met Rissa in Corinth, she had noted Rissa's obvious sympathy toward Lawrence. But now Rissa stares out the windows at the vagabond ex-slaves gathering to wait for Eliza's food and says disparagingly that if the war is not stopped, the Southern ranks will surely swell with Northern volunteers, since it is so very clear that the black man is meant to be in servitude and the way of the South preserved.

Whenever Rissa talks like that, Eliza leads her away with a hot tea, taking her into the front room to choose a book left by the Colonel's family, one of which would surely distract her mind. Other days, Rissa is as charming and lucid as in those early days in Corinth, obviously the woman to whom Ben was so lovingly devoted. But as Rissa deals with her body's betrayal, which Eliza knows is, no doubt, a torturous barren landscape that no one else could fathom—she discovers that she herself feels an aching loneliness, hard to describe.

Most like a cotton thread, a piece of lint floating with no tether to earth.

For over the months, despite their differences, she and Rissa have formed a close bond, and now Rissa cannot be counted on to be Rissa at all times. It is a new kind of sorrow, and with it, a new kind of worry.

The future was a desert I did not know how to cross.

Chapter 29

Rissa's silver comb, her gold ring, her cameo pin, her sterling silver brush, which she had so carefully moved while following Ben since the outbreak of the war—all went the way of her sapphire brooch to Supply Officer Tom Saxton in exchange for meat, sugar, flour, fruit and salt. He is Eliza's banker of sorts—her pawn shop for sure—always willing to exchange what she has for what he has. "So where's your husband?" he asks one day, looking at Eliza knowingly. "If you're with child, you must have a husband. So?"

O, Dear One, was it visceral? How did he know? Did he pick it up by the merest suggestion? Despite my skill in imitating those I studied—Rissa and the other officers' wives—how did he know that I was not one of them, not really? Was it obvious in the way I wore my warmest dress, the one Preston Cummings bought me and insisted I wear when he had kept me in Nashville? And the elaborate fur coat, the one that I buttoned around me, my warmest, that hid my changing body better than any I could have borrowed from Rissa? Licking his lips, looking at me, he always threw off suggestive remarks and watched for my reaction, which instinctively I knew how to give back, bantering as I had heard so many times while growing up, thinking how to disarm him without causing aggravation. No, not ever aggravation, never cause aggravation, since aggravating him would not be to my advantage, especially now when he stood between Rissa's and my (as well as the child inside me) ... yes, he stood between all three of us and the threat of starvation. Relishing the fact that I knew how to do this, I realized I also enjoyed this, saying back: "Yes, and my husband, if he were here, would likely offer you a drink and show you the door. In fact, shall I show you it now?"

That taunt, she knows, doesn't make a bit of sense, since they are standing inside a warehouse where he has taken her to give her a piece of beef, but the meaning is the same. He laughs, his voice deep and liquid with lust. "I hate women who only tease. Let's barter. Three pounds of prime beef for an hour?"

"I'm not what you think. Never have been."

"Of course not. And I'm Abraham Lincoln on vacation." He points to the wrapped meat she holds. "Come back when you run out of that."

Walking away, she knows he is watching her. And all the while she is hating him, hating what he instinctively knows, hating what she can't seem to ever quite hide.

The air warms; the ice on the river melts. Fish come to the surface, and she encourages the ex-slaves to catch them, any kind really, to bring to her so she can boil their bones. Irving too brings her fish since he has taken up fishing to fill out his diet. And always she offers him cooked food from her kitchen when he drops by, which is almost every day. As the stories of her food travel, the crowd waiting outside her kitchen spread to later hours, hours in which white people have begun appearing too—some Blue Coats along with desperate country people, others because they simply want to taste what is so renowned.

One noon, as she steps out of her kitchen to serve the day's meal, she sees on the street Tom Saxton himself, riding a gray horse dragoon-style with his stirrups long while he leans back. How splendid he looks, which he obviously knows, as he nods to those who look his way and cannot look away, dazzled by his splendor. Controlling her distaste for the fact that he has come to look at her, she nods and smiles. She needs him: That above all else holds her eyes smiling on him as he watches, then rides on.

Inside her, the baby is a quiet, hard seed, hanging silently on to its bed of nourishment, fluttering but not yet ready to roll and kick. But every day she feels its impending birth with deepening anxiety. Can she provide for it? Who can deliver it?

Discreetly she asks among those who wait outside her kitchen if there is a midwife among them. But there are hardly any women in the group, much less one who has birthed a baby. The winter sky, usually dishpan gray, begins to open with wide splashes of sun breaking through. And in those brief moments, some citizens in the city forget that they are like prisoners in their own homes. And Rissa acts more like herself, as if she were forgetting that she does not have much more life to live. Ben's letters continue to come, not often, but steadily.

Dear Rissa,

Do you remember Parson Thompson's old gray horse, the one who broke loose from its pasture and went wandering? Remember how Parson Thompson sent word out everywhere and even offered a reward? Then in the middle of his praying at the Sunday service (and shouldn't he have had his eyes closed?) he spied his horse passing by the church's open door and went running out of church, yelling, "Whoa, Old Gray, Whoa!" The rest of us innocent, heaven-seeking, good people stayed with our heads bowed for a good long while until finally the parson's brother stood up and said, "Amen."

How many of these joyous memories of our youth do you have? O, Rissa, how I miss you. I long for you so. Sometimes, here where I am, the thoughts of you are all I have to keep me sane and connected to this earth. I know that I will be back with you soon and my memories of being here will fade like dyed cloth left out in the sun. But some days it is very, very hard to miss you so sharply.

I know you are well and that Eliza is making your days as comfortable as possible.

Last night I had a terrible dream, a result of my heated and contorted brain missing you, no doubt. For I dreamed that I returned home and you received me coolly, and immediately afterward you got in a buggy with a young man and left in a cheerful and fastidious manner. My heart was practically bleeding from sadness, and I decided to follow, and when I arrived at the party, you were in fine glee, entertained by two nice-looking gentlemen. You still wouldn't notice me. The tears gushed from my eyes, and I thought you observed me crying, and that you told me that I had brought this on myself, and then you left me and rejoined your two favorite beaux. I wanted to get my double-barreled shotgun and blow them to bits, as well as myself! I awoke then and realized it was only a dream, thank goodness. I don't know why in the world I should have dreamed this. I suppose it is only my wildest fears manifesting themselves, since being away from you contorts my mind and makes me almost crazy.

My darling Rissa, God knows you are my only source of happiness, and were it not for you I would recklessly thrust my life into the thickest of any battle regardless of consequences. May God bless you, and keep you safe till I return. Tonight when you are asleep, reach out, and if you feel a warmth in the space beside you, know it is I in my thoughts and dreams to be with you.

Forever yours, devotedly, Ben.

Never did Rissa read Ben's letters to Eliza. Instead, Eliza found them afterward and read them herself, silently. Indeed, she even memorized certain passages and let her mind sing the words in silence all day, throughout every day. Never had she heard such words spoken. Never did she know such could exist between a man and a woman. And then in early April, Rissa asked if Eliza would take a letter for her, meaning that her hand was too weak to write long, and there was much she wanted to say. "So will you?" Rissa, sitting in a chair, looked in the mirror at Eliza, behind her, who was brushing her hair. Rissa was having a particularly lucid, good day.

"Of course."

The Colonel's family had left many writing materials. Holding them, Eliza felt that the war had never even happened. Her own pen and papers on which she had been writing her letters to Dear One, the ones that had been lost in her travels and now that she had been rewriting and adding to them in between the hours of caring for Rissa, were showing the strain of being worked over. But on the letters to Ben, there were as yet no stains or frayed edges. They were clean and lovingly written, stark white, velvety ink, crisply folded.

Dear Ben,

I have asked Eliza to write this for me, for I feel more like talking to you than writing. Besides, I have found that she has a very nice handwriting, and so, I shall put her to work, as you would teasingly say. Just now Eliza and I sit by the fire in this nice room which you so lovingly secured for me, and I think of you, my darling, and how much you have always put my comforts and wishes first. Why! Only this morning, I suggested to Eliza that we take a ride down through the woods to Parson Thompson's meadow, and then remembered that I am here and not there and that we live now in a different time. Our childhoods and days of discovering our love are passed. But the feelings we had then have not dimmed, no, not ever dimmed, not in the least. I know that you must be in difficult surroundings and that you try to allay my worries by saying you are suffering no hardships. I too am well and growing stronger every day. I can't wait until we are reunited. I have a surprise for you, my darling, and will give no hints until summer, when surely you will be released and be somewhere that I can meet you. I can tell you in person then. Though I will say, the tiniest of things can be the grandest of surprises.

Keep well,

Your loving wife, Rissa.

Eliza looks up. Rissa is smiling in a cloud of her own thoughts, her just-brushed hair splayed on the pillow, her eyes nearly closed. Eliza holds the writing pen above the paper, knowing that Rissa's "surprise" means the child inside her, knowing too that Rissa assumes that she, Eliza, in her silence, had accepted Rissa's offer to take the child when it is born. Why not? Wouldn't any sane unmarried woman with child think it most sensible to give it away? But now is not the time to discuss any of that. Eliza herself is not even sure what she will do. Instead she dots the *i* in *Rissa* elaborately and draws a line under her name, as Rissa always does. Then in an impulse, she writes:

As dictated to me, Eliza Goode, in the afternoon on a fine cold day. We wait for you.

"Shall I mail this now?" she asks Rissa, standing up.

"Yes."

The letters pass only from one Federally occupied area to another, but, still, they move more slowly than Eliza or Rissa likes. So Eliza finds a quicker route. As efficiently as bags of flour and boxes of ammunition, Sergeant Saxton can pass them through supply lines from Clarksville to Boston. And in the month of April, Eliza never hesitates to ask him to do so.

My Dear Ben,

We are well and feeding the multitudes that wait in the yard outside the kitchen of this house each day as Eliza cooks. It turns out she is a renowned cook with unexpected and amazing talents. How she learned this, I shall never know, for she is secretive and elusive. I am lucky to have her with me, however. I realize this. It has been the most extraordinary and unfortunate circumstances that have brought her and me together. And if I didn't need her so at a time when I am regaining my health, I would have sent her packing. She is unrefined, as you know, strangely educated, and imperious beyond belief. But I won't go into more, just now. Only know, hurry home to my waiting arms.

As Rissa dictates this letter, it is hard for Eliza to write it, especially because Rissa cuts her eye at Eliza the whole while to see if the message and intended meanness are getting through. After Rissa returns to bed, Eliza seals the letter with a fist, knocking it hard on the dining room table, then walks out the door to take it to Sergeant Saxton to pass along. Halfway there, she begins laughing. Walking and laughing. As she passes others on the street, she knows she looks suspiciously loony, but why care? Giggling, looking up at the sky, she laughs at the peevish, childish temper that Rissa had displayed, her moods that rise and fall like sea tides.

And it came to me: Who was I to be insulted? I, who knew nothing of what Rissa was facing, each day, as inch by inch, second by second, her life was draining away? Quite the contrary. I was swollen with Life, its very promise pitching and rolling inside me now, which no doubt made Rissa outright hate me—not me, but Life's energy in its fullest expression. It was then, in that moment, that I discovered a renewed respect for her, which reignited my patience. Now I knew how to forgive her cutting remarks, her often disdainful looks and comments and the erratic moods that hurled our days into misery. This must be what it felt like to really give up the sour obsessive feeling of hurt. I myself was nearing eighteen, an old eighteen. By fall I would be a mother. I needed to learn how to be that.

Accept and Forgive—I repeated it day by day. It was the right and real thing to do. One, though, I dared not take on: the one who ignited the living seed inside me. That was too complicated.

Soon after Eliza's eighteenth birthday, on April 28, 1862, New Orleans fell. She learned it from the papers that Sergeant Saxton gave her. She read how the citizens had resisted: crowds running through the streets brandishing knives and pistols. Wagons rattling over the streets, hauling cotton for burning on the quays, along with crates of sugar and rice that were then thrown into the river with cries that at least the damned Yankees would not have them.

She also later learned that on May 15, General Benjamin Butler, who was placed in charge of the occupation of New Orleans, issued Order 28 in response to some New Orleans women spitting on the occupying soldiers—one even emptying a chamber pot on a soldier's head. The order said that any woman who showed insult or contempt for any Federal officer would be treated as *"a woman of the town plying her avocation,"* which was shorthand for "prostitute." *Heavens! Avocation, my foot! It was a full-out bona fide vocation!*

Clearly, the occupation of the great city was a contentious affair, and now Eliza began wondering about her mother and

Madam Francine. She imagined them spitting on Blue Coats in the street, even putting a portrait of Benjamin Butler on the inside of their chamber pots, then finally accepting the occupation of the city and even allowing the occupiers into the grand house on South Basin Street. More than once at dinner, Madam Francine had said to her veshyas, "Always remember, no matter who they are, no matter where they come from, under their britches, they are all alike."

Federal or Rebel—what would it matter when money was to be made.

****

In mid-August, when Eliza was upstairs bathing Rissa, she heard a great turmoil in the streets. "What in the world?" She hurried to the window, holding up her soapy hands, and looked out on a ragtag company of Confederates dashing up and down the street. They rode thin, wormy-looking horses and were dressed in dirty butternut clothes, but they had a determined fire in their eyes. In a matter of hours, they tossed the town into turmoil.

Watching wide-eyed and excited, Eliza and Rissa stood at the window, listening to hoofbeats sounding up and down the streets. Within the day, the Union Army surrendered without a fight, and for the next few weeks, the Rebels strutted about the streets, some even waiting outside Eliza's kitchen door for what they heard was a meal beyond compare. Down near Dunbar Cave, a band of Rebel guerrillas set up camp. And since they were no part of the Rebels who had recaptured the city, there was no one in charge over them. For the short while that the city was back in Confederate hands, the ragtag guerrillas rode in and out on their scruffy horses, buying supplies, lingering on the streets to talk with the Rebel soldiers on guard duty and soon even stopped by Eliza's kitchen for a meal.

Dear One,

As you might have imagined, it was bound to happen. It was a hot summer day when I walked out from the kitchen with my kettle of soup, and there, hunkered among the ragged few of the guerrilla band who had been coming by in the last few days, was Ned. Squatting, holding a tin bowl, he looked at me, dressed in butternut deerskin, grinning, his hair wild but his eyes less demented than I had seen him last. "Hello, Eliza," he said. "I heard you was here. I didn't know about that, though." He pointed to where the child now had swelled me to a size that could not be hidden. All day now it kicked and squirmed inside me. In fact, I had taken to wearing Rissa's robes that could be belted loosely and swept around me like a tent.

"Ned," I said, "I have worried about you."

"No need to. Is the child mine?"

I was so stunned by his question, I stood paralyzed. His eye might not look crazed, but his brain was clearly infected by his same fantastical dreams.

"No, Ned," I answered as gently as I could. "But how glad I am to see you. As my brother, you will know that I will always care how you are."

He screwed his face up in disbelief, his lips pursed. "I was home for a while. I guess you are interested to know of everyone. Madam Francine is rich as Midas. Your Mr. Preston looks odd—not himself at all. He has broken out in rashes and often holds his hat over his face. And your mother has taken sick."

I gasped. "What?"

"She's contracted The Disease." He smiled cruelly. "Thin as a grass blade, fevered, making her twice as desired, you know. She'll be rich too by the time this war is over. That is, if she can hold up."

"O no, Ned. How long?"

"A few months for sure now. She's treating herself with her herbs and things. She could go for a long while, you know."

Quickly, I turned, taking my soups to others, glancing back, watching Ned, who was hungrily eating. Yes, I knew that what he told me was very likely the truth. My mother was a prime target. Tuberculosis had long been known as "The Prostitute's Disease." The thin, fevered look was even considered an aphrodisiac, a thrilling eroticism.

Ned himself looked so poor, so trod-upon, so loose in the world, so without home, friend or family, I could not help *but stare at him several times as I walked among those who reached up with their bowls and spoons. He might be in the grip of a madness that I could only fear and not understand, but my heart went out to him even while it trembled. Ned here! Ned now close enough to haunt me.*

But in September, the Federals came back in full force, driving the careworn Rebels out, who rode off on their emaciated horses while the guerrilla band followed. Eliza stood at Rissa's window, looking hard through the glass to try to be sure that the one she saw in the rear of the guerrilla band was indeed Ned, riding at a gallop on a crooked-legged buckskin no bigger than a pony.

Immediately, the city settled back into Union occupation, and in late September some Clarksville women, who had seen Eliza walking to the wharf, brought her two loose-fitting muslin dresses, known as "comfort clothes." The callers sat in the parlor of the Colonel's house while Rissa, who needed help now getting down the stairs, joined them. And it was clear that Rissa enjoyed them as much as if she were back in Brookhaven, Mississippi, receiving friends. "We expect the little one in only a matter of a month," she said.

Eliza sat primly on the piano bench, answering their concern with the made-up fact that her husband had been taken prisoner just as Rissa's had, and that she hoped he would be paroled soon.

"Like General Buckner," one of the ladies immediately added.

"What?" Eliza turned, her heart tripling its beat. "Buckner—has he been released?"

"Yes. I read it in the paper yesterday. Exchanged for a Union general and released. On his way west, it said."

Eliza quickly looked at Rissa, but the meaning of what the visitor had said escaped Rissa. She looked exhausted and detached. Her eyes were half-shut and rimmed with dark circles.

"Did the paper say that anyone else was released with him?"

"No."

And then the visitors changed the subject, speaking of the recent recapture of Clarksville, while all the while Eliza could not stop thinking about Ben. Was he on his way right then, that moment, to a place in Confederate control where she could take Rissa to him? Her mind skipped, thinking, where, where possibly: Richmond, Charleston, some place in North Carolina? There had been no Confederate victory since Ball's Bluff; much of the South was now in Federal hands. Where could he safely go? As Rissa swayed in her chair, nearly asleep, Eliza went to her, and with that as a signal to the visitors, they got up to leave.

On the way to the door, Eliza asked the parson's wife, the one who led the visiting party, "I wonder, do you know of a midwife? Someone who might—"

"Of course, my dear. I'll send a note right away to my cousin. She has a woman who works for her who has served in that capacity. They live in a hamlet not more than ten miles from here. You needn't worry. I'll get back to you soon."

But soon was not time enough.

That night, Eliza went into labor. Rissa, aroused by the crisis, crawled down the stairs for what Eliza told her to find. She brought back upstairs a paring knife and kettle. She found Eliza's bag and pulled out the necklace that Eliza called for. And she lit two candles in the window.

Eliza held the birthing beads that she had been given that day on the plantation where Quashi had taken her, and as the pains rose and waned, she squeezed and counted the beads as she recalled the slave women had done that day. "It's too early," she kept saying. "Too early for it to come. It is not time yet." And then after several hours, Eliza could see that Rissa was afraid and weak and yet bravely whispering encouragement over and over. "It will be fine, Eliza. Simply fine. The child will be perfect, perfect, a son no doubt. A son for Ben. Think only of that. Think of a strong, fine son. And he will soon be here."

"We need help. Go, Rissa. Go across the street and see where Irving is. He might know of someone, a midwife. Maybe one of the doctors from the Union hospital will come. Can you? Can you make it that far?"

"I will. I will. Yes, you're right, Eliza. You're always so smart."

She turned, pulled a shawl over her head and held on to the wall, making her way to the stairs and across the street. How she walked to Irving Lowry's, Eliza would never know.

Maybe she hung on to the wrought-iron fence for as far as she could, then hunching in pain, walked quickly to where Irving Lowry was just coming home from a church meeting, and seeing two candles in the window, which he and I had decided could be a signal that we needed help, he met Rissa halfway.

Poor Irving, surrounded by women for more than half his life as a teacher and father of daughters, he took up his role in the bedroom where I labored to birth the child, with Rissa aiding him the best she could. He boiled water in the kettle in the fireplace. He found clean linens and warm flannel and laid them by my bed.

Near three a.m., the newborn fairly leaped from my body, no bigger than a small rabbit curled in a dream sleep. But then it unfolded in Irving's hands like a letter ready to be read. And it squalled so loudly, belting out a song that I swear sounded as if it were a one-note celebration in joining our party, that we all laughed. We laughed so loudly that the room soon filled with all our mingled sounds.

Irving swaddled the child and handed it to me. I looked down at the girl-child's face and whispered, "Welcome, Chantilly," for it seemed that instantly I knew what her name should be. For a long while, I simply looked. Looked at the tiny face whose features whispered traces of me, and at the dark, dark hair and turned-down ear that whispered of her father. I rubbed my lips together, overwhelmed with emotion. Trembling, I stroked her head over and over in awe. Water came into my eyes as if washing away all chances that I would not see clearly, for I knew that I was now looking down into my arms at the mind of God. At least, at the earth's great creator's wish. How the seed was set into motion did not matter now, not so much to me, and certainly not at all to the Great One, who cared only that Chantilly took her first strong breath in affirmation that she was supposed to be here. My emotion so overflowed that I knew what I was feeling in its purest form was what we call love. My heart verily burst with it. I felt it completely, and instantly could name it.

I handed her to Rissa. "Here, hold her," I said. Silently, all the while I was telling myself: Let her think what she will. For we both know she will not live long enough to take the child. And I would never—not even at threat of my own death—ever now give her up.

Chapter 30

A letter from Ben came that next week.

My darling Rissa,

General Buckner has been gone from here now for several weeks, and it appears that I have been overlooked in being paroled for the time being. It is a dilemma for me, since the Federals insist I give my oath of allegiance to the Union in exchange for parole. However, do not worry; I sense they will lift their stringent requirements and let me go soon. Then I can come to you where we can be safe.

My greatest challenge here is being so alone. Never did I know that loneliness can become an illness, eating at my heart, chewing my strength. It is thoughts of you that keep me strong. I know you have your own challenges, and I take comfort in knowing that Eliza is with you and caring for you. She is such an exceptional person, so many talents and steadfast qualities. Indeed, you and I were lucky to come upon her in our travels. I know she is writing letters for you, which I hope is a sign that you have bonded in a way that helps you both meet these difficult times.

A thousand loves to you, my dear and affectionate wife. O, for one embrace this morning.

Your affectionate husband,

Ben

"Let's tell him," Rissa says, lying in bed, holding the baby whom she has begun to call Tilly, stroking the baby's hair. Eliza sits on the foot of the bed, preparing to write a letter for Rissa.

Whenever Eliza and Rissa aren't holding the baby, she stays in a basket on the foot of Rissa's bed. Now Rissa is so weak and so gripped by intermittent spasms of pain, that she can no longer stand up. The cancer must be spreading, now on its way to block her most vital organs. Often when Eliza looks at Rissa, she has to resist sucking in her breath, startled by how Rissa seems to change hour by hour: Her eyes are sunken, her face is an ashen color, the tips of her fingers, blue.

Every few hours, Eliza breastfeeds the baby and then hands her to Rissa, who, quite studiously "burps" her, then laughs. Both Eliza and Rissa spend hours singing, cooing to the baby, delighting in every sound she makes. The newborn's grunts, crooked smiles, even the squalling for food are occasions to laugh and forget what they desire to forget.

Rissa cradles the baby until Tilly falls asleep.

"I'm not really comfortable telling Ben about her," Eliza says.

"Oh, but she is such a joy!"

"No. I don't want him to know."

"I assure you, Eliza. It won't be a reflection on you. I can tell him in a way that he won't care. News of her can inspire him, make him hold on to his strength. That's what we need to think of—him. Not your shame."

Eliza freezes at the sound of the word. She studies Rissa's face, which seems innocent of what she has just said and its possible effect on Eliza. The word seems to hang in the air like a bad smell. Eliza pulls her lips back, preparing to say something mean and cutting in return, but refrains.

"Rissa, I myself will never be ashamed of my child. So she herself will never be in danger of feeling it. But how can I be sure that telling Ben about her wouldn't unsettle him? If you and he are to raise her, shouldn't you wait to offer the fact that she came from me?"

"Oh, I suppose I see your point. Yes, perhaps we should wait. The surprise will be worth the wait, after all. No doubt, he will call for us to meet him soon in someplace safe. And I can just imagine the moment in which I will descend from the carriage holding Tilly in my arms and how I will hand her to him. And the look on his face! Oh, my! Can't you just imagine it!"

"I can."

"And he will even think that I birthed her myself, and that she is his, for we did indeed, before he rode off to Fort Donelson..." She smiles suggestively, flashing her eyes.

Later she dictates this benign letter:

Darling Ben,

I am distraught with thoughts of your postponed release and focus on getting so strong that I will virtually bound out of the carriage to meet you when you send word where I shall come to you. I will have then the surprise I promised. For it is here with me, and I delight in imagining the look on your face when I show you it.

Yesterday we had a fine onion soup, a French recipe it seems. I don't know where in the world Eliza has gotten all these ideas for soups. Well, I guess I do know, since she has confided in me what I will tell you later. In any case, they can be most tasty while other times they are so bizarre I cannot digest them. She is simply too creative for her own good.

Ben, I wish to apologize for the row I made with your father over Fernwood. I know I made you miserable in my protestations. I beg you to understand how difficult it is to be a woman and denied the property I am due, which is not really a matter of the property but a matter of respect. I know you said you understood that, but I need to hear you repeat it just now.

I wait for you my darling. Stay strong in my love, which never wanes.

Rissa

Eliza blots the ink and folds the letter carefully. But before she takes it to Tom Saxton to pass it along the Federal supply route to Boston, she opens it back up and writes quickly a last line:

There is now a baby in this house. It is mine. And she is exquisite. She is beautiful in her own right and is growing even more beautiful sleeping in the arms of Rissa.

Stay strong. We wait for you.

Eliza.

Hourly, Eliza gives Rissa valerian root tea to help her handle her increasing pain. Rissa sleeps fitfully, and Eliza sits beside her or else lies on a palette on the floor to sleep for a few hours, the baby in a basket beside her.

In a lucid moment Rissa sits up and blurts a memory as if from a dream. "Imagine, Eliza, there I was in Mississippi, in one of the only places where a woman can own property. And yet, my dowry was immediately taken by old Fletcher McFerrin. I don't care if he is Ben's father. He is nothing like Ben. Stingy and mean. As brittle as old straw. I hate him. Hate him! Think of this: There we all were at dinner on New Year's Day when he announced that he had rewritten his will. His great plantation, Fernwood, is to be bequeathed to Bennett, which then, after Bennett's death, is to go to the worthless McFerrin relatives in Memphis. Old Mr. McFerrin announced it all and passed me by completely! Me! Me! Who was due Fernwood and could receive it under Mississippi law. I even quoted to him the Married Women's Property Act—the one so hard fought for in 1839—allowing men to deed property to their wives. 'Yes, but the law does not require that I deed it to my wife or to you,' he retorted, the putrid old man. I assure you, it was not a matter of property, it was a matter of principle—that he bypassed me, to insult me. And when I fought him over the next weeks and months, he said that if I showed this side to Bennett I would drive my husband to drink and vicious associations."

Eliza shivers. *Vicious associations:* another catchword for "prostitute." She rings out a wet rag and wipes Rissa's face. Wildcrafted pain cures are losing their power.

Suddenly the baby shrieks. Eliza rubs Tilly's stomach, tight with colic. Suddenly too Rissa begins to scream, her back bowed in pain. Eliza puts her hands over her ears. In desperation, she pours more valerian root tea. From a bottle she finds in the Colonel's bedroom, she pours straight bourbon into Rissa's mouth, and then, Eliza holds her warm hand on Tilly's stomach and rocks her.

Only after nearly an hour does the dying woman and the newborn fall silent and asleep.

It is then that Eliza vows that she will have to resort to an extreme plan. For how much longer can Rissa stand days like this? How much longer can she, Eliza, withstand watching this suffering while being so powerless?

Two days later at nightfall when Rissa is having a rather pain-free hour, Eliza picks up the sleeping baby and says, "Here, Rissa. Can you care for her while I go into town? I forgot we are almost out of firewood for the cookstove. And I can arrange for some to be delivered tomorrow."

Rissa perks up, her eyes gathering a sparkle. "I would love nothing more."

She reaches out for Tilly and then holds her, looking down into the baby's face. "You won't be gone long, though?" Anxiety colors her voice.

"No. And I will send Irving over. I'll stop to speak to him on my way out. And here is a rag soaked in breast milk. If Tilly fusses, let her suck on that."

"Good. And I will rely on Irving. He is always of good help."

Eliza then goes to the room where she keeps her things. She puts on the exquisite dress that Preston Cummings had bought her. She twirls up her hair. She looks into the mirror and finds that what beauty her face has always held is there still, only now with it is a womanly cast. Quickly she has recovered from childbirth, but her cheeks are still glowing with full flesh left from her pregnancy. And her breasts, always ready to nurse the baby, now swell against the dress's fabric. She pulls a white shawl over her shoulders and walks down the stairs. It has to be this night, at this time, she knows, for she has always heard that breastfeeding keeps one safe from pregnancy, and she feels certain about how to do this. She knows what she can make happen.

I simply walked down to the river. I went along the wharf

until I saw a gathering of soldiers and asked where Tom Saxton was. I knew he lived in a barracks somewhere on the wharf; after all, the Union holdings could not go unattended. He was in charge of the guards that were posted all along the waterfront by the warehouses.

Bonfires from the shantytown threw a yellow glow against the sky. I knocked on the barracks door and asked for him. When he came out, I told him that I needed something so very desperately. Of course at that, he smiled suggestively, but I rushed on telling him that what I needed was a vial of opium. When he said what I expected, that he did not know where he could get such, I told him that I knew. Truly, the rarity of such a drug would make it hard for anyone to procure it. And if any were there in the city, it would be for Union use, for the worst of cases, for the worst of suffering.

It was then that I told him that if he would send a courier along Federal lines to the house of Madam Francine on South Basin Street in New Orleans—and quickly—and there mention my name, give the note that I had written, which I addressed to my mother, I would give him in payment what he had so long hinted at wanting. He reached out and squeezed my waist. He ran his hand across my face. But I drew back. I said I would not complete the bargain until I saw him send a courier with my note. After all, I was a good businesswoman when the moment demanded it. And I also knew my mother would not deny my request for the vial of opium. It was always available at that house.

When the courier—a small young man, so young that hardly any hair grew on his face—vowed that he would take the first steamboat in the morning to New Orleans, I didn't doubt him. The look on his face at the mention of the address and the mission revealed his dedication to do what was asked. No doubt he would have scratched his own itch by the time he got back.

It was there then, in the dark corner of one of the warehouses, that I let the Federal Tom Saxton collect his part of our bargain.

****

Five days later, Eliza went back to pick up the package that the courier had brought from the house where Eliza was raised. Soon, Rissa was sitting up in bed working on a piece of embroidery that she had started.

With her increased comfort, the household had taken on a new calm. It was not just the reclaimed calm of where pain had been eased, it was also the calm of acceptance.

When Rissa fell asleep, Eliza went to her bedside and picked up the piece of embroidery Rissa had been working on. In quiet sadness, Eliza saw that it was a mourning portrait, a custom that many housewives practiced when a family member died— it commemorated them with the lost one's likeness stitched into the cloth, surrounded by the classic symbols of death and everlasting life: the urn, the weeping willow in the background, a dove with a branch in its beak. The date of the family member's death was always stitched on the bottom.

Eliza rubbed her fingers across the embroidery that was almost finished in what was a very close likeness to Rissa's own face. And in the space where the date of death was to be inscribed, Rissa had embroidered: November 1862.

On the next morning she rallied for a few hours. And in that time she requested that Eliza write another letter for her.

Dear Ben,

It is a beautiful, crisp fall day. Outside my window, I can hear the birds preparing to fly farther south. Their chattering is almost a noise. It reminds me of our excitement, a household in a rush, preparing to travel.

In the event that anything should happen to me, and that I would not be able to meet you when you call, I would like to ask for one last promise. Please stay faithful to me, my darling Ben. My last wish would be that you keep my memory present and vivid, not ever to let fade the feeling of our love. I request then that should I not be with you that you would not take another wife in my absence. This request gives me comfort, for I know then I will in that way be with you forever.

Your adoring wife,

Rissa

Eliza writes the letter and seals it. Then she places it in the Colonel's parlor on his desk under the weight of a blotter.

Three days later, Rissa dies while Eliza sits quietly by her side, holding Tilly.

Rissa had opened and then closed her eyes. Once, she reached out for Eliza, then withdrew her hand. Her chest rose high, then shrank, and the struggle was over. The blessing of opium had ushered in a peaceful death.

There are many things to handle now: a burial, which with Irving's help and also with the women at the church, Eliza arranges for the next day.

It is cold and rainy. Eliza wraps Tilly in a blanket. She stands by the graveside until the service is over. She goes home, then comes back an hour later, alone, and puts a bouquet of holly leaves on the grave. She stands a long while, thinking. She stays until the baby cries with cold.

That night she takes up the letter that Rissa had dictated. She looks at it for only a short while, and then with certainty, she tears it up and puts it in the fire and begins writing another, weaving in even a story that Rissa had told her.

Dear Ben,

It is a beautiful, crisp fall day. Outside my window I can hear the birds preparing to fly farther south. Their chattering is almost a noise. It reminds me of our excitement, a household in a rush, preparing to travel.

I have been thinking of certain things, and would like to say that if anything were to happen to me, and I would not be able to meet you when you call, I would not want to sentence you to a lifetime of grief. My wish would be that you keep me in your heart as a memory, that you take from me what I gave you in our time together—the certainty that there is such a thing as everlasting love. But I wish no hold on your future. If you find another that you can love, take her with my blessing, dear Ben. Your happiness is my most fervent wish.

Now, tell me again that lovely story of when you and your roommate at VMI hid Professor Jackson's fifth lesson on the—what was it?—the proper position for artillery? You were so bad, knowing that Professor Jackson—who ironically would be renamed by this war "Stonewall"—memorized every lecture and would be lost without his notes. But you hid them, and when in response he canceled the class, you celebrated in having the whole afternoon to play.

My bad Ben. My mischievous darling. How I long for you. Of course Eliza is doing the best she can to amuse me. But in truth, her stories are boring. It is you I need.

Your devoted wife,

Rissa

PART III

FINDING ELIZA AGAIN

Chapter 31

Holding the last of Eliza's letters, I simply stared at the yellowed paper in my hand. Over the past months, I had spent so much time with her, imagining her; I did not want to believe that Eliza's life ended during the occupation of Clarksville in the way that Hadley accepted—and in the way that the newspaper article seemed to verify.

Yet when looking at all the facts in play, I saw how Eliza could have been accused as being in collusion with the occupiers. There was Eliza's wildcrafting and the runaway slaves that she fed each day, which could have easily fueled rumors of suspicious behaviors akin to practicing a kind of witchcraft. They were rumors that also could have taken flight similar to the rumors that spread after Major Morgan's suicide. Furthermore, wouldn't Ned, during his time in Clarksville, have had time to fuel those rumors, if not start them? Eliza's obvious closeness to Tom Saxton could certainly have led to rumors that she was conniving with the enemy, at the least, be far too close to the Federalists for any secessionist's comfort. Eliza was simply too unusual with her extraordinary beauty, her steel-like strength, her guile, her undiscriminating kindness. She was bound to arouse discomfort and resentment in those around her. History was filled with similar sorts of people who suffered for their uniqueness.

Yes, it would have been easy to brand her as a spy, to get rid of her in any convenient way, such as to set fire to the house where she was living. But what about the child? What about Chantilly? She somehow survived.

She was not mentioned in the newspaper article. She might indeed have been the link to Eliza's letters. Could she have been the one to hand the letters down through the generations? Indeed, how had the letters themselves survived the fire? Had Tilly somehow preserved them and passed them down? That could explain how Hadley found them—overly generous Hadley, volunteering to help clear out a distant relative's house who was being moved to a nursing home. Which was just like Hadley, aiding with gusto someone she hardly knew. Actually in writing Eliza's story, I now understood how someone shame-driven would turn feverishly to doing good works, hoping to spark admiration in others' eyes if not in her own. I had already sensed that whatever Hadley was hiding, she was hiding because of shame.

Yes, it could all fit; but still, there was part of me that refused to accept the end of Eliza's story, as Hadley believed it. In two days, I would fly to Clarksville to meet her. Over the past week I had used my usual attempts to reach her: e-mailing and calling, but still I got no response. Carefully I put all of Eliza's letters back into their gauze wrapper and locked them in a filing cabinet in my study. I could hear Caleb downstairs going out the back door to work, calling up, "See you tonight." And I called back to him, "Yes, have a good day," and then the phone rang.

"Cuz!" Hadley's laugh was boisterous. "Are you packed?"

"Hadley, how are you?"

"Fine. Fine. As fine as can be."

"So where do we meet?"

"I get there before you, so I'll wait in the baggage claim. I've rented us a car. We'll have all weekend to see where she was, or at least try."

"Hadley, you read all the letters in this last batch?"

"No. I admit I only scanned them. I read carefully the last one when she begins pretending to be Rissa McFerrin to Ben.

That leaves us no facts, though, how she came to her awful end. I assume it had something to do with her being so close to Tom Saxton. Maybe we can find out something in Clarksville when we get there. Certainly we should visit the city's archives. And by the way, Susan, the pages you gave me in Costa Rica are simply lovely. I feel so close to Eliza now. I can almost hear her breathing. At times, I pretend she's standing right beside me. How you do it, I'll never know. I don't think I could have found anyone else who could have put the letters together like this."

"So does this mean you're now ready to focus on your own life? Look, Hadley, you have to stop using this Eliza story as a distraction. It's time to face up to whatever is keeping you from taking care of yourself. "

"Yessss." She drew out the sound flirtatiously. "But first I want to see what you've written from the last letters. So far, all I see is that Eliza was pretty conniving. Impersonating Rissa to Ben was not exactly exemplary behavior. It was a horrendous lie, in fact."

Hadley's talent for redirecting a conversation was sheer perfection.

"Look," I said impatiently, "I feel that you want to see Eliza as unredeemable. But she wasn't. I see her writing to Ben, pretending to be Rissa as a loving thing to do. Wait till you see the way I've written it. Besides, if Ben knew that Rissa had died, don't you think he might have lost his strength? Don't you see Eliza realizing this? By the way, did he make it out of prison, what happened to him? Do you know?"

"No. Maybe we can find out when we get to Clarksville. But now, Susan, I want to make this clear. I don't see Eliza as someone with no moral compass at all. That's never been so. I love her. I'm enchanted by her. I want her life to inform mine. After all, she is part of our family. How did you feel when you realized who Tilly was?"

"Amazed. The least thing I expected was that Eliza became a mother. And she was such a good mother."

"Yes, an amazing mother." Hadley's voice lingered on those words, deepening their meaning.

"Hadley, do you want to know what I really think now? You want to see Eliza as unredeemable because there is something about yourself you consider unredeemable."

"Ah! Smart, cuz. When we get to Clarksville, I'll let you into my little hell. I know now you won't let my, well, actually huge transgression out into the hard, cruel world. But, now ... well, I've got to run. Got someone to put to sleep." She laughed loudly and hung up.

****

While I began doing all those things that one does before going on a trip: packing, filling the fridge with food for the one you love, cleaning the sink where Rufus, the roach, still visited each night for water and crumbs, my mind kept asking, *Who? Who might fill in the facts?* Before I met Hadley in Clarksville, I wanted to try harder to pry open her past. After all, the last time we had met, her revelations had unhinged me.

Already I'd contacted everyone in Hadley's family that I could think of, and they'd all stonewalled me, leaving me only with the idea that something had happened that had cast Hadley out of her family. I knew I had to look further afield, and then I began to think back to the summer day when she had first called me. I remembered our meeting in the Boston hotel and how she had been so insistent that we had not seen our Aunt Ellen and her husband, Arthur, that day near the elevator. Why? Why? And why had I not thought of this before: to simply call Aunt Ellen and ask, find out for sure. How stupid I'd been, for of course this is what I should have done months before: Find Aunt Ellen.

I called information in Ocean Springs and asked for Aunt Ellen's phone number.

A minute later, I had her voice on the phone. "Aunt Ellen?"

"That depends on who's calling." A chuckle and then, "Is this someone related?"

"Yes, Aunt Ellen. It's Susan Masters in Boston."

"Well, lands! I haven't heard from you in a coon's age. How are you, sugar?"

I laughed. "Fine. Fine. And Arthur?"

"Oh, he's got gout. Has to sit with his toe on a stool and have me wait on him all day. Otherwise I'd of made him answer the phone. Susan, Susan! It's so good to hear from you!"

"Did I see you up here in Boston last summer?"

"Well, I don't know. We *were* there. Arthur just had to see the Red Sox. Were you at the game?"

"No. I think I saw you at the hotel."

"Oh, yes. I thought that was you. You and Hadley, but then of course I didn't want to have her see us."

"Why?"

"Didn't your mama tell you?

"Aunt Ellen, my mother died two years ago."

"Oh, yes. I'm sorry. She passed after your father, didn't she?"

"Yes. And no one in Hadley's family will tell me anything—not about why they had a falling out."

"Oh, and a falling out is certainly what they had! I'm surprised you didn't hear." And then she whispered, going on quickly and bluntly like most Southerners who love knowing the inside of a dramatic story: "Hadley lost her son. Had to give him up in her divorce. The court said she was a bad mother ... gave all custody to the father. About killed Hadley's mother."

"But why? No judge does that unless there's a dire reason."

"Drugs. Hadley was on drugs. She's an addict. Got all she wanted 'cause she's a doctor. They sent her to a rehab place and took away her license for a while. I'm quite sure she was never cured. A person can't get that out of her system once it's in, you know. You can turn a cucumber into a pickle, but not ever back into a cucumber."

"So ... that's—"

"Yes. That's why. 'Bout killed all of us. There's just some things you can't forgive."

"Hmm." We chatted a bit more about family and gout and the Red Sox, then I hung up.

At the same time that I was shocked, I was also relieved. It all fit together now. And I had some idea of how I might deal with Hadley, for even if Eliza had died as Hadley believed, she had lived beyond her shame and had indeed become a mother, and those two things could very well save—if not heal—Hadley. I was also desperately hoping that there in Clarksville, we would somehow unearth new reasons to believe that the newspaper article about Eliza's death was false. Eliza living. Eliza living on—that would be shockingly powerful. Too powerful for Hadley to ignore.

I flew into Clarksville from Nashville, and just as she promised, Hadley was there, sitting on a bench in the baggage claim section, grinning. Her hand was on a red suitcase, her eyes sunken and circled, her hair still dark like Eliza's and swept up under a fedora as if she were in the last scene of *Casablanca*.

"Have you been here long?" I asked.

She stood up. "Only ten minutes. You are always good for your word, Susan. Now where are the pages you've finished?"

****

At the hotel, we sat in Hadley's room. She said she'd reserved separate ones because she got up so often in the night and didn't want to disturb me. She looked thin and pale, but clearly she was holding up well. She did not yet look that desperate way when life is ebbing, and this encouraged me. While she held the pages that I had written and read the first few, I looked out the window and drank a glass of ice tea.

She rattled the pages. "These are lovely, simply lovely, Susan. Look at all you have brought to life!" She then put them down on the bed. "I'll read the rest tonight. Let's go explore. Let's try to find where the Colonel's house was, before it burned at least."

"Hadley," I said firmly, "I called Aunt Ellen. I always thought that I saw her last summer in the hotel when you and I met. Remember? And I never could quite erase that mystery from my mind."

"That makes sense." She reached for her purse, as though to go out, but then stopped at the door and looked back at me. Finally now she was taking note of what I had said, paying attention. I was encouraged. Had I finally caught her, brought her down from her flight, which for months had made me feel as if I'd been holding on to a string tethered to the leg of a frantic bird?

"Of course that was a sensible thing to do," she said, looking at me. "So you talked to Aunt Ellen?" She then sat down on the bed as though exhausted, and looked at her hands. Her fingers were furiously scratching her wrist. Her skin looked thin and raw. "You know now. I'm putrid scum." She laughed bitterly. "Yes, so you know. I'm the worst of the worst, a mother who lost her own son."

"Hadley, how did this happen? It can't be as bad as you make it sound."

"Oh, but it is. Jack is the love of my life. And now I am allowed to see him only two weeks each summer. In fact, Susan, that's where I was when you kept calling after we met—off at a dude ranch trying to rekindle a relationship so contaminated it feels embalmed."

She stood up and walked to the window, looking out so she didn't have to face me.

"And the irony is, it started so simply. We went on a skiing trip. The three of us: Jack, who was five at the time, Rick, and me. I broke my leg. I took a week off but simply had to go back to work. There I was spending hours in the OR, giving anesthesia with my leg in a cast. I started telling myself I needed something to help me get through the days. I talked myself into taking just one little shot of fentanyl to ease the pain, to take away the stress. I felt I deserved it. After all, it's natural to give fentanyl all day to patients. It's counted each day, but it's still easy to falsify patients' records. After a few weeks on it, I craved it in a way that I can never explain. If you want to know the anatomical explanation for it, I can give that to you too: How I opened the reward pathways in my brain—the same ones that light up when you hear someone say, 'I love you.' Or those other great pleasures: eating, sex. So yes, I kept taking fentanyl until my goddamn pathways were distorted, insatiable in fact, and then ... yep, I was ... totally helpless. You see, cuz, dear cuz, I'm a druggy. A junky. An addict. Is that what Aunt Ellen called me? My mother too, if she'd gotten a chance? Here I was: a medical school standout, a frigging god, or better, a goddess. For years I had been putting patients to sleep and bringing them back, so of course I could do this to myself. That's what I told myself. Turns out my intellect and power were my enemy."

She went to the bathroom for a glass of water. When she came out, I said, "I suppose you were at risk being around such powerful drugs all the time?"

"You got it, but that's no excuse. Other physicians get snared by drugs, but sleep doctors have the most deadly weapons. Here, I'll give you a little crash course, then the next time you're at a cocktail party you'll be scintillating. Like, throw around this fact: that abusing pain killers has been around forever, certainly since a pharmacist's assistant in the late 1790s discovered nitrous oxide and passed it around as a party favor. It wasn't used as an anesthetic until forty years later. And you know what? Physicians die of overdoses just like anybody else. So now, let me get to how I was particularly perfect for this, a perfect target: the fact that I never want to admit a weakness. That I'm smart as a whip and am always expected to be smart as a whip. Hell, I was the head of every class and wanted to be the head of every class! So I found something to ease me from *all* expectations, even my own. And in that, I set off the craving. Everybody thinks depression causes drug abuse, but that's backward. It's the craving that sets off the depression. Even now I can go into the stall in the bathroom where I gave myself shots of fentanyl and on a brain scan my amygdala will light up like fireworks. You see, my brain is changed, not just for the time being, not just when I was shooting myself up, but like, for life ever after—forever."

"That's a strong word: *forever*. But Aunt Ellen said you went into treatment. And you *are* practicing medicine again."

"Only by the skin of my teeth. And not without a bunch of legal requirements. Look, you have to know how bad I was to know who I am. I wore long sleeves to hide needle marks. I began giving myself shots between my toes. I wore glasses in the OR so no one could see my pinpoint pupils. I lost interest in the academic side of anesthesiology and was interested only in the drugs—*and* getting some for myself. And then I was reduced to what addictionologists know: that my brain on drugs simply disappeared. On drugs there is no cerebral function—none at all. The only thing at work in an addict is what is left: the brain stem. I was an animal, reacting. No cortical function. No thought processes whatsoever. What made me human was ripped away."

She turned and started rummaging through her suitcase. I wanted to reach out and touch her, but I sensed she would have drawn away. Instead I reminded her, "But it wasn't always like that. You are clearly functioning now. You are okay."

"No, I am not okay." She looked up, rubbing cream on her arms. "I live with a chronic craving and the truth that I lost my son. I destroyed a family. And I can't go around admitting my weakness. For the longest, I couldn't even admit to you that I'm an addict. Physicians are different. Think about it: How can I tell anybody the truth? Do you think anyone would let me put them to sleep if they knew my history? Do you think any surgeon would work with me if I told them? Listen, Susan, all that saved me were the colleagues in my practice. They called in an interventionist, because they feared that if they personally confronted me about my drug abuse, I might be so shamed that I'd overdose. So they hired a stranger: someone whom I'd never met. And when *he* put it this way: that I was endangering others, putting my patients at risk, that I was not performing up to my and their standards. Well, *that* I could understand and accept. He promised that if I did everything he asked, I could come back and take up where I left off. So I went to rehab, a special place for impaired physicians. It was hard. And long. Eventually, I was allowed back into my practice but only by a legal contract. You see, I can practice as long as I am in ongoing rehabilitation— meaning that I have regular drug tests. I am monitored every day. And I should be. Anyone who is an unfit mother, who has pissed off her husband so much that he thinks I am an ex-con who can explode at any minute ... well, I deserve cancer. I deserve to be burned alive in this house that I built for myself."

"Hadley, that's cra—"

"Crazy. Yes. Say it. And you are welcome to think so. But you are not me. And you don't know what I face."

As usual she was one step ahead of me. There seemed nothing now that I could say to unblock her. Instead I changed the subject: "But if you think your life should take the same path as Eliza's, she didn't do anything to bring on her death. In fact, I'm not sure she died at all."

"What do you mean?"

"I can't explain it. I've just spent so much time trying to bring her back in a way that we can see and feel, I can't accept that her life ended here in the way you think."

****

It was mid-afternoon when we got into our rental car and drove over the main streets of Clarksville. The trees were leafless, and the November air held a damp chill. Bare tree limbs reached toward an overcast sky. It even felt that it might snow. When Eliza was here, that November of 1862, it must have been this way.

The feel of the little city seemed to echo from when she lived here. A train trestle, in sun-bleached wood, crossed over the swampy area near the river and headed across the open ground. It looked much as a wooden train trestle would have looked in the nineteenth century.

We were so close to Fort Campbell, which was constantly sending troops to Iraq in a conveyor-beltlike way—some to there, some back—that Hadley and I both felt a sense of sadness every time we saw soldiers on the streets. Units jogged up the stairs on the walkway near the river as a form of conditioning, running up with their voices chanting their drills. It was heart-breaking to think that there was no substitute for war in our time of 2004, as there had been no release from it when Eliza lived here.

While Eliza was in Clarksville, she must have learned of the Battle of Shiloh in that April of 1862, that it had been a bloodbath beyond anyone's imagining. Probably she read of it in the papers, as well as of the fall of Memphis and Corinth. If she had not died as Hadley supposed, she would have known of the Battle of Stones River in Murfreesboro, Tennessee, on those last days of 1862—a battle so close to Eliza, and so vicious, that no doubt she would have learned of it and realized its importance for the Union. Following the humiliation of the Battle of Fredericksburg, the Stones River victory erased all doubt that the Union was faltering, so on that first day of January 1863, Lincoln had what he needed and released his executive order freeing all slaves in the territory under rebellion.

Discussing all this, Hadley and I found a pub with a roaring fireplace and stopped for a late lunch. Watching the owner shove pizzas into a blazing furnace on a wooden slide, I knew that Hadley would not be patient. And as soon as he turned toward us, Hadley called, "Know much about Clarksville during the Civil War?"

He wiped his hands on his apron. "My favorite hobby." He was portly and short, reminding me of how I had written of Irving Lowry. I half-expected him to say his name was Irving, but instead he introduced himself as George Milford, and then eagerly made a list for us of the antebellum homes still intact. Three of them were on the street where I figured that Eliza and Rissa had lived.

As quickly as we could, we drove there. We parked the car and walked. Remembering how she described the house—and that it was brick—I assumed that not all of it had burned. Perhaps it had been rebuilt and even now existed in a remodeled version of itself. But we found nothing that we thought could be it.

One which seemed similar, we walked around, standing on tiptoe to peek into the windows. It had been converted into a museum and was closed for the day. A black wrought-iron gate framed its front yard. It was brick and beautiful, just as Eliza had described the Colonel's house. We walked up the front steps and across the porch to look into the windows of the front rooms. As we did, we heard a woman's voice call from across the street, "They're not open till tomorrow."

We turned.

"We know," Hadley called, and walked back down the steps to meet her. "We're just interested in the house. Do you know anything about it?"

The small, friendly woman came toward us, pulling off her work gloves. I saw now that she had been raking her yard. The rake was lying on top of a pile of leaves. Eliza had described Irving Lowry's house only a little: the tall windows, the dark-red brick, the double doors. But as I looked across at the house from which the woman was now coming toward us, I knew instantly that this was Irving Lowry's house. The brick barn was still behind it, converted now into a guesthouse.

"Hadley," Hadley said, introducing herself. "And my cousin Susan. We're trying to find out if one of our relatives lived here during the Civil War."

The woman nodded. She held out her hand. "Rose Lowry. I grew up here. Born and raised."

I'm certain that I gasped. Certainly I was struck speechless, which didn't matter, for she had obviously inherited the Lowry gift of gab.

"Been the city librarian for five years, but retired now. Yes, you could say I'm a classic cliché: old maid librarian. But it's not all true. I was in the Foreign Service thirty years. Female Foreign Service officers were forbidden to marry. Couldn't belong to a political party either. Now I'm retired and can do damn well what I want. So I'm engaged to a widower and am a Democrat, though not a diehard one. I swing, as they say. Now, what might I help you with?" She smiled. Wrinkles circled through her wide, soft face like the lines in a cinnamon bun.

I pointed toward the museum. "We've heard stories about a house that was once here that burned."

"Oh, yes, we heard that story too. And that two spies were burned to death there. It was during the Civil War, the Union occupation."

"Goodness!" Hadley's voice was breathy with emotion. "We think we know who lived there. But two? You said two were burned to death there?"

"Yes. My grandfather told the story. It'd been handed down to him, he said. He used to take us to the Lakewood Cemetery and show us a headstone. He said it was the woman who was found burned in the house. It became a sort of ghost story for us, you know." She chuckled.

"Oh, my!" Hadley and I said at the same time.

"But my grandfather always said that the woman in the grave was not the one who lived in the house. He said it was a great mystery. And there is a grave next to hers that is marked simply 'Unknown.' As children, we liked to add to the story, like children do, you know. We'd pitch tents in the yard over there behind the museum, and all night scare the pee-doodle-squat out of each other, saying we heard a woman screaming in the house."

"Did you ever hear anything about a child being there? Might the child have been given to someone to raise before—"

"No. I never heard anything like that. But then, it happened near a hundred and fifty years ago, if indeed it ever did happen. People add to stories as they are handed down, you know."

It didn't take Hadley and me more than ten minutes to drive to the cemetery that Rose Lowry had pointed out. And there my heart sank lower than I thought I could bear. Despite what I knew the facts were supposed to be, I was never prepared to see Eliza dead.

On the first tombstone was: *Eliza Goode*
Birth, unknown. Death, December 31 , 1862.
And beside it, the gravestone *of UNKNOWN*
Death, December 31 , 1862.
A short distance away we found: *Rissa Elizabeth McFerrin*
May 3, 1833—November 5, 1862.

Chapter 32

It is strange to learn how you react when you are asked to save someone or are led to believe that you have the power to save someone. If you ever consider not answering the call you quickly find that hesitance vanishing and then become so obsessed that you could easily be labeled bona fide crazy, at least for the time being. Then, when you sense that you are failing, you become as if some poisonous insect has bitten you and are aware of having only so much time left. Even before Hadley and I parted at the airport, I began feeling this way. We were both so despondent over finding Eliza's grave, we were speechless, unable to grasp that the story was over and that I could not wring more out of it. What else could I do to affect Hadley's life—or at least what was left of Hadley's life?

"Please go into treatment," I said as we walked to her airport gate. "For my sake if not yours." Then I added quickly, "Treatment for lymphoma, I mean."

"See." She looked at me and smiled sardonically. "This is what happens. Once someone knows my past, they tiptoe around every word. Even now our friendship, the time we've spent together, it's not the same."

"I'm sorry. I didn't mean—"

"Forget it, cuz. Just know I love these." She hugged the leather folder where she kept the pages I had written. "I can't thank you enough."

As Hadley walked down the hallway to board the plane, she kept turning to wave at me; then she slowly disappeared in the crowd until I was left looking at the space where she had been. It was eerie how we were tied to each other now. In what happened to her, I felt my own self-worth and fear of failure at stake.

During the next week at home, I could barely sleep. Then I got an e-mail from Hadley: *I am home; I am as fine as can be. I am rereading your pages and am stunned at Eliza's transformation and strength. But I am still so sad at what we found in Clarksville, even though we shouldn't have been so shocked. After all, we knew how her story ended. But I have to say, seeing her grave has affected me beyond my ability to express it. Thank you, though, dear Susan, for these lovely pages.*

The next day, I knew what I had to do. I booked a flight to Jackson, Mississippi. Caleb was too busy to go with me, so I left alone on a Tuesday morning from Logan airport.

On the flight down to Mississippi, I looked out the window, down at the earth that we were skimming over. I kept rubbing my arms and tapping my foot nervously under the seat in front of me. Too distracted with my hysterical need to affect Hadley, I couldn't read or do anything else.

When the plane landed in Jackson, I rented a little Ford Focus, gas thrifty and easy on my pocketbook.

Following Highway 55, heading to Brookhaven, I nervously blended in with the speeding traffic—the pace actually fit my own feverish mind—and when I drove through the little city of Crystal Springs, I got off at an exit to find places where Eliza had been when she passed through nearly one hundred fifty years before. I imagined her at the train station, which was no longer there. Her world had simply disappeared, swallowed into our speeding, electronic, hyper-paced one; and perhaps we are none the better for it.

I got back on 55 and, for the first time in my life, broke the speed limit as if my own life depended on getting to Brookhaven before late afternoon.

As I drove into the little city, I didn't even stop to find a motel.

I feared that the county office with property records would close before I got there. Walking in, after asking to see microfilm, or whatever they had to show old records, I found myself in a back room no bigger than a closet. Many records had been converted into computer files, but not those that went back as far as I wanted to go. So I studied on microfilm the property taxes paid in the 1840s. It didn't take long to see payments for Fernwood, an eight-hundred-acre plantation near the Pearl River. Quickly, I got back in my car, racing the fading daylight, and drove to the plat where Fernwood should be.

In my excitement, I unrealistically expected to find a large tract of land, still intact, with outbuildings, perhaps even a grand house remodeled and beautifully kept. Instead, I pulled over and parked on a street in a subdivision, taking a deep breath in accepting that this was now Fernwood. Yes, this was as close to finding Bennett McFerrin's home as I would get.

Despondent, I decided that I might as well go to a motel and give up on finding anything more about the McFerrin family on that day. Aimlessly, I drove through the subdivision. And when I saw a one-lane dirt road taking off at the back of it, disappearing into woods, I drove onto it. Instantly, brush and vines grabbed at the sides of the car. Now I was really glad I had the tiny car. Beside the roadway was evidence that kids played there: soda cans, an old campfire. Farther along, beer cans and whiskey bottles dotted the brush on either side of the car.

Any number of times I nearly stopped to search for a place to turn around. If my car broke down, I'd have to walk out, and I didn't like that feeling. Already I was several miles into the thick woods, as abundant with kudzu as any place I'd seen. But I kept going, feeling that, if nothing else, I was where Ben and Rissa had once been.

A brick chimney rose out of the kudzu, and I parked and went to it. The remains seemed to have once been a church. An old graveyard was behind the crumbled foundation. Rimmed in rusted barbedwire, the gravestones were neatly arranged east to west. Instantly, I realized that I was in a cemetery where many slaves were buried, for customarily, they were interred with their heads pointing to the east, which some believed meant they wanted to be positioned toward Africa. I walked among them.

The names on the gravestones were Mini, Tom, Luther, Martha—
no last names at all, except occasionally when their masters were
named. And then, I walked among rows that clearly marked the
graves of those buried after the war, when freed slaves took the
last names of their masters or else names they particularly liked.
In a row nearby I came upon one, which when I realized what it
meant, I simply stood before it, staring, so stunned that I shook
my head back and forth with my eyes blurring with emotion.

*Delia McFerrin born a slave, died a free woman, June 4,
1901.*

And beside it: *Quashi, beloved husband of Delia McFerrin,
born in bondage, released into heaven free, March 29, 1891.*

McFerrin. The name practically screamed in my mind. But
Delia McFerrin? Had she been here after the war? Had she
taken a name that she chose? But why?

Quickly I got back in my car, turned it around and drove out
of the remote woods as fast as I could. It was too late to go to
the public library. It had already closed. It was dusk now and an
orange sunset was spreading across the sky.

The city cemetery had to be somewhere within the city limits.
The town was not that big. Surely I could find it before dark. I
turned on the car lights. I drove by a number of churches. And
then on a sloping hillside, I saw a long row of headstones.

With my car parked on a grass road inside the cemetery, I
got out and walked. I practically ran through the rows. An old
clapboard church was over to one side. It was clearly remodeled
and preserved, from how far back, I couldn't tell. When I walked
close, I saw a plaque on the doorframe: 1885. Behind it was
another old cemetery, its pathways mowed, the wrought-iron
fence around it, rusted but intact.

I walked quickly down the rows between the headstones. My
eyes were like a bird's, piercing distances, searching hungrily for
one thing. And then three rows over from where I was standing,
I saw it: the name. I ran. I stood before it and stared for a long
while. I actually put my hand up to feel my face, for my skin
and body seemed so completely numb with the realization of
what I had found. In joyous stupefaction, I read on the tall stone
headstone the simple words:

Eliza Goode McFerrin, beloved wife and mother.
April 9, 1844—October 22, 1930.

And beside it, four other headstones:
Bennett Buckner McFerrin
December 3, 1832—February 25, 1917.

Chantilly McFerrin Lovett, beloved wife and mother.
September 3, 1862—August 20, 1903.

Todd Randolph Lovett, beloved husband and father.
July 8, 1860—August 20, 1903.

Another small tombstone with a tiny angel statue was near the foot of Eliza's.

Robin Rissa McFerrin, our beloved,
April 22, 1865—April 23, 1865.

There was only one more excursion that I needed to take, and I had to wait until morning. That night, I slept barely two hours. My mind swam with images of what must have been their life—hers and Ben's. And then in the morning, I stood at the door to the public library before it was even opened. My search would be a long shot, but I also knew Eliza. If she finished her story, as I suspected, she would not have put it where it could not be easily found. She never intended for her letters to *Dear One* to fade and go unread. Oh, no, not with Eliza's hawklike mind, and—to put it bluntly—her ambitious ego. She intended for her life to count for something, even if to resurrect herself in her readers' eyes. Eliza was too big in scope to write and hide what she wanted to pass on.

"Archives? Well, yes, we do have substantial archives." The librarian, a large-boned woman with a tight perm, led me into a back room. "Not too many people come asking to see what you're after. But we do have a whole file of old journals and things that people left here in the '40s. A lot of children of those who lived through the Depression wanted to drop off their parents' memoirs. Not much else to do around here during the

Depression but write about it!" She laughed.

Near the end of the second hour that I sat in that dusty little room that smelled of mold and floor wax, I found a yellowed stack of paper in a file folder titled *My Grandmother's Memoir*. And then the opening words: *My grandmother, Eliza Goode McFerrin, gave me these papers on the occasion of my marriage in 1903, five months after my mother and father were killed in a carriage accident. My grandmother came of age during the Civil War, and she said she wanted to leave a record of her experiences. My sister has other parts of this memoir, and I regret to say that this journal is not intact, for it is difficult to understand it, disrupted as it is.*

Rissa Eliza Whitfield, Brookhaven, 1959.

I opened the collection of letters and read the first few right there, sitting as if in a trance.

Dear One,

If you have the imagination that I expect you have, you might already know what I now tell you. For after I sent my note to my mother via Tom Saxton's courier, I knew that then my mother would know where I was. That was a fact that both pleased and gave me great apprehension. All these long months, I had longed to let her know where I was; I missed her, if not her exactly, then the fact of having a mother. Especially since I was now one myself. And so I was revealed: She could now write me, find me, and worst of all, might want to still "deliver" me to the one with whom she had made that evil deal...

And then over the next few weeks, the most horrible, shocking development took hold. I never would have predicted that my actions there, during the occupation of Clarksville, would have exposed me to such wild suspicions. But they did. Just as before in my life—as after Major Morgan unwittingly killed himself— rumors ran wild. Townspeople began being even somewhat afraid of me, stepping off the curb when I walked by, as if I held supernatural powers. And then with Rissa dying, those suspicions seemed to escalate. Some even entertained the idea that I had snuffed out her life, since I began wearing her clothes out in the open. With darling "Tilly" I even attended church and

went to soirees at various houses, with Irving Lowry escorting
me. O! We were a scandal. Out of our naivety, we became what
we least intended.

That December, just before the ground froze, Ned—sad,
lost Ned—rode into town on his pitiful starving horse, leading
a small guerrilla band. He circled the house where I stayed,
calling me a spy and a whore, inflicting the worst damage on
my already sinking reputation. In horror, I watched him ride
out of town, screaming a rebel yell that shivered my soul. A
Union guard shot him in the back as he was near the end of the
street, and his body lay on the ground until it was picked up by
his guerrilla band and ridden off. Sadness, relief—two warring
emotions so wedded within me that I suffered as if brought low
with an illness.

It was a week later that I began to feel a tightening of
suspicions around me. I was barred from church—the elders
simply met me and Tilly at the door and said we were no longer
welcome. I was refused service at the local store when I went
to buy clothes for Tilly, putting Union money on the counter—
money I had desperately secured from the Union supply officer,
Tom Saxton. Even Irving Lowry turned away when I saw him
in his yard. He was simply withdrawing from me, since I know
he could not bear to shun me disdainfully, as others were doing.

In the last week of that December, I stood on the front porch
of the Colonel's house and watched in disbelief at what I saw:
a carriage coming up the street, Mr. Cummings in the driver's
box, my mother inside. They had not come to collect me as a
debt, but to see me out of curiosity and to relieve what little
conscience they had—at least my mother. Him—I doubt I would
have ever questioned his motives, except that he was dying.
Riddled with aggressive syphilis, his skin was rotting off. Ulcers
dotted his arms and neck as far as I could see. Skin that was
covered by clothing was no doubt ulcerated too. How lucky I
was that he had contracted it after I was far away from him.
"Here, look, Eliza! Look what I have brought you?" my mother
cried, coming to me, holding out a vial of opium. "I thought you
might need more. And I decided to bring it myself." But her eyes
burned so feverishly, I recognized death hanging on her, just
as I had seen it on Rissa. Preston Cummings reached for Tilly

who was in my arms, and in a moment of simple acceptance, I let him hold her. But then as he cooed, I shrank with disgust that he should even touch her. The fact of her seemed to soften him, though. He looked at me with eyes blurring with emotion. He was simply tipped over by the hard sure fact that he had not much longer to live and was facing such a horrible death. A raging course of syphilis was well known to all of us: skin rotting to the bone, the brain eaten away from the inside out, insanity and death the end result. He simply wept the whole two days he and mother lived in that house.

She was so consumptive that she was barely a hundred pounds. Her head swiveled on her brittle neck like a pod of dried berries on mountain ash.

"I'm sorry," she said to me, her voice a hoarse whisper, holding Tilly, looking down at my child lovingly while glancing at me. "We are fortunate ..." her head tilting, gesturing toward the front parlor where Preston Cummings was dozing in one of the Colonel's chairs, "that he did not touch you before he did. For that is his nature."

When I took Tilly and walked to Tom Saxton to send my most recent letter to Ben—which I always signed Rissa, in that sense, keeping her alive for him—and there receive his most recent reply to me (for we now wrote to each other as often as the posts could take them), I was walking back, holding Tilly in one arm, pressed against my shoulder where she slept, while in my other hand I shook Ben's letter open to hungrily read:

My Dear Rissa, I cannot explain now how it has come about, but I am able to be where you can come to me. Apply for a pass to the ferry stop south of Columbus, Kentucky, where we can visit my relative. Please make the trip quickly. Dress warmly. All my love is with you, and with whom I know you will bring. Such life, anointed at this time, is a declaration and command to shield it, to accept the joy that it inevitably will bring. No matter the grief, no matter its pain, we must embrace the future. I am eager to meet what you bring. And to learn its name.

Ben.

I folded up the letter, struggling to get it stuffed into the pocket of my coat. At the end of the street, I looked up and screamed in horror. The Colonel's house was ablaze, and I instantly knew what my mother had done: given her opiate to not only herself but to him, then set the house ablaze. It was she whose charred body was found in the house. It was he who was buried beside her. And with them, the evidence of my past was below the earth.

I ran then with only the clothes on my back, and Tilly in her blanket, to Tom Saxton, who with some enticement wrote the pass I needed to travel through the Federal lines into Kentucky which was under Federal occupation too. Ben, in desperation, had escaped Fort Warren, slipping through one of the musketry loopholes in the room where he got his drinking water, then scaled the seawall and swam to shore. He made it to some Buckner relatives in Kentucky.

"You've been here for hours."

I was stopped in my reading by the librarian coming to the door.

"Don't you want to take a break and go out for something to eat?"

"No." I looked up, startled. "But I'd like to copy these. Do you have a Xerox?"

"Of course. It'll cost you, though. A nickel a page. Here, let me take those and I'll do it for you." She reached for them.

"No!" I grabbed them away. "I'll do it."

I copied them, and then when I got back to my motel, I inhaled them. The pages weren't many. Barely twenty. But what they held was what I thought could make all the difference to Hadley.

I called her on my cell phone. Of course she didn't answer, but I left her a message.

"Hadley, if you are so hardheaded that you erase this message before you listen to it, then I wash my hands of you. And I'll write your obituary with the headline of World's Most Stubborn Bitch Is Gone. Because, get this, dear cuz, there *is* more to Eliza's story than you and I could have even imagined—and certainly more than you want to accept. If you want to know what really happened to her, and who is in that grave we found in Clarksville, meet me in Brookhaven, Mississippi, as soon as you can get here."

I then opened my laptop and went about telling Eliza's story, once again.

Chapter 33

The trip to Kentucky was not easy, though it was not far. The dark night threw a sharp chill over Eliza and the baby as they rode in a supply wagon that Tom Saxton had arranged for her. Tilly cried with cold, and Eliza huddled in a corner and breastfed her every few hours to comfort her. The moon was full, throwing a yellow glow over the covering of the wagon. The mules pulling it were stubborn and slow; the blue-coated driver, impatient and crude, cracked his whip over the mules' backs, cursing.

Near dawn, they took a ferry across the Cumberland, and there on the bank stood Ben, waiting for them. Eliza walked toward him hesitantly. Tilly was asleep in her arms. She waited for him to speak first, but he said nothing, only looking at her. He was so pale and so thin; he was a replica of his former self. His face, reddened by recent shaving, was filled with gathering emotion. His beard was gone. His mustache was clipped and darker, his eyes sunken and marked with a silent suffering that he could never speak of. In new, creased clothing, not a uniform but newly bought street clothes, a farmer's clothes, he had no semblance of a soldier. He blended into the landscape, blended in with the few others waiting on the bank for the ferry to dock.

She spoke first since he seemed unable to: "You didn't expect me, did you?"

"But I did." He reached for Tilly, and Eliza gave her to him, watching how he looked down at her sleeping face, then back at Eliza. "I distrusted my imagination, though. It supplied me with possibilities. But now..."

He came close and put his head against Eliza's. He leaned gently against her, leaving a cradled space for Tilly. Eliza was not certain, but it seemed that she felt a cold dampness in the crease of her neck and thought it was coming from his eyes. "Did she die peacefully?" he asked.

"Yes."

"And she is buried there?"

"Yes."

"And you are safe and okay and ..." His voice crumbled and stopped.

She filled in for him: "So all along you knew?"

"Yes. That you were writing her letters, then writing for yourself."

"Was it that obvious?" She tilted her head and smiled playfully at him.

"No. But there were certain little phrases. Little things that no one can imitate when you have been with someone as long as I was with Rissa."

"Oh, I'm so disappointed in myself!" She shook her head and creased her lips teasingly. "I thought I was better than that." And then seriously, "Do you forgive me—forgive me for pretending to be her?"

"A part of me wished it."

"Ben, we have no expectations—Tilly and I. We are perfectly capable of making a life for ourselves ... separate from anyone, anyone at all. And therefore you—"

"Shhh. I know. I know every bit of that. I also know that if you were dropped in the deepest hole on this earth, you would come walking out fine. If anyone can outlast this war and a hundred others, it is you. And I simply want to do that—outlast everything with you. Since the first time I saw you, part of me has loved you. It might seem that my saying that diminishes my love for Rissa, but it doesn't. When I was locked in a cell alone, not knowing if I would ever be released, knowing that I was losing her every minute and not being able to stop that—it was clear that if I didn't hold on to my ability to love, I would lose my life too—if not in fact, then in being one of the living dead as I have seen so many become in this war. No. Love is intended to be passed on. It is bigger than we can know."

Dear One,

Little more do I need to say about us, Ben and me. Not about how we stood on that riverbank and held each other with Tilly between us for seemingly an eternity, and then moved on to take up life as best we could, making our way to Fernwood, where along the way we stopped at an inn. There, in our private room, after putting Tilly asleep in a cradle made from the wood-basket beside the hearth, I undressed in front of the fire and approached the bed where Ben lay, feeling shy, as if my past life had not been my past. Never before had I felt that way about anyone with whom I had given my physical self to. I have no ready words to describe what I learned. The physical, wedded to the feeling that two people know each other through their minds and feelings in a way that cannot be duplicated with any other person—well, for less of better words, I will say only that I finally came to know what can exist between a man and woman. With Ben, I simply came to know the deepest of feelings in its most elemental power.

We made our way to Fernwood as quickly as we could. Ben accepted the inevitable end to the war. And there we lived, waiting out the final blows, knowing the fate of the South was sealed when Jeff Davis asked all the seceded states to join in a symbol of unity by fasting on one chosen day, and the governor of Georgia replied that no one told him when to eat!

After the war, Ben entered politics as a Republican, spurning the terrorist groups that held their evil feet on the necks of the black race to keep them from voting, owning property, becoming what we helped Delia and Quashi to be: merchants in the town with a saddlery of their own. We went so against custom in politics and lifestyle that we were scoffed at and occasionally shunned. At times I felt in danger, but I had been there before. It bothered me in a way I was used to. Outlast them, that's what I knew to do. Outlast them, that's what we did—Ben and I.

So now, no more about the war or about Ben and me or about the three other children we had as our own. My story now is only about you. If you do not yet know of love, of what it can do, then I am—by now when, no doubt you are reading this—below earth imploring you: Learn it. Learn it as the elixir to still all wars—especially the ones within us. Drink of it deeply. Know how to give and receive it. And if perhaps you can find room within you, might I ask for a little favor? Yes, a little favor from you. It will require time. It will require of you imagination and even perhaps forgiveness. For of what I ask, Dear One is—let me live on in your dreams.

****

Hadley arrived that afternoon at Brookhaven, driving over from her practice in Laurel. She knocked on the door of my motel room and stood there, wearing a trench coat and looking hopeful but with a defiant glare in her eye—as if saying, I dare you: Go ahead. Show me something I can believe.

Quickly, I explained how I had found the pages in the town library. I didn't want to say more. I knew I could not say through conversation what I could say through what now glowed on my computer screen. "Here." I pushed the laptop toward her. She picked it up and sat down on the bed.

I walked out and went to the vending machines for something to drink. I stood and watched the door to my room. I didn't want her to come out without my knowing it, and I didn't want to go in and be with her as she read. She needed to receive what I had written in silence, in privacy. As I waited, I could hear myself breathing.

After about a half-hour, she opened the door. With a stunned, thoughtful expression on her face, she then realized I was standing, waiting for her, and she laughed. She exploded in loud laughter, but it was not now boisterous and overwrought. Instead she ended with a forceful, ha! then coughed. "Isn't that just like her—I mean the way she grew into the old woman who wrote those pages, saying she needed to say no more about her and Ben, and then going right on and saying everything! Everything!"

I didn't want to break the spell. So I only nodded. And then I walked to my car and held open the door. "Shall we?" I asked boldly.

Since I now knew the way, I drove confidently. Neither of us spoke; what we knew we were about to face simply made every word we could have said seem jarring and wrong.

I pulled onto the grass road in the cemetery. When I got out, Hadley quickly followed. She was now almost running. When I saw her locate the name on the headstone, I slowed to watch her. She approached it, then stood, as I had myself earlier, silently reading, realizing slowly and deeply what it meant.

She then turned and looked at me and said simply, "She lived."

"Yes. And lived well. For a long time too. And surrounded by those she could love."

I then told her that the memoir I found had been placed in the library by Rissa Eliza Whitfield, Eliza's granddaughter.

Hadley turned, startled, and looked at me. "Do you know what this means? Before Mamaw Masters died, I heard her speak of her great-grandmother Ellie Whitfield. That must have been a nickname for Rissa Eliza."

For a second we breathed in silence.

"Oh, God." Hadley stared at the headstone. "Tilly is something like our great-great-great-grandmother. And that means—"

"We are related to him too. Preston Cummings."

"And also Benjamin McFerrin, through law, at least." She looked at me, her eyes locking mine. "He brought up Tilly, even though she wasn't his. He gave her his last name. And of course we can figure out the rest, because Eliza wanted to hide that fact. She never wanted Tilly to know who her biological father was. And probably she gave her letters and last pages to her granddaughters only after Tilly was killed, for this makes it clear: Tilly and her husband, this Todd Randolph Lovett, died on the same day, so it must have been some kind of an accident. Yes, that's what I think: that Eliza kept the truth from Tilly, then passed the pages on so her granddaughters could know the truth about their mother's birth. Telling the truth in her letters and placing them in different places to be found gave Eliza peace."

I looked at her, nodding, appreciating how she had reasoned all this out. "Certainly it says a lot about family—strength mixing with weakness, that good could trump, well, less than good. And Eliza *was* good." I then laughed a deep raucous laugh of my own. "She played a trick on me too. Because all those long days when she was in that house with Rissa—that must be when she wrote her letters. Or rewrote them. For she would have lost the early ones when she fled the first camp in Mississippi, then in Nashville when she escaped from Preston Cummings. So she gave us her life in letters, as if she were writing them as she lived it."

Hadley laughed. "Well, she was one heck of a writer."

I laughed again. "Definitely."

"And now we know for sure: Eliza wanted us to know her," I added. "She must have assumed we'd be good, strong people. People who could accept her for who she was."

Hadley laughed then, softly. "And I think we are that, don't you?" Then playfully, she said, "At least I am. I don't know about you."

I laughed with her. "This has been quite a trip, hasn't it?"

"Yes. Definitely, quite a trip."

Hadley then became quiet. As I watched her, a swell of emotion caught my breath and I held it, hearing each heartbeat. Rarely had I been as close to someone as I was now to Hadley. She had come to me and asked me for something and I had given it, not knowing if I would succeed. In an uncertain world, this was at least certain: I was in the midst of one of the most magnificent experiences of my life.

****

I flew back to Boston that night. Before I left Brookhaven, I saw Hadley off, not knowing what she would do now, but feeling that she was about to make some new decisions. I called Caleb from the motel room. "I'll be home at ten," I said. "And you won't believe what we found."

"What you hoped?"

"More than I hoped."

"And Hadley?"

"She's going to be fine. At least, I think she's going to *try* to be fine."

A week later, Caleb and I received a post card.

I have started radiation. 70% chance, they say. But you know these damn doctors—they measure everything in numbers. Even the things that can't be measured.

Susan, do you remember that lipstick that I hid from you when I was nine and you were in college? Well, I put it in the zipper pocket of your purse, thinking that when you came across it, you would be stupefied with delight. And you were.

Helping someone stumble across what they have lost feels like magic. We felt it then when I was nine. And now, you have done this for me. At the risk of sounding melodramatic, I might say it this way: I lost my will to live, and you led me to where I could find it. But then, we both know now where our magic came from. Eliza has been a part of us, all along.

Love and thanks, Hadley.

****

Two weeks after I received Hadley's card, I took all of Eliza's letters and wrapped them in new ivory linen that I knew would last and be strong. I took them to the Boston Public Library and left them with the librarian there who said simply, "Thank you." She then gave me a receipt for my donation, saying that at the end of the year I could claim a credit on my taxes.

I smiled and walked out. Eliza would have liked that. She would have heartily approved.

Even now, whenever I think of the fractured, desperate searching that Hadley and Eliza set me on, I call up a warm, amused feeling. For if indeed Eliza was intent on achieving an immortality of sorts by trailing out a story behind her, somewhat like chimney smoke from a quenched fire, then I too had become part of her plan. And we were more than happy to be her chosen: Hadley and I.

With us, she will always be immortal.

Author's Note

It was inevitable that I would write a Civil War novel. After all, everyone in my immediate family is named after Robert E. Lee: my grandfather, Robert Lee; my father, R. Lee; my brother, Rhitt Lee; and I, Shelley Lee, as if carrying part of the famous general's name would be an instant job recommendation—at least in the South.

The story of my family's love affair with the general's name was so amusing that when my mother was chosen to be on a radio show during a visit to New York in 1949, the producers invited her back at the dawn of television to appear on one of the first quiz shows, "Two for the Money." There in 1954, my parents bantered with the show's emcee about their love affair with Robert E. Lee's name. His punch line was, "I don't suppose anyone in your family is named Grant?"

In 2004, searching for a Civil War story to bring to life in a novel, I looked on a website where family members of those who fought in the Civil War post anecdotes. I found there a few sentences about a Confederate officer, taken prisoner at the surrender of Fort Donelson, who sent a note to General Ulysses Grant asking permission to ride into Clarksville to find someone to care for his seriously ill wife. If granted this permission, he promised to then report back to General Grant as his prisoner.

Such gallantry is so typical of the Civil War, and today seems unbelievable. Indeed, the idea that Grant allowed this request was intriguing, for what if this Confederate officer hired a camp follower, a prostitute, to care for his wife, who then, after the wife's death, could impersonate her?

To study a young woman emerging from an underworld, dealing with shame, employing all her talents toward survival—and learning that more can exist between a man and woman than physical desire—wouldn't this be a fresh approach to a Civil War novel, one that would illuminate much of the women's side of the war that has yet been untold? The fact that I grew up near Clarksville, Tennessee, which was occupied by the Union Army for the entire war, gave me confidence in setting the pivotal scenes of the novel there. Furthermore, since the occupation of Clarksville would be the time when my character Eliza would emerge from her past, there would be an intriguing echo for the book's title.

These thoughts were the seed for *The Occupation of Eliza Goode*.

Since the message sent to Grant was supposedly factual and shared by a family member, it seemed that each chapter leading up to that message and afterward, should also be rooted in some historical fact. So began years of research, which I knew would please my chosen audience of book clubs. These readers, most often women, are intelligent, well-educated and eager to experience something new and lasting by the choices of books they read. I learned this most particularly when I was a newspaper columnist for four years leading my reading public through novels in a newspaper-based book club, "Novel Conversations." So although *The Occupation of Eliza Goode* is a novel, I wrote it with historical facts informing each chapter, with the sources and other fascinating information listed at the end of the book.

In particular, the character of Rissa McFerrin draws heavily on the background of Jefferson Davis's wife, Varina. The scenes of officers' wives following their husbands have been greatly enriched by *Reminiscences of a Soldier's Wife* by Mrs. John Logan, published by Scribner's in 1913. One can read almost the entire book before learning that Mrs. John Logan's name was Mary. Her reminiscence of being sixteen and seeing Lincoln ascend the stage to debate Stephen Douglas is simply too riveting not to borrow for this story.

The letters expressing his love that Bennett McFerrin writes to his wife are drawn from and inspired by letters from the Sixteenth Mississippi Infantry written home to their wives, as well as by the letter from Sullivan Ballou to his wife on the eve of the First Manassas, featured in Ken Burns's documentary, "The Civil War." The photograph that I always considered to be "my Eliza," I first saw on the cover of *Storyville, New Orleans* by Al Rose, taken sometime during the years of 1898 to 1917 by Ernest Bellocq when prostitution was legalized in New Orleans. Living with that image for so many years while creating Eliza, I was thrilled and relieved to discover that the photograph is in public domain, and therefore available to be on the cover of this novel.

On my way to writing the end of *The Occupation of Eliza Goode*, an unexpected, wonderful thing happened: I became less of a regional citizen and completely aware of being an American. Frankly, I don't think that is a slight reason for any of us—especially in this Civil War sesquicentennial—to pause for a moment in our crazy, techno-driven lives to revisit, and relive through the power of story, the war that saved us.

Shelley Lee Fraser Mickle

Sources

Listed in the order in which they informed the story:

The Civil War—A Narrative, by Shelby Foote, Random House, 1958.

Civil War websites, posting by families related to Union and Confederate soldiers.

Soiled Doves: Prostitution in the Early West, by Anne Seagraves, Wesanne Publications, 1994.

Sarah Morgan: The Civil War Diary of a Southern Woman, edited by Charles East, Touchstone, Simon and Schuster, 1992, published by arrangement with the University of Georgia Press.

Being Good: Women's Moral Values in Early America, by Martha Saxton, Hill and Wang, 2003.

The Everyday Life During The Civil War, by Michael J. Varhola, Writer's Digest Books, 1999.

The Other Civil War: American Women in the Nineteenth Century, by Catherine Clinton, Hill and Wang, New York, 1984.

Storyville, New Orleans, by Al Rose, The University of Alabama Press, 1974.

Public Women and the Confederacy, by Catherine Clinton, Marquette University Press, 1999.

Fanny Kemble's Journals, edited by Catherine Clinton, Harvard University Press, 2000.

Women in the Civil War, by Mary Elizabeth Massey, University of Nebraska Press, 1966.

Queen New Orleans: City by the River, by Harnett T. Kane, William Morrow & Co., 1949.

The Americans: A Social History of The United States 1587-1914, by J.C. Furnas, G. P. Putnam's Sons, 1969.

Gentlemen's Blood, by Barbara Holland, Bloomsbury Publishing, 2003.

Tramping with the Legion: A Carolina Rebel's Story, by C. Eugene Scruggs, Trafford Publishing, 2006.

The Story the Soldiers Wouldn't Tell, by Thomas P. Lowry, M.D. Stackpole Books, 1994.

The Cambridge History of Medicine, edited by Roy Porter, Cambridge University Press, 2006.

Lincoln—A Novel, by Gore Vidal, Random House, 1984.

The Complete Civil War Diary of John Hay, edited by Michael Burlingame and John R. Turner Ettlinger, Southern Illinois University Press, 1997.

The Republic of Suffering, by Drew Faust, Vintage, 2009

Rise to Greatness: Abraham Lincoln and America's Most Perilous Year, by David Von Drehle, Henry Hold and Company, New York, 2012.

The Civil War—An Illustrated History, Geoffrey Ward, Ken Burns, Ric Burns, Alfred Knopf, N.Y., 1990.

"Ripple Effect: The Battle of Ball's Bluff and Its Aftermath," by Kevin Allen, *The Zouave,* Summer 1994, pages 3-5.

Edible Wild Plants—A North American Field Guide, Sterling Publishing Company, 1990.

Sixteenth Mississippi Infantry: Civil War Letters and Reminiscences, compiled and edited by Robert G. Evans, University Press of Mississippi/Jackson, 2001.

First Lady of the Confederacy: Varina Davis's Civil War, by Joan E. Cashin, The Benap Press of Harvard University Press, 2006.

Mary Chestnut: A Diary from Dixie, Gramercy Books, Random House, New York, 1997.

Civil War Academy. Com, "Ball's Bluff."

Reminiscences of A Soldier's Wife, by Mrs. John Logan, Charles Scribner's Sons, New York, 1913.

www.usa-civil-war.com/Manassas/manassas_1-2.html

Nannie E. Haskins Papers 1863-1917, originals in the holdings of the Tennessee State Library and Archives.

Historic Clarksville 1784-2004, second edition, published by The City of Clarksville.

Personal Memoirs: Ulysses S. Grant, The Modern Library, Random House, New York, 1999.

Internet sources on Bedford Forrest.

I Rode with Jeb Stuart, by Major Henry B. McClellan, Da Capo Press, 1994.

So Far from Dixie: Confederates in Yankee Prisons, by Philip Burnham, Taylor Trade Publishing, 2003.

Fort Warren: New England's Most Historic Civil War Site, by Jay Schmidt, UBT Press, 2003.

"Collateral Damage," a DVD on Drug Abuse and Anesthesiologists produced by Phillip Boysen and John Santa. Also information from interviews with Dr. Shirley Graves, Professor Emeritus, University of Florida.

Scenes in Clarksville are derived from the author's personal notes during a visit there in November 2004.

NOTES

Madam Francine's room is drawn from a description of the bedroom of the famous Madam Kate Townsend in *Storyville, New Orleans,* by Al Rose.

Statistics of immigrant women, lack of employment and prostitution are from *Public Women and the Confederacy,* by Catherine Clinton, Frank L. Lement Lectures, Marquette University Press, 1999, as well this chilling fact: "When Walt Whitman's brother died in Brooklyn in 1862, his sister-in-law was five months pregnant. She turned to prostitution to support herself." P. 12

Eliza's girlish use of language was formed in part by the voice of Sarah Morgan in *Sarah Morgan: The Civil War Diary of a Southern Woman*, edited by Charles East, Touchstone, Simon and Schuster, 1992, published by arrangement with the University of Georgia Press.

Madam Francine's parlor house is drawn from descriptions of Hattie Hamilton's establishment on South Basin Street in New Orleans in the late 1860s when practitioners of the purple arts were more gracious and professional than those of the Storyville days when prostitution was legalized in New Orleans from January 1, 1898 to 1917, when the U.S. Navy closed it down.

The legend of *Jazz* was found on the Internet, which, although the Internet is a flowing river of information and often suspect as to accuracy, the following information seemed tailor-made for Eliza's story: New Orleans was the only place in the New World where slaves were allowed to own drums. Those with European horns added a music that grew into what was known as playing Jass. One legend tells that the word Jazz grew from the custom of prostitutes wearing the smell of jasmine so that they could approach a potential customer with, "Want a little jas'?" Of course brothels and parlor houses always employed musicians; Jelly Roll Morton is one of the famous founders of jazz who worked in brothels. Over time, the J for Jass Music was often erased on blackboards to read Ass Music. Eventually dance halls changed the spelling to Jazz.

The character of Delia is partially formed from

information in *Fanny Kimble's Journals,* edited by Catherine Clinton, Harvard University Press, 2000.

Duels

Duels were so common in New Orleans that they were like daily sporting events. As farfetched as it sounds, physicians were even known to duel over the diagnoses of their patients. For a man to be called a "fire eater," was taken proudly, and proudly displayed.

The carnage of the Civil War helped to wipe out the practice of dueling; there was simply no longer the stomach for such ridiculous bloodletting. A missing arm or wooden leg was proof enough that a man had faced an enemy with honor.

Soldiers & Camp Followers

General statistics of the war list that three out of five soldiers died of disease, mostly from measles, smallpox, dysentery or typhoid. Approximately 90,000 men were diagnosed with venereal disease. Eighty percent of prostitutes were under the age of thirty; forty percent under the age of twenty; sixty-two percent foreign born; and most died within four years of venereal disease or alcoholism. We can assume that this was the fate of Ellen, Fanny and Amalee. Tuberculous as the "prostitutes' disease" is documented in *The Cambridge History of Medicine.*

Germ Warfare

Preston Cummings's part in a plot to use germ warfare is drawn from information in *Personal Memoirs: Ulysses S. Grant*, The Modern Library, Random House, New York, 1999, regarding germ warfare, page 590. Also *Blood on the Moon: The Assassination of Abraham Lincoln,* by Edward Steers Jr., The University Press of Kentucky, 2001. Until the cause of yellow fever was discovered by Walter Reed to be borne by mosquitoes, there was so much ignorance of the disease, those plotting to unleash an epidemic in Washington assumed that victims' clothes could transmit the disease.

The Battle of Fort Donelson

As soon as Fort Henry fell in Kentucky, Grant marched

some 15,000 Union infantry to be within striking range of Fort Donelson. When the day turned unseasonably warm, the men dropped their blankets along the way to lighten their load without realizing they would later pay dearly for that decision.

Another 10,000 troops traveled by steamboat, along with Grant's floating headquarters, *The New Uncle Sam*. On February 12, Lincoln's birthday, Grant sent the President a telegram: "I hope to send you a dispatch from Fort Donelson tomorrow," which can be interpreted as Grant's intended birthday gift to the President, especially since there had not been a significant Union victory as yet. With Lincoln's son, Willie, lying ill, only eight days from death, Grant's message could not have been anything but a welcome distraction from what would be Lincoln's darkest days and deepest sorrow.

Inside Fort Donelson, the four Rebel commanding officers—Generals Floyd, Buckner, Pillow and Colonel Bedford Forrest—bickered and worried, knowing that they were frighteningly outnumbered. The fort was rustic, a stockade with crude log huts to house soldiers. It was never designed to withstand a heavy attack. Each officer was in a particular personal danger. Floyd, the ranking general, was a former U.S. Secretary of War who had taken the Rebels' side after secession, and fled Washington for the South—but not before he shipped guns to the Confederacy. If he were captured, he would be tried for treason.

Gideon Pillow, second in command, had fought with Grant in Mexico, where Pillow earned a reputation for being manic and impulsive. Buckner, having fought in the Mexican War with both of them, feared what Grant knew: that Pillow was likely to dart from one direction to another—that is, just the kind of adversary Grant relished.

Then there was Colonel Bedford Forrest, who had been galloping his cavalry restlessly, most likely already realizing the odds and looking for a way out of the fort.

Every day Buckner walked the grounds: handsome, meticulous in his uniform, fighting his gloominess and tendency to dote on what he knew that Grant knew. His only comfort was knowing two cards to play against Grant: First, he and Grant had attended West Point together where they had shared a close friendship. And, a few years before, when Grant had been in California, where he was dismissed from the army for drunkenness, Buckner had loaned Grant money to pay his way home.

For weeks, the Rebels had worked to fortify the fort. On the eve of the battle, it held 17,000 men, including artillery and cavalry. Twelve cannon were aimed down the river from where the Union gunboats would come. Feverishly, the Rebels dug rifle pits, throwing yellow clay onto logs in a three-mile arch to protect their supply base: the little country town of Dover.

The night before the attack, Grant called for an additional 2,500 men left at Fort Henry, who then began moving up during the cold night. Near midnight, the weather turned to twenty below. In the kitchen of a farmhouse, Grant spent the night in a feather bed. A few miles outside the fort, his infantry lay exposed on the ground, miserable, having thrown away their blankets, and most often sleeping in pairs with arms wrapped around each other, praying that in the morning they could get their fingers warm enough to pull a trigger.

At dawn Grant awoke in charge of his first big command—27,500 against 17,000. Thus far in his life he had failed at every business venture he had tried. With a wife and children to support, he feared poverty above everything. When he was offered a commission in the army, his father sent word: "Be careful, 'Ulyss,' you're a general now; it's a good job, don't lose it."

On the morning of the attack on Fort Donelson, Grant, an avid horseman, rode his favorite horse among the popping of skirmish fire and hung back from the fort, waiting for his gunboats to catch up. At three that afternoon, he launched the attack and rode to a ridge to get a good view.

The Union gunboats came down the Cumberland River, firing away, just as they had in Kentucky at Fort Henry. The Rebels' big guns fired back, falling short. But as the boats came closer, Fort Donelson's cannons found their targets, and in a matter of hours, the gunboats limped back toward Kentucky.

The Rebels stood and cheered, thinking they might indeed hold the fort.

That night, another snow fell. In the dark, the Rebel generals began shifting troops in the howling wind, with snowfall muffling footsteps and the clang of gun wheels. When the sun rose, Pillow sent his regiments forward, cracking through icy brush.

Bedford Forrest began slashing his way through the Federal line. Blood stained the snow, and by dusk, 2,000 Rebels lay wounded or dying, along with 3,000 of Grant's army. But the road to Dover was open, so that even if the Rebels might not hold the fort, they could at least slip out through the night and escape to Nashville. Which is exactly what Pillow decided to do: get out in the dark, head the seventy miles to Nashville, save his troops and join in the defense of Nashville. He rode the line to assess the best points for escape. Yet when he saw his exhausted men, he went to the hotel at Dover to tell Floyd and Buckner that he had changed his mind.

Stepping inside the small hotel on the edge of its creek, he reported, "We are doomed."

Floyd looked at Pillow. "I turn command over to you, sir."

Pillow quickly added, "And I pass it, sir.

"Well then, I assume it," Buckner said and sat down at a desk. "Now, give me pen, ink and paper, and send for a bugler."

Overhearing this, Bedford Forrest stormed out. In the cover of darkness he led about 1,000 men, riding double, across the swollen creek in front of the Dover hotel, and headed to Nashville.

Buckner sent white flags and the bugler toward the Union line. A courier galloped with Buckner's note to Grant asking for terms of surrender.

Soon, Grant sent back: "None. Only unconditional and immediate."

White flags of surrender snapped in the wind as men on both sides walked through the lines, mingling and talking, waiting for Grant to appear. His horse could be heard cracking the road ice as he traveled to the Dover Inn. He walked inside, sat down with Buckner and shared cornbread and coffee, and the two talked as old friends. Buckner remarked that if he had been the commanding general during the fighting, Grant's troops would not have been able to get up to the fort as easily as they had. And Grant replied that if Buckner *had* been in charge, he would not have tried it the way he did. Then Grant delivered the surrender papers for Buckner to sign.

Buckner refrained from reminding the new Union general

of his embarrassing past, and Grant graciously avoided rubbing in his old friend's current embarrassing failure. Two red tips of puffed cigars glowed in the room, then Grant announced he was taking over the Dover Inn as his own headquarters and was sending Buckner north to a Federal prison. He opened his wallet, offering Buckner money, to which Buckner shook his head in decline, then stood to be escorted out by Grant's guards.

At the river, Generals Floyd and Pillow frantically arranged an escape. When a steamer arrived with a reinforcing regiment from Mississippi—too late to be of help—Floyd jumped aboard, then quickly ordered the steamboat to Nashville. The soldiers, who had just disembarked, stood on shore howling when they realized they had been left to be captured.

Pillow, rushing up and down the bank, couldn't come up with anything other than a scrow, big enough for only him and his chief of staff. Quickly, he jumped on and became a dot heading down the river, bucking on the waves.

When Grant learned of this, he said he was actually pleased that Pillow had gotten away, for it was much more valuable that Pillow be a general calling the shots against him than to be his prisoner.

Ready to look over the fort that he had now captured, Grant rode to the site of the battle and found some 14,000 Rebels—often said to be "the cream" of Confederate volunteers—shivering with cold, gray from gunpowder, standing around, glad to be alive, chivalrously waiting to be sent north to prisons. Later, Grant would write in his memoirs that his commissary general of prisoners reported issuing rations to 14,623 Fort Donelson inmates at Cairo, Illinois, on their way to northern prisons.

Reporters rushed to file their stories on the first real Union victory, as well as the battle to introduce Ulysses S. Grant to the country. In a matter of days, the general took on the nickname of Unconditional Surrender Grant to fit his initials, while from all across the Union, boxes of cigars arrived at his headquarters, sent by a swelling number of fans.

Discussion Topics

As the author researched the history for this novel, she passed on extraordinary information, such as that several in Lincoln's cabinet wanted to let the South go and expand into Canada, creating a separate nation with that land acquisition; also that germ warfare was attempted by trying to release a yellow fever epidemic in Washington, D.C. Did these facts astonish you too? Were there other facts that you learned, expanding your knowledge of the Civil War and your realization of how it changed America?

Hadley has a hard, sad life. When you learn what is driving her, is there information about her daily challenges that is new to you?

When Rissa dies and Eliza takes over Rissa's identity in the letters she writes to Bennett, do you view her act as immoral or generous? What are all the ways in which her act can be viewed? How much of loving someone is the desire to protect them?

There are many mothers in this story. How are they each different and what do they share: Eliza's mother, Hadley's mother and then Hadley as a mother herself, as well as Eliza?

Susan realizes that Eliza was a marvelous storyteller, just as she attempts to be. Hadley places her faith in the power of story to inform her life. Is the power of story diminishing in our present culture? Are there stories that influence your life?

What in reading this book will you remember as part of your identity as an American?

CPSIA information can be obtained at www.ICGtesting.com
Printed in the USA
LVOW08s2158150614

390168LV00003B/244/P